D0622036

F R A N K   L E E

JOMO

A MAN IN TIME

FRANK LEE

JOMO

A MAN IN TIME

TATE PUBLISHING
AND **ENTERPRISES**, LLC

Published by Tate Publishing & Enterprises, LLC
127 E. Trade Center Terrace | Mustang, Oklahoma 73064 USA
1.888.361.9473 | www.tatepublishing.com

Tate Publishing is committed to excellence in the publishing industry. The company reflects the philosophy established by the founders, based on Psalm 68:11,
"The Lord gave the word and great was the company of those who published it."

Book design copyright © 2016 by Tate Publishing, LLC. All rights reserved.
Cover design by Norlan Balazo
Interior design by Shieldon Alcasid

Published in the United States of America

ISBN: 978-1-68164-778-4
Fiction / Science Fiction / Genetic Engineering
16.01.22

For Jason Barry and Lisa Gunberg Wartner,
our children who continue to inspire us every
single day. We are blessed.

What a man thinks of himself, that it is which
determines, or rather indicates, his fate.

—Henry David Thoreau, *Walden*

Author's Note

THE VOICE, LARRY Calvert, interjects his own experiences or feelings from time to time. For the reader's ease, these segments are written in italics.

Also, some of the main characters have African names. Please review the pronunciation guide before beginning.

This novel is fiction; however, most, but not all, subjects of science or genetics are generally accepted knowledge.

List of Main Characters

Jomo Jorland (*jo*-mo)

Nice Nkoe (*nee*-kay en-*ko*-ee), who becomes Nice Jorland

Per Jorland (pear)

Michel (mi-*shell*), French male gender

Julie Brooks

Tambo (*tom*-bo)

Haakon Bjornson

Jomo Nkoe (*jo*-mo en-*ko*-ee)

Nonkipa Nkoe (non-*kee*-pa en-*ko*-ee)

Hald Aarbakke (*are*-bok-ah)

Prologue

"*MR. CALVERT, JUST start where you grew up.*"

"*Hold on a bit. I love sitting here on my own front porch overlooking the Chesapeake Bay. I know I've got leaves to rake, but they can wait. I think this interview might work if you follow my rules.*" *Larry Calvert leaned forward to freshen his coffee, then sat back and took a sip.*

"*Okay. I grew up in the Washington DC, area. My father worked at the Pentagon. He was in World War ll. He was a Staff Sergeant in communications, top-secret codes, and encryption. He was there on D day. In fact, he landed on Omaha Beach in the same LST (Landing Ship, Tank) with General Eisenhower, supreme commander of the Allied Forces in Europe. They were side by side till the defeat of the Nazis in France and allied troops marched down the Champs in Paris.*

"*As a young teenager, I met President Eisenhower when my dad and I paid a visit to their small retirement farm near Gettysburg. I'll never forget when they first met eyes. They greeted each other as good old friends. We were introduced to his wife, Amy, as we toured the house. Then he gave me a Coke, mixed two scotch and waters, and we settled down on the front porch. They never talked about his presidency, only the war.*

I listened to them talk for a while, and then I blurted out, "You live near Gettysburg, sir. How do you think General Robert E. Lee, the leader of the Southern Army, felt after hearing Union soldiers were being buried on his front lawn?"

They both put down their drinks and Ike turned to me with a surprising look. "That is beautiful land overlooking the Potomac River, Lawrence. General Lee and his wife owned the house and all that land, which is now Arlington National Cemetery. They inherited it through Lee's wife who was a great-granddaughter to George Washington's wife, Martha."

He looked to my father and then looked back to me. "The first Union soldiers buried there were in 1864. Lee had lost at Gettysburg, and the Civil War was all but over. How he felt? No general takes defeat well, Lawrence. I'm sure it was personally disheartening to him and quietly he must have known it was the end for him." He paused as if in deep thought. "And how would you come to ask that question of me?"

His eyes lit up when I told him of my great interest in the battles of the Civil War and all the Saturday afternoons I'd studied the geographical battle layouts at the Smithsonian Institute.

"In Washington, it's who you know not what. So strings were pulled, and before I knew it, I was throwing my white dress hat in the air at Annapolis. As a kid, I learned to swim in the

Potomac, so I thought I could best serve my country in Naval special ops. You know, frogmen. When I was five, I'd ride on my dad's shoulders as he swam across the Potomac from Georgetown to the Virginia side. There were remnants of an old bridge foundation that I remember. You've got me going way back. I used to ski down Jenkins Hill in DC. Now it's called Capital Hill. Sorry, I'm getting off the subject. Where was I?"

"You were on frogmen, sir."

"Oh, yes. Just before the early days of the Vietnam War and just before he died, President Kennedy started a new unit called MACV-SOG. It was a joint operation composed of the new Navy Seals and agents of the CIA. I ended up in SEAL Team 2. All good men. We were the tip of the spear.

"It was 1967. I'd made lieutenant the day before my orders arrived. The next five years, my missions went from secret pilot rescue ops into the Ho Chi Minh trail in Southern Laos where the Viet Cong were holding one of our own, to a subop deep into Hanoi Bay to capture a VietCong general. I led covert ops in all the campaigns, including Tet, Steel Tiger, Tiger Hound, and Cambodia. Somehow, by God's grace and mercy, I returned from a lot of one-way missions, where the odds were I'd be killed or captured.

"I got a chest load of decorations that never could console the loss of so many heroes I knew personally. One of them was a good friend who saved my life by taking a bullet. As I kneeled in the mud, holding his head out of the water, he witnessed to me. He said he wasn't afraid to die because Jesus was coming

to take him by the hand. He smiled so peacefully and told me to pray for his wife, and then he breathed his last breath. So that was the beginning of my life as a Christian. My future changed dramatically after that moment. I cried a lot, and then I put it behind me. My unit was deactivated in 1972. I retired from the Navy. I'd held the line, and I was proud. I have never participated in any Vietnam veteran events or parades.

"After the war, my father handed me a letter from the Smithsonian Institute. They were looking for a new director and had received a letter of recommendation from President Eisenhower a few months before he died. Now I'm retired again. I was director of the Smithsonian for forty years. To this day, I think my dad and President Eisenhower hatched the plan, but I could never get my dad to admit it. The first day I walked into my office, it felt like home."

"That's quite a life story, Lieutenant."

"Call me mister. That was long ago. I'm lucky to be alive. So we agreed on only two questions. That was the first."

"Yes, sir."

"Now, about your second question: the story behind the story."

"Yes, sir. The story behind the story."

"To tell the truth, I'm not sure where to start."

"Why?"

"Because I was so much a part of it."

"But that should make it easier. I don't understand."

"Per was my best friend. Look, the Smithsonian Institute is huge. Overwhelming, yet the stories all come down to personal."

"What do you mean?" the interviewer asked.

"That beat-up space capsule. It's not about the capsule. It's about the heroes. The astronauts and their courage, and it's what you came here for."

"Oh, now I understand."

"You asked me about the human genetics story, question number two."

"Yes, sir. Just go."

"The story of Jomo transcends the past, present, and future like no other story in the institute. So if you're ready, I'll pour you another cup of coffee and begin. You can push the recorder button now."

"Sir, I pushed the button fifteen minutes ago."

"No problem. I know. That happened when I was being interrogated once."

Modern autoroute E23 from Geneva to Lausanne, Switzerland, was once—between ten and fifty thousand years ago—a single path traversing the Northern shore of the second largest lake in all of Europe. For centuries before recorded time, tribes, traders, and travelers journeyed this very path in search of…

In modern times, this storied crescent-shaped lake is known as Lake Geneva by the Swiss. But in Lausanne, a holdout of French speaking Swiss prefer the upper speak: they call it Lac Leman.

Exiting luggage at Genève Aéroport, a man on a mission caught the next cab in line.

"Vidy. You know Vidy?"

"Yes, sir, Vidy section of Lausanne. On the shore. Yes, sir, I know it. We should be less than one hour. It looks like a storm coming," the driver replied in thick Swiss English.

The fare settled in as the cab headed North then Northeast on the auto route. This was no typical businessman or banker, and the driver watched him closely because this man was visibly agitated, opening his pouch to read and reread a letter.

The once sunny morning was quickly turning gray. A freezing rain was blowing in from the Northwest, and both men occasionally looked to their right to see the backside of huge white caps that would run their course all the way to the Southern shore and French soil. It was November, and Europe was settling in for another winter.

As the driver neared Lausanne, he said, "This is the turn to Vidy, sir. Where is your destination? Do you have an address?"

The man gruffly replied, "IOC."

"Yes, sir." The driver watched in his rear view mirror as the man placed the letter into its envelope and stuffed it into his goatskin pouch. A car cut him off, and he had to pay attention to his driving.

As he returned his eyes to the mirror, the man pounded his fist on the pouch and cursed in an African language.

The man looked up. "You spy on me! It does not matter. Are you proud of your country?"

The driver stammered, "Why, yes, I am. I am very proud to be Swiss. I am a proud Swiss. This place is my heritage. Why do you ask?"

"Then you understand."

Miffed, the driver asked, "Sir, understand what?"

"Because of your answer, I will tell the story of why I travel your autoroute on our return to Geneva."

The cab continued, windshield wipers on slow speed, and then turned left onto an expansive and well-manicured lawn leading to a low modern glass building. On either side of its regal white marble portico, two guards awaited their arrival.

The cab pulled up directly in front. A guard approached and opened the door for the man. He turned to the driver. "Wait here. I will not be long."

"As you wish, sir."

The Swiss guard spoke officially in French, "We've been expecting you, sir. I trust your flight from Kenya was fine."

"Yes, fine," was his abrupt reply. "I do not want to sit or wait. I have traveled five thousand miles to deliver this letter. You must bring me immediately to the committee."

"Yes, sir. That has already been arranged. They are waiting."

"I am sorry. I did not mean to be rude. Accept my apology. I am tired."

"Apology accepted, sir."

A firm knock on the heavy oak door was followed by a single word. "Enter!" A security guard opened the door and announced to the room, "I present the Kenyan ambassador." The man nodded a look of thank you to the guard, then walked straight to the head of the long mahogany table and unexpectedly slammed down his goatskin pouch.

The ambassador stood erect. When offered a chair to sit down, he declined. He was full-blooded Maasai draped in traditional red tribal dress. Striking ornaments crowned his ebony head and multiple strands of African beads adorned his neck. From the pouch, he curtly produced an envelope and placed it at the head of the table.

In Queen's English, with a Kenyan accent, he spoke. "My president expresses his extreme dissatisfaction. You will find his official letter of protest in the envelope. You will not belittle my homeland, my very core of life. This is not between my president and all of you. No, it is between you and our people. Our pride. Our heritage. I travel here in search of justice, not politics, and not caving your vote to world hysteria! Without justice, none of you are worthy of your office or your fine suits and your extravagant expense accounts!" With that, he turned and strode back to the oak door, firmly closing it behind him.

The letter was quickly passed around to the committee. No one spoke. Silence said it all. Finally, the committee president spoke to the four women and ten men. "I now convene this special meeting of the executive committee. May the secretary make note of the letter delivered by the Kenyan ambassador. We will begin with old business."

1

Twenty-Five Years Earlier

IT WAS EIGHT o'clock in Kenya—a new day in the eternal equatorial cycle. Nice Nkoe and her mother, Nonkipa, left their *boma* to make the weekly ten-kilometer trek to market. With empty baskets balanced on their heads, they walked as one, patient with each step. To the Southwest was majestic Mt. Kilimanjaro. To the North, South, and East was the endless expanse of African Savannah—the Serengeti.

Dressed in their colorful *kikois*, and occasionally greeting friends, they spoke softly in Swahili as they made their way along the path that shortcut the dirt road leading to town. After several kilometers, the elder remarked, "I see you have not forgotten how to carry a basket."

"You taught me well. Sometimes I carry a stack of books on my head when my arms get tired. The men always notice that." Both women laughed. Talk was comfortable. "We've walked this path together so many times. When I was young, I learned every root that crosses it so I would not trip and spill my basket. I followed all your steps."

"As I followed my mother's. I have watched you carry since you were a child, and now your walk flows like the mist in the early morning."

"Oh, Mother." Her stride was elegant, aristocratic, purposeful, and enchanting. She was twenty-one and home on vacation from the University of Nairobi. It was a happy time with no pressures, just the easy rhythmic chores of daily life.

As they neared town, the driving sounds of African drums grew louder and louder. Nice's steps became lighter, lifted by the rhythm. Everyone was in a good mood when the drums came to town during market. Nice was glad to be home.

Arriving at market, there was no time to rest. They quickly wove their way through the farmers displaying their vegetables, fruits, and prepared spicy foods, as well as crafts, all spread out on large rainbow-colored cloths. The chatter was lively, and buyers enjoyed it as much as the sellers. Nice thought, *I love this place. It is my home and always will be.*

Finally, with baskets full, the two women set down their loads next to a small table at the outdoor cafe to rest and talk over a cup of coffee before the long trek home. Nonkipa decided to use this moment to talk with Nice about her future.

"Nice, do you have a plan yet for after graduation? I've asked you every year."

"Mother, I love you. Why must you always bring this up every time I'm home? I'm twenty-one years old. I'm sorry. I'm not mad at you, but you have to stop asking me that same question. I'm going to make something of myself. I'm different. There is no way that I'm going to fail in life."

"Yes, you are different from the girls with whom you were raised. They're all married now. Never kept up with school."

"Not just that, Mother. I earned high grades all the way, better than the boys and now better than the men. I got out of circumcision by running away while the others froze with fear. Thank God!"

"Yes, I remember that day. You were eleven years old. I told you to run and stopped them when they tried to chase you. Later I brought you water and food where you were hiding in the bush, and your father surrounded you with thorns. That night, I did not sleep for fear an animal would find you. The next morning, I told them if they went after you when you came home, they would have to deal with me."

"You never told me that before. I will always be grateful to you and Father. I worked and paid my way through the university. I even have a small apartment of my own. I'm proud of what I've accomplished so far."

"I know all these things, and your father and I are proud of you."

"So please stop asking me what I'm going to do every time I come home or what I'm going to be."

"I'm sorry, Nice. I never meant to upset you. Your father and I only want the best for you. You're our only child."

"Then let me go. Just let go, Mother! I know this will always be my home, and I can return any time and be welcome."

"You are right there. We'll always love you."

"So please understand me. I'm building my future every day. Graduation is in a few months, and I'm sure I can steal a good job from the men in my class. I know I can make a stronger impression than any of them."

"Perhaps that's what I meant when I said you're different from the other young women. It's your confidence. You've always run to danger and excitement. You must have it your way. You think you can do it all."

"You finally see me. I love the countryside, but I know there's so much more out there."

"We love you, Nice, and I promise we will not hold you back. I can handle your father. Don't worry about him."

"Oh, Jomo. I love him, but just because he's a farmer doesn't mean I've got to whistle cows all my life. That's his life. I wish I had a brother, though, who could take over some of the chores. I know you two get tired."

"We make do. And we are thankful for what little we have. Listen, after you leave to go back to Nairobi, I'll have a long talk with him. He'll come around."

"Thanks, Mother. I knew you would understand."

"I do. I raised you. You always were determined, and I respected that about you."

"Thank you, Mother. I love you."

Suddenly, Nice pushed back her chair. "Excuse me, Mother. I'll be right back." She walked straight to the street where six climbers who were passing through to the Kilimanjaro trail head were talking with two men.

"Stop!" She pushed her way to the center. "Do not give these two men any money! This one is a fake policeman, and the other is part of their money scam!"

He gave her a push. "Kupata mbali, mwanamke!" (Get out of here, woman!)

She put her finger on his chest and repeated, "You are a fake policeman and a scammer! You're nothing but common *shiftas* [bandit]!"

The six looked at her, and then at the two, stunned. They thought they had broken a local law.

He slapped her again and tried to grab her wrist. "I kukukomate!" (You're under arrest!)

Before one of the tourists could intervene, Nice countered with her palm to the underside of his chin, breaking one of his front teeth as his jaw snapped shut. "You are not police! I know them all here! This is my town! You two get out of here before I call the real police! And don't come back!"

She smiled to the climbers as the two men took off running. "Hope you have a good climb." With that, she returned to her chair. "Scammers, Mother, only scammers, common shiftas."

"That's what I mean, child. You run to danger."

"Ha, no, I walked."

They both had a good laugh, and each ordered a second cup with the little change one of the climbers gave Nice.

"He got what he deserved, but you must learn to be more careful with that quick temper of yours. You are too impulsive."

"Oh, Mother."

"No, I mean it. What if they really were police, say from another district or county? You would be on your way to prison and a terrible beating."

"I knew I was right. I learned how to defend myself from a Frenchman I met near the university. He taught me how to really hurt anyone who threatens me. I'll show you."

"It's not about defending yourself, it's about making big life mistakes."

"I can take care of myself."

"You're not listening to me now. You're impulsive, and you may do something or say something you'll regret immediately or perhaps many years later. Or, my dear daughter, you might even cause pain and sadness to those who love you. It can grow the wrong way. Sometimes I feel Nairobi has taken my child."

"I will not promise, but I will remember what you said."

"Good, my daughter. You will be better off in life." Nonkipa gently put her hand on her daughter's and spoke softly, "Take a long look inside and always *walk in the truth*."

"Mother, what do you mean? What is truth?"

"Truth will take convenient forms. *The Truth* is never changing. It is eternal."

Nice was adjusting the angle of the sun umbrella when she whispered, "Have you noticed the white man with the camera sitting to our left? I think he's been following us since we bought the vegetables." Nonkipa turned. Grasping his chance, the stocky short man rose and approached their table. His gait was spry and expression genial.

Nice curled her toes in the hot soil. Her childhood was of the bush, but four years in Nairobi had made her street-smart. Glancing at her mother and then squaring her shoulders to the man in khaki, she challenged in English. "Why are you following us?"

"Please, excuse me. I mean no harm. Yes, I have been following you."

"Why?" she interrupted, her upper body leaning toward him. Nonkipa observed her daughter's boldness with the man. He placed his cup on the small round table, and with a sincere smile, he asked, "May I sit?"

"Yes, you may."

"My name is Marcus Balieau. I'm a fashion photographer from New York City. I've just completed an assignment in Mombasa and decided to come to Oliotokotok to see Kilimanjaro closer before going home. I'm overwhelmed by the stark beauty of your country—the colors of the earth, the sounds, the music, the people, the smells. Some say, 'To drink from the cup of Africa.'"

"But why are you following us?" Nice countered, growing impatient with the stranger and his odd exuberance.

"I was taking photos of all the action in the market when I saw you from a distance. I caught up to you and photographed you buying vegetables. Your dress is so beautiful, and all the colors of the market blend with you to create a palette of color. As I was photographing you, I had an idea. Please bear with me here." Reaching in his camera bag, Marcus withdrew a business card and gently placed it on the table. "I have associates, close friends, with the Ford Modeling Agency in New York, and I think they'd like to meet you. You have a very cosmopolitan look."

Nice glanced at her mother, then turned to Marcus, lifted her chin, and again squared her shoulders with him.

"What is your name?" he pressed on.

"I am Nice Nkoe. Here is my mother, Nonkipa."

"Where did you learn such eloquent English?" Marcus continued in a friendly voice.

"I'm a student at the University of Nairobi, and yes, the Queen's speech is eloquent. So?"

"What are you studying?"

"My major is economics. It's none of your business, and why do you ask?"

Marcus smiled. "Have you ever thought about becoming an international model?" He looked at her with a barely visible turn of his head.

Nonkipa's eyes wandered to the other side of the market square where children were laughing and playing an ancient game with sticks and a tiny ball.

"Excuse me, Mr. Balieau. My mother doesn't understand English very well," Nice spoke softly to Nonkipa in Swahili. Several moments passed before her mother looked at the man's camera and slowly nodded.

"If you would like, I'll give you both a ride home in my jeep. Those baskets of yours look heavy. On the way, I'll explain about visas and green cards, but first we have to see how the camera's lens sees you."

As the jeep jostled off into the bush, Nice was secretly relieved she would not have to carry the heavy basket home in the hot sun.

Nearing the small settlement of about twenty huts, Nice's father, Jomo, appeared on the path, whistling two cows back from the communal pasture.

Slowing the jeep, Marcus asked in a lighter tone, "Nice, may I take pictures of you with your family?"

"Of course, if I'm going to be a model, you'll need pictures of me, right?"

"Yes! Yes, Nice, these will be the first of your career."

Jomo's mouth dropped at the sight of his wife and daughter in a jeep with a stranger. He and Nonkipa seldom came in contact with tourists. He gave a loud whistle different from the herding whistle.

As Nice climbed out of the jeep, she called to him, "Father, we met this man in the market. Marcus, please meet my father, Jomo Nkoe. Father, please meet our new friend, Marcus Balieau."

Seeing the cameras, Jomo challenged the stranger. "If you want pictures of my family, it will cost you two hundred Kenyan shillings."

Nice translated then turned to the elder. "But this is different, Father. He's from New York. I might get a job in the United States with his help." She brushed him off as she turned toward Marcus, rolling her eyes. "His gruffness hides the lamb."

Out of nowhere appeared two Moran wielding spears, and they were not smiling. Marcus suddenly realized he was not in a touristy village that sells curios and acts out war dances.

Instantly, Nice took charge of the situation. She pointed to the two and spoke softly but with authority. "You two, you are both acting like no-good thugs. Lower your spears now and go back to your cows! There is no danger here." Gesturing to Marcus, she said, "He's a good man, and he's no danger to the village or to me. Now, go!"

Jomo, with the authority of a village elder, countered his daughter. "No, they stay until he leaves!"

At this, the two men stiffened and brought their spears closer to Marcus. Sweat broke out on his forehead, and he looked to Nice and Nonkipa, his only allies. He was a stranger and not welcome.

Nice took a step forward and ordered her father. "They go. Now."

Hearing her daughter, Nonkipa walked boldly to the young men and pressed their spear tips to the dirt.

"I am your father. Do not tell me what to do."

Nice stepped back, offended by this sudden anger, but she recovered to position herself between Jomo and Marcus. "Yes, I will." Then without waiting for his response, she repeated the orders to the two. "Now, go. Get away from my house!"

The two gave a nod and returned to their herd. As they disappeared into the bush, Jomo muttered, "I used to have power."

With fear written all over his face and in a near panic to calm the tension, Marcus reached in his pocket and pulled out a fistful of paper and coins totaling 290 Kenyan shillings. With a smile, he handed it all to the elder who was holding a *rungu*. Jomo counted the money and approved with a smile.

"Father, you're lucky he shows kindness after you were so rude to him."

"Get on with it," Nonkipa interrupted in her very best broken English.

Marcus was a pro. Quickly, as the trio was uncomfortably jockeying for the camera, he produced two more cameras. They hung at his side like he was a gunslinger. Focusing his eye through the viewfinder, he saw Africa. He hummed to himself as image after beautiful image clicked off.

In the middle of the frame, Nice was taller than her parents—a modern woman. In her elegant way, she completed the bond of this family unit. Her face and happy expression bridged the gap between the old and the new.

One of the cows, impatient to return to the boma, tugged so hard on Jomo's rope that it pulled him out of the picture's frame. Nice laughed with Nonkipa at his futile attempt to get back to his place in the photograph. The second camera whirred as Nice held Nonkipa's shoulder.

Nice was a natural. Without losing contact with the lens, she reached a graceful arm of assistance to her father. Together, they now held the rope. Marcus's lens zoomed in on Nice's dancing eyes and mysterious yet engaging smile. "Simply beautiful," Marcus murmured to himself as the last frame clicked. He knew the images and beauty would surpass anything he'd done. Nice was a natural.

Nonkipa invited Marcus in for *chai*. Once inside the dung hut, Marcus watched as Jomo produced a blackened chunk of cedar and a ten-inch twirling stick. In the blink of an eye, he had a tiny amount of dried grass smoking and then burning. Picking it up, Jomo carefully transferred this to the fire pit; fire primitively made so fast, Marcus didn't have time to capture it. He thought of asking Jomo to repeat it for the camera, but he'd already pressed his luck with this protective father.

Nonkipa boiled the tea while the four settled in. Marcus's eyes had fully adjusted now. The hut was surprisingly cool and refreshing with no odor. The dirt floor was as hard as cement and well swept. They sat on six inch stools and a few more were stacked in a corner. The beds were simple, made of woven branches over a crude but strong frame then covered with animal skins.

This is cozy, he thought. A faded picture of Elvis was nailed to the wall. To the left, on a small table, was an old black-and-white photo—now turned orange from age— of two young warriors with smiles as wide as the African plains. They were kneeling over the huge head and black mane of a male lion they'd killed. Only one of them held a spear.

Jomo blew a little air on the fire and without looking up, said quietly, "That is a picture of my father and his good friend. His friend was not a Maasai. He was Kikuyu. In those days, a friendship between tribes was not common. Tribes kept to their own. Territory and defending it cost many lives. His friend, though, had Maasai relatives West of Nairobi, so it worked. They were young. The photograph was taken by a white explorer." The elder stopped, gazed into the past, and then continued. "That was the old Africa, around 1907, near the Thika River, Northeast of Nairobi.

No white person has ever seen the photo before *your* eyes have."

Nice sat down as she translated to Marcus. The elder waited for her to catch up to his words. Marcus bowed his head toward Jomo. He gave a silent thank you when he heard the last sentence.

The smell of the tea began to permeate the hut as Marcus listened to this man whose face looked so of the earth. Jomo continued, "In those days, it was part of the passage from boy to man. Now, a young one may brag that he is not afraid to kill a lion with a spear, but all Maasai know the lion is a very dangerous opponent. Now there are national parks where the lion is protected. Maasai still have ways to prove their courage, though. A boy must kill a big animal." Jomo got up to pick up the picture. He looked at it real hard. "It may be stolen valor. That's how it is today." He returned it to its place.

"My father's good friend was called Kamau wa Ngengi, but between the two of them, his nickname was Jomo, the proper name he would take on later in life. He was truly a great warrior all of his long life. He outlasted my father and was, some think, a hundred years old when he died. They both became men that day long ago because each of them said the other had killed the lion. Now *that* is a man's friendship."

The family laughed as Nice finished translating then added to Marcus, "We laugh because Father has told us that story so many times."

Marcus joined in, and the hut became a place full of merriment and love.

Behind the photo, Marcus spied a book covered with a skin of some unknown animal, maybe a small square of warthog skin. "May I look at your book?"

"Yes. It came in the mail long ago. It was my father's book. He gave it to me before he died. On that day, he told me to learn to read."

Marcus carefully removed the dusty skin from the book and, with his other hand, lifted it gently. He blew the red dust off the cover to reveal an American classic—*Green Hills of Africa.* "May I open it?"

"Yes, you are our guest."

Marcus opened the cover to read,

> My dear NKoe,
> To my best and trusted,
> A tracker, you are relentless
> A friend, you are loyal
> A man, you are humble
> Carry on, my good friend.
> Ernest Hemingway

Amazed, he read it again then paged to the copyright, 1935. It was a first edition.

Jomo spoke quietly without looking at Marcus, as Nice translated, "Open it to page 100. There is a photograph of my father sitting in a tent with him."

Marcus opened to the page, and there he was, Ernest Hemingway. He quietly returned it to its place and commented, "This is a good book."

"Yes, Nonkipa and I have not read it yet, but Nice will read it to us someday."

"It came in the mail?"

"Yes, in the mail many years ago. I was young. I remember when a letter arrived from Nairobi to come and get it. That man was a hunter and a good white man. He traveled as a young man through the Serengeti in 1933. My father was his guide and tracker and most of all, to keep him and his wife safe."

Marcus nodded. "Yes, he came to Africa about that time. His wife's name was Pauline."

Jomo continued, "There was a lion he wanted to kill for a trophy. It was a man-eater. Very dangerous. My father led him to it, and it was done. After he returned to America, he wrote that book about Africa and sent it to my father to read. My father only knew Swahili. We saved the book."

This family is good, and this is a special time for me to be so welcomed into this circle, Marcus thought. "May I take a few more pictures of you, Nice, inside your home? The lighting is very good right now."

Jomo listened then Nice translated for him, "Of course, this one is for free," her father said like the punch line to a joke. Laughter again filled the hut.

"I must go now because I have a long drive back to Nairobi." As they went outside and stood near the jeep, Nice translated for Nonkipa.

"I think it is good you have come into our life. I like your plan for Nice." Nice was happy to hear her mother's words and support in front of her father.

Jomo looked straight at Marcus. "I neither like you nor dislike you. I have not decided on you. Your spirit appears good, yet you speak of taking my daughter. If you are truly good, you would not take her. I will keep her here. We need her to cook and tend the cows as we grow old. We have no son. No, you cannot take her," he said with a wry smile.

Unnerved by Jomo, Marcus pressed on and found himself responding with the same speaking rhythm used by his hosts. "Thank you so much. You are good people. I will try to help Nice be a model." With that, he started the jeep and left. Glancing in the rearview mirror, it was beginning to sink into his New York state-of-mind just how much of a change this would mean for Nice and whether she could handle being a model.

The Nkoe family held hands and watched until the stranger was out of sight. Only a dust cloud marked the road on the horizon, and then it disappeared. Nice reached into her basket and pulled out the card:

Marcus Balieau

Fashion Photography

New York City, New York, USA

Nonkipa smiled. Jomo frowned.

Nice returned to Nairobi to continue her studies. Before long, the traffic and the hustle and bustle of city living and upcoming final exams had made that short holiday fade into a distant memory.

Arriving home after a long day of classes, Nice found a manila envelope postmarked New York City in her mail slot. Nearly two months had passed since Marcus had taken the photographs. She climbed the steps to her apartment, wondering and hoping.

She closed the door, sat down on the couch, ran her finger over the name Marcus Balieau, and then carefully opened the envelope. In it were five photos Marcus had taken that day and a letter. She read the first two sentences out loud to herself:

Dear Nice,

Your photographs have been well received at the Ford Modeling Agency in New York City. They believe you could have a great career as a model. Enclosed is a flight ticket to New York.

Our state senator, a friend of mine, has intervened on your behalf after he saw your picture and heard the story of how I found you. You will need to go immediately to the U.S. Embassy. Because you will have employment when you arrive, they have already prepared a Visitor Visa for you and you will not require most of the usual paperwork.

Looking forward to seeing you.
Marcus Balieau

Nice threw her hands high in the air as she jumped up and yelled and twirled round and round the room. "I am going to New York to be a model! I'm going to America to be a model!"

2

So long ago, yet that was a day easy to remember. At that very moment, as Nice was dancing around her apartment in Nairobi, a colleague of mine by the name of Dr. Per Jorland was pinned down by gunfire from six Somali poachers in a remote area of one of Kenya's many national wildlife preserves.

Per and his company were subcontracted by the Smithsonian Institute to assist the Kenyan National Park Service in a series of genetic projects on endangered and protected species. Seems that Per, a warden, and a few trackers from the Kenya Wildlife Service had accidentally stumbled on some poachers at an elephant graveyard and before they knew it, were backed up against a cliff with only large boulders for protection.

The standoff continued for hours, and not knowing how long it would last, Per and his men conserved ammo and water. Daylight turned to dusk, and then began a long uneasy quiet in the penetrating blackness. Per discussed their options in brief whispers. Since they could only estimate the enemy's number, a scout had to assess an escape on the right and the left. Per volunteered for the right, and a tracker named Tambo went to the left. An hour later, after silently moving only an inch at a time, Per reached a boulder on higher ground from which he could make out shadows about sixty feet away. He waited and watched and wondered what Tambo was finding or whether he was even still alive. Per thought perhaps he had been killed in the darkness.

The total silence gave no clue how many men the shadows hid or if it were something completely different, maybe a pack of wild dogs. It was too dark. Per's heart was pounding as he struggled to control his breathing. *No*, he thought he saw something. All his senses were on high when he heard a faint groan of pain and then another. *Maybe we wounded one or two, but not all of them*, he thought. A low guttural groan came again but louder. *With that guy in pain, they're bound to be down there, alert, with guns ready*, he thought.

Just then, when he had determined escape by this route would be impossible without casualties—maybe all of them—a poacher lit a cigarette, and in that brief few seconds, Per could make out five men sleeping on the ground with their guns leaned against a rock. He started back carefully, but before he could move more than ten feet, he heard the rush of a pride of lions attack the poachers and their helpless cries as they were easily overwhelmed and torn limb from limb in a feeding frenzy.

Per rushed back to the warden and Tambo was already there. They ran a mile downwind and waited till morning to return to the jeeps.

A front page story on Per and Tambo with pictures of the mutilated bodies appeared in the Nairobi paper two days later. When Per got back to the States, I asked him about it while fishing on the Chesapeake Bay.

With a smile, all he replied was, "Yes, Larry, that was a close one, but really, lions, poachers, danger, that's what you're saying when you say Serengeti."

I laughed as I was reeling in my line. "Is that all?"

"No."

"Well, what?"

"Well, it's about turn off and turn on, Larry."

"Go on."

"You know already. There are critical times in life when you turn on. Turn on to a higher place of awareness, existence, achievement, maybe even destiny. The rest of the time you're running on idle. Some idle fast, some slower."

"I know what you mean, Per. I almost cheated on a test in college but couldn't and left the cheat sheet in the dorm."

"No, Larry, you've got the idea, but I'm talking about those huge ones you know are wrong, but you do them anyway because at the time the options make sense. It's impulse, pure and simple impulse. Right or wrong. Maybe I'm selfish. Maybe I think of myself first too much."

"Such as what?"

"How we started crawling over these rocks. I could have had a bullet or knife in me in that darkness, but the option made sense. Later or within seconds, you face the consequences right or wrong."

"Do you look for situations where you can apply this?"

"No, but I don't shy away from them."

"Why?"

"Why?" Per repeated.

"Yes, why, Per? Seems like a life of making decisions in wrong situations can be a no-win situation in the end. I mean sooner or later the odds will get ya. You're talking impulse decisions, sometimes not well thought out. Listen, life decisions are better and a lot easier when you pray to God for guidance."

"No. Well, you've got a point. I guess being single makes it easier. I don't know. Look, this, what we're talking about, is not an everyday thing for me. You know that. Most of my time is spent at the lab in sterile scrubs evaluating what I've gathered in Kenya. I'm a scientist. No, really, Larry, I'm a scientist. I'm not impulsive in the lab."

"Per, you're an adrenaline junkie I want on my team any day! That's who you are."

"Thanks. I don't talk much about it."

"Well, I've had my own adventures, Per. After all, I didn't end up director of the Smithsonian without a little checkered past, eh. Checkered ain't necessarily bad. No regrets, no baggage. Duty, honor, country. That's what I give to every day. It's easy to live with that. So I'm a little like you. There's a lot we have in common. Someday I'll tell you a few."

"I've heard a few from others already. Hanoi Harbor? Really? I'm honored to go fishin' with you, Larry."

"Well, isn't this a kumbaya."

"Let's change the subject, okay?"

"Yeah."

"We're digging a hole with no ladder here, ya know?"

"Then what?"

"What you say?"

"Get the net, Per. If I boat this, you owe me five bucks for first fish!"

She poured a glass of tepid water from the sink, held it to the window to check its color, and sat down, wet from perspiration. Her heart had slowed, and the reality of the letter in the package began to sink in: adventure, hope, money, and escape from this crowded, unforgiving, male-dominated city. She was leaving for New York. Really.

That evening, she celebrated with friends at a locals-only watering hole near the university. By the time she left, everyone in the place had read her letter. They all knew her and wished her well in New York. She was escaping.

The next evening, she got a call from an acquaintance that she frequently met at that same bar. He always spoke quietly and was a gentleman to her. He was handsome and knew how to treat women.

He was French, and she knew French as a child, but she learned the subtleties of the language when spoken by adults from him. She liked him and thought often of taking him as a lover. He listened. He looked her in the eyes when he spoke. He held his wine glass in a certain practiced yet nonchalant way. He was a Parisian, and she trusted him. His name was Michel. She did not know his last name. A year or so ago, he had told her he had been to New York.

"Hello?"

"Hello, Nice, this is Michel."

Nice answered in French, "Oh! I am so happy you called. I am leaving for New York."

"Yes, I know, Nice. I heard it from your friends. I am so sorry I missed your party last night."

"That's okay, Michel. It is true I am leaving soon. I have a job or, let's say, a modeling tryout. I hope to pass it. My plane ticket and hotel are paid for."

"That's wonderful, Nice," he answered thoughtfully.

"If I don't pass, I'll have to return. I have no money." There was a silence. "Hello, Michel, are you still there?"

"When do you fly out?" he asked in a probing way.

"The day after tomorrow, it's a morning flight. Why?"

"I have an idea. May I see you tonight? I know where you live. You told me long ago, and I wrote it down. Better yet, may I come over now in about three hours? We can talk a little. You see, I've been to New York. I have friends, well, they're really business associates there."

Nice thought, and then said, "I suppose. Yes, come over."

"Great, I'll bring some good wine."

"Good then. See you in three."

Michel's knock came on her apartment door exactly three hours later. She opened it to see him in his usual elegant yet relaxed attire. In one hand he held a bottle of Vouvray, and in the other, he pulled a medium sized black rolling suitcase suitable for a model. "Come in, Michel."

"Why, thank you, Nice."

She opened the cupboard and took out two of her best glasses, wine glasses she had been given at a British Embassy party several years earlier. She rinsed the dust off them and then dried them properly. Michel approached from behind her and popped the cork. He poured the wine, and they sat down to small talk, a little about what to expect.

Nice kept eyeing the suitcase. Finally, she asked, "Did you bring me that suitcase to use? I already have one but not that nice."

Michel put his glass down and looked her in the eyes. "Yes, Nice, I brought it for you to use on your trip. Listen carefully to me now." He dropped his tone of voice lower, more serious, with a thicker French accent than she'd ever heard. "I have a business proposition for you, Nice. You can take it or leave it. Do you understand?"

"Yes, Michel, I understand," she answered slowly while stiffening her body language and crossing her legs.

"Then I'll tell you. There are uncut diamonds sewn carefully and professionally into the zipper of this suitcase, 100 high grade diamonds from Somalia."

"Somalia? What?"

"Yes. Well, technically off the Somali coast but not in international waters."

"I thought I knew you, and now you say you deal with the Somalis? They are despicable killers. Al-Shabab has terrorized our people for years, and I hate their despicable sharia law. Michel, what? I want no part of this. I think maybe you should leave."

"Nice, please listen. I do not—no—I've never even spoken with a Somali. You have my word."

"Then who? Tell me."

He freshened his glass and savored a sip. "Nice, these diamonds are from a clandestine deep water mining ship off the Somali coast. A Russian ship. This deal is with the Russians."

Nice answered in a concerned voice, "Russians?"

"Yes, Russians," he answered with a slight smile. "Diamonds have no international boundaries. It's hard to trust the Russians, but it works both ways. They trust me, so I trust them. That's how it works. Simple yet complicated."

"I see. Would you please refresh my glass?"

"No, you don't really see, but I trust you. Do you trust me, Nice? This is important, so think before you speak."

"I do, Michel. I do trust you."

"Good. Then you would become a link in the operation. I chose you because of your confidence." Michel gestured toward the suitcase. "See for yourself. You cannot tell by looking at it, and diamonds have no smell for the customs dogs."

"Michel! I don't know!"

He continued, "When you leave the airport, go straight to Central Park across from the Guggenheim Museum, Southbound on Fifth Avenue, and sit on a bench you will find there. My business associate will already be sitting there, and he'll exchange this suitcase for an identical one. In it, you will find a very large perfectly cut, highly valuable diamond, maybe fifty thousand US dollars, a reward for your work. Also, there will be two thousand dollars for you to buy new clothes. Wear your best clothes on the plane. Do not put any of your favorite clothes in the suitcase, only jeans and sweatshirts. After the exchange, you will never see them again."

He reached for his wine upon finishing but never took his eyes off her. She said nothing, almost in shock.

"You have until nine o'clock tomorrow morning to decide. Call me exactly at nine with your decision. If you agree to it, say 'Roses are Red.' If you don't for any reason, say 'Violets are Blue.' Nice, I like you. I will understand, and I promise I will hold nothing against you. Do you understand?"

Nice held her chin high and took a deep breath. Her heart was pounding. She thought, *My God, he's a smuggler. He's a diamond smuggler. What will I do?* Then she answered very slowly, "Yes, yes, Michel, I understand completely."

He stood up with a smile and finished his glass by swishing it in his cheeks to savor it. "Enjoy the rest of the bottle." They shook hands. "Oh, and if you say 'Roses are Red,' you must take me off your cell phone." He glanced at the suitcase as he left. She watched him from her window as he walked away and melted into the early evening rush hour crowd.

She hid the suitcase under her bed and slept in fits. Nine o'clock the next morning, she dialed Michel. As he answered, she felt out of body as she heard herself say "Roses are Red."

3

THE FOLLOWING MORNING, she presented her coach ticket and boarded a plane to New York and into her future. She had told a friend to tell her parents her flight ticket was dated, and she had no time to go home for a good bye. She would write them a letter.

On the plane, Nice met a woman sitting next to her. She tried to appear cosmopolitan, "So what brings you to be on this flight to New York?"

"Oh, allow me to introduce myself. My name is Jane Clark. I'm returning from a visit with my son who is in the military and serving at the US Embassy in Nairobi. It was good to see him. He's a lieutenant and a good one. I'm so proud of him. So how 'bout you? Why are you off to New York?"

Nice hesitated and thought, *Don't say much, keep it simple, don't let her pry.* "Oh, my name is Nice Nkoe. I live near Kilimanjaro."

"But what brings you to be on this flight to New York?"

"I was with my mother when we met a man in the market. He said he was a photographer. He took some photographs of me. A short time later, a free plane ticket and money arrived at my apartment. He said I would be a good model in New York, so here I am," she answered lightly.

Jane noticed her finger twitching and asked, "Are you nervous?"

"No."

"Well, I'll be honest. You seem like a nice young woman. Listen to me. Many young women come to New York with high hopes, some maybe with a suspicious connection like yours. Here's the truth: New York is big and ruthless and devours women like you every day just as fast as they arrive."

Nice began to shake, and she struggled to control it.

"It might be high class prostitution. You're beautiful, or it might even be slavery–prostitution where you wake up in Dubai or Hong Kong. Some are just used and then murdered."

Nice started to break down. She thought, *She's right. I could be in big trouble—smuggling, prostitution, murder!* She woke up from her thoughts as Jane pressed on.

"Nice, are you running from something? Have you done something wrong? I know when things don't add up right away. Here, take my soda. You can tell me."

"Yes, thank you. No, I am not running, but I do feel like I am over my head here. But then, maybe that man—his name is Marcus Balieau—maybe he is real, and it will all turn out." She shed a tear.

"Tell you what. I like you. My husband is a detective for the NYPD."

"What is that? NYPD?"

"It's short for the New York Police Department." Jane laughed. "He's Irish, what else would he be?"

Nice shifted in her chair but did not laugh.

"Maybe we can drive you to the hotel. What hotel is it, Nice?"

"The Waldorf."

"The Waldorf? Very expensive."

"Yes it is, but no thanks. I will just take a cab." She thought, *I must trade suitcases. I will be late. Then what? He will think I stole them.*

"Why not? It'll be easy to drop you off. I don't understand. Besides, you can tell us about the Serengeti. We'd like to go there someday."

She is pushing me now, Nice thought. *She suspects something, and her husband is a New York policeman. This is all falling apart. He will find the diamonds if customs does not.*

"That sounds very good to me, but please, I am going to take a taxi cab. I have always wanted to take one."

"They aren't that special. Just expensive, and you can't have that much money, right?"

"Please, Mrs. Clark. No, thank you."

"As you wish, Nice Nkoe. Then here's my phone number." She pulled a scrap of pink paper from her purse and handed it to Nice.

Nice looked at the number and put it away. "Thank you, Mrs. Clark."

"Call me if you *ever* need help. I'm just a phone call away. I have a feeling about you and your free ticket. Nothing is free in New York. Nothing."

"I will remember you, Jane." Nice avoided eye contact and slept the rest of the flight. She lost her in the crowd at JFK Airport. At customs, the dog ignored her, and she managed just enough cool to pass an inspection.

The taxi driver from the airport was a nameless, faceless sort of man with an acne complexion, yellow teeth, and an accent Nice was not familiar with. He had an annoying quirk of snapping his neck bones with his right hand and kept looking at her in his rearview mirror.

Finally, Nice blurted, "Quit looking at me!"

He replied, "I see things all the time. Sometimes I ask for money. Like you."

"I will report you."

"No, you won't. The ones who give me money are up to something. I don't miss much. There's something good or bad in every face."

"What do you mean?"

"Know when you're over your head. Desperation. You may give me money before this ride is over."

"Why do you say such a ridiculous statement?"

"New York. You're in New York. I could tell by the way you looked at your bag as I put it in the trunk. You're worried about it. Maybe smuggling? There's something about your bag. Like I said, something's up, a beautiful woman like you. There must have been a wrong turn somewhere."

"Stop talking and drive! Just shut up!"

"Where to now, ma'am?"

"I want you to park in the Southbound lane in front of the Guggenheim."

"Righto, ma'am. Fifth Avenue, Southbound."

The cab stopped across from the Guggenheim. The driver got out, opened the trunk, and gave her the bag.

"Told you. Something's up," he whispered.

"Shut up," she whispered back. She rolled the bag over to a park bench where a well dressed man was sitting, placed it next to him and then sat down. He never looked at her but showed a large semi-automatic pistol with a silencer in his suit. He spoke confidently and quietly.

"Well done, Nice. Ordinarily, I would have killed you here with two bullets. Just a robbery gone bad, you know. You're a mule, but the Frenchman likes you, I guess. You are pretty. Our paths may cross again, so always follow the rules."

With this, he slowly got up and walked away with her bag. Nice heaved a huge sigh of relief and tried to compose herself. She sat on the bench for several more minutes and then returned to the cab.

The driver got out and commented, "Different suitcase, ma'am. You owe me a hundred bucks plus the fare, don't you? Or I could make a call."

"Yes, I will pay you. I do not like you. You are like a troll in a storybook that took money from anyone to cross a small bridge. Shut up and take me to the Waldorf Hotel. It is on Park Avenue, if you don't know."

"I know. I live here. That's the dumbest thing you've said so far."

As they sped off, she sat in silence, thinking of what her mother had told her about impulsive bad decisions and regrets.

"My lips are sealed. Welcome to New York."

She had just checked into her room when the telephone rang.

"Hello."

"Hello, is this Nice?"

"Yes. Who is calling?"

"Nice, this is Jane Clark. I'm calling on my cell phone from my car. I met you on the plane. My husband is next to me. Could he talk with you?"

Nice's heart raced. She thought, *A detective.* She pulled herself together and then answered, "Why, I suppose that would be all right."

"Hello, Nice. My name is Joe Clark, NYPD."

"Yes, Mr. Clark."

"Sorry if we're disturbing you, but to be honest, my wife, Jane, had a feeling about you on the plane but couldn't really say why. We know that your story about staying at the Waldorf checks out now."

"Yes, I am fine, thank you." She thought, *He suspects something? Maybe that taxi cab driver—*

"It's just that your story seemed rather, may I say, unlikely? Then again, every day someone tries to make it here in New York. Would you be willing to come down to the precinct so I can meet you?"

Nice's palms turned sweaty. "I would rather not. I will be very busy first thing tomorrow morning at the Ford Modeling Agency, but thank you for caring."

"Well, how about this? I'll keep track of you for a while just to make sure you're not in trouble. How's that?"

"That would be fine, sir."

"Good then. Welcome to New York!"

"Thank you, Mr. Clark."

"Goodbye."

"Goodbye, Mr. Clark," Nice said as she put the phone down and began to shake. She looked out the window and saw a black-and-white police car parked in front of the hotel. She thought, *He suspects something. I have to be cool.* She looked out the window again, and the police car was gone. She reached in her pants pocket, pulled out the pink paper, and threw it in the trash, and then she retrieved it and wrapped the diamond in it. She opened a loose electrical outlet to hide it in overnight.

New York wasn't what she'd expected—no, in some ways it was better. She held her head high and walked confidently to breakfast at a corner diner just down the street. She was worried about her money and now, detective Clark. Aside from the flight, hotel vouchers, and two thousand dollars in cash sent by Marcus and the two thousand from Michel for clothing, she was broke. Four thousand was barely enough to catch a plane back to Nairobi if it all fell apart.

The 11:00 a.m. appointment came fast. As the cab driver from South Africa let her off, he told her in Afrikaans, "There's a saying here in America, 'Never let them see you sweat.'" She thanked him for his advice with a smile and a five dollar bill, and then tipped the doorman liked she owned the place. Just a few deep exhales to relax, and the elevator doors opened. Nice Nkoe from Oliotokotok, Kenya, walked casually but confidently into the Ford Modeling Agency's reception room.

"Hello. My name is Nice Nkoe. I have an appointment at eleven."

"Yes, Nice, good to meet you. I'll notify them that you've arrived."

"Thank you. Shall I sit?"

"No, that won't be necessary. Oh, Nice, there was a Joe Clark who called for you this morning. I told him you had an appointment for eleven o'clock. He said he'd try later but left no number."

"Thank you." But she thought, *Good, that'll get rid of him.*

"They're expecting you," she said with a light chuckle. "They're probably walking down the hall right now."

"I thought I was meeting one person. Who are they?"

As the receptionist answered, "Marcus Balieau and the company president, Sarah Jones," Marcus opened the door. The two entered all smiles. Nice thought, *Marcus looks different, so New York.*

He walked straight to her with open arms. "Nice, oh, Nice, how are you? How was your flight? Did you enjoy your stay at the Waldorf?"

"That will be three yeses, Marcus. New York is fabulous. I saw the Statue of Liberty coming in on the plane. It feels strange but good to be in America. I love it here already."

"Yes, Nice, I've come here today to introduce you to my good friend, Sarah Jones. Sarah, I'm honored to introduce you to Nice Nkoe from Kenya."

"I'm so pleased to meet you, Nice," Sarah said with a comfortable professionalism. "I feel I already know you better than most of the young women who come to me for the first time. Marcus's photos of you and your family are striking. If you catch on quickly here," she said with a cocked head, "we'll have a great business relationship."

"Why, thank you."

Marcus interrupted, "Don't you just love her Queen's English?"

"Yes, elegant. Confident but not stuffy or what I hate, haughty! Modeling at this level is all about first impressions." Sarah put her index finger to her chin. "Nice, you're an interesting woman. Did you learn the Queen's English from your parents?"

"No, when I left home for Nairobi, I was broke as a bone. I was lucky to pay for my university tuition, food, and books. I was hungry that first day and told myself I shall get a job before the day is done."

"And what was that job, may I ask?"

"Yes. They took me under their wing. They paid me well. I was a part-time nanny for two children, so I had my own apartment to get away, you know. I tended to the children of the British attaché to Kenya. When they interviewed me at their home, the two children came to me. I got the job right then. The attaché's wife taught me how to speak and conduct myself. She called it Received Pronunciation. I owe them."

Marcus laughed deeply and then moved things along. "Let's go back in and see what we can accomplish."

"Marcus is right, Nice, we don't have much time. In the next hour, we'll teach you how to enter, walk the runway, and exit. The rest, and that's 95 percent, is up to you."

"Okay, I'm ready," Nice answered as they walked down a long carpeted hall lined with framed photos of men and women. They entered a special room of mirrors with an expensive parquet floor and a shocking pink floor length curtain at the far end.

Nice looked around. "I've never seen a room such as this. The floor looks as beautiful as the best woodwork in Africa." Then she caught herself with the advice of the cab driver and pulled herself together before they sensed her rising anxiety. She looked at both of them. "Okay, show me how it is done."

Just then, a beautiful thin woman entered and waited for her cue. When it came, she did the walk—the runway walk that fashion empires have risen with, fallen, and then risen again in this great city. Marcus followed every movement the model made, looked to Sarah, and then back to the model.

Sarah said, "Pauline, please repeat the steps for Nice three more times. Then you may go, with our thanks."

Nice watched carefully, and Marcus watched Nice, thinking, *I hope I wasn't wrong here, judged too quickly, maybe built her up too much.*

Then it was Nice's turn. A carnival like meld of African drums and hot Cuban salsa filled the room. She smiled at Marcus, kicked off her shoes, and entered from the curtain. As she walked toward Sarah, she locked eyes. She struck three poses exactly as the professional model had done and then walked back to the curtain as if she was walking the path with her mother.

Sarah commented with a pleased voice, "Again, please, again."

Nice repeated the walk ten times. With each time, she became surer of herself. She almost lost herself to the drums.

Finally, Sarah said, "Nice, that's enough. I've seen all I need to see. Marcus was right! You're one of the few naturals I've ever seen but don't get a big head here."

Marcus laughed, relieved.

The words echoed through her mind. "I'm hired?"

"Yes, Nice, you're fabulous! I mean it! You're just who I'm looking for. I'm putting you on the fast track. You will start in an important showing on Saturday. You'll be wearing something, say, international whimsy. You'll wow them. My staff will help you organize your life in New York. Until then, we own a suite at the Waldorf where you can stay until you've found a place of your own. We'll have to clean you up though. Your feet are atrocious. Calloused. That may take some time. You won't be wearing anything revealing on your feet until. But that's Africa. Aren't you all barefoot there?"

To Nice, that touched a nerve, and she couldn't hold her tongue, "Excuse me, Ms. Jones. Not to be impolite, but I live in the city of Nairobi, and you don't know what you are talking about. There are tall buildings there also and nice cars and restaurants and smart people at the university. What you just said is very demeaning to me and the women of my country. All women don't—"

Marcus eyes rolled as he interrupted, "This is wonderful, Nice! You've passed one of the hardest tests in the modeling business, and I just know you'll be a star."

"I have to go, but I'll see you with all my girls tomorrow morning. Nine o'clock sharp." Sarah shook hands with Marcus and gave Nice a forced pat on the back, then left quickly in a slight huff.

Nice looked at Marcus, and he looked at her. She gave him a huge hug, a kiss on the cheek, put on her shoes, and they left together. They took separate cabs; he to his life, and Nice to hers.

That evening while lounging on her clean sheets at the Waldorf Hotel, she got a phone call.

"Hi. Is this Nice Nkoe?"

"Yes, I am Nice."

"My name is Ralph Lauren. I'm a fashion designer here in New York. I just got a call from Sarah Jones at Ford. You met her today, yes?"

"Oh, yes. Sarah Jones. Yes I did."

"You were to report to Ford tomorrow, but plans for you have changed. I've hired you through Sarah. Do you understand? I'd like to see you tomorrow morning for a general meeting of all my girls."

"But, Sarah hired me today. She said—"

"I know. She told me."

"Then?"

"She had second thoughts about you. That's why she called me."

"But she said I would be in an important showing."

"I'm sorry, Nice, but that was another designer who she thought might hire you. That was a big show, yes, but you will not be in it. The deal didn't work. I thought you would understand right away."

"I did not think—"

"Listen, Sarah hires out models to occasions, parties, magazine shoots, and some shows. That's all. Very few get hired full time or what we call a full contract."

"I did not know all this."

"I understand. How could you know? New York is a tough town. It's never easy, not even for me, but she said you have potential."

"Potential?"

"Yes, potential. I have nothing to lose, and you and I have everything to gain. That's potential. Modeling is part threads but mostly is mystic. That's why Sarah called me. You either have it or you don't, and you, Nice, have it."

"I am only myself."

"To be honest, that is the only reason I'll give you a chance. Actually, I haven't hired you yet, but I'm considering hiring you to be a fashion model for my company, for my line of clothing. I'll have you try out on a small show. It won't be glamorous. If you do well, I'll take you on at base salary plus a little cash to get started. You'll get no special treatment, and you'll have to work your way up in the company like all the other girls. Oh, and you'll have to move out of the Waldorf. That was an agreement from Sarah at Ford. How's that?"

"Oh, thank you, Mr. Lauren. I will not disappoint you."

"I'm sure you won't, Nice," he replied with a chuckle. "I have left the address downstairs at the front desk. Be here at 9:00 a.m. sharp."

"Thank you, and goodbye, Mr. Lauren."

Next morning came fast. Everything was coming fast. In the Waldorf lobby, everyone seemed so impersonal. Only the doorman, who she'd given a tip upon arrival, gave her a "good morning." Exiting the hotel to catch a cab, she noticed the trash in the gutter. Her hair she'd worked on so long flew apart in the wind, and the early sunrise was giving way to a dreary day. Nice slapped herself hard to escape the trance that is New York. *I can do this.*

The taxi driver looked in the mirror but said nothing. He took her fare at the Ralph Lauren office building and gave an uninspired thanks in a Russian accent. Nice was alone in New York City. It hit her as she walked into the building. She was homesick.

There were twenty girls in the meeting room. Mr. Lauren had not arrived yet. She found a seat and sat down.

"That's *my* seat! Move it or lose it!"

She looked up to see a pencil thin blonde, maybe Eastern European by accent. Three friends backed up her order with looks of total attitude. When the blonde started to pull Nice up by the hair, Nice drove her fist right under the center of the blonde's rib cage. Instantly, the girl couldn't breathe. As she was turning pale in panic, Nice quietly whispered, "I don't know who you are or your name, but never touch me again."

She sat back down and noticed that Mr. Lauren had entered the room. Ever the eagle eye, he caught the tail end of the tiff by the body language of the four women standing over Nice.

Ralph quietly said to himself, "Welcome to New York, Nice. I see you know how to handle yourself." He walked to the podium, stood to the side of it, and kicked it three times. "Everyone, sit down. Girls! Okay, this is going to be short. I'm sorry to say the Miami show has been canceled, so all we have is the small retail show at a Target store this weekend. Only seven of you will work that one, and you know who you are. The rest of you, feel free to book the Miami date any way you can. We have a newcomer to our team who will try out at the Target retail show. No secret, she auditioned yesterday with Sarah, and I thought she'd fit in showing our fall line—that is, if she tries out well. That's my decision, and it is final, so please don't waste my time. Nice, will you please stand up?"

With ankles shaking, Nice stood up and looked around to see the neutral looks she'd already seen at the hotel. She had a job to do.

"Nice, I want to see you first in my office after this meeting. We'll go over company policy, and I'll introduce you to Jean Paul, my production manager." He looked across the room. "All you girls know he's the best in the business. Listen to him, follow his direction. Be on time, and you'll learn the secrets to success in this business."

Later in a private dressing room, as she was getting a mani-pedi, Jean Paul got to know her better.

"Actually, Nice, I'm a Frenchman, but I've lived in New York for twenty-five years. I've worked for Mr. Lauren for most of that time. By the way, you're from Kenya, right?"

"Yes, Kenya, near Kilimanjaro. I am proud of my country."

"Please excuse me, but might you know any French?"

"Oh, yes, Jean Paul, mostly what I learned on the playground as a child and also Swahili, of course. I was in grade 4, and I had a girlfriend from France. Her father was working on a water project. On the playground, she taught me French, and I taught her English."

"You're speaking Queen's English. I love it. It makes you so, so, so above."

"Ha, I only speak it when I want to make a point or just for fun. Otherwise I just speak in the common English—like *gonna* instead of *going to*. You know."

"Oh, yes, I think we'll get along fine, and I expect you'll have a great career. I'll help you. French will be our thing, okay? Please though, try to get back to speaking the Queen's English. It's not so important with your close friends, but I mean especially at formal parties, interviews, company client meetings, you know—your aura. Nice, it's how the public sees you. It will help your career. I'm sure!"

Mischievously, she answered him in seductive French, "Okay, Jean Paul, that sounds good. I will do that. Thank you for the advice."

Jean Paul expressed a pleasant surprise. "Nice, that certainly does not sound like a child's basic French."

She smiled closed lipped and thought of her conversations with Michel but said nothing of him. "Thank you again, Jean Paul."

With that, he left, and Nice smiled as she exhaled.

That evening was her last night at the Waldorf. She had hoped to stay there for at least a few weeks. Mr. Lauren had given her a starting money advance but only enough for her to find an apartment and eat. She wrote a letter to her parents and tried to explain why she had left them. As she signed it, she tried to hold back the tears, but a few fell on the page.

The next morning, she checked out and sat in the coffee shop, reading the classified rentals with her suitcase by her chair. The waitress was nice. She was from Dubuque, Iowa.

She told Nice about her first week in New York. This little friendly exchange buoyed Nice's spirits. She waved as she left the shop and walked out to the street.

The New Jersey Target store was not at all what Nice imagined it would be. She tripped just before emerging from the curtain. There were shoppers in sidewalk dress and men with dozer hats. Some leaned or had their hand on the small catwalk. Elevator music filled the air, and an announcer spoke too loudly over the microphone as he introduced the models.

The small crowd did not seem to even notice her as Nice began her pose in an expensive fall jacket and designer jeans. A two year old started screaming. Nice thought, *There is no magic here. I feel like an invisible nobody. Keep smiling! No one seems to care in this city. Dammit, everyone, look at me. I am a beautiful bird in the tree right above you! I don't think I have what it takes.*

Then, just as she finished her last pose, a little girl dressed all in pink accidentally threw her teddy bear in her exuberance. It landed at Nice's feet. As she bent over to return the bear to the youngster, a fashion photographer caught the image of the model and little girl as their eyes met. And what a photo it was. The next day, the tabloids got ahold of it, and instantly, the world of fashion wanted to know who she was, who this fresh, new face was. The phone was ringing off the hook in Mr. Lauren's office. Then came the interviews and appearances and how she was discovered in a little off-the-beaten-path town in the foothills of Kilimanjaro, Kenya. All the world loves a good story. It worked because she truly had a good story to tell.

4

One Year Later

NICE AND JENNY were best friends. They'd met that first week when Jenny's brother, who also worked for Mr. Lauren in productions, introduced them.

The girls met for a short lunch in New York City.

"How ya been, Nice? I haven't seen much of you lately. Got your message you wanted to get together. I've missed you. So what's up?"

"I have to talk to someone."

"Okay, what?"

"This modeling is, well, sometimes I think I'm going crazy."

Jenny listened.

"This job's all happened so fast. I've come from a Nairobi apartment to five star hotels in Milan, Prague, St. Petersburg, and Rio de Janeiro, and that's just the last month. It's been a change, all right, almost too much."

Jenny interrupted. "I should have it so tough. Look, I haven't had a vacation for a year and a half. Quit whining!"

"I don't know if it's the people, the schedule, or maybe me, but one thing's for sure, *I* haven't changed. I'm not complaining. It's just all been a little bit too much."

"You look tired, Nice, and yes, I'm a little jealous, but you're my friend, and I'm going to let it go right here, right now."

"I am. Yeah, I'm stressed out and tired. Last week, an Italian guy called me a supermodel. I smiled and thought to myself, 'You don't have a clue who I am. A year ago I was sleeping in a dung hut in a tiny village in Africa, happy with my mother and father and cows.'"

"Well, your life's a lot different from mine, but I do know we've all got a destiny and a purpose here."

"What kind of talk is that? Destiny? What are you now, some kind of Tony Robbins? Just talk!"

"When you know your purpose, it'll be easier for you."

"What?"

"Well, I don't know, but I do know or I think this happened for a purpose."

"Like what?"

"Well, here we are. We're here in this diner today right now instead of each doing something else. A lot of times, there's a reason for this. Some kind of force guiding your or maybe my destiny down the line. Maybe soon, maybe later."

"Wow!"

"Yeah, wow! That's what I think too, but ya can't think too much either because then you're trying too hard to steer. Do you get me, Nice, like steering?"

"Well, yes, I do. Maybe that's why I'm worn out. Maybe I'm trying to control myself too much. You know, I am too much, and yet I must. To be successful, I have to even watch how I speak to strangers. I mean, I must use the Queen's Speech even when I check into a hotel."

"There ya go, Nice. We're here in this diner right now, probably for a reason we may never know."

"Jen, this all sounds really interesting. I mean, maybe believable, but so what?"

"Well, then, how about this? That guy who took photographs of you in Kenya, and suddenly you're a model in New York. Do ya think he just dropped out of the sky into your life, into your dusty village in a rental jeep?"

"Jen, I—"

"No, Nice," Jenny interrupted. "First he had to come to Africa, Kenya, and then your daily life with your mom in a market, and then he finds you. I'm telling you, it can't be all by random. *All this!* Oh, and a little girl throws a teddy bear!"

The ladies fell silent, each lost in their own thoughts.

"I like this diner, Jenny. Do you come here often?"

"No, I only come here on Saturdays when I can get away to Manhattan for some shopping. I like it too 'cause it's old fashioned New York." Getting down to business, Nice changed the subject. "Well, what's going on? You said on the phone you have someone for me to meet."

"Yeah, well, I thought about what you said the last time we were together. The men you meet in fashion, I mean. It occurred to me yesterday that I have a guy for you to meet, well, you know."

"Jenny, what's he like?"

"Smart, no, I mean brilliant, about six feet tall with sandy hairs and blue eyes, and very good looking. How's that for a start? He's a little older than you, and he works with the bigwigs down at the Smithsonian in Washington, DC."

Nice put down her fork. "Wait, is he single? What's wrong with him? There must be something. Maybe geeky? Maybe he's the smothering type?"

"Be serious! Of course, he's single. I know because he's my boss at AnGen. You know, the place where I work. He's gone a lot, so he couldn't smother you."

"You work for him?"

"Well, he says we all work together, but yeah, I do work for him. He owns the company, signs my checks. He's really special. I like him but just as a friend. His name's Per Jorland."

"Okay, where does he live?"

"Out in Rockville, close to the lab. Look, I think, at least, he'd be fun for you to talk with. You're from Kenya, right?"

"Yes."

"Well, small world, he gets over to Kenya three or four times a year, sometimes more."

"Hmm."

"We've got a lot of gene projects going on there with exotic animals. The biggest is gene therapy for an African elephant disease. It's very high tech, splicing in a healthy gene to stop an inherited liver disease. Maybe you'd like him. That's *all* I'm saying here. He's an adventure sort of guy, drives a sports car and he has a good sense of humor. He's fun."

Nice frowned a little. "Okay, Okay. Are you talking about a blind date?"

"God, no. He's throwing the office Christmas party next weekend at his townhouse. Knowing him, it won't exactly be a slick bachelor pad, but it'll be fun! Wanna come? Nice, this is so not a big deal. You can be my guest."

Nice paused before committing. She finished what she was chewing and answered. "All right then, give me the address, and I'll give you a call." Both were getting up and walking toward the cash register.

"Thanks, Jenny. This one's on me. Might be the best check I'll ever pick up."

"Anytime, Nice. See ya next week!"

At Per's townhouse, about twenty men and women were standing in small groups around the room, relaxed and having a good time. Per made sure he talked with everyone. He had just finished talking with a doctor of molecular cell biology from Johns Hopkins when Jenny approached with Nice.

"Dr. Jorland, I brought my friend, Nice. I'd like to introduce you to her. She's from Kenya but lives in New York City now. You're bound to have something in common."

Per, reaching a hand to this beautiful woman, looked at Nice. "Hello, Nice, it's a pleasure to meet you. Please call me Per."

Nice extended her hand. "Thank you, Per. Wonderful party."

"Well, thanks. It's all I could do to call the catering company. I'm not really the entertainment type. My brother calls me the doesn't-get-out-much type."

Nice laughed. "Just the same, Per, you throw a good party. Look around." She gestured with a graceful arm.

"Jenny said you're from Kenya. Let's go out on the patio. Tell me what area and town you grew up in." Closing the door to the deck, the sounds of the party faded. It was a little bit cooler outside, and he gave her his sport jacket.

"I'm from a small town in the foothills of Kilimanjaro called Oliotokotok. I grew up in the countryside though. We had two cows."

"Two cows? Your family farms?"

"Yes, we're simple country people."

"Then how on earth did you end up here in the US? That's a big change."

"Well, I moved to New York City about a year ago. I'm a model. My agency got me a green card and paid my way. I work for Ralph Lauren, the designer."

"That's quite a story."

"My parents still live in the same village, but now they have four cows. I send them money." Nice laughed comfortably. She liked Per. *Gentle but strong*, she thought. She showed her neck, unaware as she spoke.

It suddenly hit Per. He could smell her perfume as she moved closer and brushed the back of his hand. His mind was moving so fast with this beautiful woman. "Wait, I know that town. It's near Amboseli National Park, a little Northeast of Kilimanjaro. I've had coffee at an outdoor cafe there, a place by the market."

Nice was stunned. "You know that place? I had coffee with my mother there just before I left for New York."

"It's a small world, Nice. If you grew up in the countryside in that area, you're probably a Maasai. Am I right?"

"Yes, I am Maasai. My last name is Nkoe, Nice Nkoe," she said lightly.

They looked each other in the eye as they leaned on the patio railing, quietly talking. The party continued on without them. The guests and everything else were completely forgotten until they were interrupted when some came out to say their good byes and thank Per for the party. Nice and Jenny were the last ones to leave. On their way out to the cars, Jenny asked as she fished keys from her purse, "Well, was I right? What do you think?"

"Mm. Oh, Jenny, I like him."

"Told ya."

"He asked me out on a date. He seemed a little shy about it, but I said yes right away."

"Know where you're going?"

"Not really, he just said it should be nothing special, and I like that."

"Call me sometime. Tell me how it went."

"Will do. See ya."

"Yes, see ya."

The following weekend, Per took the train from Rockville and caught a cab to Nice's apartment. It was about 3:30 p.m. when he climbed the steps to her brownstone and buzzed her apartment number.

"Hi, Nice. It's Per. Are you ready for a little fun on the town?"

"Yes, oh yes, Per. I'll be right down."

Per breathed a sigh of relief. She hadn't backed out. He motioned to the driver to wait. She opened the door looking fresh and dressed elegantly yet casual. "A wonderful day for a date, isn't it, Per?"

He took her hand as their eyes met.

She thought, *I like this. He feels natural as if I've known him longer. The magic is still between us.*

As they settled into the seat, Per said to the driver, "Please take us down to Battery Park."

Nice tilted her head quizzically. "Battery Park? The Staten Island Ferry?"

"No, but close. The tour boat to the Statue of Liberty."

"Right on, sir," the driver said as he turned to comment and see Nice. "I know it well."

"The Statue of Liberty? I saw it from the plane, but—"

"Yes! I thought you would really appreciate her after living in New York now for a year. I was there once as a kid—a school trip—so it'll be special for me too."

Nice laughed. "Per, I already knew this would be fun. I mean, you're fun without even trying."

"Try? Oh, I'm doing my best. You're worth trying for!"

They took the tour, both fascinated by the stories and history surrounding Lady Liberty.

"I'm glad you brought me here."

"It was the only place that makes sense."

Inside the base were aging photographs of immigrants arriving in America. One photo caught Nice's attention. "I like this one, a woman and her three children each with a small suitcase. That's how I arrived. Do you like children?"

"Oh, yes. When they're young, they are our dream. When they're older, they are our hope."

"What do you hope for them?"

Per thought for a while about her question. "To be better stewards of our beautiful earth, our plants, animals, our land, and seas. There is a constant stream of interaction of processes and mysteries that maintain our beautiful planet."

"Someday, I want children."

"I have a brother."

"I was an only child," Nice replied.

"Any parent would be proud of you."

"You don't know me," she smiled as she took him by the hand and slightly squeezed.

"We'd better get back to the boat," Per said. They ran and caught it just in time.

Back at the pier, they stood waiting for a cab. Nice took his hand and breathed deeply. "I feel great after the wind and that fresh harbor air."

"Well, then it's time for me to do something that I've always wanted to do."

Nice hesitated, turned toward Per, raised her chin, and closed her eyes, expecting the perfect New York kiss. It didn't come. Finally she asked, "Then what would that be, Per?"

"Something a little sensuous."

She thought, *What could be better than a kiss? He missed his chance.* Out loud, she asked with one raised eyebrow, "Again, what would that be?"

A cab pulled up, and, as they got in, Per said to the driver, "Take us to the Plaza, please."

"Right, sir. The Plaza Hotel."

"The Plaza?"

"Yes, Nice, the Plaza." They headed up Broadway.

"Why the Plaza?"

"It's kind of a secret. You know, a personal secret."

"Tell me."

"Well."

"You can tell me."

"Okay, I will tell you. I've always had a dream to have cheesecake and coffee at the Plaza with a beautiful woman, a beautiful woman like you. I think I'm—"

Nice laughed and put her arms around him. "You think you're what?"

"I think I'm falling in love."

"Me too," she answered as she pulled him to her, and they kissed.

The maitre d' seated them, they ordered and for the first time, neither spoke, each waiting for the other. Finally, Nice blinked her eyes in playful fun and asked, "What is it like to be a scientist?"

Per smiled at the simplicity of such a complicated question. He put down his fork and took his napkin to his lips. "A scientist is an explorer in an ever enlarging frontier, no matter what the discipline. Those in original research, like me, must have a passion for truth that must last a lifetime."

"I understand."

"Some, those who lack the passion, invariably cannot continue past their doctoral dissertations. They become stagnant."

"But don't you ever get bored from working the same problem so long?"

"Like a humble me, most of the really great scientists are or were of intermediate intelligence—smart enough to dream of a possibility but not so brilliant as to become bored."

"So that's how you seem so fresh and interested, like now, our first date?"

"One could say that, and through examination of your deductions through the scientific method, you probably have a solid hypothesis worth further exploration," he said with a laugh.

"You are fun to be with. I always thought scientists were stuffy."

"I'd start on evolution of a theory, but this cheesecake is calling me. How 'bout more coffee?"

"Sounds great, but you're talking all around it."

"What, around what?"

"What's it like?"

"Oh! It's fun, fun to do what I love."

"But it can't be all fun. Modeling's not all fun. Sometimes I sleep till ten, get up, and don't know what to do."

"You're right. Sometimes I'm in the field, miserable from tsetse flies or mosquito bites. Dengue fever's not fun. A flat tire in lion country's not fun. Coming home to an empty townhouse is not always fun."

"I'm sorry I asked."

"Truth."

"So how *did* you become a scientist?"

"As a kid I was fascinated by nature. I would watch a colony of ants for hours or catch and examine anything that slithered or hopped. College was biology and chemistry, then some postgrad teaching at Stanford, PhD, but I wasn't the university type. I broke away from the tenure state-of-mind. Sound boring?"

"No. What is tenure?"

"You don't know?"

"Not really. Something about time served?"

"It's when you lock into a university for all your life, and then finally get your fat pension when you retire. It's a fork in the road for most future scientists. I did it my way and started my own company."

"Tell me about that."

"I had returned to my office after teaching a vertebrate zoology undergrad and there was a letter from the Smithsonian Institute on my desk."

"Was it good news?"

"Yes, I couldn't believe it. It was an invitation to interview for an elephant gene project the institute was starting and funding in Kenya. I'd never even been to Africa."

"And you passed the interview?"

"I was so nervous but didn't show it."

"I know about that."

"So I went from barefoot and knee-deep in the swamp by my house to improving the gene pool of the African elephant in Kenya."

"What is the biggest mystery in biology?"

"Easy. It's the origin of animals. It's called the Cambrian era explosion, where fossils of advanced symmetrical marine animals suddenly appear in rock strata from 540 million years ago. The next older rock strata layer, the Precambrian, reveals only simple one-celled organisms like bacteria or algae but no transitional animals. The mystery, Nice: where did all this immense wealth of functional genetic information suddenly come from to build them?

"Many of these marine animals were closely related to lobsters or crabs with hard segmented shells. These were very complicated animals with complicated body plans like stereoscopic eyes, articulated legs, muscles, digestive tracts, hearts, and brains. Modern molecular biology and mathematical population genetic models have proven that the old Darwin theory of random mutation and natural selection cannot explain their sudden appearance in the indisputable fossil record."

She took a graceful sip of coffee. "That's fascinating. So you are a scientist."

"Yes." He smiled and nodded confidently.

"So what are you thinking with that smile?"

"Okay, I am thinking a line I heard long ago around a campfire in the bush."

"Tell it to me."

"I heard it from a PH, a professional hunter, in Kenya. It goes like this: 'The most dangerous big game hunting in the world is a woman.'"

She laughed. "You give me far too much credit. If you're hunting me, I cannot tell."

"Hunting? I'm just trying to get through my first date since I can't remember. What about you? What matters to *you*?"

She answered without hesitation, "Money."

"Only money?"

"Yes, money."

Per smiled and then broke into a light chuckle. "Well, I guess you could have said world peace."

"What is funny about that?"

"Oh, nothing. It's just a beauty pageant joke. But what's it like, modeling? I mean. I know nothing about that world."

"Oh, glamorous. Arrogant people."

"But what's it like? I told you—"

"It's…," she couldn't get started.

"You're African. So what's it like?"

"There were these traditions for the women where we'd all dance in a circle while the men watched. You know, demeaning fertility dances and suggestive moves. I never liked going to the middle."

"Were you shy?"

"No, it all seemed so primitive. I tried to tell my mother, Nonkipa, after one of those days. It was a special holiday."

"Like a county fair?"

"Yes, there were tourists bused in. Imagine, five buses of gawking tourists wearing khaki shorts, belt packs, and expensive cameras slung over the shoulders."

"What did she say?"

"She was not at all like the other mothers. She encouraged me to study hard so I could one day leave and compete with men."

"You were lucky to have her."

"Yes, she helped me get into the university."

"But you're a model. Why are you willing to go to the middle now?"

"That was old and primitive and in front of—"

"In front of what?"

"The old women who tried to circumcise me. I hated them."

"Now I understand. I know that tradition."

"When I was about seventeen or eighteen years old, I was in a high school boarding school. My parents were too poor to help with tuition, but my marks were so high above the boys, I had a scholarship."

"I've only known you for a short time, but you must have had a serious side if you got high marks. How did that feel, I mean, being better than the boys?"

"I *was* serious. I fought my way. Growing up poor, knowledge was a life or death issue. I was so scared."

"When?"

"In order to earn a scholarship to secondary school, one must score high marks on the three day national test called KCPE. It covers math, English, government, geography, you know, everything. Only a few qualify. The rest must carry on for life with only a fifth or sixth grade level. Their mothers cry. They are locked out with no future."

"So you scored well?"

"Yes. I felt I knew all the answers, but I was shocked to find I scored highest mark of all surrounding districts. That day was the most important day of my life. After that, I knew nothing could stop me."

"Nice, I've taken a lot of tests. They were hard, but none so important."

"So I knew I would not be poor if I was smart. There was a bird that woke me up every morning at just the right time. It was a little sparrow. I would rise, rub my eyes, and step to the window. Rather than fly, it would spread its wings and let me touch them. It turned its head to look at me with one eye. I always looked for its mate, but it was always alone."

"That's incredible! Wild!"

"I think it was telling me to fly away."

He took a sip of coffee to wash down his cheesecake. "That's quite a story."

"Yes, so here I am in New York, and I'm in the circle and I love it."

"You flew and—"

"When that photographer came, I flew. I ran to danger. Later, I thought of the possibility that he could not have been a photographer but involved in human trafficking. I was lucky. I'm the bird, and I have a song to sing. I love the excitement of a big show."

"Tell me." He smiled.

"Sometimes it's hard to remember who I am. There's so much illusion. My only responsibility is to be on time, look fresh, make people want to be like me, oh, and buy the clothes I wear. It's all about image, illusion. Maybe that's why I'm attracted to you."

Per looked up, pleasantly surprised. "Why's that?"

"A scientist sees through illusion. You're real."

They turned to listen to the end of a piece a violinist was playing near their table. Per laughed. "Sometimes I run to danger, too. Sometimes it runs to me or sometimes I just stumble upon it."

"I don't know if you're saying something funny or you're thinking of some of your adventures."

"Adventures?" Per straightened up. "I own a business. Any adventure is a side perk of what I do. You know Kenya, the Serengeti. What I do is not a travelog. I'm fighting for the survival of an exotic species. There are only three species of elephant left on earth."

"I am sorry. I only meant to say, as a model, I run to it in my own way."

"I see that. In a dicey situation, I think you would be fearless, and I'm attracted to you."

"We are opposites—illusion and science. I like that."

"What don't I know about you?"

"I have a bad temper. My mother warned me about it just before I left."

"What do you mean by bad?" Per stiffened. "I haven't seen that side."

"Oh, here comes the scientist, always searching."

Per chuckled. "Just wondering."

"You don't want to know."

Per looked up, swallowed his cheesecake, and put his fork down. "Yes, I do. I would really like to hear this. There are different layers of bad. There's naughty bad and then there's really bad—damn near evil mixed with a tincture of dishonesty and secrecy." He hesitated. "So where does your bad fit in?"

"Sometimes I just go into a rage, do something, but can't remember it. Or sometimes, if I know I'm right, I'll punch someone in the face."

"Really?"

"I didn't tell the full story."

"What story?"

"I tried to kill the woman who was pulling me into the circumcision hut."

"Tell me."

"I told my mother to hide me in the bush, but that night I found a tree limb, a club, and went to her hut. I was so quiet and was just about to enter her hut and smash in her head. Her dog barked, and when she lit her lamp, I ran back to the bush where my mother found me in the morning. Per, I hated her so. I told no one. Not even my mother."

"I'm glad you failed. The police would have taken you. I've known men like that in bars. They're dangerous but never a woman. Sounds like blind passion to me. Any of your distant relatives like that? You know, heredity?"

"Warriors. Many warriors."

Per nodded. "Oh yeah, that makes sense."

"So now you know."

"Have you gone like that lately?"

"Just before I left home, I broke a man's front tooth."

Per finished his coffee and looked her straight in the eye. "This is getting a little dark, Nice. I hope you never flip out on me!"

"No, no, no. I would never!"

Per relaxed and put his napkin on the table. "Well then, very interesting. You're a very interesting woman. That pretty much ends it."

"Yes, yes, Per. I would prefer that."

He smiled. "How 'bout we leave? Great talk. Great coffee. Great cheesecake!"

On the way home, Nice asked the driver to stop about four blocks from her apartment. They got out and walked hand in hand. For a time, both were silent, and then Nice asked quietly, "I've been here over a year now, and there's a question women talk about often in the dressing rooms."

Per smiled, not knowing what to expect. "And the question?"

"Do you believe in love at first sight?"

"I didn't really know until today. Yes, I believe I do. I'm a scientist, so part of me says it's just hormones gone wild, but it sure feels good. How about you?"

"I'm different. I am wary of men. You taste right when I kiss you, and I like your eyes."

"And you, Nice, you don't need perfume."

"And you don't seem to care that I'm a model. A New York model. I like that. Here's my apartment."

"It's been wonderful, Nice. Let's do it again." He started to move closer for a goodbye kiss, and she stopped him.

"Would you like to come in? You don't know much about women, Per," she said with a laugh. "Just for an hour or two. It's not late."

"That would be, I mean, I would like that very much."

"Well then," she said with a smile, "what are you waiting for? Open the door, Per."

5

Two Years Later

THE ANNUAL PARIS Spring Fashion Week could only be called one thing: ordered chaos. Jean Paul, the slender man with exploding energy, the guy every model loves like a brother, shouted, "Keep moving, girls. You're looking fabulous. Debra, I love your style! You're up, doll. Go, go, go!"

Back in dressing area blue, eight girls were changing and having their makeup checked. They were on the catwalk in five to eight minutes. It was bedlam—a mishmash of shoes, belts, bras, hair poofers, and attitudes. A cut from Pink was blaring from the showroom. The house was packed. This was the big time, what every aspiring model around the world hoped for, the Holy Grail of international modeling. This was every little girl's dream come true: the Eiffel Tower, the boats going up and down the Seine, the Louvre Museum, croissants in a sidewalk cafe with rich, strong coffee in tiny cups and beautiful clothes, the latest designs on your body, walking down the walk, living the dream.

"Last month my husband and I had sex almost every night."

"That's a joke, Nice?"

"Yeah, we had sex almost on Monday, almost on Tuesday, almost on Wednesday." They both howled.

Nice turned to her friend Ariana. "When this is over, I'm taking a long rest."

"Me too."

"Leave all the glitz."

"Don't have to convince me."

"I need to get back to what counts. Don't get me wrong, I enjoy modeling. It's fun when you're out there, but I'm tired."

Ariana imitates John Paul, "Nice, you look absolutely fabulous!"

"Good try. I need some quiet." Nice laughed.

"I know what you mean though. I'm beat too, but the *big* money and the perks aren't bad either."

"Perks? Did I hear perks? Tell me!"

"I've got a new guy. We're off for a few weeks to a fabulous spa on the Black Sea after our last show here. Lie in the sun with my sunglasses and straw hat, daily massages, sleeping late. Ah, then I'll be ready to go again. Know what I mean? How 'bout you? You're married, right?"

"I'm on a plane back to the US, back to my husband, Per. He's great. Tomorrow's our first anniversary already. I cannot believe it."

"Huh, one year of marital bliss. I'll bet!"

"Don't get cute. We met at a Christmas party. Get this, he knew the little town near where I grew up. He's flying home tomorrow from Kenya where he has a genetics project on elephants. It's complicated DNA and gene stuff. I can't explain it, but he's perfect for me, you know? He's smart, sexy."

"That's great. Don't explain it. I damn near failed every science course, and we're on in a few minutes."

They both laughed. Ariana turned her head as the stylist gently turned it back, touching up her eyelashes. "Elephants," she said out of nowhere.

Nice smiled. "Yes, African elephants. You know, the big ones? Trunks. Tusks. Trample. Some of it's hard, dangerous work."

Looking at her friend in the mirror, Ariana summed it up. "Someday I'll get married, just not yet! Hope I get a man as good as yours, sexy."

Nice returned the look, and they both laughed. The noise was getting louder.

"Yeah, he's sexy enough, but it's not all a bed of roses."

"Oh?"

"I want children, and it just isn't happening. We're trying hard to have a baby, but it's not working. It's not me. We argue about it. Sometimes I'm just a bitch about it all."

"Did I hear bitch?"

"Yeah, a real bitch. A few months ago we were out to dinner at the Four Seasons in Manhattan."

"Sweet!"

"No, not sweet. Big night. His birthday. We argued over trying to have a baby. It was a thousand dollar dinner. I started it. I was too loud, and people began to look at us. Then the maître d' came to our table and gave us the nod. You know, that nod like an Americanized French shrug."

"Paparazzi catch you?"

"No, but it was embarrassing. We left."

"You've got to get control of that bitch thing, Nice. Be cool. Babies come when you least expect them." She laughed.

"We're trying hard. We're going in-vitro."

The noise was deafening.

"What did you say, Nice? I'll meet you? You're going to meet *who*?"

Nice shook her head but Ariana was gone. Jean Paul's voice was frantic over the music. "Girls, girls, girls, you're on. Go! Go! Go!" The door opened, and the music exploded as the models made their way to the curtained entrance.

Ariana stepped into the spotlight and began her walk. As she reached the end and began to pose, Nice entered the spotlight. The music was peaking and instantly there was a low roar from the crowd. She did her walk, that languid walk she'd learned on the path she knew by heart. *It's hard to see with cameras flashing, strobe lights, and the deafening music. It's an exciting ritual*, Nice thought. As she neared the end of the runway, she paused to strike three poses. On the third pose, Nice spied Marcus just below her, capturing the moment. *Marcus, you wonderful man, thank you*, she thought as she blew him a kiss. Their eyes met, and he flashed a big smile, nod, and wink.

The following day, Nice took an airport limo home. Dressed in faded jeans, a turquoise silk tee, and Jimmy Choo sandals, she looked every bit the supermodel she was as she stepped from the car and retrieved her Louis Vuitton luggage. Unlocking the door, she went in, dropped her bags in the hallway, headed to the refrigerator, and hit the play button on the answering machine.

> You have two messages.
> First message (in French):

> "Nice, it's Jean Paul. You were *fabulous* in Paris. Mr. Lauren has some new ideas for summer fashion. They're on the drawing board now. Get some beauty sleep, take a rest, and I'll call you."

Nice thought, *Oh, Jean Paul, the hardest thing about modeling is, I think you know it by now, I'm not that fancy lady in the spotlight. I'm just a country girl.*

6

Second message: "Hey, happy anniversary, Nice. Can't believe it's been a year already. I'm on my way home. Should be there in about an hour, and I'm really looking forward to this evening alone with you. See you soon, sweetie."

NICE SMILED WHEN she heard the message. She too, was looking forward to a quiet evening at home. With Per in Kenya and she on a European Fashion Tour in France, Italy and Monaco, they had not seen each other in two weeks.

Per touched the gift wrapped package on the seat next to him. Inside was an ebony carving of a Maasai man and woman. He turned the radio on to 109.4 to catch up on the evening news.

And now for all you science buffs, it's that time of year again. The Nobel Committee announced the recipients of the annual prize in economics, chemistry, medicine, and physics, as provided for in the will of Alfred Nobel, the Swedish industrialist and inventor of dynamite who died in 1896. Dr.

Lowell Blakely got the call from Sweden this morning. He'll be receiving the Nobel Prize in Medicine and Genetics at the gala awards event this December at the Stockholm Concert Hall. Dr. Blakely will be taking home a gold Nobel medallion and one million dollars in cash for his work on human DNA, the twenty-three human chromosomes that make us what and who we are.

Our true genetic heritage may be at stake here. Could humans someday reach immortality? Artificially enhanced humans are now thought to be possible someday. Dr. Blakely's only comment to the media was this: "We've learned a lot, but we have far to go. I am thankful for this honor. I have plans to write a book. The team working with me is brilliant." In other news, there was…

Per, disgusted, turned off the radio. "Blakely? That damned Blakely! I'm not surprised," he muttered under his breath, disgusted. "And who writes this trash they read on the air? Immortality? Huh?"

Nice's career had taken off like a rocket, and it wasn't long until they bought a beautiful nineteenth-century Tudor on the Potomac, MacArthur Boulevard, in Bethesda. It's probably my favorite drive inside the beltway. Every time I drive

MacArthur, I imagine it as the old horse-and-buggy road in the eighteenth century. And I've got memories about that road.

I attended St. John's College High School, a military prep school founded in 1861. It was the late fifties. The building was the crumbling old Russian Embassy by National Federal Park. The neighborhood was a ghetto. There were no guns then, and fist fights were a part of everyday life with the locals. It was a game.

They called us Mopheads, Johnnymops, or Mailmen because we wore the grey, old style West Point uniforms. When things got really dicey, like when we were outnumbered, we pulled off our garrison belts and used them as whips for protection and, of course, win. It was one for all and all for one. We were tough.

I played football. No glory. We played on a hundred yards of baked dirt where I almost lost my front teeth. If you got in trouble, you held an M 1 rifle all day above your head. Every day was hell week.

Things got better when we moved to the new school on Military Road, Northwest of Rock Creek Park. Better because now we could drive. We all had hot cars. Our parents had money, and they were generous with it. When the school bell rang, it was like the start of a race at Le Mans to get to our cars and hot rod past Glen Echo Amusement Park and up MacArthur to a genuine hamburger and malt like that one in the movie Grease. It was all about girls. I was a teenager with a red Chevy convertible, but I still knew how special it was to grow up on the shores of the Potomac. Guess that's just the Smithsonian in me.

I think Per was a little uncomfortable in his new digs at first. I stopped by to see the house, and the first thing he said was it was such a long walk from the living room to the kitchen. My favorite room, though, was the study done in two hundred year old maple. The desk was royal, but what really caught my curiosity was the expert knife carving of the name Ulysses S. Grant on the lower right drawer. President Grant never lived there so I wonder what sort of conversations happened in this room and why his name was carved there.

I liked that Per hadn't changed. I had so much going at the institute, I needed a good friend to relax with, and that's what we did. Relax. So enough from me. Back to my story.

Per called to Nice as he walked through the front door, "Where are you, honey?"

"I'm in the kitchen. Just heating up some soup."

He stepped into the room and dropped his bag. Nice, barefoot and wearing no makeup, was at the stove, stirring a pot.

"God, it's been a long time," Per said, holding Nice in his arms. "Two weeks! I really missed you, sweetie. I was lying in a tent on the other side of the world thinking of you, and I *really* missed you!"

"And I missed you more, Per. This one seemed too long. Two weeks is far too long. Life's just flat. Life's flat without you."

"Well, we'll find a way to make up for those days, won't we? I have a few ideas."

Nice stepped back and looked at Per with mischief on her mind. "Ideas, like what? Maybe I've got a few ideas of my own. Maybe they're better than yours."

"Well, it looks like we've got more ideas to work on than Thomas Edison!"

Nice laughed and wrapped her arms around him and held him close.

"Thanks for the Makonde, Per. It makes a beautiful centerpiece."

"I bought it from an old man in a small village, a master carver. I watched him finish it. He said a good spirit had already moved into it before he first held it. I'm glad you like it. Say, did you hear the news? It's all over the radio."

"What?"

"My old professor from Stanford, Dr. Blakely, got the call from the Nobel Committee today. He'll be in Sweden in December to accept the Nobel Prize for his work on DNA."

"That's wonderful! Are you going to call him?" Nice asked as she came out of the kitchen with two glasses of wine and sat down next to him on the sofa. Noticing his dejected eyes, she asked, "What's wrong, Per? You're always happy when you come home from a long trip."

"Sure, I'll give him a call. Don't want to, but I will. All right, I'll say it. It just doesn't seem fair. Maybe I'm jealous. Human genome research gets all the recognition, all the excitement, all the praise." Per stumbled, looking for the words to explain.

"What do you mean? I thought you liked your work. You're successful. You own your own company. What more could you want?"

"I'm doing the same thing, but it's on African elephants, and it's just *Big Deal*! If I could start over again, I'd be in human genetics. That's where the action is, that's where the grants are, that's where genetic cures for disease are, and that's where all the money is." He turned to her with a smile. "But then I never would have met you."

Nice thought for a moment and said, "Money? We have money. There's a Maasai saying about being careful what you ask for. It goes something like this: 'There might be a snake in the beautiful basket.'"

"Right, and there's another about the grass is always greener. I know," Per replied.

They stood up together, and she wrapped her arms around him. "I love you," she said, gazing into his eyes and ran her fingers through his thick, sandy hair. "It's never too late for a good looking smart man like you to change your profession. You know I'd stand by you all the way."

Per, feeling a little better at her words, replied, "Thanks, I needed that."

"Come on, I'm starving."

That was a carefree yet professional period in Per's life. His business was growing, and he'd found who he thought to be the perfect girl, but there was something between them I wasn't aware of at that time.

Per was sole owner of AnGen, a small biotech company dedicated to the practical research in animal genetics and disease intervention. He coined the business name AnGen, short for "Animal Genetics." When DNA research boomed, Rockville became the mecca of biotech scientists and their private companies due to the close proximity to Washington, DC, and what else: grants. Per was lucky to avoid the Washington funding two-step. I personally saw to it that our budget always included his work in Kenya. We were tied for the long haul. I liked him from the start. He was an extremely bright biologist, plus he was tough, so I didn't mind being his angel.

This was their first anniversary. After a year of dating, they were married in a quiet ceremony in the party room at the Kenyan Embassy in Washington, DC. Tambo, Per's trusted friend and tracker from Kenya, was Per's best man, and Jenny, Nice's best friend, was maid of honor. Jomo and Nonkipa Nkoe, Nice's parents, were guests of honor. Tambo had accompanied them on the flight from Nairobi.

Nice wore a silk Kanga *accented by three-in-one necklaces and bracelets made of colorful Maasai beads. Delicate thong sandals completed her wedding outfit. Only two photographers, Marcus and a trusted paparazzi, were allowed in to record the ceremony for the star-thirsty public. Nice had always told Per, "For the rest of my life, I will never spend another night in a hut," but when Per pointed out a story in Conde Nast about honeymooning in Tahiti, the pictures of romantic huts at the end of long docks into aqua-blue waters changed her mind. And Tahiti it was.*

Nice was an only child, and her dream of a family of four or five children became a frequent topic of their future plans. Per was all for it. His only brother was a confirmed bachelor. Who would carry on the family genes? With their incomes, they could afford it, but as of their first anniversary, they were still working on having even one child. Frustrated from trying, they sought the help of a fertility doctor.

After dinner, Per helped clear the table.

"Oh, by the way, did you see your mail?"

"No, not yet. Why?"

"You got a letter from the Smithsonian today. It's on your desk in the library. You go. I'll finish up here, and then we'll have dessert. Take your time. It's great to be home together. I love you."

Smithsonian Animal Gene Pool Project
900 Jefferson Drive SW
Suite 1002, MCR 304
Washington, DC 20560

Dear Per,

Again, congratulations on your work on the African elephant gene therapy project. You will be relieved to know future funding for AnGen/Kenya has been approved for Phase II. The Kenyans have given you high marks on your fieldwork. On another more urgent matter, we have "one upped" the American Museum of Natural History. A perfectly preserved bull wooly mammoth was discovered by a Saami (Lapp) family above the Arctic Circle in Northern Norway. Its location is an ancient ice field in Finnmark. Excavation began a few weeks ago and is near completion. The Smithsonian has paid the Norwegians for DNA tissue samples to be used in cloning and for a sperm sample from the bull. Per, the timing is perfect. We recently received funding for our new Resurrection Biology Project. The goal is to recreate a recently extinct species. Another team will begin work on the passenger pigeon.

I'm sending you to secure the samples before the mammoth is airlifted by helicopter to a Lapp mountain cave for further study. Returning to Maryland at once, you and your team can then begin initial genetic assessments on the samples and attempt to bring a sperm sample back to life. It is our hope to mate this Saami mammoth with the clone of the 20,000-year-old Jarkov mammoth found in Siberia 1997.

Dr. Hald Aarbakke will meet your arrival at the Oslo airport. It'll be cold there, Per. Your Scandinavian blood should love it!

Sincerely,
Larry Calvert
Director, Smithsonian Institute

Later that evening, after making love, Per broke the news from the Smithsonian Institute.

"Larry Calvert wants me up to the Arctic Circle in Norway as soon as possible."

"The Arctic Circle, really?"

"Yeah, there's a frozen mammoth that he wants DNA and sperm from, and it has to be done before it's airlifted from the ice field to ensure there's no mistake like decomposition from an accidental melt."

"And he asked you?"

"Yeah, well, elephants, mammoths, they're pretty much the same. I hope it won't take too long."

"It's very cold up there this time of year."

"That should be interesting though. Maybe I need a cold adventure after all those hot trips to Kenya. Besides, maybe I need something new."

"How old is a find like that?"

"Wooly's been on ice for at least eleven thousand years."

"Sounds like you're in for a new kind of adventure, maybe a big hairy one," Nice said with a chuckle as she rolled over on top of him and changed the subject. "I think you're sexier than, well, you're sexy and don't even know it. One day in your life is more of an adventure than what that stuffy old Lowell Blakely and his Nobel shmobel has. Besides, I love you, babe. I haven't had an elephant charge me like you did in the last two weeks!"

Per laughed. "Wow, keep it coming. You're really building me up."

"You know I'm doing my best!"

"Every day is fun with you, and the nights aren't bad either." He turned out the light.

"I saw Marcus Balieau in Paris yesterday," Nice said. "I was doing my thing at the end of the runway, and I thought if I hadn't met him that day in the market, I wouldn't have met you. I blew him a kiss. Jealous?"

"Insanely. Come here." Per rolled over and snuggled closer. "Thanks for not talking about a baby."

I'd just walked into my office the following morning when my phone rang. It was Per.

"Larry, I got your letter, and it's a little different for me. Thanks for giving me a shot at this."

"Please don't mention it. There's a lot of PhDs around, mostly a dime a dozen. You live this sort of stuff. Sometimes I wish I could get outta here more myself, but the institute's been good to me. I've been all over the world."

"Well, Larry, I just wanted to check in to see if there's a story behind the story. You know, heads-up info."

"Other than minus thirty-five below Fahrenheit, it's pretty much just a 'bring 'em back' adventure for ya. Say, how's Nice? I haven't seen you two for quite a while except for that story in People magazine."

"She's great, Larry. After all this, we'll give you a call. How 'bout that Blakely I heard about yesterday? Just got back and heard it on the news."

"Blakely? Scuttle I heard, he was behind the curve. In fact, there was a minor mutiny 'cause his people knew more and had better ideas than he did along the way, but he—"

Per interrupted, "Got the Nobel."

"Yeah, Per, he got the Nobel and the mil."

"Well, when I heard it, I was thinking about how my life could have been."

"Look, you and AnGen, you've got something real that you can hang a hat on. You'll be fine."

"Thanks."

"Go with me here. You're fine."

"So I'm leaving for Norway tomorrow. I'll give you a call when I get back with the samples. It should be fun, cold but fun."

"There ya go, Per. Good luck, and take care of yourself!"

"Will do. Later then."

"Bye for now."

"Yeah, Larry. Good to talk to you."

7

IT WAS THAT time of year near winter solstice when the Arctic night seems to last forever, long enough to reach total blackness on a cloudy night. Snow and sky meld into a deep abyss where humans are uninvited.

The spartan camp consisted of three Saami laavos. In the center of each tent was a fire pit. Fifty paces away was the excavation site, with two other laavos set up for equipment and gear. A rectangular trench eighteen feet deep and six feet wide had been dug around the perimeter of the mammoth. Unlike the Siberian Jarkov mammoth excavation, there had been no temporary cover over this dig, and the harsh conditions left the Saami workers exhausted.

Finally, it was the last night at the site. Two Saami workers in the main laavo took turns tending the fire while they listened to Dr. Aarbakke. He pulled a paper from his pack. On it was a chart of geological time corresponding to the fossil record. He handed it to Per who studied it, then passed it on to the two Saamis. Dr. Aarbakke started, "In the beginning of the nineteenth century, a French scientist named Cuvier found huge skeletons of animals near Paris. They were so huge, no one could identify what animal on earth they were from. At that time, most scientists thought the earth to be only three or four thousand years old. Fossil bones were, until then, thought to be from animals currently alive on earth. No one had yet even imagined the concept of extinction. The bones turned out to be from a wooly mammoth. Its jawbone did not match either that of an Indian or African elephant."

"How wrong they were! Fossil records go back millions of years," Per added.

"Now, of course, we know that's not true."

"That's right, Doctor, millions of species walked the earth, and then became extinct, never to be seen again."

The two Saami were fascinated by this story of a French scientist from two hundred years ago. One of them looked to Dr. Aarbakke. "Tell us more about the fossils."

Dr. Aarbakke cleared his throat to speak, but again Per interrupted, "Modern scientists have divided the fossil record into eras. The mammoth you have been excavating lived in the end of the last era, the Cenozoic Era, called the Pleistocene Age. For three million years, they roamed the earth."

Dr. Aarbakke, surprised by Per's knowledge, interrupted, "How do you know so much?"

"Well, you might call me a bit of an amateur paleontologist. Now and then, I've gotten my hands dirty. There are a lot of digs going on in Africa. In Kenya, early human digs are common along the Great Rift. I stop in on them occasionally. My friends, the Leakeys, have an important dig going on the West shore of Lake Turkana. Let me tell ya, somehow they always find the hottest places to dig. I'll never know how they can find a few bones the size of my fingernail and call it a new human species." Then, turning to the Saami, he continued, "That area and to the South are called the Cradle of Humanity."

The Saami again asked, "Tell us more about the mammoth."

Dr. Aarbakke continued, "It's got to be more than eleven thousand years old because it's been proven by carbon-14 analysis that's about when they went extinct."

Per nodded.

Then Dr. Aarbakke caught Per's attention when he resumed. "One thing we don't know is how did such a large beast seemingly become—may I be so bold as to say— cryogenically frozen, still standing midchew?"

Per remarked, "That *is* astonishing, Doctor! I didn't know this was a rare find."

Puzzled, Dr. Aarbakke continued, "I thought the Smithsonian told you how historic this find is."

"Historic? A cryogenic freezing? How the hell is that possible? I do know about cryogenic freezing: fertility doctors freeze sperm and eggs to be regenerated years later. But could that happen?"

Dr. Aarbakke began thoughtfully and spoke, "New evidence suggests that an asteroid hit the earth around twelve thousand years ago, give or take, a couple hundred. Researchers say that asteroid hit may have triggered an extended period of unusual coldness across the entire planet. To those who have studied this period, this rapid freeze is known as the Younger Dryas, and there's a theory that this local area was already cool when suddenly a monumental rain of comets like ice balls fell from space, temporarily bringing the local area to a temperature approximating that of outer space—an intense local cryogenic quick freeze, Per, I don't know. I just don't know. There have been finds in large areas that are littered with crushed bones. No explanation. Maybe comet-like ice balls. Who knows, Per? Who knows? I just don't know."

Aarbakke continued, "But one thing both you and I know is there are still many secrets our earth and universe have yet to reveal. We tend to believe only what is in our short recorded history, yet here in this corner of the earth is a mammoth seemingly cryogenically frozen. Logic says we must accept this also as recorded history and ambient outer space must be the origin of such an event."

The two Saami were wide eyed as Per remarked, "If this is true, it's absolutely incredible, but then, you're right, we'll probably never know."

"We have no shaman here," one Saami whispered to the other in a worried tone.

"Another thing", Dr. Aarbakke looked at the three, "we've always thought the glaciers and ice fields of Northern

Norway to be only four thousand years old as in the South. With this find, we now must conclude they have to be at least fifteen thousand years old!"

Per looked up from the fire. "Flying up here for samples, I had no idea the sperm and DNA would be cryogenically frozen! If this holds true, good DNA is great, but I may be able to bring the sperm back to life. Imagine that."

"I know. I'm just as thrilled and hopeful as you are. This will be—hold on, we've got a call coming in."

The discussion was suddenly cut short when the radio crackled one last time in Norwegian.

> Repeat, we are tracking large North Atlantic storm moving in tomorrow. Have mammoth carriage and hoist straps in GO position. Repeat: GO position. Mission must be underway at 0500 hours. Repeat, two choppers at your position at 0500. Out.

Dr. Aarbakke yawned. "Tomorrow's gonna come fast. We'd best get in a good sleep. Once those choppers get here, all hell is going to break loose."

They buried themselves deep in reindeer hides and soon all were fast asleep.

The fire had reduced to glowing coals when Per woke up from a light sleep. Everyone in the laavo was wrapped up in reindeer hides and asleep for the deep Arctic night. Per got up, stoking the fire with more wood while thinking about the mystery of the beast's demise.

I wonder. What if all those animals hadn't become extinct? No, they'd be so exotic we'd slaughter them like black rhinos, Bengal Tigers, whales, and the redwoods with no conscience. Modern humans, what does that mean anyway? Dinosaurs are extinct, maybe soon African elephants. All my work. Who even cares? We call ourselves modern, yet we poison our air, water, and slash and burn the rainforests. How soon till we're extinct? Yeah, how soon? There's a God, I know, who created heaven and earth. I believe that, but after all our crimes, how will he judge us? Maybe he'll just forget our species, rearrange our molecules, and try again. Can't go on forever. There's gonna be a reckoning, Per mused.

Knowing he would never again see the hairy red time capsule in this wilderness setting, Per quietly donned his parka and high-powered halogen headlamp, then slipped through the flap. Two Saami dogs lifted their heads but did not bark. Instead, they returned their noses to the thick fur of their hind legs. It was bitter cold.

Per double-checked the many thick nylon straps, then stopped to wonder at the huge, silent form. He thought, *I'm lucky Larry picked me to be here in this place at this time. There are many others he could have picked, and yet I'm the one. This could be my big break. I'll be famous, maybe just for fifteen minutes, but I'll be famous. It's not the Nobel, but beggars can't be choosers. So what if it ends up in some dusty museum corner? I'll take it. I'll run with it as far as it takes me.*

The huge ice block seemed clearer in the halogen headlamp beam than what he'd expected. There was far less diffusion with the absence of the Arctic sun. Per thought, *What the hell's going on here? It never looked like this during the dig. It's so much easier to see through the ice with my lamp. Glad I saved it for the final inspection. I don't think any of the workers have a halogen or have been in here during the deepest hours of the night, not when it's totally black.*

A gradual ramp had been dug facing into the end of the block containing the head and huge curved tusks. The ears were smaller than the pictures of other mammoths he had seen. It's squared-off mouth still contained chunks of some kind of plant or moss. Per touched the huge block with his hands. *Was this really a cryogenic instant freeze?* In mysterious wonder, he walked around the trench to the hindquarters, his lamp seeming to create movement in the shadows.

Bending over to tighten a buckle to the carriage, Per saw an inconsistent darkness on the opposite side of the trench behind the hindquarters. He was puzzled, and thought, *Looks like a rock or could it be part of another mammoth? How could the workers miss this?*

Per's beam played across the crystals and reflected a frosted form. With an ice ax, he hacked away at one end. The cloudy apparition turned to a definite shape and color. The ancient ice was maybe six inches thick and with a few chops, became clear as a window. Suddenly, he was looking into the eyes of another face! Per stopped and muttered, "What the…" he was paralyzed, mesmerized.

His throat could not make a sound in the minus forty degree below freezing air. *What is this, a Stone Age man, not the face of a Neanderthal, perhaps a Cro-Magnon?*

The thought was so stark in his mind, he didn't know if he had muttered it or simply thought it. He hesitatingly chipped more ice away and looked in the eyes again. The face looked remarkably modern, real, and full. Not white but a light tannish cream in color. Not drawn or skinny. Not dehydrated. Not like a mummy or the iceman found in Italy in 1991. This one looked alive. The eyes were open wide, fierce, deep-brown eyes. Intelligent yet surprised, almost questioning the instant death crisis he must have found himself in. He was a hunter, and suddenly he was looking his own death in the eye. *My God*, Per thought. *It's a preserved Cro-Magnon, a Cro-Magnon warrior looking me eye to eye.*

Per stopped and stared into the eyes of the man, a man who'd been buried for thousands of years. *Is he staring at me? Is he trying to tell me, is he trying to speak?* Per thought. *Or did he speak? This is beyond ancient. Way beyond.* His heart began to pound. He could feel the aortas in his neck pumping. His hands shook, and he dropped his ice ax. He fell to his knees, humbled, and then he had to lay down on the blue ice; his light casting its beam off into space. *No, this is not real. I'm still sleeping. He's lifting me up. He's telling me, my God, he's talking. He's saying, no telling me, to go to warm. He's saying to almost walk in the truth.*

Awake, he pounded his face with his mitts. It stung, but he began to gather his senses. It was so cold. Slowly he got to his knees, and then stood. "The face, the eyes, the hair, he's real," he whispered. "I'm not hallucinating. My God, touch him. Touch his face. Say it! This is the find of the century. This is the first truly intact Stone Age man." Per took a deep breath of ice cold air and cleared his mind. *I've got to work quickly.*

It was amazing how modern and European he appeared. *Except for the matted dark brown hair and the headband made of carved ivory rod beads and some sort of teeth*, Per thought, *clean you up a little, and you remind me of that strapping young Norwegian I stood next to while we were waiting for our luggage at Oslo airport. Astonishing.* The skin, although he was looking through a few inches of clear bluish ice, was flawless, yet weathered. Not wrinkled and deeply scarred like a sea captain's, only four forehead creases arranged in a pattern. Two-inch rectangular black tattoos under his eyes accentuated the depth of his stare. Slightly open, his mouth revealed perfect dentition. The head imperceptibly merged into massive neck and shoulder muscle. The neck seemed to begin at his ears. Muscle fibers defined his skin.

He appeared strong, dignified in death, handsome even in the eerie light of the powerful lamp and the shadow it cast. A sinew necklace of huge claws hung from his neck and disappeared in the ice around the back of his head. The knots in it were evenly spaced. There was long haired black fur behind the entire body, maybe bear skin.

Per stopped abruptly to hear if any sound came from the laavo.

Silence—only wind. He gazed up. Only the soft rose of aurora borealis and distant impartial stars were keeping watch. As he stood, clouds again moved in, returning the scene to black abyss.

Carefully chipping along the torso and arm draped across it, he could see a wide cross-shaped tattoo on each breast. There were two-inch line tattoos down the breast bone. The shoulder, arms, and torso were a dark shade of cream. He was ideally proportioned but much larger than he had imagined a Cro-Magnon man to be. Drawings of Stone Age men he had seen as a child came to mind. Again, he looked back at the fierce eyes. *A hunter-warrior*, he thought. It was starting to snow lightly.

God, I hope no one wakes up and sees I'm gone. No, the hides are so thick, they'll think I'm still deep down in. Hurry. Keep working. He carefully chipped more ice away, removing a leather pouch the size of a softball by cutting the leather strap from around the man's waist. He could see every muscle fiber of the abdomen pressing against the underside of the skin. He thought, *A warrior's weapon pouch or maybe a medicine bag.* He removed his gloves and warmed the stiff pouch till it was pliable enough to open slightly. It was empty. *Why is it empty? What was in it? What was it for?*

He next chipped five inches of ice near the knees and saw two more crosses on the kneecaps. The legs were hairless. The thighs reminded him of looking closely at a frog's legs when he was a child. They were huge, and every muscle stood out with its own identity. This man had been a powerful warrior. A true man of the last ice age, killed instantly, not by another man or animal but by the inexorable forces of nature, his only match.

The left arm was draped across his lower rib cage. The massive upper arm seemed to be still pumped as if death were just an interruption. Per drew his knife from under his parka and without thinking, sawed off a one-inch slice of the bicep and laid it in the snow by his boots.

Then instead of examining it, he quickly chipped away to the dark furry loincloth, pulled it back, and carefully sawed off one icy testicle. The snow was blowing in the trench.

As he packed the two samples into a snowball and placed it in his parka pocket, he whispered, "Trade you those for my new ice ax."

With that, he wedged the ice ax under the left arm. The irony of it hit him, and he thought, *A titanium ice ax held by a Stone Age man.* Then he reached down to lift handfuls of ice and snow to pack back into the holes he had made when chipping with the ax. He stuck the leather pouch in his other pocket.

The last place he covered was the eyes. As he did, he said, "Sorry, old man, I'll be back for you someday." Per rose up, turned with a last look, and walked out of the trench. He thought, *If I tell them, they'll take him from me. The institute will say, "Thanks for finding him, Per," and turn around and give the warrior to Blakely. Blakely does the DNA, gets all the honors, press, the Nobel Prize, and the million bucks, and I get a stinking wooly mammoth, no Nobel, no mil. No way. No! That's not how it's going to play out. Not this time. Sure, I'll do the DNA and sperm research on the mammoth but secretly on the warrior. Then I'll come back and dig him up when I'm good and ready. I'll organize my own expedition. I'll be famous.* The snow was falling stronger. He couldn't see the stars anymore.

Returning to the laavo, he carefully wrapped the snowball in a red bandana taken from around his neck, and then placed the two specimens in the red Smithsonian lockbox cooler alongside the mammoth specimens he'd gathered earlier with Aarbakke.

"There," he said, "you two enjoy the trip back to the States." He quietly entered the laavo. No one stirred. He settled into his reindeer skin and soon was fast asleep.

The huge Norwegian Navy CH-53 Super Stallion chopper had already flown off to the South, dangling the heavy cube containing the mammoth. As he climbed in the other chopper with the red cooler, Per looked back to scan the surreal scene. The Saami workers had already struck camp and were assembling the snowmobiles, sleds, tents, and all the excavation equipment and gear for the trip to lower ground. The deep rectangular hole in the snow was abandoned and rapidly filling in with fresh snow. There was a stormy Arctic black grayness to the West. Time was becoming a factor. Just before liftoff, Per jumped from the chopper and ran down into the back end of the trench. Dr. Aarbakke yelled to the pilot over the sound of the rotors. "Stop right now! Don't lift off! Per's jumped out!"

The pilot acknowledged the shout and looked in the direction Dr. Aarbakke pointed. Per pulled his GPS from his pocket and quickly locked-in the precise latitude-longitude coordinates. The pilot could not get his attention with his impatient thumbs up gestures. Per ran back, climbed aboard, and waved to the smiling Saami as they lifted off. The sight disappeared into whirling snow like a dream forgotten.

No one could imagine the secret Per now carried.

8

ONE WEEK AFTER Per had returned to AnGen, everyone with high clearance was dressed in full sterile scrubs for the big one. The mammoth's DNA already had been found to be in pristine condition. But now, with such hot science in his possession, Per wasted no time to start the experiment of a lifetime: bringing potentially perfectly preserved mammoth sperm cells back to life.

Per reached surgical gloved hands into the stainless steel deep freezer, bypassing the red bandana holding the warrior's DNA and sperm samples, and unwrapped the foam covering containing the mammoth testicle. Using a sterile surgical saw, he cut off a thumb sized chunk of the inner portion. Hands still in the freezer, he carefully sliced off a three millimeter section with a scalpel, returning the large sample to the foam covering. Then he rewrapped the huge specimen, placed it back next to the balled-up red bandana, and closed the freezer door.

The entire technical staff of AnGen watched with anticipation as a lab technician quickly brought the sample to the cold room where the melting speed could be controlled. "It's unbelievable," Per mused. "The DNA and cytoplasm of the muscle sample was still healthy and viable. Won't it be incredible if old wooly's sperm is still viable?" Per joked, trying to relieve the building tension of his colleagues. "You know, they appear almost to be cryogenically frozen. This just might work," he quipped lightly. "Everyone, please cross your fingers. It's crunch time." They all chuckled uncomfortably.

He mounted the slide with the thin slice and inserted it into the huge phase-contrast microscope. Then he switched on the micro warmer and applied a micro drop of warming medium. Expertly spinning the dials with his right hand, he watched as crystals slowly melted before his eyes. Five long minutes passed, and Per began to shake his head. Then he said, "I saw movement." A long two minutes passed as everyone in the lab held their breath. Then he cried out, "Some flagella are moving. A few of them are slowly swimming! Mammoth sperm cells, they're swimming now. It's incredible. You've all got to see this!" He adjusted the microscope. "They look absolutely healthy and normal. We'll have to repeat this, but this all looks good to me."

A cheer went up from the surgery-clad group. One tech threw his surgical cap to the ceiling. The room was abuzz because they all knew what this meant for this small company.

"Wait until the Smithsonian gets the news." Per rolled up his sleeves. "We can't jump to conclusions just yet. We'll need more work with the electron microscope to verify the health of the chromatin and cytoplasm, but this, ah, now this is a great day for AnGen," Per stated, readjusting his eyes as he pushed back his chair, stood up, took a deep breath and exhaled.

As he stood up, Jenny came over and gave him a slap on the back. "Well done, Per, very well done! Nice will be so proud of you."

As the lab techs filed past one by one, peering into the microscope, each looked up at Per with wide eyes of amazement. "Astounding," the techs kept repeating.

"Ladies and gentlemen," Per said quietly, "this is truly a great day for science and a great day for AnGen. With this, we have secured our position as the leader in animal genetics research." He paused to drink in the happy mood of this room of trusted employees. "Don't be surprised if you see a reporter and cameras here next week from the Discovery Channel. In fact, I think a raise in pay for everyone starting next week is the best way of saying thank you for all your hard work and dedication. We can afford it now. Those big grants will be coming in when this news breaks." Applause started as he continued. "I think we should all take the rest of the week off and meet again back here Monday morning." The unexpected announcement was met with another round of applause.

Later, on Per's way out of the building, a security guard stopped him, "Congratulations, Dr. Jorland. I heard the news!"

"Thanks Bill. Have a good night. Oh, I'm giving you a raise!"

The following morning, Per pulled into his private parking slot, turned off the motor, but could not bring himself to open the door. Instead, he stared at the entrance to his own business, frozen in painful internal dialogue. *Are you going to go through with this or not? It's been the plan since that night or maybe you'd better wait a day and cool off. Yeah, but the mammoth worked. It's worth a try. She's been such a bitch about the baby thing. I don't even want to go home. She'll be nice for an hour, and then she'll start in on me again. No! You must be insane. This will destroy you. No, I'm not. There's nothing wrong with me. It's her. I'm going in before Bill comes out and thinks there's something wrong.* With a huge exhale, he got out and was met at the door by Bill.

"Good morning, Dr. Jorland. I didn't expect to see you today. This place sure is quiet."

Per interrupted, all businesslike, "Morning, Bill. I just came in to catch up on a few ideas I've been working on. It'll be easier to think with the whole place on shutdown, so you don't have to accompany me to the lab."

"Fine, Doctor."

Per, carrying a small high-tech cooler marked Property of Dr. Gorlin, walked through the door after scanning his fingerprints.

He got into full sterile scrubs and went to the freezer. He bypassed the mammoth specimen and reached instead for the red bandana. He stopped to listen, making certain he was alone—total silence—then continued on. As he carefully unwrapped the red bandana, his thoughts turned to that night in Finnmark and the fierce eyes of the Stone Age man. Next, he slowly went about duplicating the successful experiment of the day before, but this time on the sperm of the Cro-Magnon. Four hours later, Per returned to the lobby with the cooler held at his side.

"That wasn't long, Doctor. Glad to see you're not wasting a beautiful day working indoors. If I were you, I'd be going for a long jog or better yet, maybe fishing. I love fishing."

Per responded with an uncomfortable laugh. "No Bill, this will not be a wasted day. There's a little project my wife and I are working on."

"Have a good week, then. See you Monday, and thanks for the raise, boss."

"You're a good man, Bill."

Per pulled out of the empty parking lot and squealed his tires as Bill had seen so many times. Ten minutes later he was pulling into the fertility doctor's office. Per got out and walked up to the reception desk.

"Hi, Sandy. Here are the samples I promised Dr. Gorlin I'd be in with. There are two separate samples in the cooler." He indicated with two fingers of his right hand. "See that he gets them right away. We want to make sure they're lively," he said with a smile.

"Very good, Dr. Jorland, I'll see to it," she said as she typed the name Dr. Per Jorland and placed it on the cooler.

"Thanks, Sandy. You sure are organized here."

"We have to be! Have a nice day, Per."

Per returned to his car, turned on the music, and pulled into traffic.

He drove. Traffic, cars, and trucks were all a blur, and he thought, *Change lanes. No, why, to where? Turn around, then what? Yes, that makes sense. I have to make sense of this. Open the window, I can't breathe. Dammit, open the window! Just drive. Drive until what? Until my heart slows, yes, until I can breathe. Slow breath, slow breath. Slow it all down. Got to. I have to go home now. You know the way. Do it. Drive home!*

He pulled into his driveway, opened the garage door, and parked. Nice's car was gone. He sat there in the blackness for about a half hour, perspiring. *What is this pain in my chest? Oh, God, what in hell's name am I doing? What have I done? If Nice finds out, she'll divorce me. Worse yet, I could end up in court, jail, prison. She'd never come to see me—the man who lied, betrayed her very womanhood. Oh, the inmates would love me. I've come up with a new kind of crime, one worse than sex with a child. Those samples I took from the ice man are property of the Smithsonian Institute. No, they're property of Norway. I'd be done. My life, my business, my reputation, all would be gone. Oh, the* Enquirer. *Oh My God!*

My chest. I can't breathe. I can't be here when Nice comes home. She'll ask questions. Got to get in the house and lie down, then I'll try to call Dr. Gorlin, and try to call it all off before Nice's appointment with him. Yes, that's what I'll do. He staggered into the house and vomited into the toilet, then rinsed his mouth with mouthwash.

That evening, Nice put her hand on his forehead. "Per, are you okay? You've only said a few words all night. Your forehead's cold and wet, and you look pale. Is there something on your mind that I can help you with? Maybe give you some good old fashioned advice. You're working too hard and need a rest."

Per looked up at her beautiful shining eyes and opened his mouth to speak then looked down and thought, *Are you going to tell her? Well? Now, Per, now is the right time. Stop a lifetime of pain and secrets now. No, maybe I can control this and ask Dr. Gorlin to hold the secret. Be real. What are the chances of that? Maybe he'll call the police.*

Finally, Per opened his mouth to speak. Slowly, in a low voice she had never heard before, "Nice, do you think love is something more than merely a biological reaction?"

"Per, what on earth are you talking about?"

"That's not what I meant."

"What did you mean then? You're acting like you're out of reality."

"Why do you love me?" Per's heart was pounding.

"Per, lay down. You look like you're going to faint. I don't know where you're going here. Are you having an affair?"

"Nice, I don't feel well."

"Per, I love you. I respect you. I know we argue sometimes about a baby, but we're always honest with each other. Maybe I've been too hard on you about all that. We're best friends. If you want me to quit my job so we're together more, I will."

Per again thought, *Now tell her! Tell her you gave the sperm from a Stone Age man and some of yours to Dr. Gorlin, but you don't know for sure if either sperm would conceive. Now, tell her you made an impulsive decision. Now right it! No, you're spineless.*

Per pulled himself back together and spoke. "Nice, listen to me very carefully here."

"Yes, Per, I'm listening." She put her head on his shoulder and reached for his hand. Per began to cry softly.

He turned to her. "I guess I've been working too hard. Maybe we need to spend more time together. We're always working. Maybe I'm having a midlife crisis."

"No, Per, you're fine. You're right, and thank you for being so honest with me." She got up. "Now, you need to get to bed. We'll start fresh in the morning."

Per woke up at 3:00 a.m., went to the bathroom, and looked in the mirror. *Per, you're a God damn fool. You could go to hell for this. Your thinking is psychopathic. Can't you see it? There's no way you can win here. The only way is to hope there is no conception, or if there is, it will be from my own sperm. Maybe I can get out of this after all. Yes, after all. Keep going like everything is fine. Yeah, keep going, it's too late to tell.*

Before he turned out the bathroom light, he looked at Nice deep in sleep.

Next morning over coffee, Nice suddenly blurted out in a stern voice, "Last night you never answered my question."

"What, Nice?" He felt backed into a corner.

"You know—so answer it now, Per."

"I don't know, about what?"

"About are you having an affair, Per? I mean it! If you're hiding something, tell me right now! This is your first and last and only chance to be honest with me. So, what is it?"

"Nice, in total honesty, I'm not having an affair and have never cheated on you."

"Good, that's what I hoped to hear. No affair and total honesty." She came to him and put her arms around him, way around him. "I love you, Per."

"And I love you too, Nice."

"Let's plan a getaway. No, not plan. Let's get away after I see Dr. Gorlin, just the two of us. Do those things we talked about on our honeymoon. No more supermodel. No more scientist. Just go for three months. Who knows? Maybe this time with Dr. G will work."

One day I was cleaning out my office. I loved that office. Old walnut that I'd cleaned and dusted over the years. There were places, nooks, and, you know, there were places somehow forgotten in even such a small space where forty years can dim a memory. In the back of a drawer rarely opened, I found this curious cigar with a blue band It's a Boy!

At the time, for the life of me, I could not remember who gave it to me. I tossed it in the box. You know, the box with the paperweights, fountain pens, and old letters, thinking someday I'd recall why I had tucked it away.

Not long ago, when I decided to take on the Jomo project, it hit me! About nine months after Per got back from Norway, he walked into my office and, with a proud smile, presented that cigar! That whole in-vitro thing was tough on him, but now he had a son. So it's time to get back to my story.

No Parking. Ignoring the sign, he pulled in, slamming on the brakes. The hospital doors couldn't open fast enough for him. With their usual professional calmness, the receptionists handled him at the nurse's station like every other expectant father.

"Dr. Jorland, congratulations! You have a son. Please have a seat while I page Dr. Meorta. She's with your wife now." Seeing his bouquet, she dropped her nurse role and smiled. "Your flowers, by the way, are beautiful. It won't be long."

Per sat down in the waiting area, rifling through wrinkled old copies of magazines till he found one that looked interesting. Ten minutes passed, and then fifteen. Per returned the magazine to the pile and spoke just loud enough for the woman behind the desk to hear him. "What the hell is taking so long?"

Finally, a nurse approached him, smiling. "Excuse me, Dr. Jorland, your wife is in room 418."

"May I go up there now?"

"Yes, she knows you're here."

Nice was sitting up in bed, surrounded by fluffy pillows, wearing a lacy saffron-colored bed jacket and matching dressing gown by Givenchy when Per walked into her room.

"Nice, you look beautiful. I got here as fast as I could."

The nurse handed him the baby.

"Oh, it's our son, our beautiful son." Per cradled the little baby in his arms. Nice looked at Per with a tired but happy smile.

"Yes, Per, he's our little Maasai warrior. It all happened so fast, there wasn't time for you to get here."

"You okay?"

"Sure, just tired. I could sleep for a week. No, I believe I could sleep for two."

Per laughed at the impossibility of her statement.

"I guess the fashion world will just have to get along without me for a while longer."

They laughed softly. Still holding the baby, Per leaned over and kissed her.

"Dr. Meorta says he's very healthy," Nice commented.

Per fixed his attention on his son's face for the first time. "He has such beautiful dark eyes. They're very, well, they're very like yours, Nice."

"I know. The doctor says they'll probably turn a lighter brown though."

"He's so alert. Are all babies like that?" Per asked.

"Oh, I think so." Nice paused, and then seriously said, "I've been thinking about his name. I want to name him Jomo, after my father."

"Jomo. Jomo. I like your father." Per took time to contemplate the idea. "Yes, it's a respectable name. Jomo Jorland. It's a strong name for a son, Nice, a little of you and a little of me."

The nurse came back into the room. "Excuse me, Dr. Jorland, but your wife needs to rest now."

"What? But I just got here. You can't be serious."

"Oh, well, you don't make the rules here, hon." Rolling her head to the right, Nice asked the nurse, "Do you think he looks more like me or Per?"

With her keen eye for babies, the older nurse didn't even hesitate. "That baby is of you. Yes, that baby is of you, Nice."

Per kissed Nice and Jomo and placed the bundle in Nice's arms. "I'll be back first thing in the morning. Good night, Nice. Good night, Jomo. I'll call Dr. Gorlin first thing in the morning, I'm sure he'll be thrilled!"

"Great, Per. Bye. I love you. See you tomorrow."

"That baby is of you." The phrase kept repeating in Per's head all the way home. *"That baby is of you, Nice. That baby is of you, Nice."* He woke up sweating that night with the same sentence on rewind.

Next morning, Per was on the phone. "Hi, Sandy. Could I talk to Dr. Gorlin, please? This is Per Jorland."

"Just a moment, please."

Then Dr. Gorlin answered. "Yes, Per, so how is Nice doing?"

"Dr. Gorlin, that's why I'm calling. It's a boy, a healthy boy, six pounds, three ounces!"

"Congratulations, Per. I have to commend you on your patience. It took Nice a long time to become pregnant."

"You're telling me!"

"Those sperm samples you gave me nine months ago finally paid off. I still remember, only one conceived. I was delighted! You'll be a terrific father, I'm sure."

Per hesitated at his statement, and then changed the subject. "The nurse says he looks like Nice. Dr. Gorlin, this is truly the happiest time of my life! We can't thank you enough. You've been so helpful."

"The fun's just started, Per. Now you get to raise him as your son. He's the gift of family, love and life. Let's stay in touch."

"Yes, we will. Again, thanks, Doc." Per hung up the phone and thought, *Only one conceived. You heard him yourself, but which one? He's healthy. The doctor said so. I'll check his DNA when he comes home. It would be so easy, just a little hair follicle. No, stop thinking about all this. I don't really want to know. What if he's not mine? I might treat him different. He's my son, and he's healthy. That's all I need to know. No, it's all I want to know!*

9

ABOUT A YEAR after she had Jomo, she was at the grocery store with the little guy in the cart when she got a call from Mr. Lauren to come to his office and talk over her future. Next day, she dropped off the baby and caught the train to Manhattan. Entering his office, she was overwhelmed by the Welcome Back sign behind his desk and all the office staff that came in to give her a hug. She was back.

Within two years, her career was back in full stride. The paparazzi loved her. Whenever she and Per appeared in New York, their picture was splashed in some international magazine. The world knew her name—Nice.

It was October and she was in Paris wrapping up the Spring Fashion Tour. She was checking for messages at the front desk of the InterContinental, when to her right, she heard a well-dressed Frenchman speak. Instantly, she knew the voice by its unique lilt. She turned, astonished, and spoke in the seductively fluent French he had taught her so many years before.

"Michel, is that you?"

"Nice!"

"You're here in Paris? Are you staying here too?"

"I always stay at the InterContinental. It's great to see you, Nice. Never thought I'd see you again. Yes, I'm here on business. I love Paris in the Fall, and I always find a way—a reason—to be here instead of—"

"Nairobi? That's an easy one." She laughed.

"Well, yes, sometimes there still, but let's talk about you."

"If it's October in Paris, it's fashion week for me. Spring fashion, you know. I love it. I work for Ralph Lauren. He hired me that first week in New York. I was lucky. I love his designs. They're right for me. You know, I could get you a pass. There will be beautiful women. I'm sure you'd fit in."

"Perhaps. You look absolutely fabulous and happy. I see you're a happy woman."

"Oh, Michel," she said as she lifted her chin.

"Have you got a little time to walk or have coffee? I know a delightful bistro or we could take a walk along the Seine. The leaves are falling."

"Why, sure, I would like that."

The two left the lobby together and walked out to the smell and colors of Autumn in Paris. He still had the same smile, walk, and the Parisian mannerism she remembered from four years ago. The same genuineness she'd liked about him then. She walked close to him, almost touching. He was a friend and almost a lover from a time when she was poor and struggling. He liked her when she had nothing, unlike the men she now met, who pandered to her for her success. Compared to Michel, they were boys.

The doorman smiled, almost in surprise, to see her accompanied.

"Please wave us a cab, Peter."

"As you wish, Nice." He knew her as a regular at the InterContinental. She always tipped him generously. This Parisian, though, he'd never seen her with. He did not meet eyes with him. As he opened the cab door, Michel offered him a tip, which he hesitantly accepted. Nice, already in the backseat, never noticed this exchange. As he got in, Nice thought in quiet panic, *My God, I'm getting in the backseat with a criminal. He's a diamond smuggler. What am I doing? What am I thinking? Get out now! Quick, think of a reason, an excuse.* "I think I should, Michel, I think I should…"

"Should what, Nice?"

"I think I should take us to Pont Neuf. I love that walk along the river, rain or shine. It clears my thoughts."

"That's a lovely idea."

Nice leaned forward. "Driver, please drop us off at Pont Neuf."

"Why Pont Neuf?" Michel asked with a genuine interest.

"Oh, I like to walk to the middle and drop a flower in the Seine and, don't laugh, make a wish."

"That's what I like about you, Nice. Always a surprise waits. What is life without surprise but dull, grey, predictable? You, Nice, you are not predictable. I never know what you are willing to do or say. I see you're wearing a beautiful diamond. Is it the—"

"No, Michel, your French charm works, but I'm married. My name is Nice Nkoe Jorland now. I've got a three year old son, and I can tell you he's a bit of a wild child, in a good way. He climbs every vertical obstacle in the house. My husband takes care of him when I travel."

"I heard you caught on in New York, and then I saw your picture on the cover of *Elle*. I'd say supermodel, am I right, no?"

"Well, some say."

"Anyway, you look fabulous," he said with a mischievous laugh. "So how long are you here in Paris?"

"A few more days and then back to New York. Look, here's Pont Neuf already. Please, I'll pay."

They walked out to the middle of the bridge and stood silently, immune to the hum of traffic. As Nice saw the reflection of their silhouettes, only shoulders and faces leaning over the side wall, she thought, *Why am I comfortable with this man? What am I doing? What if Per found out? How could I explain this? I should not be here with him, yet I don't want to leave him, not now.*

Michel broke the silence. "Pont Neuf is the oldest bridge in Paris, Nice, and most Parisians think it to be the most beautiful. Just think, lovers, thieves, fools, and dreamers have stood on this bridge in this very spot since 1607—four hundred years."

"Let's walk," Nice cut in.

"Yes, the stairs."

As they took the steps, watching their footing for the black, crumbling cement, an alto sax player under the bridge blew out "Body and Soul."

"All the jazz greats played here in Paris in the fifties and sixties."

"Yes, I know. It was the Beatles that knocked out the masters, even Elvis. My mother loved Elvis."

They were quiet again. Not an uncomfortable quiet but a thoughtful one. Huge leaves carpeted the walk and crinkled with each step.

Nice picked one up to get a closer look. A tour boat made its way upstream. Finally, Nice spoke softly and looked to him as their walk fell into a lazy rhythm.

"How long have you been a diamond smuggler? How did you get started?"

"Why do you ask? What interests you so much, or am I your flavor of intrigue, unpredictability, as I said in the hotel? So what if I told you? And what would that change? Maybe it is better you don't know. We're friends. That means something to me. Friends are rare. Good friends are even rarer."

"Do you have friends?"

"Some."

"Friends you can count on?"

"You mean now? After what I've—I mean after smuggling and the people I've worked with?"

"Yes."

"You, Nice, are one of few."

A class of grade three children approached from the next bridge. From afar, Nice could hear the teacher leading a French song with a gusto she'd heard so many years ago in grade 4. As they passed, Michel held out both hands to the entourage as he did a little dance. The children ran to touch his hands, and he laughed as they passed. Their teacher gave her approval by turning her head and flashing her eyes just after she had passed.

"You do live in the present."

"As do you. A woman of impulse. Not what is right but what feels right."

"But what of secrets?" She changed the subject.

"Again, not what is right but what feels right. Why secrets? They are intriguing. Or maybe intrigue is secrets, no?"

"I ask because I have never told my husband. No, I must stop here, all this talk." She went to the railing and looked across to the island, thinking of changing the subject. "I'm married. I met him a year after I flew to New York."

"Yes, I remember. You were happy. We shared some wine at your apartment."

"Then I took your suitcase that held the uncut diamonds."

"Yes."

"I brought them through customs in New York."

"Were you scared? I was a little. You had a lot of my diamonds."

"No, but I was nervous about modeling, a job, leaving Kenya, leaving home, and being alone, nervous, but not scared. Maybe that's why I breezed through customs. No, I lied. I was very scared. There was a lady next to me on the plane who could see right through me."

"Yes, and also the stones were so well hidden even from x-rays. Truth, you were lucky. So why do you ask me about your secret? A secret is always, it is forever. To live in the present is to put it aside as not relevant."

"Not relevant?"

"No, not relevant to who you are?"

"But Michel—"

"You have a secret, no? I'll say it. You smuggled diamonds. It was easy for you. You were not caught, and who you really are has never changed. Put it all aside. You are one of few who can do that. I've met Parisians who say, 'Live life in the present.' They are liars. They show their secrets and guilt by the way they talk and act in a bar. Nice, we are the same. That's why we found each other—friends, when you had nothing."

Nice did not respond, only thinking of his reasoning. They continued walking. Michel had a patient pace of walking while talking quietly. She liked that about him.

She thought, *Maybe it's okay to keep my secret. After all, I'm still the same. Why let it bother me, and face it, it was exciting. Smuggling diamonds. The drop-off. The same feel as I walk on the runway and feel the music with eyes below me and the sounds, the cameras, the bows, the total pageantry. It's the same, only more. It's dangerous.*

"What are you thinking of, Nice?"

"If you're a criminal, then so am I."

"No, Nice, please understand. Moving diamonds about the world is no more a crime than prostitution. It's been a business all through the ages. Only governments want to control it. By control, I mean they want money for doing nothing. Not run a mine, not being involved in the transfer, no cutting, no mounting, nothing. Parasites."

Nice stopped and moved closer to him. She could smell the leaves and the Seine flow into her brain. Her head was swimming.

"What of you, Michel? Why are we friends and not lovers yet?"

"I ask the same of you. You already know why. It's why you smiled when you saw me in the lobby and called my name."

"Why?"

"It's why you brought me to Pont Neuf, to your favorite quiet place in all of busy Paris. Say it, Nice."

"Yes, Michel, I'll say it. I love the thunder."

She held both hands over her mouth at the thought of what she had just said. Michel put his arm around her. She began to rest her head on his shoulder and then stopped and pulled his arm away. An elderly Frenchman walked by, hunched over, hands clasped behind him. He wore his beret tucked in low to his eyes, as if to say, "It's none of my business."

In a lighter tone, Michel continued, "May I ask how much you sold that diamond for? I heard it was a beauty, maybe six carats."

"I never sold it. It was easy to hide. I thought I'd sell it if I needed the money, but my career took off. Besides, it's not a legal cut. There's no registration on it. I'd have to go to the black market."

"I could sell it for you by tomorrow."

"Maybe one day but not now. I don't have it with me. Let's turn around and catch the next steps up. I want to go back to the hotel."

As they walked, a breeze came up, and Michel gave Nice his jacket.

"Thank you, Michel," she said, regaining her smile. "Do you remember the night you kissed me in that Nairobi bar?"

"Yes, Nice, I do."

"We were in a dark corner, and I felt a little light headed from too much wine. I didn't even know you, still I felt safe. I mean, I felt you were not taking advantage of me."

"Yes, I remember. I enjoyed when you kissed me back. I told you I wanted to show you my world. To be honest, I wanted to take you home with me that night and make love till dawn."

"I told you I couldn't because I had an important test the next morning. Truth, there was no test, I just wasn't ready."

"Yes, and I didn't see you again for a few months, but the bartender gave me a note from you about a week later. It was perfumed and said Maybe, Nice."

She pulled the jacket more tightly around her and thought, *He's right. I do like the thrill, the adrenaline, the excitement. In fact, I need it. I always have, even at the university. I went to that bar where I met Michel. There were plenty of other colorful men there. I felt I could do it all. It all led me to who I am now.*

Michel interrupted her thoughts once again. He knew they'd be in the taxi in ten minutes. "Would you like to bring another suitcase to New York? I can have it ready and in your room by tomorrow evening. Just fill it full of clothing you don't care about, and I'll send your best across the pond by DHL. It would be a big one of the highest quality, all polished, four to six carats, not yet graded in Antwerp and impossible to trace. It would be easy, worth it to you."

Nice stopped in her tracks. Her heart began to pound, but she said nothing, only pursed her lips and looked at Michel directly in the eyes. She sat down on a bench, and he followed. She thought, *Should I go to the well again?* Then she looked ahead and behind to see if anyone was listening, "Tell me more about the diamonds I would carry."

"The more I tell you, the more dangerous it becomes for you because you've moved deeper into my life."

"Why? Why would that be for just a mule?"

"So you know the term? I trust you would not be a weak link. If not, I would have had you killed by the Guggenheim."

"Yes, the man on the bench told me that. So tell me something about what I would be part of. I mean this proposition."

"It bothers me that you seem to seek a thrill, but I do also. Antwerp. Do you know Antwerp?"

"Yes, I have a diamond necklace from there. I bought it on the Champs Elysee."

"But did you know Antwerp is the world capital of diamond cutting? Two hundred million dollars worth of polished and rough diamonds trade through that city in Belgium every day. Think of it, Nice. Everyday. All I want is a little bit of that, you and me and my trusted men."

"So where? Where would my diamonds come from?"

"Then I'll tell you. About a year ago, my men and I stole them. About sixty million dollars worth, rough and polished."

"Sixty million dollars worth? How? How could you have done that?"

"We knew when the armored car left Brussels carrying the diamonds bound eventually for Antwerp. When the armored car unloaded at Brussels airport and left, we cut the fence and drove very fast in black vans with blue police lights flashing to the plane and stole the diamonds right out of the hold. They were pulling chalks as we arrived. Nine of us, dressed in black hoodies, as police, all with automatic assault rifles, stopped the pilot from taking off. A few got up in the hold and unloaded the particular parcels addressed to middle men in Zurich. We packed them in the vans then drove right back through the fence for a high speed getaway. Later, we burned the vans."

"You didn't kill anyone?"

"No, Nice, not even one shot. The next day, I read that the passengers weren't even aware."

"You are far bolder than I thought. I like that. I could love a man like that."

"If we had to, we would have. I have never enjoyed killing. It is very messy, and the prison sentence is not convenient to one who enjoys the good life. Listen to me. It's not arms trading or stealing fine art. I do not go to the huge mines where people suffer. It's clean. Once they are in the market, they're fair game. They are only little stones. International crime, yes."

"I never expected all this."

"I trust no one, yet I trust you. Run with me, Nice."

"I want to, yet…"

"I know. To run with me, you would have to give up everything." Michel spoke softly. "Look, Nice, if you don't want to do this, I understand. We are friends, remember? It would be exactly the same as before: same suitcase, zipper, man at the drop-off."

Nice got up quickly and started walking away from him toward the stairs, up to street level, leaving the river behind. He broke into a short run and caught her on the second stair.

"I'm sorry, Nice. I'm very sorry I brought this up. May I take it all back?"

She looked at him as she removed his jacket and gave it back to him then put her hand on his cheek and said in a low voice, "One million US dollars. Cash. No black market diamond this time. The money must be in the other suitcase at the Guggenheim exchange, and this is the last time. If you and your people can live with that, then you have a deal."

They started up the two flights of the ancient stairs together. As they neared the last step, Michel spoke. "I believe that can be arranged."

"Fine." They shook hands. "I'm in room 318. So, eight o'clock tomorrow night?"

Nice waved a taxi down.

"Good, my dear friend, Nice. I will miss you."

"And I will miss you also and your way, my dear Frenchman."

Michel took her by the shoulder as she turned away.

"Nice, how much do you make a year? Modeling and magazines, I mean. May I ask?"

"Oh, I'd rather not, but about twenty million a year."

"And you would gamble it all for one million?"

"It's game on, Michel."

With that, she got in the taxi, flashed a full smile, and then blew him a kiss as she waved to him through the rear window. He smiled back, waved, and thought, *We are the same. See you tomorrow night.*

The knock came exactly at eight o'clock. Michel knew where the hotel surveillance camera was located and never looked up. Nice opened the door with a warm and knowing smile. He was dressed formally in an expensive suit and tie. In his right hand was the suitcase. His left hand held a bottle of Vouvray and two glasses. He returned her knowing smile with his own as she closed the door. He walked in, checking out her suite, and parked the suitcase by a Louis XIV love seat and then went to the table by the sofa. With a flourish, he popped the cork and proceeded with the tradition.

"The clock has started. Are you ready, Nice?"

She stood in front of him with hands on her hips as he poured. Nice said nothing but let her pursed smile and confident nod speak for her.

"The wine is tradition," he said. "Everything must be the same after the clock starts. I think this is the only time when we must be predictable, especially you, until this is over."

"I understand."

"Now, after we share a glass, I'll leave the rest of the bottle for you."

"It's the same as-"

"Yes."

They shared a glass together, knowing never again. They talked of the early days and then toasted each other to health and happiness. He swished it around in his mouth to savor the last swallow. When he started for the door with her suitcase, she stopped him. She sipped her wine and moved closer to him. "Today when we were walking, I wanted to kiss you when you put your arm around me."

"And you already know that I wanted you to kiss me. You know I want you, Nice."

"I almost did."

"Why did you stop?"

"I-"

"So kiss me now."

She moved closer to him, and they felt only each other. "I shouldn't be doing this." Nice set her wine glass down, wrapped her arms around him and pressed her body against his. "You like it when I touch you."

"Yes, Nice, you are all woman."

Eyes closed, their lips met. She moaned as her fingers began unbuckling his belt. Then slowly, she pulled away and reached for her wine as her hips began to slowly undulate against him.

Michel whispered, "I hope to see you again. We'll continue in the silk sheets with my favorite wine."

She took another sip. "This is good wine, like you. We will, I know it. I can feel it, Michel. There will be other days and times for us. We are the same. But I want you now. I'll give you everything you want and more."

"I would like that very much."

"Stay the night." She began unbuttoning her blouse.

He took her and kissed her. "Oh Nice, I can't. I've a commitment with very dangerous people. In my business—should I say our business—commitments are never broken. Just as my knock on your door, I must be exactly on time. Trust is everything."

She slowly released her embrace. "Then next time."

"Bittersweet."

He opened the door and returned to his room. Nice poured a second glass and sipped it slowly while gazing at the solitary glass left behind on the table. She said to the empty room, "Just like last time. He entered my life and then was gone, like a ghost." She laughed. "Like a French ghost." She went to the window and watched Paris come alive with the night. *Per is at work*, she thought.

The taxi pulled up on Fifth Avenue across from the Guggenheim, and the driver went around to open the trunk and her door.

"Thank you so much. It was a far better ride than one I remember some years ago."

"Thank you, ma'am, and thank you for such a large tip. Here is your suitcase."

"I always tip a professional and courteous driver, especially if he is quiet and minds his own business."

"Not sure what you mean, ma'am, but perhaps you might have had a bad taxi experience?"

"Let's just say, yes, it was bad and cost me an extra hundred dollars when I was poor."

As she took her suitcase and began rolling it into the park, she turned around with a smile. "Don't wait for me. I'll catch another."

"Yes, ma'am, as you wish."

The same well-dressed man was sitting on the left hand side of the bench when Nice approached. In her left hand, the suitcase. Her right hand was not visible as it held her black leather purse.

He spoke first, never taking his eyes off the newspaper, "We meet again. He still cares about you. You are lucky. Most don't last long. They quit when they were ahead. Perhaps you might learn from them that you're over your head. Allow me to tell you a story. Long ago there were two dogs. One chose to stay by the fire. The other left into the night, never to return. You are an amateur. Return to the fire or I can see a bad ending here."

"This is my last time and don't show me your gun. I have a 9mm Glock in the fold of my purse, and my finger is on the trigger. Now, open your suitcase and show me the money."

"As you wish." He looked about for anyone approaching. Clear. "As you see, it's all here. He keeps his word. Now, slowly take your hand off the trigger, take the money, and leave before I decide I don't like you and kill you right here for fun or how about a sniper bullet when you're on the runway? Yes, Nice, I know who you are, and I know where you live. Go back to your husband and son and leave this dangerous game you seem so attracted to. You have no place in this world of scum. Tell me, what do you really know about this man, Michel?"

"Well, I used to—"

"No, really know."

"I, I think I know him."

"There are two worlds: love or death."

"I've never heard that before."

"I am death, and he is death. Can I put it any clearer?"

Nice tried to hide a betraying gulp in her throat.

"See, that's what I mean. Now leave. I don't like working with amateurs. Take your money and leave before some asshole paparazzi catches us on a telephoto."

Nice picked up the handle and never looked back. She caught a taxi to Bank of America where she owned her secret, personal safe deposit box.

10

Seven Years Later

PRIVATE SCHOOL WAS no island from those who would gang up and bully anyone they chose. In fifth grade, young Jomo usually ate lunch with seven boys, five of whom were sixth graders. He thought the older kids were his friends until one day when the biggest kid started making fun of how he sat so straight and used his utensils and how sometimes he would speak the Queen's English as he had heard Nice speak.

The teasing went on and on. Fifteen minutes of it seemed like hours. He tried to explain how his mother had grown up in Kenya where, when proper English is spoken, it is the Queen's English because Kenya was once a colony of England.

They only laughed and taunted more. Then the big kid got up to return his tray, mocked Jomo's last words, and flicked Jomo's nose with his index finger as he walked past him. Jomo, quick as a fly, grabbed the older boy's hand with his left hand and with a vice grip, crushed it, breaking three bones.

The other sixth graders fell silent as they heard the bones snap one at a time as Jomo stared down his adversary. Then he picked up his tray and went to class.

Two hours later, there came a knock on Jomo's classroom door. His teacher, Mr. Scott, went to the door, opened it, and was handed a note from the principal's office. He read the note to himself and then looked to Jomo.

"Jomo, you are requested to report to the principal's office immediately. Do you know what this is about?"

The whole class raised their antennas because they'd already heard.

"Well, Mr. Scott, I think I do," he said as he put down his pen, rose from his desk, and slowly walked to the door.

The secretary waved him in. As he opened the door, he saw his mother and the principle, Mr. Schaeffer.

"Please sit, Jomo. I'll get right down to it here. A sixth grader claims you broke his hand during lunch today, and there are witnesses. What do you have to say for yourself?"

"Jomo," Nice interrupted, "this isn't like you! Mr. Schaeffer and I both know you never get into trouble. It's hard to believe! What's gotten into you? Just tell us what happened!"

Jomo sat up straight. "The sixth graders were bullying me about how I eat and how I talk, and it went on and on. Then the biggest guy tried to pick a fight with me by flicking my nose. I grabbed his hand with mine, and I squeezed. I heard a bone snap, and when I heard it snap, I squeezed harder so he would never bother me again. I let loose after two more bones cracked. I'm sorry. He deserved it, but I'm sorry. I did it without thinking. I just did it without thinking."

Mr. Schaeffer continued to watch the young boy, but he never squirmed. Instead, he held his head high. "Jomo, in most cases, you would be suspended for one week with probation the remainder of the school year. I think in this case, however, that boy provoked the fight. He's been a troublemaker and has bullied others, as I'm sure you know. His hand will heal, and maybe he's the one who learned the bigger lesson today. I'm going to let it go this time, but I never, and I do mean *never*, want to see you in my office again for trouble of any kind. Do you understand young man?"

Nice, relieved at his judgment, "Thank you, Mr. Schaeffer. Per and I will have a talk with Jo. He's not a bad boy. We'll see to it that he avoids trouble in the future. He loves this school so much. I promise."

"Yes, thank you, Mr. Schaeffer, you will not see me in your office ever again, I promise."

"Okay, Jomo. Nice, thanks so much for coming in so quickly. You and Per have always seemed like very good parents. I'll walk you out. Jomo, you go back to class now."

Then Mr. Schaefer asked something Jomo thought odd. "By the way, may I shake your hand?" Jomo took his hand,

"Now squeeze my hand as you squeezed Mike's." Jomo did as he was asked and watched as Mr. Schaeffer's eyes fluttered. Jomo closed the door behind him and went back to class.

"Mrs. Jorland, before I walk you out, I saw that boy's hand. Jomo really injured him. His hand has multiple fractures. Have you ever seen this kind of behavior before?"

"Well, no, I can't recall ever."

"Not *anything*?"

"Not what? What do you mean?"

"Well, how about pulling a leg or two off a spider or being mean or cruel to animals like kicking a dog? You know, I had a boy here some years back that threw a live salamander into a fire."

"Yes, I know what you mean, but no, he's not like that."

He leaned forward. "Mrs. Jorland, he just said he kept on squeezing *after* he heard the first bone crack. Do I have to spell this out to you?"

"Mr. Schaefer, I beg your pardon."

"This may be just an isolated incident, the kind some boys just go through or, and don't be alarmed, it may be a warning of worse things to come."

Nice covered her mouth in thought. "But what can Per and I do?"

"Jomo may have a mean streak living just under the surface, always ready to—"

"No, I don't think so. No way! Don't you think I'd know my own child by now? You're going too far here!"

"Look, I'm not taking sides here. I just don't want this to be glossed over too quickly."

"You and I both agree on that, sir."

"There have been studies, well done and documented, that a small percentage of young men possess what's known as *warrior genes*. This is not a bad thing. Some of the best in our military possess them, but unfortunately, so do psychopaths, even serial killers."

"Mr. Schaefer! I'm about to walk out!"

"Mrs. Jorland, please calm down."

Nice screamed at him, "I am calm!"

"Just listen to me now. I happen to know a little bit about this from my PhD work in child development."

Nice crossed her arms and tried to relax. "So tell me then."

"Thank you. All men possess the X chromosome and also the Y. The X is inherited from their mothers. Men and boys do not tend to be overly aggressive in everyday life. However, in a serious conflict or high stress situation, those who possess it can turn extremely violent or retaliatory. Some believe up to a third of all men have this shortened gene on their X chromosome, but few exhibit it due to their environment as they grow up. You know, it's the old *nature versus nurture* enigma."

Nice looked straight at him and shook her head. "You mean he inherited this behavior from me? Mr. Schaefer, that's impossible."

"Yes, it is. Think of your ancestors and what they might have been like. You're from Africa, right?"

"I don't care about your warrior chromosomes. Just shut up, and what's Africa got to do with all of this? We love him."

"I know you and Per love him. We all need to nurture him. All I'm saying is he may have a hidden feral trait you haven't yet observed. I've always believed love and nurturing can overcome bad biology." Then he lowered his voice. "Look, I'd like your permission here to allow our school psychologist to talk with him. This was, well, this was an incident that can't be brushed under the rug. I hope you understand. It's, well, I have to because it's protocol."

"Please, you don't have to tell me. He has to be able to defend himself! This is not just kids being kids! I'm not going to leave him alone on this! No! I mean it. You're going way too far with this."

"Mrs. Jorland."

"No, this psychologist's written report could change his whole life! And you know it! No, please let us talk with him first. Please, Mr. Schaefer. Please."

There was a long pause. "Well, okay. Against my better judgment, I'll write a note on my day sheet that I let this go to a meeting between you, Per, and Jomo, followed by a meeting with you and our psychologist. That will keep it off permanent records for the time being. After that, we'll see where she wants to take it. That's the best I can do here."

"Okay then, Per and I will have a long talk with him this evening, and I'll contact the psychologist."

"Now, thanks for getting here so quickly. Let's stay in touch."

She closed the door and walked back to her car, confused and concerned.

Jomo never sat at that table again.

The next day and for the rest of that year, he ate lunch a few times a week with his fifth grade sweetheart. Julie Brooks was the kind of girl fifth grade boys could only fantasize about in their first rushes of male hormones. Slender with squared shoulders, the face of an angel with a long brown ponytail, big soft chocolate eyes, and an inviting smile that still lacked permanent cuspids. She was the smartest in her room, and on school field days, she beat all the boys in the hundred yard dash, the high jump, and the long jump. She was quite a special young girl. She was a firecracker.

"Jo, I heard you went to the principal's office 'cause you broke Mike's hand yesterday. What happened? Did you get detention? Are they going to kick you out of school? You never get in trouble."

Jomo took a gulp of milk, wiped his mouth with his sleeve, and then tried to answer Julie's volley of questions. "Mr. Schaffer was there with my mom. I told them the truth. Mike's a bully, and he had it coming. He let me go but gave me a warning. At home, I thought my dad would get mad, but he didn't. Neither did my mom, but we sure talked about it for a long time at dinner. That's all, Julie."

"Well, you better not get in trouble again! You can get kicked out for that, and I don't want you to go to another school," she warned with bright eyes.

Jomo hesitated then said, "Okay, I'll say it, I won't do it again, but if I had to, if he was going to hurt me, I'd do it again. I promise you, I'd do it again." Later that day, by her locker, they sneaked their first kiss.

Little did Jomo know at that time that he and his sweetheart, Julie, would end up together all through high school.

Later that year, the Jorland family went to Jamaica for their annual holiday. Nice and Per lay back basking in the sun, while Jomo ran up and down Negril beach with his Jamaican friend Dondi and some other Jamaicans they'd just met.

"I'm glad nothing came of the whole school psychologist thing," Nice reflected.

"Me too. Well, they have to cover their asses."

"That's funny!"

"Really? I'm glad because it could have gotten very complicated for Jo. You did a great job getting rid of that goofy psychologist. These people think guilty until proven innocent. That's how they justify their jobs. This whole psychology-sociology thing in our colleges is getting out of hand. What's wrong with sticking with the greatest generation?"

"I know we haven't talked about it much, but I still think about how Jo crushed that boy's hand and my talk with Mr. Schaefer. He said I gave him the warrior gene."

"I have too, but heredity talk can get a little boring." Per paused, wondering if he should tell her. "There is a cheek swab DNA test for this warrior gene."

"What does it look for?"

"You may not understand this. There is a gene, the monoamine oxidase-A [MAO-A], on the X chromosome in most men. Those who completely lack the MAO-A but possess a variant of it have the warrior gene. It's pretty simple."

"You're right. This is too complicated for me. Are you going to check him?"

Per squirmed a little. "You know, I really don't want to know about his genes. Let's keep it simple with him. Okay?"

Nice sighed. "Okay. It's hard to believe he's already ten years old. Where have the years gone?"

"They haven't gone anywhere. Don't think I haven't noticed men look up when we walk by? You're still as beautiful as ever, Nice." He paused then said, "I saw you on the cover of *Vogue* in the airport, Nice."

"No, I don't mean that."

"Well, what do you mean?"

"Jo's growing so fast. He's a little bigger and stronger than other ten year old boys, and he's smart too."

"Well, look at me, so was I," Per countered, flexing his biceps. "So, what's the problem? In Jamaica, it's no problem, mon."

They watched a sailboat tack into the wind.

"I wonder what he'll be someday."

Per answered, more seriously this time, "He'll be what we've taught him, and what he has special to add to that. He's starting to develop."

"Like what?"

"Well, look at him. I mean, *really* hard. He never seems to run out of energy or tire out. He's amazing that way, and he doesn't lose, ever."

They both watched the boy as if he was someone else's child.

"He can outrun a fifteen year old."

Jomo was running a pickup foot race with some teenagers on the beach.

"Watch him now, the sand literally flies as he runs. He's unusually strong and confident for his age. He reminds me of you on that night we met."

"Flattery."

Nice relaxed her shoulders and lay back deep in her lounge chair. Five minutes later, she began again. "I've seen it in his eyes. His teachers have remarked about his eyes also. They turn fierce to a challenge." She lifted her head to see the boys cruising in. "Look, here they come."

Dondi looked at Jomo and motioned to Per's wrist.

"Dad, could I have your watch?"

"Why?"

"Oh, nothing." His mischievous face revealed nothing.

"I have to know why, Jo, before I give you my watch on this beach in Jamaica. This better be good."

Nice added, "Should be good. Boys, I agree." She laughed at Per's sense of humor.

"We're gonna have a contest. It's for—"

Dondi cut in, "It's to see who can hold their breath the longest underwater."

"Yeah, Dad, it's okay. I'll bring it back."

"Who's in the contest?" Nice asked, frowning.

"All the kids over there and the two big guys who are running the races. They're cool guys. The big guy says he was in the Olympics once. Hussain. They're okay, Dad. They do it all the time."

"It sounds okay. Be careful. And bring my watch back!"

"Yes, Jo, be careful, but try to win."

Down the beach, they could see a group of children and a few adults gathering in three feet of water. Twenty minutes later, Jomo and Dondi ran back to Per and Nice.

"Here's your watch, Dad. Thanks. We've got to get back."

"Thanks, boys. Dondi, don't think too much about my watch."

"Mom, can I go up to Dondi's house in the hills? We want to build a hut that'll look out over the ocean."

Nice thought for a while. "Well, I don't know."

"We'll bring coconuts and water and sleep up there. We planned everything."

Nice looked at Per. "Okay, Jo, Dad will go with you two to help you get started."

"Time for me to have an adventure with the boys," Per said, as he mustered an adventure attitude. "We'll build an authentic Jamaican hut. Well, maybe just a sleepover hut. Nice, you can come too, but you've already spent eighteen years in a hut."

"Oh, you are very funny. I'll pass. You guys have a great time. Maybe I'll get a massage or go shopping."

The boys cheered. "Thanks, Mom and Dad."

Dondi chimed in, "Yeah, thanks. Let's go swimming. I know where there's an octopus, Jo."

Per and Nice got up and waded in the surf holding hands.

"See, Nice, he's just a normal kid."

Bright and early the next morning, Per and the boys set out for Dondi's village in the mountains. A local cab picked them up at the resort, and soon, they were speeding down the highway, away from town and the seven miles of beach.

Per was in his element and smiled as he breathed deep the thick sweet smells of the interior, of the bush, of the cane fields, and the diesel engines of cane trucks.

The cabbie drove much too fast, and Per asked him to slow down with the youngsters in the car. A mongoose crossed the road left to right, and the driver commented, "Good luck for us today." Dondi and Jomo had their eyes on everything they passed, with Dondi teaching Jomo *Patua* as they rode along.

After forty-five minutes of bumping over ruts in the dirt road, they finally arrived at Dondi's simple house. His mother served the trio a traditional Jamaican breakfast of salt fish, *ackee*, and *callaloo*. Doling out a second helping, she quipped to Per with hands on her hips, "That boy grows fast. What do you feed him, food imported from Jamaica?"

"Jennifer, to tell you the truth, I have asked myself that same question. I'm just glad he's a happy healthy boy." Per looked at the boys who were busy chowing down. "You two sure are two peas in a pod. Finish up, boys, and we'll be on our way. Jennifer, the breakfast was delicious. Thank you for your hospitality."

"Bye, Mom," Dondi said.

Jomo added, "Thanks, Mrs. Thompson. Sure was good!"

As the trio left, they each grabbed a jug of water she'd set out for them. Jomo stopped, turned to Mrs. Thompson, and pulled out a chocolate bar. "I carried this for you, Mrs. Thompson."

She kissed him on the cheek.

Dondi and Jomo, machetes in hand, took the lead as they started out on the path leading toward the mountain. Per followed close behind. The three slipped past villagers' huts and gardens, over a stream where women bathed and washed clothes, and through cane fields. The path leading to the mountain began to rise. Still early morning, the tropical sun was already beating down on their backs, warming them as they walked along.

They continued to climb and soon came upon a barely visible entrance to a cave where Dondi said he'd found pictures of people and animals on the walls inside.

Dondi said to Per, "Nobody knows about it except my friends and my mom and her friends. You're too big to get through that place!" The boys laughed as Per crouched down to look smaller then crouched down farther.

"Still too big," shouted Dondi. The boys were laughing at big Per.

Then Jomo asked seriously, "Dad, can I go in there with Dondi to see the pictures?"

"Well, I don't know. Dondi, is it safe to go in there? I don't have a rope."

"Sure it is, Mr. Jorland. It's dark and there are a lot of bats, but it's not hard to get in there for me and Jo."

"Well then, okay, but be careful, you two!" Per reached in his small pack, produced a pen flashlight, and gave it to

Dondi. "You two just look at the pictures and then come right back out. Do you hear me?"

"Okay, Dad, we'll be careful."

The boys disappeared feet first on hands and knees into the side of the mountain. They descended twenty-five feet down a twenty degree slope. Footholds were easy in the porous rock. The passage opened up to a cavern about the size of the interior of a double-decker bus. They stood up, and Dondi played the flashlight over the far end. Thousands of bats lined the ceiling, and the fresh guano was slippery. There they were, pictures of animals and stick people painted in red and yellow. They carefully walked over to look at them closely.

"See, just like I told ya," Dondi said.

"Yeah, they're really cool. There's more over here too. Shine the light over here."

"My Mom said they're really old when I told her about 'em."

"Dondi, I drew some pictures like these that I saw in a dream before I woke up once. I showed my Mom. She liked them and she put 'em up on the refrigerator."

Dondi thought and then asked Jomo, "Do you think if I painted over them with brighter paint, tourists would pay me to go in here?"

"No, they'd be scared to go in here. Let's go. My dad said come right out."

The boys ascended the narrow passage and soon were out in the hot sun.

"Did you see the pictures?"

"They're really cool, Dad! There are red animals and yellow people holding long sticks. They're on all the walls everywhere and some are really pretty. Kind of like paintings."

"Think I just missed the best part of the hike, boys."

"Told ya," added Dondi.

"Okay, give me back my flashlight, Dondi, and let's get going."

They pushed on, the boys using every chance to slash and beat at anything, any vine in the path with their machetes.

"Jo, your mother walked a long, long path such as this one every week growing up in Africa. Sometimes, in the dry season, she would walk six miles just for water, and there were always lions and other animals to watch out for."

The boys ruminated over the specter of meeting a lion on the path as Jomo's mother must have at some time, maybe at their age. He impulsively said, "I would kill it. I would have to kill it if it tried to eat me."

Per had to laugh to himself.

The trio continued to climb. Per brought up the rear, watching Jomo, and then came that internal dialogue that would sometimes continue for days. *Look at him, no really look at him. He is of you, Nice, of you, Nice, you, Nice. Is he really my son? Stop it. Stop asking that question. What if, look at his eyes, even his teacher thinks he's different? No, he's mine. He's my son, he is my son. I never want to know.*

Then, he had a flashback to the man in the ice and continued with his internal struggle, *Thick neck and shoulders, strong legs. Look at Jo's shoulders and legs. He's strong, sure, but that means nothing. No, he's mine. He is of Nice and me. Stop all this, just tell yourself to stop all this. This is the last time, the last time.*

They reached the summit and rested. Per noted the boys were drinking more water than they should to last for the rest of the day and an overnight sleep after building a hut. He said nothing, wanting them to learn from experience instead of telling them everything. His time in the African bush told him they had six hours of water before they'd run dry and have to return to the village.

Again it came to him, *Thank God, I'm thinking about something else. Good, Per. He's real good, Per. He's healthy and happy. Do you really want to know anyway?*

All three stood for a few minutes, while Dondi proudly pointed out the faraway sea, the beach, the morass, and fields of cane. The ten year olds lost all interest in building a hut and decided a little campfire would be good even though the temperature was eighty-five and humid.

"Dad, do you have any matches so we can make a little campfire?"

"No, Son." He caught himself. "No, Son," he repeated, "but I'll show you both how to build one without matches."

The boys followed him, and soon, Per found a dry stick he could use for twirling, a small chunk of dried tree bark, and some dried grass.

"Now watch closely, boys." The boys moved in with their eyes a foot from the demonstration. In a few minutes, he had a small smoking fire and sent the boys running for sticks. Per watched them, smiled, thought of his supermodel wife, and commented, "Your mother can build a fire much faster than I!"

The rest of the day was spent sitting around the campfire telling stories. Dondi told one about a mermaid he saw in his dream at the Blue Hole, a place where the sea comes out of the earth as freshwater.

Then, Jomo lifted his water bottle and said sadly, "Dad, I don't think we have enough water to stay much longer."

Per thought to himself, *This was a good lesson to be learned. He called me Dad. I like that.*

They put out the fire carefully and descended, Dondi to his home and Per and Jomo back to the beach resort.

Later in the hotel pool, the three came together in neck-deep water and did their threesome hug.

"I love you, Mom and Dad."

Nice and Per smiled and said at the same time, "And we love you, Jo." Nice kissed Per then turned to Jomo, "By the way, Jo, who won the contest on the beach?"

"I did."

"So how long did you hold your breath?"

"Three minutes and twenty-two seconds."

11

Nine Years Later

PER'S YOUNGER BROTHER, Marty, was single and loved the outdoors. He was a solid sandy haired man with an infectious smile and a quiet confidence that could instantly put anyone at ease. His hands were as big as bear paws, and he could draw a fifty pound bow as if it were a toy. Per and Marty weren't just brothers, their friendship ran as deep and wide as the Mississippi. After high school, he started a small hunting gear store up on the New Hampshire side of the Connecticut River Valley in Benton, a hamlet about forty five miles to the North of Hanover, New Hampshire, where they grew up. In the early sixties, their parents had sold their corner grocery in old town Stockholm and immigrated to the United States. All they knew was how to run a small grocery store, so when 7-Eleven began selling franchises in 1964, they bought one and built the 7-Eleven that still stands near the Dartmouth campus. Per and Marty put in many hours behind that counter.

Between the two of them, Per was the A student. He chose Dartmouth in his hometown but only got the full ride from Stanford, and that's where he ended up.

Marty's greatest success was the guide-outfitter service he ran out of the cabin in the White Mountains he and Per had constructed years ago before Per became too busy to hunt. His name was well known in bow hunting circles nationwide because of his many videos on TV and magazine articles written on the sport, and his business flourished on internet sales in spite of Benton's population of 364 souls.

One fall evening, Marty called Per and insisted his brother bring Jo up for a deer hunt. "Jo's nineteen now, and I'd sure like to spend some time with him before he leaves the nest. I've penciled you both in for next week at the cabin. You'd better say you can make it. How about it?"

Per thought about his brother's offer and agreed, "Sure, we'll definitely be there. Jo's been restless lately. A bit of time in the woods would do him good. You know, Marty, sometimes I think life in the city is smothering him. Maybe it's the growth spurt he's in now. I don't know. He's changing."

"Hey Per, that's what kids do! He's been in a growth spurt now for what, nineteen years? Don't you remember how we were at that age? There's nothing wrong with Jo that a few nights around the campfire with us can't solve."

There was a pause then Per replied, "So true, Marty, so true. Okay, then put us down for next week, and I'll let you know for sure tomorrow after I check with Jo and Nice. Maybe I need a week more than he does."

It was still dark when they pulled out of the driveway for the eight hour drive.

"We haven't driven alone together for a while, Jo. I think this week will be good for us."

"I was just thinking the exact same thing, Dad."

A hundred miles went by in a blink with Jomo napping most of the time. Conversation ranged from questions about his girlfriend, Julie, to a story Per told about two rogue elephants attacking a small farming village in Kenya and how his friend Tambo was almost killed trying to dart them. Before it was over, every hut and structure in the village was leveled by the five ton beasts.

Crossing the Massachusetts border, Per glanced at his son and asked, "Would you reach back in my pack and get the paper bag out of the left hand zipper?"

Jomo rustled through the gear and pulled it out. "Here it is."

"Open it. It's a present for you."

Jomo reached in like a child opening a Christmas present. "Hey, it's an old leather pouch. Thanks."

"Sure, it's important to me. It's a very old pouch I got on a trip long ago before you were born. I'd like you to have it.

It's been in my pack pretty much all your life, and it's very special to me."

"What's it for?"

"Well, it might be a hunter's pouch or maybe it was a medicine bag. I don't know for certain, but I do know it has always brought me good luck." Per looked at the road. Then with a smile, he added, "Maybe it'll bring luck to you."

"Come on, Dad, you're a scientist. Do you really believe in luck?"

Contemplating his life, Per responded slowly, "Well, no, but after living with this old pouch for twenty years, I can tell you there's more to it than you could ever guess. I've done well in life, I married Nice. What could be better than that? Tie it around your waist under your shirt. Who knows? Maybe you'll become attached to it. I know I am."

Per took his eyes off the highway long enough to watch Jomo tie the strap around his waist. He gazed out the window at the road ahead and exhaled softly, an uneasy feeling settling in. *It was an impulse. Maybe I should have kept it in my pack*, Per thought. *It's too late now. It's his.*

Per began the internal dialogue that plagued him. *Yeah, maybe it's just the city that's stifling Jo. Maybe I shouldn't have given him that leather pouch.*

They arrived at the cabin midafternoon. Marty burst out the door with a broad smile when he heard car doors slamming. Jomo, stretching, was already breathing in the pine and birch aromas.

"'Bout time Per got you out of the city and brought you to the woods," Marty called to Jo. Approaching the two arrivals, he exclaimed, "Jo, you've grown like a weed since I last saw you! I didn't expect to be looking straight eye to eye at you," he said, engulfing him in a bear hug.

Per interrupted, "Spoken like a true uncle, Marty."

They all talked and kidded around as Marty helped unload their gear and carry it inside.

That evening as they sat around the campfire, Jomo listened and learned. Marty and Per had bowhunted together as young brothers. They told one story after the next, trying to outdo each other.

Marty looked straight at Jo. "Are you ready for this, deer hunting with a bow?"

Per interrupted, "Yeah, he's ready, Marty. Three years ready. Been bringing him to the range. He's a natural."

"Good, 'cause as I remember, Per, you really never could shoot a bow."

Per let out a groan. "I call cheap shot. Look, you became a pro. Why even compete with that? Besides, in Africa all I need is my .300 Winchester and a pocketful of bullets. Why fiddle with a silly bow and arrow? Marty, I hate to tell you, but you're back in the Stone Age. So you got a problem with me?"

Marty and Jo laughed at the brotherly response.

"No way!" He threw his hands up. "I give, before you DNA me to death."

"Don't you ever, and I mean ever, try that again."

Marty said, "Want to wrestle for it?"

Per put it to rest. "Pass me a beer, bro." They all laughed.

Marty punched Jo in the shoulder. "Jo, how old are you now? I haven't kind of kept track, yet."

"Nineteen. Why?"

"Want a beer?"

"Sure, Marty. Bud's okay. I usually go with Blue Ribbon, but Bud's okay."

Per cocked his head slightly and smiled to his son. "Then have a Bud at Marty's cabin."

Jo popped the top, "Can do."

They all laughed.

Jo leaned over and flicked Marty's hat, "Where'd you get that hat?"

"It's a banana hat. Mostly cowboy, mostly Mexico. Mexican cowboy. I got it on a pig hunt from a farmer I'll always remember and respect."

Then it was Jomo's turn. Marty reached into his breast pocket, pulled out a tin of Copenhagen, and expertly placed a pinch in his cheek. His grown-up nephew was about to tell his first story at the cabin. "I read this in a hunting magazine." He added a log to the fire and began. "Two guys were on a bow hunting trip in Northwest Ontario. They were hunting for a trophy black bear. On the last day of the hunt, they'd been up in their tree stands for three or four hours when a huge black bear came down the game trail, nose in the air. It smelled the bait, stopped for a long time, and then continued on over to the bait.

"The guys were up in two pine trees on opposite sides of the bear. One signaled to the other to take the shot. That guy waited for the perfect shot." Marty and Per hardly moved. "He drew his bow and let loose the broad head arrow, hitting the bear just above the heart, a little high for a quick kill. This huge bear panicked, ran in a quick circle, and in an instant was climbing the nearest tree, the tree of the hunter who fired the shot.

"Bears can climb a pine really fast, and it was only about thirty seconds before the mad bear with the arrow lodged in its chest was trying to grab the guy's boot with his teeth and claws. Before long, the bear grabbed his leg and pulled him right out of the tree. The guy fell thirty feet, broke both legs, and instantly, the bear was down on him.

"That bear mauled him. The guy rolled in a ball and covered his neck and face, but the bear bit him in the back of the neck, killing him. All this happened so fast, the guy's hunting buddy couldn't get down his tree fast enough, although he was yelling and shooting his .40 caliber pistol.

"Finally, the bear fell dead from the arrow and bullets."

When Jomo had finished, there was a long silence while Per and Marty digested the story.

Marty looked at the fire. "When you go hunting for big game, it's true, things can go wrong in a heartbeat. That's the way it's always been since the early humans hunted on the savannahs of Africa, right, Per?"

Per readily agreed, having lived with the unpredictability of wild animals, and having had a few close ones himself.

Talk wasn't necessary as they watched the flames. It was a memorable night for three guys and family in the woods under a canopy of a million stars, breathing the crisp and clean air.

"Time to turn in," Marty advised. The two men rose, brushing off their pants and adjusting their suspenders.

"Can I sit by the fire a little longer, Dad?" Jomo asked.

"Sure, Son," Per replied, as he glanced at Marty.

"I'll check your bow and make sure it's silent," Marty called back over his shoulder. The brothers walked toward the cabin. Jomo heard the crackle of oak leaves, measuring their steps in the darkness. Then he heard the door close.

Jomo found a more comfortable position to sit in, his eyes transfixed on the flames of the fire. He thought about what Marty meant by position of the moon rather than the phase of the moon. "Game are always active when the moon is directly overhead or directly on the other side of the earth regardless of its phase." He reached under his plaid jacket, untied the leather waist strap, and held the pouch out in the firelight. It was worn and soft to the touch, thick leather with a sinew drawstring. A faded red drawing of a four legged animal was barely visible against its dark brown background. The sewing was uniform and expertly done.

Someone who really knew about leather, he thought as he reached inside it to find it was empty. *I like it though*, he thought, as he retied it around his waist. *I don't think they'd mind if I just lay down here close to the fire for a while. I'll put a few more logs on, and I'm in a field of flowers. They move in waves with their whites and reds. It's cool but not cold. Spring. Snow, blue ice, mountains in the distance. A woman and a child laughing, and the flowers separate as they move—no, float closer. I'm happy to see them. The child runs to me, and we fall into the flowers, rolling and laughing, the smell of their petals fuse with their laughter. Now she comes to lie with me under the warmth of the sun. We kiss, and the child pulls on my hair. She whispers in my ear, "Toruk." I see my reflection in her eyes. I am strong. I am in love.*

Jomo slowly opened his eyes to see the fire was but a bed of glowing coals. A spark brought him to his senses. He rose, doused the fire pit, and walked to the cabin. It was starting to snow lightly. As he quietly opened the door, a faint recollection of a dream crossed a distant part of his mind and then disappeared. He found his bunk in the dark and was asleep in a minute.

The next morning came quickly. Marty gently rustled Jomo's shoulder. "It's time," he said quietly.

Jomo sat up and looked out the window. It was black. The clock read 3:00 a.m. As he put his feet on the floor, a strange recollection of his dream came, and then instantly disappeared.

Marty whispered, "Your dad's feeling under the weather, so it's just the two of us. We'll only take one of the four wheelers in case he feels better or changes his mind."

Marty was a man of few words. As the teenager hungrily attacked his breakfast, Marty stuck two bars in Jomo's shirt pocket. "Pemmican," he said. "And here's some paint for your face." While they went over the hand signals, Jomo stuffed down some bacon and five eggs.

Next, he went to the mirror and smeared on alternate stripes of black and green. As he applied the paint, a flash of his dream came again.

I was crouching in the tall weeds. I was hiding from something that was hunting me.

Marty called, this time a little louder and impatient to get Jomo's attention, "Hurry up, bud. It's time to shove off. Let's go!" He closed the cabin door. "There's just a light dusting of snow," Marty noted as he pulled out a brown plastic bottle, poured some of the liquid on a rag, and wiped down Jomo's boots. "Deer urine," he said. They wiped it all over themselves. "Use some more. I've got plenty of this stuff."

They got on the four wheeler and quickly left the light of the cabin behind them. They rode down a dirt road for what seemed like a long time. The deer urine made him lightheaded. Hairs on the back of his neck stood up, and his nose became his center.

Suddenly, Marty stopped the machine, got off, and whispered with a hand gesture, "Up the logging road." Without the headlights of the 4×4, sight was impossible.

"I can't see a thing," Marty whispered as they started out.

Unconsciously, Jomo took the lead. *Animals had walked here recently*, he thought.

The snow softened their steps. On and on they went. Marty tapped the back of Jomo's shoulder. He turned to see a hand signal close to his face. They turned onto a game trail worn deep by generations of deer. Soon the clouds gave way to fading starlight that eerily revealed they had been traversing a steep glacially scraped ridge in total darkness.

They came to a clear cut at the base of a forested hill of red spruce, red oak, and sugar maple. In its center, among some volunteer beech saplings, were the four mock scrapes in brilliant green moss, just as Marty had described the night before.

Jomo watched as Marty dropped deer urine on the first and then kicked the moss down to bare dirt with his boot. On the second, he kicked again. On the third, he kicked harder and dropped the hock gland from the huge buck he had shot last year. The fourth scrape was left alone. Marty eyed the licking branches above the scrapes and then dragged the deer urine rag between the scrapes.

A hand signal told Jomo where to set up. They separated. The scent of deer was overwhelming. He settled into a dense thicket of briars, and instantly his body formed into a loose ball. He could see the scrapes. The one with the hock gland was a mere fifteen paces away. He could not see Marty but knew he was about thirty paces to his right. Dawn was arriving as darkness turned to dim light. It was time to rest. Newly fallen leaves from the oaks and maples were turning brown and gave the silent forest a nutty aroma. A fox slipped by three feet away, not aware of him. Jomo memorized its scent.

Then two small bucks appeared at the edge of the forest. They went directly to separate scrapes, pawed around, and quickly left. Time passed. Jomo could smell the big one before he saw it. It stopped at the edge of the clearing and then went to the scrape in front of him. Nose down, it sniffed the hock gland and snorted so loud it spit out a huge mouthful of acorns. Earth flew from its pawing hoofs. It abruptly stopped broadside to lick the branch above the scrape.

Jomo drew his bow from a kneeling position and shot the buck in the heart. It went down where it stood.

"Great shot, Jo," Marty whispered. They dragged the buck fifty paces away from the scrapes, and Marty pulled out a leather folding case with two gleaming skinning knives of odd shapes. "You take this one," he continued. Marty guided Jomo's hand with firm surety when the initial incision was made into the steaming animal. Jomo's senses were completely in focus. The sight and smell went to his head.

"Go get the four wheeler, will ya? I'll finish." He checked his watch. "It's seven. We'll be back for another breakfast before eight." Then with a kind smile, Marty offered, "I'll put my tag on this one. Maybe you'll get another deer tomorrow, Jo."

Jomo set off at a fast lope, his heart still pumping from the adrenaline rush. Before long, he was at the four wheeler. Warm from the run, he dropped his bow and jacket in the weeds and jumped on. "Ah, crap," he muttered. "The key's been left on. Battery's dead." With a bounce, he was off the machine and headed down the dirt road at a fast pace. Thoughts of the morning hunt only made his feet go faster.

Per was sitting at the kitchen table in his long underwear as he shot through the cabin door.

"Dad, I shot a big buck!"

"Hey, that's terrific! That brother of mine is quite a guide! Are you back already for another breakfast?

"Not yet. Marty's still back at the scrapes dressing the deer. The four wheeler's battery was dead. Left the key on. I just ran back to get the other one."

Per dressed quickly and then left in the pickup with Jomo in the lead on the other four wheeler.

Marty was waiting at the logging road when they pulled up. "Jo, I saw your tracks head off toward the cabin. How'd you get back here so soon?"

"I just ran back. Where's the deer?"

Later that night after Jomo went to bed, Marty turned to Per and said in a slow, puzzled tone, "That son of yours must have run nine miles this morning, Per, at a sub-five minute mile pace!"

Per looked at Marty, startled. "What? No, that can't be possible. He was on the track team in high school, but he wasn't that fast."

"Believe me, Per, a sub-five minute pace. That's world class."

The brothers stared at each other and then burst out laughing and shaking their heads.

"Someone's math must be way off, Marty. As I recall, you got a D in math!"

The following morning, Marty was awakened by Per's frantic voice. "Jo's gone!"

They looked at the clock. It was 3:30 a.m. In the kitchen, they found a note.

> Morning Dad and Uncle Marty. If I get a deer, I'll call you on the cell phone.
>
> Love, JO

"What if he gets lost?"

Marty turned to his brother. "He won't get lost. He's got a feel for nature. He ran through the woods back to the shack yesterday after shooting the deer, didn't he? Nah, he won't get lost. Let's leave him alone. Don't call him. It's the right thing to do."

"Then it's your call, Marty." Per opened the door to see Jomo's tracks disappear beyond the reach of the kitchen light. Turning, he reached down and put the cover back on the face paint.

Marty thought for a while, then spoke to Per seriously, "Per, he's nineteen now. I think you might be still treating him as a kid. He's grown, and he's tough, but he still talks like a kid. I'll bet he talks like an adult, though, when he's not around you and Nice. You know how it is. He's the next generation. We're old to them. He holds his words, thoughts. I like him. He's breaking his own mold, and it won't be long before he's on his own. I can see it, can you?"

Jomo walked for a half hour before he nosed the scent of a deer. It smelled sick. He passed it by. The next one came soon after. In the dark, he knelt down, felt the size of the hoof print on the road, put his nose to it, and then rose. It was an alpha deer. The scent led him down and across the ditch into an oak forest. Jomo began to trot through the darkness. He smiled. He felt alive. Rather than tiring from his pace, his legs felt stronger and stronger with each mile. Thick weeds, brush, rocks, he was as surefooted as his prey. Hunter and hunted, locked in the life-and-death dance that played out for millions of years before them. The trot turned to a lope.

Patiently tracking, changing directions, sensing fear, and panic, his eyes opened wider in the dim. His tongue dropped deep out of his mouth for more air. A low fog hovered over the valley as the sun revealed its delicate curtain. There was neither cold nor warmth, only the chase. He knew he was close. Then, as he rounded a low rock outcropping, he suddenly stopped. He could hear it. It was three and a half hours before he saw the huge buck. It was early light. He knew it was the same one. It was breathing hard and on its haunches. They locked eyes at thirty paces. The buck was slow to get up on all fours at the sight of the relentless human.

Jomo broke into a smooth run. The big deer flagged its white tail and ran down a steep ravine of jagged boulders. It was running for its life. Jomo's legs did not fail him down the descent. He saw saliva on the side of a rock. The deer was tiring. The scent took him back out of the ravine up toward the saddle of a low mountain with a white rock near its peak. He also was breathing hard. The climb was dangerous at this pace. He was so close, he could see the underside of the big deer's cloven hoofs as they rained down softball-sized jagged rocks.

When he reached the saddle, he stopped to rest. He was far from the cabin now. Suddenly, the deer charged from his left behind, and as Jomo wheeled, the deer reared. Lowering its head, it deeply gored Jomo's right shoulder.

The impact knocked his bow off, sending it clattering to the ground. The buck reared again. Jomo dodged to the left and grabbed the base of the huge antlers as they came down at him. They struggled for maybe thirty or forty seconds when, without warning, the beast bellowed and fell to the ground dead, eyes fixed on him.

Jomo laid down with his head on the neck of the beast, his shoulder bleeding, and looked up to see two ravens circling. He blacked out. When he awoke, he stiffly reached for a pemmican bar, took a bite, and then pulled out his cell phone. It was nine o'clock.

By the time Per and Marty arrived, Jomo had field dressed the big buck as Marty had taught him and dragged it down the mountain a good fifty yards. His shoulder was still bleeding and had begun to swell.

Per took Jomo by the arm to evaluate the severity of the wound. "When we get you back to the cabin, I'll have to sew that up. The survival kit's in my pack. There's no anesthetic, just dressings and a bottle of Cipro to stop any infection."

Jomo replied with a grimace, "Thanks, I'll take it. A little closer to my neck, and he might have killed me." He was tired.

At the dinner table that evening, Marty remarked for the second time, "That's the biggest buck I have ever seen around here. It may be a Boone and Crockett. Yeah, I'm sure, a Boone and Crockett record. Jo, you're one lucky kid that its heart burst before you were seriously hurt."

Marty paused and thought, "Funny thing though. I've been hunting deer all my life and never seen a dead deer with a burst heart. Never. Never even heard of it."

Marty looked to Per and raised an eyebrow. "But I guess there's always a first time."

Per changed the subject, "I'll change the dressing again after dinner. It looks like the bleeding's stopped."

While they laughed, Per flashed back to the fiery eyes of the warrior in the blue ice. He was deep in the vision when Marty brought him back.

"Jo," Marty asked, "what really happened up there? Something doesn't add up, but I can't put my finger on it."

Jomo replied simply, "Like you said, Uncle Marty, I guess I just got lucky. Maybe it's my lucky leather pouch."

Marty looked up. "What lucky pouch?"

Jomo casually replied, "Oh, just a leather pouch my dad gave me." Jomo went outside and forgot to show it to Marty.

Later that evening, Per unexpectedly rose, left Jomo and Marty at the campfire, and went back into the cabin.

"Where ya going, Dad?"

"Oh, I'm just going back to the cabin to straighten out some of the clutter in my pack. I haven't cleaned it out since my last trip to Africa. You two stay here and keep the tall tales going."

Marty looked up. "Okay, Per."

"I won't be long," Per said as he closed the cabin door behind him and went over to the big black plastic trash bag in the corner of the kitchen. Quickly, he opened it, and there on top was Jomo's bloody gauze dressing he had changed earlier. Per thought, *I'll bring it to the lab to find out once and for all if his DNA is from the Cro-Magnon. This muscle and blood will tell me everything I need to know and more. I've got to know. I've got to know!* He found a clean baggie in a drawer, placed the gauze in it, sealed it, and placed it in his pack in the small bedroom. Then with an exhale, he walked out the door and back to the campfire.

On the way home Per thought, *I feel closer to Jo than ever before, and I think he feels closer to me. He looks me in the eye when he talks to me. He smiles. It feels good. It makes me feel like I've been a good father.* Then his mind wandered. *Maybe Marty's right. What really happened with that buck? This was a good trip for us. He's changing. Different from when we left, but it's a good different. I feel like he's a new person I want to know better. I don't only love him, I truly like him.*

Per looked over and saw Jomo sleeping.

Later, Jomo woke up and watched the signs on the freeway passing by. "Dad, can I move up to the cabin for a few months? I'm not ready for college."

Per frowned but didn't take his eyes off the road. "Jo, we've talked about this for six months. Now the college year's started. Julie went. So that's out. Your mom and I don't understand you. Now it's the cabin? I'm not going to ask you about your future anymore. Comes a time everyone's got to find their own way. The decisions you make now could make or break you. Believe me, I know. We love you, and you're always welcome, but you can't take up residence in our house. It saddens me to say this, Jo."

"You're right, Dad, I don't have a plan. Just go with me here. I could get into any college with my grades, but I'd rather live in the woods. I'd read books and live off the land maybe for a few months."

"Excuse me, Jo. I've got to laugh a little at your live-off-the-land idea." Remembering Marty's comment, Per thought for a minute, "Well, I guess you're old enough, but let's talk it over with your mother. If she thinks it's okay, then I'll give Marty a call, how's that?"

Jomo smiled. "Thanks, Dad."

As they approached the exit, Per thought, He's nineteen. *My God, why did I do that? Why did I go back for the gauze? I've gone nineteen years without facing this. Why now? I should just leave this alone! Just stop! Okay, calm down. If he isn't my son, I'll do a complete electron microscopy on his muscle along with the Cro-Magnon's. That's what I'll do.*

Just then, they pulled into the driveway, and Per came back to reality.

12

THAT WEEKEND AFTER Jomo and Per got back from Marty's, the phone rang. Per answered. There was a number on the caller ID he didn't recognize.

"Hello. Jorland residence."

"Hello, Dr. Jorland, this is Julie. May I please talk to Jo if he's home?"

"Well, hello, Julie. It's been a while. How's your first year at Yale coming along, and what classes are you taking?"

Julie, very quick as usual, replied, "I know you're a Stanford man. I like it here. I like Yale. It's hard, Dr. Jorland. I'm really studying more than ever, but I'm doing pretty well." She paused then said, "I think I'll major in mathematics."

"Hey, that's great, Julie. Yes, I am a Stanford man—Go Trees! Hold on. Let me call Jo to the phone. I know he's around here somewhere. Oh, and good luck, you'll do fine."

A minute passed, and then Jomo answered, "Hey, Jul."

"Hi, Jo, how did the deer hunt go at your uncle's cabin? Did you get one?"

"I'll have to give those two yeses, Jul. I got the first deer, Marty gave me his tag, and I also got the second. The second one got me first, and then I got it back. It's a good story. I'll tell you sometime. Next time you're over to the house, you'll see the horns over the fireplace. Marty says they're maybe big enough to go in the record book. How about you, Jul? How's it going at Yale? Is it any fun or all work? Tell me the truth, Jul!"

"Oh, it's going okay. I've made some new friends in the dorm. We're all freshman on our floor. It's going good, but I sure miss you. I really mean it! Not really homesick, but I miss you."

"I miss you, too, Jul. It's all different now. I'm here, and you're there. Phone calls are good, but I'd sure like to be with you."

Julie brightened up. "Well, that's what I'm calling about. I've got a great idea that I think you'll like."

"Okay, go!"

"Next weekend is homecoming, and it's a very big deal here."

"Yes?"

"Bands, the football game, parties, Fall colors on campus, and all that. Jo, I want you to come for the weekend, maybe two or three nights. It'll be perfect. I've already checked with my friend's boyfriend, and he could put you up in his dorm room. He's got fun friends you could meet. They're from all over."

"Wow! That sounds like a great time."

"Well then, are you coming?"

"I'm going to London with my mom, but that's not for two weeks." He thought for five seconds. "Yes, Julie! I'm as good as there! It'll be great to see you!"

"When you get here, I'm gonna plant the biggest kiss on you right in front of the dorm, and I don't care who's watching!"

"Maybe I should get in the car right now. No, I'm just kidding."

"So it's a deal! I want you to be here Thursday afternoon around two."

"I'll be there."

"Okay, then. I have to go. I miss you!"

"And I miss you. See ya!"

Jomo arrived at two on the dot, and first business was to collect that kiss as promised. The weekend was off to a great start.

"I'm off classes till Monday. I'll show you around today, and tonight there's a great student party off campus. There's gonna be a reggae band, dancing, and pretty much a good time without alumni around. Tomorrow, we'll figure out what to do, maybe help with the freshman float, take a drive in the country, you know. I know a place where the frats have their keggers. It's a farm owned by some rich alumni. It's called Trillium, and it's beautiful in the Fall and very private," she said with a look. "I'll bring a blanket."

"A blanket?"

"Yes, Jo, a blanket."

"Are you—?"

"Yes, Jo, sex. That vow we made years ago makes no sense anymore. I want you. I've always wanted you. Ninth grade, it was kissing but we're way past that now."

"Jul, why didn't you tell me sooner? I was afraid I'd lose you if I—"

"No, Jo, you wouldn't have. It's the other way. I've been waiting. And waiting and waiting for you."

"Really?"

"Oh yeah." She laughed. "It's not all about books! I'm gonna love you, Jo, I'm gonna love you."

Surprised, Jo moved in for a kiss.

"Don't talk. It'll happen naturally. Oh yeah, and before you leave," she whispered in his ear, "after that, I've got a surprise, someone I'd like you to meet."

"Who could there be here to meet besides you?"

"I arranged it, Jo. I'll be honest here, I want to be with you, so I want you to go to Yale, and we can be together."

"But who do you want me to meet?"

"His name is Billy Bye. He's the track coach." She put both hands on his shoulders, looked into his eyes, and lightly shook him. "Jo, you set a few school records."

"Barely. So? That was high school, Jul. Yale is Ivy League. It's the big time. I don't know."

"I've talked to him, and you could maybe even have a full scholarship if you try out and make the team."

"As usual, you've got it all figured out, don't you? But then, that's not a bad thing, either." He nodded.

"Well, yes, but it's a good idea, don't you agree? This way we could be together."

"When's this? I mean, when will I see him?"

"I've set the meeting up for tomorrow afternoon, Jo. You don't have to run, just talk to him. This would be for next year. Five seniors are leaving. The timing's perfect."

To Julie's surprise, Jomo drew back a little. "Well, I'll talk with him, but I have to tell you, I've been thinking about not going to college yet. I just talked with my dad about it a few days ago. Maybe I'll go up to Uncle Marty's cabin for a while."

"But this is a year from now, Jo," Julie responded, disappointed but still trying.

"Okay, Jul, I'm making no promises, and thanks. I'll see him tomorrow. Now, let's get on with the weekend!"

Miffed by his attitude, Julie put on her best smile and thought, *He doesn't get it. I set it all up, and, well, I don't know anymore. Maybe I've got to move on, yet I feel like I love him.*

The weekend with Julie was a total success, thought Jomo on his drive home. *I guess I wondered if we'd still be as tight as before she left. Now I know, and now we know. We might be in love. Did I really say that to myself? I think she was a little upset why I didn't get any more excited about that track coach. Oh well, she's beautiful, and the weekend was great!*

Jo opened the windows, reached down, turned up some rockin' country music and adjusted his sunglasses as he drove home.

Sure is a nice day. So, I'll continue with my story.

One day, I was in my office arranging some papers for an upcoming board presentation, when Per gave me a call.

"Hi, Larry. It's Per Jorland"

"Per! I haven't heard from you in quite a while."

"I know. I've been busy."

"How's the Kenya project coming?"

"We're plugging along, just plugging along. Say, Larry, that's not what I called to talk about."

"Well, here I am."

"Are we on a secure line?"

"Secure line? Why, yes, my office has the only secure line in the institute. Why? What's this all about?"

"I'll come right to the point, Larry. I've been doing some DNA and electron microscope studies on my son, Jomo. Larry, they're extraordinary."

"Your son? How so?"

"All I can say now is that they're different. He's different."

"Per, this is coming pretty fast. Would you slow down? What do you mean by different?*"*

"Larry, I'd rather not say much more over the phone. Instead, I'd like to send some of my early results to you—that is, if it's okay with you."

"Well, sure. Now you've really piqued my interest. Just send it on over, and I'll be glad to take a look."

"No! No, Larry, I'd rather send it to your house so no one else reads the cover letter and sees my preliminary results."

"Sure, Per, if you wish. If it's really new stuff, maybe I'll get it published for you in the Smithsonian magazine."

"Well, that's an idea, Larry, but I think a little premature. After you read my cover letter, you'll understand what I'm into here. This goes way back, back to that dig in Norway. Remember Norway, the mammoth?"

"Norway? I remember that one. That's nineteen or twenty years ago. What a disaster! The female elephant that carried the baby had a total emotional breakdown when she gave birth to a hideously malformed hairy baby. But back to you. Now I'm really interested, Per. Send it to the house, and you can trust me. When it hits my eyes, it's classified, my friend."

"Good, Larry, I'll send it off today."

"Looking forward to it! And it's really good to talk to you."

"The same here. Goodbye for now, my friend."

"Yes, you can count on me, Per."

"Okay. Bye."

"Bye."

13

Sixteen years had passed since that bittersweet goodbye at the InterContinental with Michel, but Nice still hoped to see him again every year when she checked into the Paris InterContinental.

"Yes, Nice Nkoe Jorland. I have a reservation for room 318."

"Yes, Mrs. Jorland, your usual room. Just sign. It is ready for you."

As she signed in, she thought, *I'll ask if he's staying here. What room he's in. What are you thinking? Stop this. You're not lovers and never were. But you kissed him. You wanted him. You don't even know his last name to ask. You're married, so get him out of your mind. You're weak, Nice. No! Just ask her now!*

As she put down the pen, she looked up and asked in a breezy voice, "Could you please tell me if a man by the name Michel is staying here or perhaps been here recently?"

"Michel? You're looking for a man named Michel?"

"Yes. He is a Frenchman. Very polite, good looking, dark hair, about fifty years old."

"Michel. That is such a common French name. Do you know anything more about him?"

"Yes, well, no. I have to admit I don't, but he told me he always stayed here when in Paris. Think! You must know him!"

"I'm sorry, Mrs. Jorland. You could leave a message, but this hotel is so big and international, I doubt it—"

"But surely you must know him!"

"I am truly sorry, Mrs. Jorland."

"Then I will have to find him another way." She turned, visibly disappointed, and walked to the elevators.

That evening alone in her room, she impulsively called room service for a bottle of Vouvray and two glasses. The steward arrived quickly with the bottle on ice in a beautiful silver bucket and two sparkling crystal glasses. She avoided them for a half hour and thought, *Look at you. Have you completely gone insane? It's been sixteen years. He's not thinking of you. All these years he never called you or left you a note at the desk. You've gone over the edge, Nice. No, I'll pour two glasses and imagine he's here on the couch next to me. No harm in that. Maybe he never contacted me because he loves me and doesn't want me to get caught up in his dangerous world. Maybe he's actually here in Paris. Sometimes I get a feeling—a rush—that he's near and he's thinking of me.* She set the glasses on the table, pulled the bottle from the ice, popped the cork, and delicately poured both glasses. Next, she lit a candle, took a long sip, and let her mind float to that walk on the Seine sixteen years ago.

Suddenly, the phone rang.

"Hello, Nice Jorland? Is this room 318?"

"Yes, this is Nice."

"We have a call for you from a hospital in Nairobi, Kenya. Will you take the call?"

"Yes, please connect me at once," Nice ordered, thinking the worst. Per was in Africa.

"Hello, Mrs. Jorland?"

"Yes?"

"This is Dr. Winston. I am chief of emergency medicine at Kenyatta Hospital in Nairobi. This connection is not good, so listen to me closely. I am sorry to inform you that your husband, Per, has been bitten by a cobra. He could die. They were in Tsavo National Park in thick brush country when the bite occurred. He was rushed out of the park, and they met up midway with our ambulance carrying antivenom from our emergency room. We got to him in short time, but the bite is very serious. I shall be honest with you now. He is not doing well, and there is the possibility he could die. He is in and out of consciousness. When he is conscious, he is coherent. We are doing our best for him, but his condition is critical at this time. Do you understand me?"

Nice fell to the carpet. "Oh God, don't let him die, not Per. No! No!" The phone slipped out of her hand as she started to cry then she heard the doctor calling her name loudly. She pulled herself together.

"Mrs. Jorland, he is awake at this moment. Would you like to talk with him?"

"Per! Per! It's Nice." She waited for his response, but none came. "I love you. Please do not die on me!"

Then, Per's voice was faint. "I love you, Nice. This is a tough one. It happened so fast." Then a long break as he contemplated his plight. "The doctor said I could die. I could die right here in this hospital far away from you and Jomo."

"Per, listen to me. You are not going to die! Say it! 'I am not going to die!' Say it, Per, 'I am not going to die!'"

He started to fade off. Nice barely could hear him say, "I am not going to die," and then he was back again. "Nice, I've got something I have to tell you. It's important, something you need to know." He tried to find the right words. The connection was breaking up, fading in and out. "Jomo... Jomo...the father...I am...Jo is not..."

Nice heard the phone hit the floor, and then the doctor was back on the line. "Mrs. Jorland, we will call you if or when his condition changes. Will you be at this number for another day or two?"

"Yes, Dr. Winston, I'll be here for two more days. No, wait, I'll catch a plane for Nairobi tomorrow."

Dr. Winston became almost abrupt with the hard facts. "Mrs. Jorland, I am afraid that will do no good. He will either get better or die, and it would all happen before your arrival. You would do better just to wait by the phone. Good bye for now," he said as he dropped his professional voice. Then he added, "try not to worry. I shall call you again later this evening, and please know he is in good care."

Jomo was splitting wood at the cabin when his cell phone lit up. Caller ID showed it was from his mother on location in Paris.

"Hi, Mom, how's the weather in France? Having a good time or are you working too hard?"

"Jo, listen to me. This is serious. I just got off the phone talking to a Dr. Winston in Nairobi. Your father is very, very ill, in critical condition from a cobra bite. I was able to talk to him for a few minutes, but he wasn't making sense at times, and his voice was very weak. Oh, Jo, he could die over there." Nice started sobbing.

"Should I come to Paris or meet you in Nairobi? Do you have the telephone number of the hospital and this doctor who's taking care of Dad?" He could hear her crying. "He is not going to die! What are his chances? What did this doctor say to you?"

"Jo, he said to not go. There is nothing we can do at this time. They're taking good care of Per, and he'll call if his condition changes."

"When?"

"He told me later this evening. I'll phone the moment I hear anything."

"I love you, Jo."

"I love you too, Mom. Call me again this evening, will you? I want to make sure you're okay."

The call came in from the hospital in Nairobi at 4:00 a.m.

"Mrs. Jorland, this is Dr. Winston. I am very happy to inform you your husband has taken a turn for the better. He was wheeled out of critical care an hour ago, and if all goes well, he will be out of the hospital and back in the US in about one week. Did you hear me?" There was static on the phone line.

"Dr. Winston, thank you for all you've done for Per. Thank you for saving his life." The connection was breaking up.

"You're welcome, Mrs. Jorland. We are all very happy for you. Goodbye for now."

Nice shared the good news with Jomo, and a week later, Per was back home.

One morning, he walked into the kitchen, poured himself a cup of coffee, and sat down next to Nice at the breakfast nook.

"Hey, you, how are you feeling this morning?"

"Much better. I think I've turned the corner. I can't say for sure though. I'm pretty stiff."

Nice pinched his cheek playfully. "Well, you look better anyway. We almost lost you, you know." Her tone of voice changed after an uncomfortable pause. "Say, do you remember when I talked to you in the hospital?"

Per thought for a minute and then said, "Not too well. I thought about that call after I woke up today. It's like trying to remember a dream. I remember I was sweating so much, the phone was wet, and then I had no strength to even hold it up anymore. Why?" Per fidgeted in his chair at the tone in Nice's voice.

"Well, you were trying really hard to tell me something, but the connection wasn't good, and you kept fading in and out. You were trying to tell me something important, something I needed to know, something about Jomo." She waited for a response from Per, but there was only silence. "Is any of this ringing a bell with you at all?"

Per hesitated and then looked at Nice quizzically. His brain instantly came to attention, but his body language showed a relaxed person. He looked down at his hands, wondering if this was the right time to have this conversation, if ever. Was he brave enough? "Nice, I can't remember. I can only recall you telling me something about not dying, not dying on you."

"Hmm, it must have been something about Jo living at the cabin then." She looked at him oddly. Something didn't seem right, and then she brushed it off. "Oh well, no worries. I'm glad you're feeling better. You sure gave us all a scare. I am grounding you from any traveling, sir, for the next few weeks."

"That sounds good to me, Nice. I guess I'll head in to the office for a couple of hours tomorrow. I'm getting behind schedule on a few projects."

Nice got up to refill their coffee cups.

That was your time to be honest with her. Are you willing to live with this secret and take it to the grave? Per thought, bothered by his own dishonesty. *If you never tell her, will you ever have any peace?*

14

Two Years Later

PER'S LINGERING EFFECTS from the cobra bite had long passed, and it was time for a return trip to Kenya. This time, Jomo would accompany him. Now twenty-one, he was a young man and had not seen his grandparents Nonkipa and Jomo Nkoe since he was twelve.

The morning after they arrived, they talked freely with the warden, Robert Brown, in the Illiki Cafe at the Nairobi Ambassador Hotel.

"Per and I go way back. Remember those days when you were in school, and Per would be gone for a week or two?"

"Of course, I remember."

"He was probably with me in one of Kenya's many game reserves. On this occasion, Jomo, we'll be taking you deep into the Mara where no tourists go. Our project with the African elephants is in phase 2 of a long-term gene therapy. We've enjoyed great progress, haven't we, Per?"

"That's right, Bob, slow but steady progress."

The warden took a sip of coffee. "At first, our genetic work with that population was quite primitive."

Per looked to Jomo. "Then in '96 came Dolly, the sheep cloned in Scotland and recently, cracking the African elephants' genetic code. Today, there are labs in the US that can analyze a hundred complete genomes in one day. Incredible. Now, African elephant DNA from tusks can even identify what country in Africa the illegal tusks come from. If only we could keep these beautiful animals safe from illegal traders and angry farmers."

Bob continued, "The Mara is a huge game reserve on the edge of the Northern frontier that stretches from Mt. Kenya to the Great Rift Valley. All of the wildlife runs free here—spectacular herds of millions of wildebeests and others who accompany them, such as zebra, gazelle, impalas, elands, giraffe, lions, leopards, elephants, and birds migrate back and forth from the Tanzanian Serengeti to the Mara every year."

Jomo listened intently. He'd heard Per talk about the Mara, but the warden's every sentence was fascinating, almost lyrical.

The big man opened his napkin, pulled two pens from his breast pocket, and quickly sketched a red ink map of Lake Victoria, Kenya, and Tanzania. In blue ink, he drew the Mara River originating deep into the interior to the Mau Escarpment and some of its tributaries. "Rain comes and goes with the seasons on the great savannahs, and the animals always follow the water. Each migration must cross the Mara River. This important river flows to Lake

Victoria. I am very concerned because it appears to be slowly drying up. Some are cutting down the Mau Forest at the escarpment, its very origin. If it dries up, hundreds of thousands of exotic animals will die.

"Per has told me you have an extraordinary feel for the wild, which you instinctively seem to be able to cope with whatever card nature deals. Well, this place, the Mara, will challenge all your senses. Many have ventured in never to return. Here, the laws of nature are written with teeth, claws, horns, hoofs, and thorns. If you get into trouble here, getting out can be difficult. This, Jomo, is the *nyika*, the great wild, the impenetrable expanse that for centuries denied white explorers the passage from Africa's Eastern shore to Africa's Western shore. The Maasai call it *Siringit*. It means 'endless plain.' Respect the Siringit. It will patiently pry or sometimes quickly find your weakness, your humanness. I have one piece of advice for you: if you are hurt, never let them see you limp."

The warden checked his watch. "Tambo is waiting outside with the jeeps by now. We should go. Oh, by the way, Jomo, you are not authorized to carry a gun, so Tambo will have a spear for you in the second jeep." He stood up from the table first, a man oozing confidence.

The drive from Nairobi was dusty and hot. Per had ridden it many times, but this was Jomo's first adventure into the Mara. The road was crowded with signs. One in particular caught Jomo's attention:

Beware! Elephants Have Right of Way!

This was a trip Jomo had looked forward to for a long time. Per and the warden were going deep into Maasai Mara to take blood samples from a large matriarchal herd that had been spotted by a bush plane a few days earlier.

Jomo rode in the front seat to hear Bob on the first leg of the drive.

Bob talked loudly over the hammering of the tires. "The samples will be part of a twenty-five year, three generational assessment of phase 2, a serious liver disease characterized by sticky blood platelet blockages in arterioles within the liver that appeared ten years ago."

Per leaned forward from the backseat to explain, "It's similar to having a slow motion heart attack, Jo, but in your liver. The vessels that deliver oxygen and nutrients to their massive livers are occluded, and soon, large areas of the liver die."

"Thank you," Bob continued. "Per and his gene therapy work are maybe the last hope for survival of a portion of the African elephant population. Per and his colleagues at AnGen have identified the elephant gene that encourages growth of new blood vessels to bypass the blocked areas. The lab results of these blood samples are extremely important. Their germ-line approach is targeted to inheritance of healthy, functional liver genes. By deleting the defective gene in either the sperm cell or the egg cell and replacing it with a healthy, functioning gene, the defective gene is not passed onto the next generation. It is truly cutting edge therapy."

Jomo thought for a minute, and then remarked, "You mean you can change an inheritance in a single generation?"

Bob responded a little louder to make his point clear, "Yes, Jomo, what we're doing is a profound inheritable change within a single generation. It's truly cutting edge in gene manipulation. Gone are the days of adaptation over eons. We're running out of time for these beautiful creatures."

"Can that be done in humans too?"

Per looked to Bob and answered, "Well, Jo, you're old enough to understand the significance of your question. Yes, it can, but that is not our mission. There are, no doubt, a select few scientists doing just that behind closed doors, genetically altering the next generation of babies to make them stronger or better in some way. I appreciate your curiosity. It's very controversial. We're after the survival of the biggest vertebrate in the animal kingdom."

Bob looked to Per and raised his eyebrows.

They stopped for several days' worth of supplies at a park ranger lodge about thirty kilometers inside the park boundary. Hours after leaving the main road, they followed a narrow, almost impassable, four-wheel-drive road paralleling a seasonal river bed.

It was hot and dusty. Per, in the first vehicle with the warden, was better off than Jomo and his three newfound tracker friends. The second, an open Toyota jeep, was loaded down with stinky gasoline jerry cans, and their tracker/ driver insisted on tailgating the first vehicle so closely, they were barely visible in a thick cloud of red road grit. Occasionally, when the cloud did lift, the four could be seen with bandanas tied over their faces, their reddish caked eyes and smiling white teeth peeking out. Per looked back and smiled at the unusual site. Abruptly, Bob stopped the rover. The trackers in the second vehicle were out in an instant and trotting in a line, with twenty-one year old Jomo in the lead. Per turned to see the three erect camouflaged figures led by a bigger man, his son.

There were fresh elephant tracks everywhere. One tracker spoke in a hushed tone to another. The words were acknowledged with a nod.

"What did he say?" asked Jomo, not fully understanding the term even though Nice had taught him Swahili as a child.

Mbitha, the third tracker, retrieved a clean bandana from his shirt pocket and wiped the cracked clay from his eyes. While pointing, he translated, "The tree got even with the elephant."

Jomo surveyed the scene. The young bull had mistakenly, while eating, uprooted a tall baobab tree. The tree had fallen on him, breaking his back.

Crouching with eyes to the soil, the warden explained to Per and Jomo that this was a fresh track of a very old African bull. The head tracker again spoke in Swahili.

Calling to the warden, he said, "Ahmed Usho," referring to the legendary old tusker bull killed in the 1970s. "This is a big one."

Per replied, "This is not part of the mission protocol, Bob, but that old one has eluded us for so many years. Permission to try to get blood samples from him?"

"Thanks, Per. Have at it," the warden responded. "Have at it, if we can find him! He's about as dangerous as a mad black mamba!" Then he muttered under his breath, "Hope we're not biting off more than we can chew."

Per mumbled, "Me, too. Okay, it's a go, men. Let's do this." Per motioned to Jomo and the trackers to find the old tusker.

The twelve thousand pound bull had a front foot with a long, wide cleft in it that made him easy to track. Grooves in the soil showed his tusks were so big and heavy, he had to rest them. Somehow, he had eluded park management for years because he had rubbed off his transmitter. He probably even wandered beyond park boundaries and successfully eluded poachers as well. Ten years ago, this bull had been held for three days in captivity at the Tsavo National Park headquarters. At the time, he was thought to be fifty years old, one of the many healthy bulls Per had worked with in phase 1 of the gene therapy project so many years ago.

Bob and Per remained in the rover, while Jomo, spear in hand, trotted off into the bush. The trackers followed single file, rifles held loosely in hand. Before long, there were only three men trotting in a line. In his excitement, Jomo had broken into a blistering pace and was nowhere to be seen up ahead in the dense bush. Still on the huge bull's scent, Jomo came upon a wild dog, alive but barely breathing. Its neck was sliced and bloodied from a wire snare, probably intended as campfire dinner for Somali poachers. Jomo thought of Bob's words on the drive: "These ruthless criminals had been shooting critically endangered black rhinos with AK-47s, in spite of the dead-or-alive bounties on them. They saw off the horns and sell them into the Asian folk medicine market, leaving the dead animal to rot."

The pathetic dog, near death, looked up at him. As Jomo bent over to release the snare, two nomadic male lions entered the clearing from his right. They circled to the left to attain a superior downwind position, their unblinking eyes assessing Jomo's strength and aura and measuring that against their hunger.

Jomo readied his spear. Icy stares were exchanged. The black maned one lowered on all fours and snarled with his huge canines as if to strike. The brother completed its circle to a position directly behind. Jomo instantly feigned a charge with his spear, then pivoted, and caught the one from behind with a spear tip to its neck, not deep enough to severely injure it. The dust flew. He howled and lay down. As the other stopped short its charge, Jomo quickly touched his spear tip to its shoulder. The black maned lion quickly understood and came to the aid of his brother.

The two turned to look at Jomo and the dying dog as they disappeared into some wait-a-bit thorns.

Jomo continued the pursuit. When the three finally caught up to him, Mbitha commented, "Do not run so fast. You do not carry a rifle. Did you see the two lions eating the dog?"

"No, Mbitha, I didn't see them eating the dog."

"They could have taken you from the tall grass as you ran like a deer. You must keep closer to us, young Jomo. You do not know the Siringit."

"Thank you, Mbitha. I will follow your lead, but I do not think they could have taken me."

Mbitha smiled and offered him the fist bump. "I think you can lead. It is good that you lead. We approve how you track."

The troupe spotted the old tusker three miles to the South and radioed the warden and Per. An old bachelor, he was alone, resting in the shade of some flat topped thorny acacia trees. For Bob and Per, it was an easy darting and routine blood sample. The beast was tired and didn't object to the humans' intrusion. He was hot and appeared to be in great need of a mud hole to cool down.

Per watched Jomo examine the beast lying on its side in the tall grasses. Tambo stood close. "See, Jomo, the elephant's bright red color comes from the clay of the Siringit. Its right tusk is long, curved, and heavier at the end, while the left is straight, slightly shorter, and worn on its end." Watching Jomo examining the left tusk, Mbitha added, "Elephants and all other animals are left handed. See, he digs with the short one." Tambo smiled.

Once the antidote was given, the group retreated to the rover except for Jomo who remained at its side.

"What the hell is he doing?" whispered the warden to Per. The trackers took a few tentative steps forward, their vintage high caliber rifles at the ready position.

"Wait, I think he'll be okay. Lower your guns." Per held up a closed fist to indicate stop.

The tusker rolled to one side slowly and then awkwardly rose to his knees. When he stood up, his tattered ears flapped noisily as he shook off the drug. He was wild. Jomo did not move. His trunk began a systematic investigation of Jomo from head to foot, and then foot to head. An area on its huge forehead between the eyes was pulsating.

The trackers watched in amazement as the huge animal continually attempted to put the tip of its trunk into Jomo's mouth and continually returned to the pouch at his waist. "In all my years, I've never seen anything like that. Who is he? Are you sure he's your son?" The warden asked. "That wild bull should have killed him by now."

"My God, what's the bull doing?" whispered Per.

Shikuku replied in an unbelieving breath, "That bull is telling Jomo he recognizes him, and everything is okay. He is talking to Jomo through his forehead with low sounds. Now see, Dr. Jorland. He is showing young Jomo his scars."

Per shuddered. "He is different. I heard the story of a forty year old African elephant female introduced into a zoo population of about twenty elephants. There was no fighting for the pecking order seen. Rather, all the elephants gathered lovingly around the newcomer as she carefully showed them all the scars from her life in the wild. The larger scars, perhaps from a lion attack, were compassionately examined by both the elder males and females. Once I was stung by wasps on my foot. An aggressive dog I didn't know approached me and licked my swollen foot for three minutes. I never imagined I would ever see this behavior, much less with my son."

The elephant and Jomo continued to interact, and then the beast turned and lumbered off downwind to the South. At about a hundred paces it stopped, raised its trunk to Jomo, and continued on. Jomo replied with two open hands at his sides.

It was near dusk. Tents were up, and the campfire was going strong. Shikuku, the best cook of the trackers, was separating out a thick bed of hot coals for the Dutch oven. Crouching by the field kitchen, he turned to see Jomo's arrival back in camp with two guinea fowl he had caught by hand. Tambo just shook his head and said to the warden and Mbitha, the other tracker, "I cannot believe what that boy can do."

The warden responded, "I know. There's something different about that boy. I've never seen anyone like him."

The following morning, they awoke to find outside their tents a solitary set of elephant tracks bearing the telltale cleft.

Jomo opened the flap of his tent to see Tambo crouched over several tracks. Tambo looked up at Jomo then said, "Tusker stood here motionless after we fell asleep. No one heard him come or leave."

The trackers looked at Jomo at a distance as they began breaking camp. All were quiet.

The silence was broken by Bob's satellite telephone. Tambo and Per could see something was amiss. When he'd hung up, the two approached him. Tambo stood quietly as Per spoke in a concerned tone.

"What's up, Bob? You've got that look like something's going to happen, and it won't be good."

"Right, Per. Remember when I told you and Tambo about those bloodhounds the Congo started using?"

Tambo answered, "Yes, Bob, that was maybe six months ago, right?"

"That's right. Well, those hounds have proven to be a great success in tracking ivory poachers in Virunga National Park. Many of the poachers have been tracked down to their village and either killed or captured by an elite force of Congolese Rangers."

Per interrupted, "But why are you telling us this now and why the sad face?"

"Because it was about that time we ordered two trained bloodhounds from Switzerland."

"So?"

"They arrived this morning by plane. They were already getting used to their new home at park headquarters. I should be happy, but that phone call was about one of our elephants in the study. This morning, she was found about sixty kilometers from here with her face chopped off."

"Oh my God, Bob," Tambo uttered.

Per was speechless. Then he stated, "That's about two, maybe three, hours away. What can we do?"

Bob straightened up to shake off the news. "Looks like the hounds will go to work their first day."

Just then, Jomo arrived. "What's up, Dad, something's happened?"

Per answered, "Ivory poachers killed one of our study elephants, Jo."

"Oh no."

Bob broke in, "I know you three were planning on leaving to see Jo's grandparents this morning, but we might as well get samples from her before she decomposes, and our Rangers may need your assistance. From what I was told, there could be as many as a dozen criminals, and they will be armed. This will be very dangerous."

"Bob, you know you can count on us," Per volunteered as Jo and Tambo nodded. "This gets personal, very personal," Per added with a tone of boiling anger.

"Alright then, men." Bob looked at the sky and horizon to the Northwest. "They're already on the way to the scene. If we leave now, we'll arrive about the same time."

Bob was right. They arrived before the Rangers when they were near by following the circling vultures above the site. As they drove up, a small group of Maasai men and women greeted them as though they had been waiting all morning. Some had been crying. As Jomo hopped from his jeep, he could hear the chatter of Swahili intensify from the onlookers.

Tambo questioned the group for leads, while Jomo approached the dead beast with Per and Bob. Jomo tried unsuccessfully to cover his nose to the overwhelming smell.

Bob commented, "One day old kill, and it's already starting to swell."

He held Jomo's shoulder as they examined the body. As he was taking photographs, he spoke quietly, "She was five years old, Jo," he said with a tear in his eye. "I knew her mother. I first saw her when she was just a baby, about a week old. She'd play and run under her mother's legs, and she loved to splash in the Mara River."

Jomo kept shaking his head from the pain of what he saw. Bob continued, "See there, AK-47 bullet holes into her knees so she would fall. I cannot even see the bullet holes between the eyes because her face was completely hacked off by axes and machetes to gain an extra foot or two of ivory. I hope she was dead when they began chopping. They try to conserve bullets."

Per approached with his kit. "Let's get it done, Bob. Let's get the liver samples before they arrive with the dogs. Once they get the scent, there's no holding them back."

The small gathering of Maasai moved in closer to see Per and Bob do the job no one envied. The vultures surrendered their positions at the feast as the two professionals worked quickly.

They could hear the hounds before they saw the two military converted Toyotas. Seven well armed men in camouflage emerged and approached the scene just as Per and Bob were finishing their work. As Bob looked up, the seven fell into a loose line with eyes forward. It was easy for Jomo to see who was in charge here.

"Men, you all know Tambo from Kenya Wildlife and Per Jorland. Please meet Per's son, Jomo Jorland. They will, I am sure, be of assistance in our mission."

Jomo went down the line to shake hands with each man. By their looks, he knew they took their dangerous work seriously. As Jomo returned to his position next to Per, one more man approached the meeting with the two most beautiful bloodhounds Jomo had ever seen. He set two dishes on the red clay and filled them with fresh, cool water.

"Bob, I'd like you to meet our two new soldiers in the fight. Here are Dodi and Abby. They arrived this morning from Switzerland. A note said they are the best of the best." The two hounds drank all the water and then went directly to Jomo.

The man with the leashes watched this and said, "Jomo, I think they like you more than they like me. Why don't you be in charge of Dodi? I mean, hold her leash. She'll do the rest."

"Yes, sir." He gave Dodi a scratch behind the ears and took her leash. The dogs were reluctant to approach the body, but with some reassuring coaxing, Jomo got Dodi to approach the bloody scene while Abby followed. Jomo picked up a splinter of flesh and tusk carelessly hacked off, smelled it carefully, and then put it to the dogs' noses two times. They understood and began to yelp and circle the scene. Within five minutes of double checking, the men were on the trail with Jomo, spear in hand, and the hounds in the lead. Mbitha and Shikuku followed far behind in the big Toyotas.

As Dodi and Abby lead the men to the West on an unused game trail, Per whispered to Bob, "These dogs really are highly trained. Did you notice how they quit yelping about a kilometer after their initial discovery of the scent?"

Bob returned his thought, "Yeah, they're worth it, all right. Kenya tax money is not being wasted. I like that."

He motioned for all to stop. "We're headed toward the Mara River, men. It is about seven kilometers ahead. They may be camped along the river to escape into Tanzania or Kenya. I suggest we stop about two kilometers out and send scouts so the dogs don't give us away when they know they're getting close, okay? You two will go forward with Jomo here leading you to the camp." He put his hand on Jomo's shoulder.

The two looked at Jomo and nodded in surprise at the statement. "Jomo, you use your spear to be silent. I know you can handle this."

"Yes, sir." Jomo gripped his spear with authority.

Soon there were three, with Jomo in the lead. They found the camp along the river as Bob had predicted. It was empty, save for one filthy Somali poacher covered by flies. He was cleaning the flesh from two beautiful white tusks.

Jomo whispered in anger, "Those are the tusks!" Jomo made the plan, "I'll circle around to the right. When you see me in position, walk in behind him with your guns, but do not shoot and warn the others who may be returning soon. He'll run down that path toward me when he sees you. I'll be waiting with my spear as he enters the bush."

The Rangers listened to his plan and agreed, but one added, "You only have one spear. Here, take my Rambo knife. You may need it. Do not endanger your own life, and our orders are to kill if needed."

"Thank you, sir. I will take it." Jomo strapped it on.

According to plan, the Rangers started in, rifles at ready, when they saw Jomo wriggle the bush far down the path. Suddenly, a second poacher emerged from the thick bush to their left and cried out to the one fleshing the tusks, who then grabbed his machete. They both ran for the path, with the second only seconds behind the first. The Rangers, in hot pursuit, knew the plan had changed, and Jomo was unaware he was in danger.

At the precise moment, Jomo stepped out with his spear set. Realizing he'd been tricked, the poacher bared his teeth and raised his machete to attack, but Jomo's spear found its mark just as the machete missed his neck by inches.

The Rangers were yelling to warn him, but Jomo heard the second poacher running toward him. His spear was stuck in the man's chest, so he drew his Rambo knife. The second came in fast with his knife, but there was no struggle as Jomo stepped aside and tripped him. Quick as a fly, Jomo was down on him, squeezing the blood from his knife hand as he slowly overpowered the arm strength of the man who had cut off the face of the elephant. When Jomo's knife slowly entered his skin, the man's eyes opened wide and revealed his true soul: the evil eyes of a filthy feral tomcat.

A dream flashed through Jomo's mind in a millisecond: a bear, claws, blood, and a fire-hardened spear tip into the heart of the beast.

The man let out a wild cry as he felt the knife slowly pierce his skin, his chest, and wind its way between ribs, muscle, and nerves till it came upon the live pounding place. He reached up and felt the cold hilt with his left index finger, looked at his once partner-in-crime laying awkward with a spear in his chest then attempted to stand but collapsed into a thorn bush, dead.

The two Rangers rounded the corner to see Jomo standing over the two and wiping the blood off his knife.

Later, the elite squad killed the remaining nine poachers by ambush in a hail of bullets. It was a good day for the new bloodhounds.

That night as they all sat around the fire, Bob stood up as if to give his statement more meaning, even official. "Jomo, what you did today, after what I've seen in you these days, and your leadership, I tell you now, you are welcome into our fraternity of warriors to save our beautiful animals from extinction. You are a true warrior to the cause, and you are good for Kenya."

In the light of the huge bonfire, all the men of the squad filed by one by one to look Jomo in the eyes and clasp hands.

When Mbitha came by last, he said, "As we told you last night, you are Maasai."

Three Rangers tended the fire at the camp that night. The bodies had been photographed, logged, and moved two kilometers upwind to avoid drawing in predators. Per was almost asleep in his tent when the satellite phone rang. It was Nice calling from the States.

"Hello."

"Hi, Per. It's Nice. Can you hear me?"

"Real clear. How are you?"

"Just fine, Per. Everything's okay here. Catching up on my sleep, grocery shopping, you know. How are my mom and dad getting along? I'll bet Jo is sure glad to see them."

"We haven't been to see them yet. We got held over an extra day in the bush. We're deep in the Mara, camping right now."

"Why?"

"Poachers killed one of our study elephants, a five year old."

"Oh no!"

"We had to drive deeper in for her samples. Then Bob, the warden, went after them with his best men, his elite Rangers. Jo and I went along."

"Well, did you catch them?"

"Yes, we caught them alright, all ten of them. I'll tell you about it all when I get home."

"No, tell me now. The reception's clear. Did any of you get hurt?"

"Well…"

"Per, you sound kind of worried. Is there something I should know? Is Jo okay?"

"Oh yes. He's fine."

"Then what? Why are you talking so quietly? What's up here?"

"Well then, I'll tell you. We tracked the poachers with bloodhounds. Bob sent Jo and two Rangers ahead. They found the camp and Jo—"

"Jo what?"

"Jo killed two men, one with a spear and the other with a knife, Nice. He killed two men. He killed two poachers."

"Oh my God, Per."

"Yes, Nice. That's all I can say, too."

"And how does he feel about that?"

"It doesn't appear to have affected him, not at all, Nice. Not sad or happy. If anything, maybe a little more serious but still the same Jo that we know. Oh, oh, he did say he saw the second man's eyes and should have waited till the Rangers arrived."

"Per, I'm speechless. With a spear and a knife?"

"Look, Nice, all I can tell you now is I love you and I'll watch him. Tomorrow, we're driving to see your mom and dad. They'll be good for him."

"You're right, Per. Get his mind off it in case. I love you."

"I love you too."

"Bye."

"Bye, Nice."

15

PER'S WORK WAS done. The warden returned to park headquarters with Mbitha, Shikuku, and the tents and gear. Per, Jomo, and Tambo drove on for a long awaited visit with Jomo's grandparents Nonkipa and Jomo Nkoe.

The tires of the jeep made conversation all but impossible, so the three were alone together in their own thoughts. Jomo thought, *What was that dream I had last night? Oh, a woman and a boy. We're walking hand in hand through a field. A field of flowers. I love you, Tuk.* The jeep hit a deep rut, came to a stop, and Jomo was jolted from his thoughts. A herd of goats were crossing the road ahead.

Per glanced over, "I thought you were sleeping."

"No, Dad, just a dream I was trying to remember."

Tambo gunned the jeep and continued on slowly.

Nice's parents had received her letter about their visit this month, and each day, they kept a close watch for the jeep that would carry their grandson to them.

Tambo explained to Jomo, "When you see a beautiful photograph of thousands of African game grazing in the foreground and Mt. Kilimanjaro in the near distance, it was probably taken in the Maasai Amboseli Game Reserve. Back some years, too many tourists and tour vehicles had ruined the park. Now, only Maasai such as your grandparents are allowed to live here. They live simply in the traditional ways of the old Africa."

Following Nice's advice on how impolite it would be to arrive empty handed, the trio stopped for gifts at the market in Oliotokotok. For Nonkipa, Jomo bought a *kikois*, a beautiful hair ornament with a matching bead necklace, a two foot mirror, three ten pound bags of sugar for their chai, four boxes of laundry detergent, a five gallon drum of lamp oil, sandals, and a chocolate bar. For Jomo, the grandfather, Per bought a hundred feet of rope, a high quality African machete, six bowstrings, a bicycle chain, three quarts of oil, sandals, and a chocolate bar. Impulsively, Per bought twelve bottles of Tusker beer and ten pounds of Kenyan Arabica coffee. One more chocolate bar and a new pair of Nike shoes for Tambo rounded out the shopping spree. Tambo smiled and nodded his approval at their wise choice of gifts as he laced up his new shoes. They found the Nkoe pair many miles down a four-wheel-drive road out of Oliotokotok. Jomo hadn't seen his grandparents since he was twelve years old. Per knew the road well because he had stopped in through the years to check on their health and make sure they had money and anything else they needed. They savored the stories about Nice and her world travels and had told Per so many stories about Nice when she was a child over the years.

The elders were tending the cows when Tambo, acting as translator, called out to the two in Swahili.

Tambo announced grandly, "Nonkipa, Jomo, your grandson and Per from America are here to see you. Come see. It is true."

"Shikamoo," Jomo called out a respectful greeting to an elder.

"Marahaba," Nonkipa replied to her grandson.

"Habari?" asked Jomo. (How are you?)

"Mzuri," Grandfather answered. (I'm fine, thanks.). "Habari ya safari?" (How was your journey?)

"Wazuri." (Good.)

"Unaitwa nani?" Nonkipa asked, teasingly testing her grandchild's Swahili. (What is your name?)

"Unaitwa Jomo," he said with a grin. (It is Jomo.)

Grandfather Jomo commented, "Nonkipa, he speaks Swahili. Nice has raised him Maasai."

"Of course. Did you think our daughter would leave and not take us with her?"

"No, no," the old warrior smiled at his mate. "You are right. Her letters have said we are in her heart. This we have never questioned, just as she has been kept in our hearts."

Nonkipa shook her head and remarked, "Enough about Swahili. Our only grandchild, Jomo, and our son-in-law,

Per, are standing here outside in the heat of the day. Please come into our home. It is time for celebration. Come in, Jomo. Come in, Per." Nonkipa stepped aside to wave her guests inside. "You, too, Tambo, you also come in!"

Tambo stopped translating to let the elders talk between themselves.

Per and Jomo had to bend over to get through the door of the dung hut. But once inside, it wasn't long before Jomo asked his grandfather about the old photo of the two men who were about his age posing over a huge black-maned lion.

Jomo asked, "Grandfather, that old yellow photograph. Is that you holding the spear?" Tambo translated.

The elder was quiet for a long while and then turned from the photo to answer his grandson's question. "No, young Jomo, that man is not me. That man holding the spear is my father's friend. The man not holding the spear is your great-grandfather. That spear you see in the photograph is the one over there by the bed," grandfather Jomo said, pointing to a corner in the room.

The elder Jomo looked over and back again, reexamining both the photo and the spear, then continued, "My father's friend in that old picture is named Jomo, as I am, and as Nice and Per named you. I have proudly carried this name my father and mother gave me, and so I see have you. I tell you this, your great-grandfather and Jomo Kenyatta were best friends as young men. They are the two young Moran in the picture."

Jomo waited patiently as Tambo completed the translation. Tambo dropped his mouth as he finished the elder's last sentence. Looking up, Jomo was truly speechless. "Thank you, Grandfather. The trackers told us last night at camp about the great leader of Kenya, Jomo Kenyatta."

With a twinkle in his eye, the elder nodded, and then smiled. "Now hear me. It has never been said who actually killed that lion, even though you see who holds the spear. That spear has been my spear for a lifetime. It was my father's, and it was given to him by his father. On that day, both claim the other had killed the lion. Even to this day, Kikuyu still believe Jomo Kenyatta killed it because it is he who holds the spear triumphantly, and Maasai still believe your great-grandfather got it because the spear tip is of the Maasai Tribe. A Kikuyu tip is shaped differently. It was their secret. It was a bond meant to last a lifetime between the two. Now, young Jomo, this secret is passed on to you. I was a child. The very day he died, he told me. My Father killed the lion but both became warriors that day."

As his translation came through, Tambo almost fell off his chair as he said the words.

Jomo nodded. "Thank you, Grandfather. I will carry the secret."

That evening, as the men sat around the fire in the square hut, the arrivals listened as the old man spoke of the way it used to be. Nonkipa prepared *ugali* over another fire just outside the entrance. She seasoned it with curry, and while serving it, she spoke to Tambo, smiling. He turned to the visitors, saying, "Eat." He motioned. "Dip the ugali in the coconut sauce. This is very special because this sauce is only made for honored guests." Bread was passed around with *calabash*, finishing off the meal. Nonkipa explained while Tambo translated with a grin, "For calabash, certain grasses are burned inside a large gourd. The soot deposits impart a distinct flavor. This soot also helps the fermentation process. Next, a mixture of cow blood and milk are added and then left in the gourd for several days. This gourd ends up smelling a bit foul."

Per looked at Tambo. Then they both frowned and held their noses.

Nonkipa continued, "The calabash is decorated with Maasai beads to make it look more edible." Jomo was starving. Nonkipa nodded appreciatively as her grandson dipped and retrieved an immense handful of ugali followed by another. They all laughed.

"Thanks very much, Grandma," he mumbled between bites. He didn't know if a joke was being played on him or not.

They were all sitting on six inch stools. Jomo's knees were eye level with those of his namesake. Nonkipa joined the men as the elder Jomo began his story. "I was both a warrior and a herder as a young man. As a young warrior, there were no boundaries. I followed the migration for hundreds of miles of the Siringit, the area now known as the Mara, but the story is not about me.

"Your great-great-grandfather was a Moran in the 1800s. The Maasai tribes were savages and murdered many of the European colonists. Sometimes entire caravans of whites and their black slaves were murdered. The Maasai were the most feared of all the tribes in all of Africa. This freedom struggle was known as Uhuru. Finally, in the 1890s, when our tribe was weakened by white man diseases, our chief, Olonana, was forced to sign a treaty, and that is when we lost our freedom, and boundaries began to close in on us.

"These boundaries caused us to lose traditions. Our young people moved to the city and left ceremony and tradition behind. Often, they show no respect to elders. What is now happening to our tribe is not good. It is sad. It would take a great chief and leader to bring time back, young Jomo."

There was a long silence before he continued, "Even the title of Moran has lost its respect. Most all of them now are nothing but a gang of troublemakers, not the true revered warriors of long ago. Back then, it was a true honor of passage, and a young man gained much respect."

Young Jomo shifted in his small chair as his grandfather looked into space as if to remember. "I will tell you a story how bad it is. About one year ago, some Moran held a roomful of girls hostage at a high school. They terrorized the girls and the teachers and took away some of the girls to be their wives. When the police caught them, they resisted and were shot. No, Moran are no longer real warriors as I was or my ancestors."

The grandfather stirred the coals slowly and drew two curved lines in the embers. Again, there was a long silence before he continued. "These are two horns, big black horns," he said. The old one told of a near-death encounter with a water buffalo once when he was herding his cows in dense brush. By firelight, he showed the foot long scars in his back.

Young Jomo waited for the appropriate time while the vision of the attack was sufficiently ruminated over by the men, and then he removed his shirt to spin the story of the big buck that gored his shoulder. This caught Per's attention because Jomo had never told Per or Marty he had first run it down in darkness for three and a half hours before the attack. Per thought, *My God, that explains why its heart burst.*

The weathered elder traced his finger along the two year old wound and nodded with respect to young Jomo. "You lived because your spirit was stronger than the animal's. The animal had to give you his spirit. That is the way of all nature."

Nonkipa came over to trace the scar of her grandson, and then she covered it with her warm hand.

Tambo spoke, "Your grandfather Jomo is a true bushman."

The elder interrupted, "Let me tell you of the dangerous elephant hunts of long ago using only bows and arrows. One brave warrior would taunt the beast, getting it to chase him. He would run very fast and lead it into an ambush. Then there would be a hail of death, and the tribe would eat."

Per noticed the instant the old man spied the pouch tied at his son's waist.

"May I see it?" he said with all seriousness to his grandson.

"*Ndiyio* (yes)." Grandfather carefully untied it by the flickering firelight.

Per held his breath, watching with anxiety, but remained quiet.

The fire crackled. "This is an animal skin I do not know." The elder slowly examined the pouch's texture and sewing and then stroked it against his cheek. "It's spirit is old," he said as he looked up, eyes wide in the dancing light. "Older than my years," he added with a well timed chortle.

Tambo settled in, readying himself for a slow, amusing story. Instead, grandfather's deep eyes, in all seriousness now, returned to the pouch. The flames sparked.

"This pouch is your guide. This pouch is your strength. Keep it close to you at all times, Grandson."

Again, there was quiet as a warm breeze entered the hut.

"How did the spirit bring you to this pouch?"

With that translation, Tambo leaned forward intently. There was a hesitation as everyone looked into the glowing embers of the fire. Nonkipa stopped making noise with her work. Per froze and held his breath.

As young Jomo opened his mouth to speak, there was a great commotion outside the hut. Cows and goats were bellowing and bawling. The clatter of a water drum upended in the mayhem interrupted Jomo mid sentence. A goat came crashing into the hut, almost tripping over the fire.

"Simba is back," Nonkipa cried.

"Aiee, aiee," shouted the old man.

As one, the men emptied out of the hut, spears in hand. The incident was over nearly before it began. A lion had unsuccessfully tried to penetrate the thorn bush fence.

"We rebuild the boma all the time," the elder Jomo commented.

"Simba, with its great claws, cannot pass through the sharp teeth of the thorn bush."

The lion's low growl soon became less and less distinct in the darkness until it finally blended with the sounds of the night.

The men returned to the hut to find the fire in total disarray caused by the goat's panicky retreat. The hut was filled with smoke, making it hard to breathe. The fire was quickly rebuilt just in time for Nonkipa's proud entrance with a gourd full of fresh cow's blood, a gift from a neighboring boma. Grandfather Jomo partook first and then passed it on. Tambo was next to take a long draw.

He then took a hasty second and motioned to the next man. Young Jomo and Per respectfully declined. Things were happening too fast for them in this once serene place. Later that evening, to everyone's surprise but Per's, his son requested a try at the red delicacy. He placed his lips to the gourd and tasted followed by a full swallow.

"You are Maasai," the elder softly exclaimed. "You are my grandson." Nonkipa looked on with a smile.

The next morning, Nonkipa cooked a breakfast of a flat semi-sweet doughnut, which is dunked in chai. Jomo commented, "I like this sweet tea. What's in it?"

Tambo answered, "Just black tea, milk, ginger, and sugar, Jo, lots and lots of sugar. Remember the bags of sugar we bought? Pass me the mangoes." Tambo, a bachelor, appreciated the home cooking and went back several times for more, always thanking and praising Nonkipa for her fine cooking skills.

Standing next to the jeep when it was time to leave, Jomo opened a sealed bag containing a large photograph album of their life in the United States. In it were many pictures of Nice. Faces close, shoulders touching, the weathered pair examined the book with reverence; their fingers slowly and carefully passing over each photograph. Nonkipa told of the times she carried Nice on her back. Her eyes turned a watery glaze as she recounted the time Nice had left for America so suddenly, and yet they understood why.

As Nonkipa started to hand the book back to her grandson, Tambo's eyes brightened with glee. In his most respectful Swahili, he guided young Jomo's hands to present the book to Nonkipa, translating. "This is for you to keep. We love you," young Jomo repeated the words in Swahili with a smile and a hug for both.

Tambo bowed to the old warrior and his wife and hopped in the jeep to start it. The grandfather spun around and pranced back into the hut. Quickly returning, he placed the ancient spear in Jomo's hand. "This was my father's spear. Now it is yours." Motioning to the pouch at his grandson's waist, he continued in a serious tone, "This spear will please the spirit in your pouch." He looked up at Per with a broad but quizzical smile. Per looked back reassuringly.

The spear was long and straight with an extended thin razor-sharp tip. Nonkipa and elder Jomo held hands as he began his final oratory. "This spear has killed rhinos, elephants, and lions. It has never broken. It is a proven spear. Before a Maasai boy can become a Moran, he must kill Simba. Soon your Simba will come to you, Jomo. You live in the city, so your Simba will not have a black mane, teeth, and claws. No, young Jomo, your Simba will be a great sadness, an opportunity, a disappointment, or all. You must prepare, for how you handle this Simba will determine your future life and manhood. You must know yourself."

Just then, with a mischievous grin, Tambo hit the accelerator and the brake. The jeep lurched forward. There was general laughter lightening the mood, and then came the long goodbye hugs between Per, Jomo, and the elders. "Goodbye," Jomo kept repeating softly until the vehicle crawled around a bend in the road. His grandparents disappeared from view.

More than a few tears came from Grandmother Nonkipa and Grandfather Jomo. They stood in the same spot, holding hands and looking at the horizon long before turning to tend the cows.

16

BACK IN NAIROBI, it just didn't seem right to accept valet parking after such a dusty drive. Besides, the white clad valet surely wouldn't want to sit in red grit fresh from the bush.

The Ambassador Hotel was abuzz with activity. Beneath sparkling chandeliers, dignitaries were gathered in small circles, cocktails in hand, and speaking in what seemed to be every dialect in Kenya, and there are many. White gloved waiters offered trays of hors d'oeuvres and glasses of brandy soda, Johnnie Walker soda, gin and tonic, beer, and plain soda water on ornate huge silver trays. Even Tambo finally broke down frustrated in trying to translate for Jomo what some of the lively conversations were concerning. The mood was light and festive.

The dress code for the event was formal, so the three, still dressed for the bush and smelling strongly of the fire in the dung hut, felt out of place. At least half the men were dressed Western in tuxedos, their companions in expensive form-fitting gowns. Others were attired in full formal Kenyan tribal dress, the traditional ornamental dress reserved for special national events or diplomatic ceremonies.

Per was the sole white man to be seen as they walked across the marble lobby toward the main desk. Jomo, his grandfather's spear in hand, decided there was no way to hide it, so he carried it proudly knowing technically it is no longer legal to carry a spear in such a public place. The three indeed stood out, a contrast to the formal festivities.

"Where did you get that old spear?"

Surprised at the question asked in such perfect English, Jomo turned to see three handsome young Kenyan men staring at him. They were dressed in a sporty yet formal way.

"It was given to me today by my grandfather. It was passed down from his father," Jomo replied, quickly tightening his grip on it with one unseen finger.

The taller older one of the three examined it at a distance, making no attempt to touch it. Noting the markings and the shape of the tip, he commented with knowing reverence, "You're a lucky man to own such an old Maasai spear. Are you Maasai?"

Jomo relaxed, a young man who was proud of his heritage. "Yes," he replied in Swahili. "My name is Jomo. My mother is Maasai. Please meet my father, Per, and this is our friend, Tambo."

Per and Tambo nodded.

"We are Maasai too," they chimed in, almost in unison, lips opening to broad white smiles. The three were friendly in an arrogant sort of way—self assured would probably be a better description.

In the swing of things, Tambo, a known Maasai himself, removed his sweat-stained hat and interrupted with a question in his best slang Swahili, "What's the do?" He was a tracker and a bushman but his countryside dialect and charisma were accepted anywhere.

The tall athlete answered in English as if to let Per in on the answer, not knowing Per was fluent when he wanted to be.

"This is the yearly fund raising party for the Kenya Track and Field Olympic Team. We're on the team that will be competing next year in Delhi, India. We'll each give a short speech of thanks soon. Tomorrow we'll go on the traditional *team into the bush* run. You know, raise the team spirit and have some fun at the same time. No coaches." Tambo could not resist the temptation of the moment. Flashing back to when Jomo left him in the dust while tracking the bull elephant, he commented in English, "This guy can really run," putting his grip on Jomo's shoulder.

Jomo raised his chin. Per noticed the conversation change in direction.

The older athlete laughed loudly. "Oh, of course. He is Maasai, isn't he?"

After a brief huddle, the younger queried, "Have you got your shoes, Jomo?"

"Of course, I ran a little track in high school," he replied. "You can call me Jo."

"Alright, then, shall we say eight o'clock tomorrow morning here in the lobby? Here, Jomo, take my card and call me if you change your mind. I'll write my cell phone number on the back." He looked at Per. "Don't worry. He'll be home by two o'clock. We're going in now. I think our coach is almost done." He motioned to Per. "Come and sit at our table."

As the three sat down in the banquet room next to the podium, the coach of the Kenyan team was wrapping up his speech.

"So for the forty seventh time—"

Laughter interrupted the coach.

"I repeat, thank you for your continued support. But before I close, I must address one controversy facing Kenya and all other countries sending their athletes to India next year.

"As you all know, the International Olympic Committee is under intense pressure from some countries to lift its ban on genetically enhanced athletes. Science is moving fast, my friends. It is nothing like cheating through doping. There is no test. Our Kenyan runners have 1,000,000 years of genetic evolution before them to create the great runners we are now. In one or two generations, enhanced athletes may be superior to us. We do not know. So far, they are not, and further, it's next to impossible to prove. We must do all we can to lobby the committee to continue the genetic doping ban. Competition must remain pure, and you can count on me to be heard at the international conference next month." There was a long applause.

"Now, on a lighter note, let us hear a few words from our runners, our national heroes, the athletes who wear our Kenyan colors!"

There were three open jeeps and an SUV for fourteen of the most elite runners in the world, plus Jomo.

Traveling through the early morning traffic from downtown Nairobi then Northwest toward the Rift on Nakuru Road was not for the faint of heart—rude taxis, careening buses, and decrepit 18 wheelers, each challenging for their share of the road. This, all this played out with seemingly random pedestrians darting through: push carts and donkeys trying to hold their positions, encroaching vegetable and fruit stands, children dressed in school uniforms, shoeless women bent over under enormous bundles of brushwood, and police racing around in orange painted lorries.

Some time far out of the city limits, the four wheelers took a left turn onto a dirt road that was barely wide enough if two cars met. Thirty more minutes on the dusty road brought them to an isolated stretch where no villages or people were seen. The fourteen Kenyans knew this place well as it was the traditional stretch of road where the national team had played out their annual run for team bragging rights for over forty years.

As they got out of the jeeps to have a few laughs, stretch their legs, and get ready for the races, one of them turned to Jomo. "This is a special place that not many know about. To us, it is an honor to run on the same road and in the legendary footsteps of Kip Keino of the 1968 Mexico City Summer Olympics, probably Kenya's most famous runner of all time. He grew up much further up the road near Eldoret. He trained in the Nandi Hills there at about 6000 feet altitude and went on to win the 1500 meter. That victory marked the beginning of Kenyan long-distance running. He ran a couple times on this road when some of the team came up from Nairobi. We've been coming here ever since."

Jomo heard this and gave his thanks that they would include him.

That was a day Jomo and the Kenyan athletes would never forget. Regulation track events were casually paced off on the desolate dirt road, and the various running events were played out in the bush of their homeland. Jomo consistently, soundly, beat their best. The day was capped off with a grueling ten-thousand-meter run by specialists only. Jomo was first to return to the jeep and sat with his legs up under a colorful sun umbrella, sipping a chilled sport drink and laughing as the other runners came in one by one.

Jomo's casual revelry under the sun umbrella was short-lived when the second place Kenyan accused Jomo of arrogance to his hosts. When he took a swing in his fit of anger, Jomo blocked it and countered with a fierce blow to his nose. The runners chose sides with their teammate, and they left Jomo alone on that desolate dirt road.

Exhausted, with nothing left to drink, he walked for miles in the hot sun and eventually caught a Southbound bus into Nairobi. When he got off a few miles from the hotel, he noticed two men were following him about half a block behind. He was tired, and when he purposely went entirely around a city block, they were still on him. He ducked in several alleys but couldn't lose them. They knew Nairobi too well. Finally, he broke into a jog and ducked into a dark alley, thinking they might pass by. The air was stagnant and reeked of stench. *They'll never come in here*, he thought.

Quietly, he worked his way back into the darkness, thinking there would be a turn soon to another street, but then he heard two voices. He faintly made out a large clear plastic bag against the brick wall. Instantly, he crouched low close behind it. The stench was overpowering. As his eyes became accustomed to the darkness, he saw it was a dead man stuffed in a plastic bag with his hand emerging from the ties. *I can't die in here*, he thought. He moved quickly to find a way out, but to his surprise, it was a dead end.

Then there they were—two silhouettes standing at the alley entrance, two men, each about 220 pounds of solid muscle. The flow of the street behind them was but a collage of fading colors. Dusk was turning to dark.

"Give us your pack and money. It will be easy, American, or we will kill you."

"No, you cannot kill me. Turn around before I have to hurt you both."

"Oh, yes, American. We will kill you. You are lost, aren't you?"

And with that, they started into the alley side by side; one holding a ten inch knife with a large blood groove, the other, methodically putting on leather gloves. As Jomo picked a spot where he would defend his life, he inhaled deep, deep breaths of the stench to load his blood with oxygen. A police lorry cruised by unaware of the scene that was unfolding to their right. Pedestrians looked in as they passed but continued, either afraid or uncaring enough to be involved.

The big man moved in first and tried to grab Jo from behind by the neck with his gloved hand so the other could stab him in the heart. Jo ducked, came up under his arm, and tried with all his strength to break it at the elbow. It hyperextended but would not snap. He yelled in pain as his arm went limp. As his other good arm quickly wrapped around Jo's neck, Jo started to lose his balance because of his pack. Before he fell, he reached around with his right hand and pressed his thumb to the back of the first man's right eye socket. As he eased his hold on Jo to go for his eye, Jo wheeled and dodged the first knife strike by the second man. The slash meant for his throat cut his left shoulder, forming a cross with the deer's scar.

Jo pulled off his pack as the first man covered his bleeding eye socket. He tripped the man with the knife and snapped his wrist as he wrestled it away. With the knife now in his hand, Jo drove it deep into the man's left lung, then crushed his windpipe with his other hand, and broke his nose and jaw with flying elbows. With that man down, he turned to the other whose face and hands were now covered in blood and beat him unconscious against the brick alley wall. When it was over, the man with the knife appeared dead, and the other was beginning the early stages of a death rattle. Jomo collapsed for ten minutes before he struggled to his feet, put on his pack, and as he entered the street, he called back, "Have a bad day."

Back at the hotel, Per and Tambo were becoming increasingly concerned about Jomo. It was well past five o'clock and nearing dark when Jomo knocked on the door. "Dad, it's Jo. Let me in."

Tambo rushed to the door and opened it to see Jo lying on the hall carpet. "Where have you been? You went with the team, but what then?"

Jomo looked up and moaned. Per came to the door and immediately knelt down to see Jo's face. "What happened, Son? You look exhausted. My God, Jo, you're bleeding."

"They left me out there in the bush with no water. They left me, Dad. I found my way home. I walked a long way on a dirt road, caught a bus coming South from Nakuru, and then walked more in the city. It was starting to get dark, and some guys tried to rob me. They followed me after I got off the bus. The driver said it would be a couple miles to the hotel, so I tried to lose them but couldn't. I took a wrong turn and ended up in a dead end alley. One guy had a knife. They tried to take my pack. I thought I should give it to them, but it had my passport and all my money. I took the knife away from him and cut him. Then I threw the knife and beat them both. Dad, I think I hurt them pretty bad, but I was only defending myself. They didn't get up when I walked away."

Per and Tambo helped Jomo into the room.

Per asked, "Why, Jo. Why did they leave you?"

"Why? I don't really know. We ran a lot of races that they paced off. It was fun. We were laughing. I kept winning. I thought it was all real casual till one guy got in my face after the last race, the ten thousand. We were all hot and tired. I won that one too. I sat in the jeep till they all came in. He tried to take a swing at me, said I was arrogant and should never have been invited along. I blocked it and hit him hard in the nose. There was blood all over as he tried again, but the guys pulled him away before I hit him again. Dad, I was just defending myself, all right?"

Per asked again, "Why did this happen?"

"I guess he just didn't like me winning their little races. Then they all turned their backs on me, got in the jeeps, threw out my pack, and left me. I finished what was left of my sport drink and started walking."

Per said, "Something doesn't add up here, Jo."

"Yes, it does. I beat them fair and square."

Per and Tambo helped him to the bathroom. "Jo, take a cool shower. I'll sew up that cut. We've got some food for you, and then you need to lie down. We'll talk about all of this tomorrow."

While Jomo was in the shower, Tambo commented to Per, "I believe him. That was harsh and not good sportsmanship."

Later that night after Jomo was asleep, Per thought, *Did he say that he won some of the races? And what, some guys tried to rob him?*

Next morning, they slept in. It was 9:30 a.m. when there was a knock on the door.

Per yawned. "That was quick. Jo, you get it. It's the coffee."

Expecting coffee and rolls, Jomo opened the door.

"Are you Jomo?"

"Yes, sir."

"Jomo Jorland?"

"Yes, sir."

"I am Detective Choge, and here is Officer Songok. May we come in to ask you a few questions?"

Per came to the door, while Tambo turned off the TV.

"It's the police, Dad."

"Please come in. We have no coffee to offer you, but it should arrive soon."

"That's okay, Mr. Jorland?"

"Yes, I'm Jomo's father."

"And?"

"He is Tambo, my colleague and tracker for the Kenya Wildlife Service. Please come in and sit down."

"Thank you. We won't be long. We have just a few routine questions."

The detective reached into the breast pocket of his suit and presented a card he passed around to the three. "Jomo, do you know anything about this card?"

Jomo took it from Tambo and turned it over to see the cell phone number on the back. "Yes, I do, sir. This is the card I got from a runner on the Kenyan Track Team a couple of nights ago at their fund raiser. We'd just come in from the bush. I was supposed to call him if I decided not to go on a run with them the next morning."

"And that day would be?"

"That was yesterday morning, sir."

"And did you go on the run?"

"Yes."

"And was there anything unusual you'd like to talk about?"

Per started to shift in his chair, and Tambo looked concerned. The detective's eyes were locked on Jomo. Jomo flashed on the day he got the note to report to Mr. Schaeffer's office in fifth grade. He sat up straight. "Yes, sir. We were having fun running these different races on a dirt road South of Nakuru. You know, the hundred meter, two hundred, and four hundred, all of them. I was winning, and they didn't like it, especially the one who tried to hit me. I blocked him and hit him in the nose. He bled all over, and they left me out there."

"Go on."

"I was so tired and thirsty. I walked a long way and then caught a bus into the city."

"Jomo, we know this already, but let me see your shoes, your running shoes."

"They're right here, sir." Jomo pointed to his shoes by the door.

"Red grit. What I would expect if you ran on a country road. We know this because we called the cell number, and your story matches. Now, about the card we found, the card the Kenyan runner gave you the night before. Jomo, police found it next to two severely beaten men in an alley about two miles from here. They're both in the hospital, and likely will not make it. So what do you know about this? Show me your hands, and that looks like a cut on your shoulder already been sewn up."

Per interrupted, "I sewed it up, Detective, last night."

"Okay, Jomo, now what? What happened here?"

"The two men followed me off the bus. I tried to change directions and duck into store fronts, but they always saw me. I ducked into a dead end alley, but didn't know it till I was back in too far. They came at me. One had a knife. He said, 'Give me your money and your pack.' I said no. Then he tried to stab me in the heart, while the other held me from behind. It was hard to defend. My pack was limiting my balance. He cut me in the shoulder."

"Go on."

"I got mad, turned, and hit the one behind me. I pulled off my pack and fought the two. Finally I got the knife, threw it, and finished them off with all my strength. Then I walked—no, stumbled back here to the hotel."

"Sounds like you had an all around bad day, Jomo."

"Yes, sir, but the morning was fun."

"What an odd response, but I guess it would be fun to beat our country's best. Look, Jomo and Mr. Jorland and Tambo, I'm trying to make sure there's nothing more to this than an attempted robbery/murder. You are a lucky man to have escaped those two, but we have them now."

"How so?" Per asked.

"Mr. Jorland, they are both hardened criminals. They're wanted for two murders in Lyon. Jomo, you either got lucky or you know how to handle yourself. Either way, they took on more than they could chew with you."

"I was only defending myself. It was life-and-death."

Tambo got up and gently moved to Jomo's side. "Who are these men?"

"Why do you ask?"

"I may be with Wildlife, but I know Nairobi. Maybe not as well as you, but I may be of assistance here. I have contacts."

"Look, Tambo, these two are hired killers. We think they are cleaners. You know, they handle internal affairs. Kill people he does not trust. I'll tell you. We found the bloody prints of both of them at the murder scene in an apartment in Lyon. Two men were stabbed in the heart, probably with the same knife as the one we found in the alley."

Jomo interrupted, "Like they tried on me!"

"Yes, Jomo. In the victims' apartment, we found evidence the dead men were involved in a diamond theft at Brussels airport some years ago. Probably an inside job. They didn't get along with the rest of the gang, we think. So he hired the cleaners. Ordinarily, cleaners never leave a trace or clue. They must have been interrupted because the scene appeared as if the bodies were about to be wrapped in plastic."

"Hired by whom? Who is he?" Per asked, concerned.

"They're our only current leads in a case we have been trying to unravel for the last ten years, and now one may die."

"I'm sorry, sir." Jomo looked down.

"Ten years?" Per probed.

Detective Choge looked at the three men. "Yes, diamond smuggling out of Africa to New York and Antwerp, we believe, and probably cut. We don't know. It's like trying to hold a fist full of water. Like a ghost you see, and then it is gone. Every few years, our sources tell us a Frenchman is active, but we have no physical description of him, no name, and even if we had one, it would most likely be an alias. We think he's the kingpin. Interpol and even NYPD are on the case."

"Do you think Jo's in danger here?" Per asked.

Choge looked at Jomo seriously. "Not unless you are involved in diamonds. Are you?"

"No, sir!"

"Then you're fine. I believe you. They probably just saw you on the bus—an American—and thought you'd make for an easy mugging. One thing's for sure though."

"What's that?" Tambo asked.

"We have one who we believe has a very slim chance to live. Who knows, maybe we'll get lucky. We'll question him before he goes to prison. That is, if he can talk. He's blind in one eye and has such a massive concussion he could end up a vegetable. But I'm always optimistic. Maybe he's got something on the Frenchman. The other one, thanks to you, Jomo, he's got so many tubes, wires, and pipes put into him, he looks like a pincushion. Don't worry though. If he dies, and probably will, I'll see to it you are not charged. This is a clear case of self defense. No doubt in my mind."

"Thank you, sir," Jomo said with relief.

"Well, that pretty much closes the case. They'll be charged today. They're off the streets. I recorded this. I hope you don't mind."

"No, sir."

"We will be going. The coffee never came. The coffee is so bad at the station. We were both hoping—"

Per jumped in. "Stop in at the lobby coffee shop. I'll call down and put it on my bill."

"Thanks, we'll do that, and the guys at the station will enjoy the story. Jomo, I've got to give it to you. You are one tough dude. If you ever plan on spending some time here in Kenya when you're a little older, we could sure use a good man like you in the brotherhood. Who knows, maybe you can help capture the Frenchman. You've literally got skin in the game," he offered with a chuckle. "Thank you for the capture."

"Thank you, detective." Jomo closed the door.

Later that morning, a call came in on Per's satellite phone.

"Hello, this is Per Jorland."

"Hi, Per, Nice."

"Oh, hi, I was about to call you. We're in Nairobi at the Ambassador. Got lucky changing our flight."

"Great. I was wondering when you'll get home."

"Be home tomorrow night, your time."

"So did you and Jo have a good time with my parents?"

"They just love him, and they loved the album with the pictures of you we put together."

"Thanks, Per. Have you been watching him after that poacher spearing?"

"Yeah, but not enough."

"What? What now?"

"This is all almost too much for me, so I'll make it short and tell you more when I get home. Yesterday, he got into a fight with a runner on the Kenyan Olympic Team, and then he put two guys who tried to mug him in the hospital. Both of them will likely die. We're free to leave the country though. A detective questioned Jo this morning. There are no charges because they're wanted for murder for killing two men in Lyon who have been traced to a huge diamond heist off a plane at Brussels airport a few years ago. They're thugs who worked for a Frenchman, a diamond smuggling kingpin, I guess. Bad guys killing bad guys."

There was a long pause that sounded like she dropped her phone.

"Nice, are you there?"

"What? Diamonds? A Frenchman? What did you say, Per?"

"Yeah, Nice, I can't stay ahead of Jo, and get this, the detective jokingly offered him a job on the force to capture this kingpin and join the brotherhood."

"He's only twenty-one."

"No, he said when Jo's older. Actually, I'm not so sure he was serious. I'm glad we're getting out of here before he does something else."

"I should say so, Per. This is all too much for me. I'm very concerned."

"Yeah, me too. I'll tell you more when we get home. See you tomorrow."

"Yeah, see you."

"Bye."

That night, Nice did not sleep well.

The next morning, Nice got a call from Michel at 6:00 a.m.

"Hello."

"Nice?"

She answered in French. "Yes, I know your voice, Michel. How did you get my number?"

"Nice, it has been so long, but I never forgot you."

"And I have never also. I know why you called."

"We both know. Can I see you before your husband and son come home from Nairobi?"

"They're coming home tonight. I'm picking them up. How did you know they are in Nairobi?"

"Can you take the train into New York? I'm at the Four Seasons, 57 East Fifty Seventh Street."

"I don't know about that, Michel. I want to, but—"

"We can either end this now over the phone or you can come to me. There is still time for us."

"But it's been so long. This is crazy."

"I know. Come to me now."

Nice hesitated. "All right. I'll be there at about one. What is your room number?"

"It's 2208. Knock quietly two times then one then two louder. Do you understand?"

"Yes, I do. Room 2208."

Nice hung up, went to the bedroom, and picked out her clothes. She checked the clip on her 9 mm, made sure there was a round in the chamber, and put it in her purse.

On the train, she was not aware of anyone around her. It was just her and her thoughts. *It's been so long. What will I say? What will he say? What if he knows Jo maybe killed one of his men? And the other? He might be mad. He might even kill me. No, not in his room. He's too smart for that, but he could kill me because I could identify him.*

She knocked, and the door opened slowly. Michel peeked out to look up and down the hall then let her in.

"Michel, you look older."

"Yes, older, but still the same." He touched her cheek. "Many of those years when you were staying at the Paris InterContinental, I was just down the hall under a different name. The hotel clerk knows me."

He poured a glass of wine and handed it to Nice as they sat down.

"There were times when I felt you were near. But why? Why didn't you?"

"I thought it best for both of us. You're married. It would only have led to pain if I had knocked. I never imagined you would be thinking of me or I would have. That was our time to make it. Live. Wine and dine. Parisians in the city we own."

"Oh, Michel. What do you know about pain when you've had people murdered?"

"That is true, but not you. Never you. Yes, two of my men in their Lyon apartment. They were greedy. They stole some of the diamonds taken in Brussels from me, but that was so long ago. Instead of killing them, I said nothing, and for the first time, broke my own rule. When they stole diamonds, yes, years later, I'd worked so hard to get out of West Africa and trusted them to move them slowly, they stole again. I could not trust them anymore. I sent the cleaners. And now I confess to you I had two mules who stole from me killed. In fact, it is right to tell you. Confessing is a weight I need to lay down. If the police had caught them, I would be done.

Listen to me, Nice. You wanted an illicit affair. I didn't, even though I knew you were down the hall. Not to count here, but who has the better moral conscience? So you say I'm a murderer, yet you've wanted to be unfaithful all these years. Who is the better? I say I am."

"Your reasoning is insane."

"Oh, what would you say to your husband, 'Oh, I had an affair, and it's over?' Do you think it would be that easy? Do you see life as just a game? To me, it is not. I have scruples."

Michel put down his wine and started pacing.

"The only reason you belittle me is you fantasized a long illicit love affair with me, and I didn't buy it. Oh, I wanted you so much. Not only sex but to run with me all the way. You always got what you wanted but not me. True, if you weren't married, you would have, but that's not how it went. One man for you wasn't enough. So I'd be the one on the side to feed your addiction for excitement. Let me tell you, it's true. You got through customs a couple of times, but you're an amateur nonetheless. Diamonds are not a world you could survive in without me. You'd be killed or caught sooner not later. So don't come onto me now thinking you have the higher hand."

"I do. How did you know? How did you find out they are in Nairobi?"

"I read it online in the Nairobi morning paper. Your son is quite a man to take my best men out like that. Professional killers. One may live and talk."

"Yes, I heard yesterday. He also speared a poacher and was inducted into an elite force, a kind of SWAT team. Government." Nice put one hand on her purse.

"Spear? SWAT team? I didn't know about that. Nice, those men he put in the hospital mean nothing to me. It only tells me my days of freedom may be numbered if one of them talks and gives clues how to find me. I had to call you. I had to see you."

Nice got up to pace, unsnapped her purse, and put it on a chair by the door. "And I also. I've never forgotten you or given up hope I'd see you again. I should have let you go, and yet I couldn't. That walk along the Seine, our first kiss, when I was with you, I went to another world, another place. Maybe a place I should have been instead of married. If I hadn't been married, I'd have run with you. We would have made a great team. I'm talking like a forty year old at a high school reunion."

"Yes, we would have."

"I've always wanted more."

"More? But you're a supermodel!"

"More passion. Yes, Michel, more passion. More of your passion and mine. Together. Deep passion. No structure, no rules, no past, no future, only now."

He put his arms around her, and they kissed.

"Michel, I only want just now. That is all I feel. No past, no future."

"Yes, Nice," he whispered in her ear.

"Make love to me now." She pressed her body to his. "You're all I ever wanted so much."

He undressed her and carried her to the bed.

"Now what, Nice?" Michel took her gently and kissed her.

She got out of bed and went to the bathroom. When she returned, she began dressing.

"I love you, but I cannot stay with you. I must be crazy."

He got out of bed and began dressing. "Yes, and I. We've only touched a few times, and yet I know also."

"We're better apart. It would never work. Not now."

"Will you tell your son?"

"Would you kill me if I did?"

"I don't think so." He stopped to think as he did his tie. "I would already have thought of a way."

Nice looked to the front room where her purse lay on the chair. "I have always known you are dangerous. I was attracted to you even in college as much as I am right now."

"Nice, you are no moth. You are the opposite. You are what all men seek. Believe me, it's the other way around. You are the kind of woman books are written about."

"Then what? I've felt you. I know you, but do I still need you? Will I need you tonight when my husband and son arrive home?"

"Only you know. Do you feel dirty from me?"

"No. No, Michel, you are no dirtier than I."

"Then what of us?"

"I know. What of us?" Nice exhaled. "Listen to me. They asked him to help capture you when Jomo is older. They believe in him. He proved himself. But I really don't know if they were even serious."

"Will you help him? I mean, tell him what I look like and where I stay?"

"No. Besides, the paparazzi would have a feeding frenzy over my past with you. I would be ruined. All I've worked for. Ruined. Police. Lawyers."

"So, I have your word?"

"Yes, and I say that because I have always separated love from business. Our business was long ago, and our love or whatever sort of insanity it is has to end now, today, Michel."

"And I." He sighed.

"Don't be so melodramatic. I love my husband and Jo. I chose long ago, even though I was weak some nights in Paris when I thought about you. I even poured a glass of wine for you. What a fool. I could have been out on the town with one of my model friends."

"But what of the police and Jomo?"

"Why do you keep coming back to Jo? I don't think he will take up the chase, but I cannot say for sure. Sometimes I think he is not of me. He's very different yet so perfect. He lives in the present. If someone tries to hurt him, he always hurts them back much worse, and I mean really bad."

"You know, if he joined the police to track me down, I would have to kill him before he kills me."

"Okay! If you try to kill him, I would kill you."

"To underestimate you could be a mistake I may not live to regret, yet I would be forced to take both of your lives only to protect myself. I'd rather see you again, even casual or even across the room at a show."

"Stop all this! Now! We can end this beautifully. Don't be afraid of him."

"I am not afraid of him."

"Maybe you're too old for all this. Diamonds. Maybe you're losing your nerve. He's already moved on. He's just twenty-one, for God's sake! Two thugs beaten in an alley. Like a warrior!"

"Warrior?"

"That's what the principal said when he was in fifth grade. He broke another kid's hand. Something about warrior genes. Stop all this! I'll admit I came here to make love. Only that. Sex, yes. Only that."

"Yes."

"Kiss me, Michel." She took him to her, and they kissed. "Bittersweet."

"I said that to you years ago in Paris, and now you say it."

"Yes, I remember." She paused to reflect. "Full circle— we're over, yet the circle remains. Do you feel it? I do."

"I like that. Now you've taught me of romance."

"I can teach you nothing! We're both grown up. Romance is the teacher, and lessons can be painful, ecstasy, or mostly in between. We are pain. So often I was thinking of you when I should have been thinking of my husband, Per."

"I see. But is your husband ecstasy?"

"That is a question you should not ask, and I need not answer. The word romance implies two not three."

"Nice, I have no words."

"Nor I. I must go now. We must not meet again. Ever."

"You have your husband and son, and I have my diamonds. Both, they shine. Both are worth it. My only pain is I cannot have what I want most."

"Choices. Listen to me, Michel. Per is not ecstasy or pain. We are somewhere in between to the good." She picked up her purse, put her hand on the doorknob, and turned to him. He came to her for what they knew was their last kiss. "I will always remember you." She opened the door, met eyes one last time, and left him with smile.

That night, they lay in bed. Per was almost asleep.

"I love you, Per. I missed you."

"I missed you too."

"But I really love you."

"It's good to be home. Jo and I really got together. Good trip. Mission accomplished."

"Good. I'm tired."

"What did you accomplish?"

"Oh, a lot. Have a good sleep."

"Night."

"Night," echoed Per.

17

THE KENYAN RUNNERS were so taken by surprise by Jomo's speed and power on that day in the bush, the news of the day's events eventually reached the ears of Don Marshall, coach of the US Olympic track and field program. Talking about it was the Kenyan's mistake. Breaking all protocol, Don invited Jomo to the US Team trials to see if there was any truth to the incredible story.

The letter of invitation to the US track-and-field Olympic trials caused quite a stir at the Jorlands.

"Jo!" Per exclaimed. "This all came out of nowhere! I knew you were good, but I never expected this! High school is one thing, but this?"

Nice turned around. "Of course, you did." She came over to Per and put her hand on his shoulder. "Remember what you said that day on the beach in Jamaica? You said, 'Look at him, Nice, he's ten years old, and he can beat a fifteen year old.'" Then she turned to Jomo and raised her index finger. "Now, Jo, you've got a few months to train, get in shape so you're ready. Think about it and make a plan."

The following day, Jomo was on the phone to Julie. She was in class, so he left a message. Before long, she returned his call.

"Hello."

"Hi, Jo, what's going on?"

"Jul, I need the number for Billy Bye."

"Just a second, it's a special number at the field house. Are you going to try out for next year's team? I was hoping you'd change your mind."

Jomo laughed. "No, believe it or not, I'm going to try out for the US Olympic Track Team! I'm going to see if Billy will let me train with the team."

"Jo! That's fantastic! Oh, Jo, I don't know how all this happened. I've got to go. Here's the general number and ask for extension 809. Good luck and call me later!"

"I'll tell you right now. I got a letter of invitation from the US Olympic track coach. He must have heard about my day with the Kenyan team."

After Jomo got the okay from Coach Bye, everyone was surprised when he left home to live at Marty's cabin. It didn't make any sense.

Julie called him and still didn't understand. Jomo had made a commitment to go to Yale and begin training under Coach Bye.

Jomo rebelled against the structure and instead, ran in the woods and on quiet dirt roads. Instead of New Haven city air, he breathed deep the clean oak forest air. Long distance was easy, but in the short ones, the one hundred and the two hundred where leg speed was critical, he'd have to dig deep. All he could tell Julie was, "I read an interview of an Olympic weightlifter who gold medaled. He ate only wild meat, everything, even raccoons as his protein source for two years before trying out for the team. He said he felt his muscles change somehow, and the weight he was once maxed out at got easier. He went far beyond where he never believed he could. Julie, I'm doing it my way!" Nice and Per understood this, but Julie thought his plan was immature and started to wonder about him. During that time alone, he trained hard, very hard.

Finally, with four weeks left before the trials, Jomo came home, packed, and left for Yale and Billy Bye. He was ready.

It was week 3. After a tough training session, Coach Bye called Jomo into his office. "Come on in, Jo. Well, you've got a shot at the Olympics. The trials are only a week away. How do you feel about it?"

"That's a good question, Coach. To tell you the truth, I'm surprised to be here. I mean, actually having a shot at qualifying."

"Don Marshall, you know about Don Marshall?"

"Yes, coach, he's the one that sent me the letter of invitation to the trials."

"Well, Jo, I know him well. He told me that grapevine story about you beating the entire Kenyan track team out on a dirt road. It was a picnic day, right?"

"Well, yes, they do it every year."

"Jo, it all sounds pretty casual to me. How do you even know for sure if they were really trying?"

"They were."

"If the Kenyan runners weren't trying, you could be in for a huge letdown. Besides, a dirt road is a far cry from a packed stadium and world televised Summer Olympics. Get me?"

"I'm telling you, Coach, they were trying. One guy even hit me because I beat him."

"Let's get back to Don Marshall. He heard the story from someone who knows the Kenyan coach. Don says you're a winner, you've got what it takes. So, Jo, have you?"

Jomo hesitated. "Why do you ask?"

Coach Bye looked at him, surprised. "I ask because I'm your coach. I can teach you. I can critique you. And, yes, help you build your confidence. An Olympic medal is the highest level of track competition in the world. You cannot be afraid of losing."

"I'm not afraid of other men."

"Jo, it's not about being afraid of other men. It's about the smart race, about maturity, and about patience. Save yourself to strike."

"If I'm faster, why wait?"

"You're not."

"Yes, I am."

"No, you're not, Jo. I haven't seen that yet. To earn the title of world champion, you must have equal parts of two things: natural talent and desire. You have more natural talent than anyone I've ever coached, and you have desire, but I think you need more." Coach Bye lowered his voice and continued, "I see you waving to your girlfriend in the stands. Sometimes you even go over to her during practice. I realize, Jo, you're not technically on the team, but this has to stop!"

"All right, coach. I guess I should tell you why. I've just been trying to keep it going with Julie. I feel like she's losing interest in me."

"I understand you, Jomo, but it has to stop! True desire means you have to eat it, sleep it, live it until it oozes from your every pore, from your every breath. Then when you're in the starting blocks, you must be peaking with that desire."

"I know all that!"

Coach Bye looked him straight in the eye. "You're all words, boy. I'll put it simply because I don't think you really understand me. You are running around for free on one of the most legendary tracks in America. There have been many great athletes before you. Listen! You're at Yale, Son, Yale University, and I'm close to losing my patience with you. Do you understand? I invited you here on a story. Show me tomorrow or you're down the road."

"Look, Coach, I can beat anyone on your team in every event. I just haven't shown it. Yes, I'm learning, but it's mostly about rubbing shoulders, leg speed, getting a good start, and avoiding intentional trips in a pack. If I really let go, I know I could blow around the outside at anytime with little extra effort. I read their faces. All pain. Giving everything to win, and yet I know I have another notch or two to crush them. No, Coach, I'm here to learn."

"And I'm here for you. To motivate you to be the very best you can be. You've got one week left. It's time to back those words you just said. Talk is cheap. I want to see your desire peak. Go ahead, Jo. You can and will do it. You can and will qualify for the US Olympic Track Team."

"Thanks, coach."

"Thank me after you win gold, Jo. Now, get out of here," he said with a pat on the back and a smile. Then as Jomo was opening the door, Coach Bye's voice changed. "Remember what I said. You're down the road."

The next day at practice, Jomo set new Yale records in the one hundred, two hundred, and four hundred. They were unofficial because records are only recognized at sanctioned meets with specific wind and weather conditions noted. Coach Bye was pleased and thought, *That little talk we had yesterday worked. Of course, that's what a coach is for.*

One week later, at the US Olympic trials, Jomo was an unknown. Per, Nice, and Julie were there to cheer him on, and Jomo had even received a rare letter from Grandmother Nonkipa and Grandfather Jomo.

In the locker room, Jomo only got trash talk like "Who are you?" and "We've seen wannabe high school heroes before." Jomo would just smile and say, "I'll give it my best shot, so all you have to do is catch me."

Running was natural for Jomo. His style was no style, simply go out fast and lead to the finish. Maybe it was the leather pouch tied around his waist.

Per kept his own theory to himself. To disclose it would reveal the secret he had confirmed with the electron microscope three years earlier. His burden must remain his for now—maybe to the grave, forever.

Coach Marshall, stopwatch in hand, watched in amazement as this unknown dominated in seven events. Nice and Per were just as surprised as coach Marshall. Jomo really wanted this.

There is no mile run in the Olympics. ESPN was first with the headline and Jomo's first interview in the locker room: "Unknown Misses 10,000M World Record By 4 Seconds."

America had found a new hero for the Summer Olympics in India.

Following the trials, the names of those who were selected for the official US Olympic Team were posted. They were told to get their affairs in order and report in two weeks to the Olympic Training Center in Colorado Springs, Colorado. Jomo, with his astonishing finishes, managed to stretch the reporting date to six weeks. Coach Marshall had to admit to himself there was something different in this young man that he had never seen before in all his years of coaching the best. Perhaps it was his eclectic self-training routine. In his own words, "I can't argue with success. An extra six weeks can't hurt."

Jomo had just finished a punishing 105-meter leg speed workout at the cabin and was preparing to roast two squirrels over an open fire when he got a call from an old friend from high school.

"Hello."

"Jo, that you?"

"Yes, this is Jo. Who are you? I think I recognize your voice."

"Yes, you do. It's Tommy John. Remember? I was third and passed you the baton to anchor at state."

"How could I forget? It's not that long ago. Where do you live now, and how've you been?"

"Didn't know what to do, so I took a little time off. You know, ski in the winter, trail run, and mountain bike in the summer. I'm in Colorado."

"So did I. My girlfriend, Julie, remember her?"

"Oh, yeah."

"We're still together. She wants me to go to Yale to be with her. So why'd you call?"

"Yale. I wish. What's goin' on, you say? What a question!"

"Well?"

"I read you made the Olympic Track Team. Crushed it at the trials. You're what's goin' on!"

"I guess it's no secret."

"When do you have to report to the Olympic Training Center in Colorado Springs?"

"About six weeks from today. Coach wanted me there in two weeks, but I did so good in the trials, he let me train awhile at Uncle Marty's cabin. That's where I am now."

"That's why I called, Jo. You need to build up your aerobic potential quickly, and I've got a way that's better than what you're doing."

"I'm interested."

"Trail running in the mountains at high altitude, higher than the training center."

"Interesting. How high are you talking?"

"Listen, I've got a lot of trail running buddies. They're ultrarunners, they're animals, Jo. On weekends, we'll pick a mountain, say within a hundred miles, but it's usually Mount Massive. The trail's good, and it's close to Leadville. That's where I live. I've done some checking. Leadville is 10,152 feet, and the training center is only 6,500."

"You didn't answer me, Tommy. How high?"

"We trail run fourteeners, Jo. Fourteeners."

"Fourteeners?"

Yea, Jo, 14,000 foot mountains! There's about 52 fourteeners in Colorado. Mount Massive peaks at 14,421. We run the trail. All kinds of switchbacks and steps way up above the tree line. We carry a pack of power drinks, fruits, and power bars. It's awesome."

"Now, that sounds like fun and something I might excel at."

"Yeah, it's fun until you puke, and you feel like your heart's gonna blow a hole through your chest! But listen, I think you could really improve your heart, legs, and lungs quickly before you report."

"You've sold me. I'll catch a plane somehow and be there tomorrow."

"Great. Give me a call, and I'll pick you up."

"Thanks, Tommy! This could be my secret weapon. I could do one or two fourteeners a week and work on my track events at the high school there."

"Oh, yeah. I see gold, Jo, lotsa gold. I'll run your stopwatch at the track. I'll research all the world record times and set up a daily progress charting system. We can do this."

"I like your enthusiasm, but I'm not in this for medals."

"That's got to be a large crock."

"If you don't know, all the better. Oh, do you like roasted squirrel?"

"What?"

"See ya tomorrow, Tommy."

"See ya."

Two days later on the early morning drive to the trail head at Mount Massive, Tommy John had a few thoughts.

"Jo, I can't tell you much your coaches won't, but the biggest thing I can help you with is just living at my place in Leadville for six weeks while you train. You'll be high altitude even when you're sleeping. If you're tough enough, running up Massive will really increase your red blood cell count. They carry oxygen to your legs. Thinner air, like fourteen thousand foot altitude, and your body naturally produces more red blood cells. Remember though, it's not a race. It's about changing your blood. Oh bud, I can cook."

"I get it."

"After Massive at 14,400, India will be a cakewalk. India's down near sea level where you're going."

"This all sounds real good, Tommy."

"Dude. This is good."

"You won't think I'm arrogant if I leave you and take a nap at the top before you arrive?"

"Now that will be a trick. A nap! Arrogant, no. In awe, yes. How 'bout I'll do the one-man wave?"

They pulled into the trailhead parking lot. Jomo's mouth dropped. "Tommy, that's a huge mountain."

"Yea, Jo. It's huge. That's why we're called ultra runners."

"I hope I can do it. Looks like there's still a little snow up there."

"We're taking the rarely used Northridge. We'll climb 4,700 feet. It's about a 12 mile round trip, and, dude, just when you think this isn't too tough, there's a class 3 ridgeline up the spine. Careful there! There's heavy exposure, so do not slip. No ropes needed, but you'll have to use your hands as you scramble. We'll descend the easy way."

They each slammed a bowl of oatmeal with raisins, donned their running packs, each holding three bottles and trail mix, retied their shoes, took long last draws from the power drink cooler in the jeep, and left a note on the windshield.

"I've run this trail many times, so I'll lead for a while. Whenever you feel like it, you can pass me."

"Sounds like a plan. Hold it, Tommy. Unlock the jeep."

Jomo reached in for the pouch and strap.

"What's that you're putting on?"

"It's an old leather pouch I got from my dad. I wear it for luck."

"Luck? There's no such thing in life. It only works in cards."

"Yeah, it does. My life's been pretty good since my dad gave it to me."

They set off on a well-maintained path through a sparsely forested boulder field of Aspen and Douglas fir that opened up into a glorious meadow of wildflowers. A mile up, the once serene path provided the only safe passage through a thirty degree scree field where foot placement was critical. Any misstep could result in a sprained ankle or worse, a broken leg. The never ending switchbacks up the steep ravine and Massive's knife ridge backbone were soon to come.

Tommy kept a steady easy pace for the first two miles till the serious ascent began. They stopped for a drink, and Jomo thoughtfully turned to Tommy.

"Do you mind if I give it a push to actually see what I've got?"

"I'm already seeing. Most guys from low altitude are puking by now. Go ahead, but don't hurt yourself. We're just making red blood cells, remember. The next time, I'll only let you walk fast."

"Right, Tommy. You're my trainer!"

Jomo zipped his bottle back in his pack, retied his shoes, and said quietly with a wry smile, "Watch this." With that, he turned and started up the first major switchback. Tommy tried to hang with him, but by the third switchback, he couldn't get enough oxygen to keep up the pace. By the fourth switchback, Jomo was so far up the ravine, he was out of sight.

Jomo was alone on the mountain. With every switchback, the trail became steeper and more treacherous. He was breathing deep. He opened his jaw and let his tongue hang out and relaxed his neck and shoulders, breathing deeper than ever before. *Think. Do not slip here or you will die. Onward. Warm. My mind and body. Connected as one.*

Yes, this feeling. The feeling when I chased the deer. Those wild eyes. Hunter and hunted. Yes, Grandfather, know yourself. Mountain is my Simba.

The last pitch far above the tree line was a 60 degree climb. Jomo stopped for a short drink before scrambling and clawing his way to the summit through sharp wet rocks and snow. He breathed deep and free and smiled at what he had done. He looked out 360 degrees over the earth and saw it as never before. He thought of the buck, the Kenyan Track Team, then came the trials to make the team, and now, soon, the Olympics in India. *My God, thank you, Grandpa Jomo. Know yourself. Know yourself.*

He lay down on a dry large flat boulder and thought, *Maybe I'll just lay down here and look at the sky as I wait for…*

And the flowers were all the colors of the rainbow. Wild flowers everywhere. Snow. Blue-iced mountain in the distance. He moves without walking. The flowers part as he laughs and rolls in them. All is peace. All is love. Toruk is by the lake. He turns to see us and smiles. The boy comes. He is me. He is my eyes. He talks to me without speaking, I am not you. Do not be afraid. I am your brother. My name is Tuk. I love you. You must return now. Always walk in the truth. We will meet again.

"You're a mountain goat!"

The words found their way deep into a back room of his brain.

"You're a mountain goat!"

The words slowly drifted down a hall of his brain until he rolled over and opened one eye. Tommy John was standing over him.

"How long have you been sleeping?"

"I don't know."

"Here, have some power drink and fruit."

Jomo, with a little help, slowly managed to stand on his own, and then he took a long drink.

"It's beautiful up here. When you called me, I was in a dream. A dream like I keep having now and then. It's like a story."

"Let's just walk down."

"Tommy, as I stood here alone, I realized that I'm really in the big show. This has all come too fast. Why am I so fast? Sometimes I feel like I'm being pushed into something I don't need. Running…big deal."

"I don't know. After today, it seems impossible, but you are in the big show with the most elite runners in the world. That's real. Which reminds me, we've got to notify your coach."

"About what?"

"You're living at my house. They'll be here anytime to give you a cup to pee in."

"Oh yeah, that pee cup after the trials. Guess I'll have to get used to that."

The two friends laughed at they descended the fourteener under a perfect blue Colorado sky.

Summer Olympic Games
Delhi, India

The Fasten Your Seatbelt sign lit up with a bell. Jomo looked out his window as the Dreamliner banked to the left to prepare for landing at the New Delhi airport. He tapped his buddy Jimmy Cooper in the seat next to him, a 5,000 meter specialist on the team. "Hey, Jimmy, take a look. There's soccer opening and closing ceremonies in Jawaharlal Nehru Stadium, and over there, see that modern one, that's the new Rama Jagarlamoody International Stadium."

"Yeah, Jo, that's a beautiful stadium. Check that track. Now that's what I call an Olympic track."

"Yes it is, Jimmy, a perfect track. Take a long look. Soon we'll be down there with eighty thousand screaming people and cameras everywhere. Are you nervous?"

"Yeah, a little bit. It'll feel good to get the qualifications over and get on with the finals."

"Jimmy, I thought I'd be nervous, but I'm not. I think this is going to be a lot of fun, and oh yeah, I've got a bone to pick with the Kenyan team, especially that 10,000 meter guy. Don't get me wrong. They're cool guys, fun too, and I respect their running, but I'm going to really enjoy pulling away from them—whatever the event—and crossing the finish line first, of course. I thought about it, and I probably shouldn't have been invited on that bush run. Oh well."

"Jo, to be honest, I'm gonna try to come in second to you in the 5,000. Hey, would you be a nice guy and draft me?"

"Sounds good on paper, Jimmy, but once the starter gun goes off, it's the fog of war. Sorry, but you'll have to catch me to draft me. If you can get a good start, tuck in behind me, and I'll take ya for a ride. Besides, I don't want to just win my events. I want to set new world records. I mean blow away the old ones. You know, give them all something to think about."

"Just between you and me, Jo, I think you can do it. I heard Coach Marshall talking in the airport to some reporters before we took off."

"What did he say?"

"Like me, Jo, he thinks you've got some new world records in your future."

"Jimmy, I can't wait to be jogging around the track with the American flag as a cape and looking into the stands to see my mom and dad and Julie. Oh yeah, those Kenyans. I'll be nice to them. You know, shake hands and try to put it all behind."

"Good plan, Jo. Be careful though. The world and the cameras are going to be looking for any slip up."

"Like?"

"Like arrogance, Jo. That's killed a lot of champions. When the Olympics are over, they just disappear, you know. No endorsements, commercials, no phones ringing off the hook, no new girlfriends. You're a hot candle, Jo. No one's ever heard of you before. Winning here can get pretty heady. I'm talkin' atmospheric."

"Yeah, Jimmy, thanks. Catch me, please, if you think I'm getting out of hand."

"I will, Jo. Be cool on the podium and especially in the interviews."

"Jimmy, you're a good friend and my wingman. We're landing. We've got a job to do."

Approaching the blocks in his first 1,500 meter final, Jomo looked to his parents and Julie in the bleachers, and then glanced at the whispering Kenyans. They knew him, and he knew them, and he knew they would try to box him in. Their plotting in barely audible Swahili reminded him of that day when he took on their whole team for an afternoon of fun in the sun. "Mimi mi duma. Wewe kushoto mimi sasa mimi kuondoka. (I am the cheetah. You left me, now I leave you)," he whispered in Swahili, just loud enough for them to hear.

They only saw his backside in the first event and in the following finals of the Games. When it was over and in the record books, his speed and aura on and off the track made him an instant world celebrity. Television and the press could not get enough of him. Paparazzi hounded him wherever he went. They talked about athlete of the century. Jomo had left his mark of seven gold medals and seven new world records for track athletes of future generations to ponder.

Smashing the nine second barrier in the 100 meter, however, caught the attention of the professional football world. Shortly after the Olympic Games, he signed an enormous contract to play for the New York Giants football team. Across the planet, he was heralded as the fastest-man-in-the-world. Jomo remembered his grandfather's advice as they pulled away from the boma. "Know yourself."

19

Two Years Later

JOMO WAS IN his second year as a wide receiver for the New York Giants football team. With the title of fastest-man-in-the-world, fans packed the stadium just to see his blazing speed and his amazing burst as he'd run to the ball. He was very difficult to play against defensively. His ability to never tire always made him a second-half threat when his defenders were worn out from chasing his every play down the field on deep pass patterns. When they defended him too loosely, he'd catch a ten or fifteen yarder for a first down. Jomo was tough, and Jomo was spectacular. His consistent game-winning catches earned him a five year, 250 million dollar contract. Nice and Per were so proud of their son. Jomo was a star.

I must interrupt here because something happened about the time Jomo was in preseason training with the Giants. It must have been August of his second year with the team. Per had walked into my office with probably the fourth packet of research

on Jomo's genetic code and his latest electron micrographic photos of muscle cells.

He was so excited. Then he started in on some other research side project he had his company, AnGen, working on. It was big, very big. Something about human disease genes in pre-recorded history.

I was really concerned. Tell the truth, I felt sorry for him. He was breaking down before my eyes. I started to think he'd better get a grip or he'd lose it all—all he'd worked for, his company, his son, and his wife. As he laid them on my desk, he was telling me an ESPN interview of Jomo would be aired that evening.

I looked at the packet, put my hand over it, looked up, and spoke slowly.

"Per, you're my best friend, and your research is truly astounding, but I can't and won't publish it."

"Larry, I've always thought, I mean, you offered to a few years ago."

"No, Per, I won't publish it in the *Smithsonian* magazine! Look, we've been friends for what now, maybe twenty-five years? That's a long time, and we've been through a lot, but this whole thing with you, Nice, and Jomo is running against my better judgment. Now you're asking me to keep silent. It's gone too far, way past my comfort zone. I'll stand by my word to tell no one, but this must stop."

"I know, Larry, but it's all so overwhelming. Maybe I won't ever have to tell them. I don't know what to say."

"Then I'll say it for you, Per. Who do you think you are? Do you think Jomo, Nice, and you are just one big science experiment? No, don't talk, just listen. I might be losing you as a friend, but I'm telling you right here and now, you better get a grip. It's none of my business why you did this crazy in-vitro thing, but as your friend, how you deal with it affects me too. You've already gotten me to swear my secrecy! That's near the same as lying. Is Jomo just a way for you to be recognized by the scientific world?"

"No, Larry, he's my son. I love him. I love Nice, and I'm so ashamed I've kept this all a secret so long, and yet I'm not! Just listen to me! What does a man do when he knows he wants a child and can't be the father, and he has a chance opportunity to choose the father?"

I listened and did not answer the question but said, "Go on."

Per was starting to break down but continued. "Will it be a warrior from the past you've just met? I saw him. He was a strong man, a proud man, not a nameless stranger or an unknown from a sperm bank. The decision was easy, Larry. I'm not insane here, Larry!"

"Per"—I sighed—"I will not and cannot play this role anymore. I don't even know if you've completely lost it or maybe you've got something there. Maybe you've got a point, a good reason, but it changes nothing. You have to tell them both! Look, his genetic code may be programmed for a life expectancy of *thirty, maybe thirty-five years. That's how long men lived in that period or, maybe he's got a genetic disease we've never seen that kicks in when he's twenty-eight. We're way over our heads here. I'm telling you, Per, he and Nice deserve to know. They have the right to know!"*

"Look Per, here's how it is. You've put me in a bad spot, but I forgive you. You told me once that you believe, but do you ever pray? My best advice? Pray to God for guidance. Truly believe. Have a talk with Jesus and confess your sins. Per, we're all sinners. He loves you. The Holy Spirit will arrange the time and place and the words you speak. When you confess in The Truth, the weight of guilt, regret, and secrets will be lifted from you, and your chains will be broken. I promise. You'll breathe deeper and sleep better, and your life will change before your eyes. Per, I learned this long ago kneeling over a dying friend. I promise you."

"All right, Larry. I'll do as you say. I don't know how or when, but I'll tell them. She's never lied to me. I'm so broken."

He turned and left with his head down. Later that day, I opened the packet to view the extraordinary electron micrographs he'd taken, and then I made a call to Stockholm. Now, let's get back to my story.

One day after practice at the Giants camp, Jomo was in the locker room talking with his good friend and defensive safety, Bobby Gage.

"Hey, man, I got a problem wit you, Jo, a big problem."

"What's that, Bobby?"

"You hit me pretty damn hard out there today for a practice," Bobby alleged, pissed off. "You rang my bell! It was all I could do not to be carried off the field. Some of the guys are wondering if you're a team player or just out for yourself. I'm defense, ya know. I'm the guy who hits hard!"

"Look, we're friends, but this is football, and it's up to you on defense to hit me hard. When coach says contact, I contact."

Bobby threw his towel across the locker room. "Yeah, but we're on the same team, bro! You put me out and I lose five million. I never met anyone like you! You only have one setting, and that's full out, and that's just not right."

"Sorry, but that's life. Eat or be eaten!" Then Jomo raised his voice. "You just give it your full out, and then you won't have to worry about me except when I fake you out and coach notices." Jomo laughed, Bobby didn't, and Jomo reached his hand out for a shake. "Friends?"

"Okay, we're friends."

A defensive coach caught the tentative handshake.

As Jomo removed his jersey readying for a shower, Bobby remarked, "What's up with the leather pouch around your waist, dude? Eddie told me you had it on under your jersey for every game last season. Lemme see that thing."

Jomo untied the sweaty leather strap that was showing some signs of wear.

"I mean it. Let me see that thing. It looks really old! Where'd you get it? It's kind of like stuff you see in a museum."

"I got it from my dad when I was nineteen. It's for good luck and it really works." Jomo walked over to the dirty clothes bin and threw in his underwear and socks. "Shoot, I won the Olympics with it," he added, handing it to Bobby.

Bobby rubbed it between his fingers. "Yeah, man, this is very cool, all right! How old is it? I mean, where did it come from? Who had it before your dad?"

"Well, my friend, I just don't know, and why are you so nosy about my stuff?"

"Hey, just asking, Jomo. Chill! It's just such a cool pouch, that's all. It might be really old and worth something, like an Indian artifact. Old, like maybe two or three hundred years old."

Jomo looked again at the pouch and ran his fingers over the sewing. There was a drawing of an animal he hadn't noticed since the day he got it as a present. He tossed it into his locker on top of some clothes. Looking up at Bobby, he said, "All I can tell you is when I was sitting in the hut in Africa with my grandfather, he sure was interested in it. He said it was older than he was, and I should always keep it with me and something about its spirit. I don't remember his exact words, but he sure had a fix on it."

"Well, you ought to check it out, man. That'd be my advice. Tell me if you ever find out. I really go for that old stuff." The two fell silent for about a minute, and then Bobby continued, "My wife and I have a whole room full of Western antiques and things. Some are over 150 years old. We've got a dining room table that came from Pennsylvania to the Red River Valley in a covered wagon, and the dining room chairs we found in an old warehouse. They're from 1841."

"Yeah, Bobby, maybe someday I'll check it out. Anyway, how does Smokey's for lunch sound, maybe a thick sirloin?"

"Now that sounds great. I could eat a horse."

"Okay, I'm buying."

"Jo, my man, that's the friend I know."

As they walked to the door, the coach warned Jomo quietly so Bobby couldn't hear, "If you hit one of my men like that again, so help me, I'll bench you! I'll bench you, and I'll tell the press why."

Driving home after lunch, Jomo got a call from Julie, now in the master's program at Yale.

"Hi, Jul, glad ya called. How ya been doing?"

"Real good." Julie paused a little too long, and Jomo sensed something immediately.

"Real good? What's wrong? Is there something you called me about?"

"I think I'm kind of happy, kind of happy."

"You're kind of happy about what, Jul?"

"I think I'm happy because I might be pregnant. Jo, are you there?"

"Yes, Jul, yes. I just never expected this. Say that again. What did you say?"

"I said I might be pregnant. I did a home test. I just had a feeling. It's only been 5 days though, but this is maybe not right."

"Julie, I'm happy, how's that?" Jomo stopped to think, "Maybe we should start planning a wedding. You know, we've talked about one."

"Listen, it's only a home test! Chances are it's for real, but I've got to see a doctor first."

"All right."

"It might take another few days to know for sure." Julie finished her sentence with her voice trembling.

"Okay then, Jul, but easy on the ice cream!" He tried to insert a little humor to calm her down.

Julie mustered a weak laugh. "Then you go easy on sending me flowers, deal?"

"That's a deal! I'll just have to wait. I won't call all hours in case you're taking a nap. I know how you don't like it when I catch you at the wrong time."

"I'll call you, Jo. Bye for now. I love you. No, I really do, Jo."

"Okay, bye for now, Jul. I love you too." Jomo was about to end the call when he heard Julie calling loudly.

"Wait! Wait, Jo! Wait!"

He put the phone back to his ear. "Jul, I'm still here."

"Jo, I lied! I lied to you!" she blurted out then continued, "I'm not kind of happy. I don't think I'm even happy at all." She paused. "I just don't know about this!"

Jomo was speechless. "Jul, I don't know what to say. What should I say?"

"I just don't feel right about this. Listen to me! I don't think I want a baby right now! I've got another year left in the master's program." She waited for his response, but he said nothing. "Jo, I think I'm okay with marrying you sometime, but no, please no, not a baby now!"

There was a long silence. Jomo pulled himself together by pulling off the road to talk. "Julie, you just told me this is not a for sure thing. Maybe it's just a false home test. You told me maybe it's false. This might be all about nothing."

"Oh, stop it with all the maybes, Jo. I'm going to the doctor in a week, and then we'll know. I'm so upset, I can't even think!"

"Julie."

"No, Jo, I can't talk anymore. I have to go. I love you. Bye."

Jomo barely got a word in. "Bye, I love you." The phone went dead. He started the car and drove home, confused, thinking, *Maybe she's right. We've got our own lives to live now, but a baby?*

Jomo tried to get his mind off Julie. That evening, as he relaxed in front of the TV at his new home overlooking the Atlantic Coast, an interesting turn of events happened. Surfing the channels, he fixed on a Discovery documentary. A new refined process had been developed for preparing samples to be tested for age with the carbon-14 technique (radiocarbon dating).

Jomo quickly reached for a pen and paper. A scientist in London was having another go at dating cloth fibers taken from the Shroud of Turin, which some believe to have covered Christ's body after his crucifixion. The Pope himself had authorized the new test, the fourth attempt to date the icon in fifty years.

The conversation in the locker room with Bobby had made Jomo curious about the pouch, so curious, he thought money was no object. Besides, he could afford it.

Suddenly, he really wanted to know just how old the pouch was. From the TV, he wrote down the email address for a Dr. Ben Purcell at Oxford. Jomo arranged to meet with the good doctor and was up early the next morning for a face-to-face call with Dr. Purcell using Skype.

"Dr. Purcell, my name is Jomo Jorland. I saw your C14 documentary on the Shroud of Turin last night."

"Is this the real Jomo Jorland on my screen? Is this the fastest-man-in-the-world, the Olympic champion? I cannot believe it!"

"Yes, sir, that's me."

"What manner of circumstance has led you to contact me today?"

"Dr. Purcell, I have a leather pouch I believe to be very old, and I was wondering if you could use your new C14 carbon dating on it? The pouch is pretty special to me, and I can pay you for your time."

"Sounds interesting, Jomo. Can you scan it and send it to me?"

"I'll send it right away, Dr. Purcell. You should receive it in a few minutes."

Jomo scanned the pouch, and a few minutes later Dr. Purcell was back. "That's a fascinating little purse, is it not?"

"It's not a purse, Doctor. It's a pouch."

"Righto, chap, you wouldn't be holding a purse, now would you?" The elderly gentleman laughed. "Well, let's see just how old it really is." He hesitated slightly before talking money. "Don't worry about payment now. I can assure you my secretary never misses a bill. Cut out a strip of leather from the inside of the sown seam so it's not damaged in the event it's found to be extraordinarily old, and then send it to me."

"I'll do that today, Dr. Purcell, and send it via overnight express. By the way, the results of your tests on the shroud were exciting."

"For me also, Jomo, but there still is more work to be done and more questions to answer. How do you think I make a living in this expensive city? Goodbye for now, young man. I'll be in touch."

"Thank you, Dr. Purcell. I'll look forward to hearing from you."

Six days later, Jomo was in the middle of doing his daily three hundred sit-ups when his cell phone rang. "Dr. Purcell, how's that test coming?"

"Jomo, we have not just run one test. This is big, young man. We've pulled out all stops to sort this thing out. We did three separate tests, and I sent a sliver of the sample off to a scientist in Germany to double check our results. It seems like we've had every chap in London with a PhD nosing around the lab, taking a look. It's been crazy! This little strip of leather has certainly caused a flap."

"Excuse me, Dr. Purcell, but I don't get it. What do you mean? How old is it?"

"Well, Jomo, I mean to tell you that pouch of yours is 12,175 years old, give or take a few years. It was sewn during the late Stone Age, about the time when the glaciers were nearly receded."

"What?"

"I repeat, 12,175 years, give or take a generation. You've got ole Bessie's pouch there, young man."

"Are you sure? I mean, that's a long time ago."

"Sure as a cock crows in the morning. There's no mistake here. The Max Planck Institute results came in this morning." Purcell changed his tone of voice. "Where on earth did you get it, Jomo?"

"It was a gift from my dad, for good luck."

"Well, where did he get it, if I may ask?"

"Not a clue, sir. I guess I've never asked him. We've never talked about it. That is rather odd, isn't it?"

"Well, there has to be an incredible tale behind it. I wish I could be there to hear it firsthand."

"I'll be seeing him soon, and I'll make sure you hear about it. Anyway, thanks for your help. Send me the bill and your report."

"Right away, Jomo, and by the way, good luck next season! Well, cheerio for now."

"Aw, right. Good bye, sir."

"Oh, before you ring off, Jomo, I must say I really want to know more about that pouch of yours. An artifact this old is extremely rare, and may I be so bold to say, I would like to be involved with any facet of its analysis and write up to the scientific world. You should know there are protocols here. You cannot just let any charlatan PhD get involved."

Jomo was taken by the surprisingly forthright statement of the noted professor. "I didn't realize, Dr. Purcell."

"I mean it, Jomo. This is a huge event in paleontology. I'd be gobsmacked not to want to be involved in this."

"Well, I have to talk to my dad, and then I'll get back to you. You got the okay from the Pope to work on the Shroud of Turin, so I'm sure you're trustworthy enough to work on this project. I want to talk with my dad about it first and see what he knows."

"Thanks, Jomo. Now I'm saying thanks to you! Isn't that a pip?"

"Bye for now."

20

"DAD, I'VE GOT a couple of days off and thought I'd come home. There's something I need to talk to you about."

"Sure, Son, it'd be good to see you. We've both been so busy. What's on your mind or do you want to wait till you're here?"

"I just need some answers. Something's bothering me."

Thinking he needed some advice, Per responded. "Okay, I'm here for you, Son."

"My plane lands tomorrow morning at nine. Can you pick me up? I'll stay a couple days, take a break."

"I'll be there, Jo," he said as he hung up the phone and turned to Nice. "He's coming home for a few days. Says he needs to take a break and says something's on his mind. I wonder what?"

"Great! It'll be good to see him. He can catch up on his sleep, and we'll get a chance to spoil him. Find out what he's been doing."

"We'll pick him up at the airport tomorrow morning at nine then?"

"No, Per. Why don't you go alone? I have a meeting, then we can get together later for lunch."

"Okay, that'll give us some time."

"Yeah, you both need that now and then."

Sensing Jomo's mood at the airport, Per suggested a drive down the Jersey coast. After a half hour of catching up on one another's lives, Jomo reached into his pack and removed the leather pouch. Looking over at Per, he said, "Dad, I've been having dreams."

Per, taking his eyes off the road, searched Jomo's face.

"Not just recently, either. I've been having dreams ever since I've been a teenager. They started sometime around that deer hunt at the cabin. I think this pouch has something to do with them."

Per pulled into a parking overlook at Long Branch. "Let's take a walk, Jo."

"Do you believe in dreams?" Jomo said.

"Well?"

"What they mean, Dad."

"I'm a scientist, but I don't think it could be proven either way. Why?"

"At first I couldn't remember the dreams, but lately I can't forget them. Sometimes they continue from one night to the next. Other times, they come over weeks and months."

"And what happens? Are they, are they nightmares?" Per asked, motioning Jomo toward a bench overlooking the water.

"In the dreams, there are several other men. We're chasing a herd of caribou. We're running on and on and on. This pouch is tied at my waist. Dad, I've only seen a caribou on TV. It doesn't make any sense," he said as he pulled the pouch out of his pocket.

"Jo, I haven't seen that old leather pouch since the Africa trip six years ago. So why should that bother you so much?"

"Wait, Dad, there's more. In one, there's a huge bear. It's dark brown, attacking and killing everyone, including the children. I spear it in the heart. There's blood everywhere. I wake up in a cold sweat, my heart's racing. It's awful!"

"I didn't know you were going through this, Jo. I've heard you mention your dreams before, but if I had known, I'd have had a talk with you about them."

"Listen to me, would you just listen! If you know anything about this, you have to tell me now!"

"Okay, I'm listening."

"I had this leather pouch carbon dated last month by a doctor in London. The lab reports came back and guess what? It's 12,175 years old! There was no mistake. He thinks it's a big deal. Where did you get it?"

There was a long silence. Per's eyes were closed as he listened to the rhythmic waves breaking. A glint of sun betrayed a small tear forming in his eye. Per had known for years this moment might come. He'd never rehearsed in his mind exactly what he would say even though he thought this moment might be inevitable. He took a deep breath, slowly exhaled, and looked at Jomo.

"Do you remember when you were a child and I talked about helping dig up a wooly mammoth in Norway?"

"Sure, it's a great story."

"Well, that expedition took place about a year before you were born. The night before it was airlifted away. I couldn't sleep. I went down into the trench late that night. My headlamp detected something in the ice. I chipped away at it." He looked straight at Jomo. "It was a preserved man from the Stone Age, a Cro-Magnon warrior."

"I have never heard about this before."

"That's because I never told anyone, not even you."

"So that's where the pouch came from?"

"Yes, but that's only the beginning of the story." Per reached down and picked up a blade of grass, rolling it between his fingers, and again exhaled. "At that time in my life, I was jealous of others who were working on the human genome. They were getting all the praise, all the money, all the credit. I was unhappy. The human genetic code was being solved, and I wasn't part of it."

"Okay, but what does that have to do with the man in the ice?"

"I took the sperm of that man, Son, and I've told no one until now." Per put his arm around Jomo. "I love you. I'm your father." Per sighed deeply. "But—"

"You love me, but what?"

"But that man in the ice is your biological father."

For a long time, father and son sat silently together, side by side on the bench overlooking the water. Jomo stared off into space, motionless for five long minutes as a ship, barely visible, entered the horizon far to the South. Working North, it slowly disappeared into a high cloud far up the coast.

"What the hell did you just say? My biological—my biological father is a Stone Age man? What the—this is sick!"

"Yes, through in-vitro fertilization."

"Stop it! Shut up! I do not want to hear this!" Jomo could not process what he was hearing. He snapped and pumped his fists. There was a long pause before he could even speak again. Per offered no words to break the silence. Jomo looked down closely at both sides of his hands as if he'd never seen them before, then gasped for breath and doubled over on the bench. He leaned over the side of the bench and threw up, then sat up but still bent over, and looked at the ground for several minutes. Per did not move a muscle as he watched this response. Then he offered Jomo a bottle of water.

In a slow, low voice dripping of anger, Jomo uttered one word, "Why?" Not looking up to Per, he repeated the word as anger enveloped him, turning his face red. "Why?"

Per tried to find some words to start, but no words came.

Jomo looked both ways to see if anyone was in earshot, and then yelled, "I don't know whether to get up right now and walk away from you forever or hit you as hard as I can!" Then unexpectedly, he attempted a right cross. Per blocked it easily and countered with a hard yet fatherly slap to Jomo's face. Surprised, Jomo lowered his clenched fist and waited for an answer, but none came.

"Why, Dad? Why in God's name did you do this to me?"

"Why, Jo? I never thought of you. You weren't even born at the time. Because before you were born, I was different."

"Different? What the hell does that mean to me?"

Per's voice turned harsh. "To you? To you? Yes, I was different than now. I had different wants, needs, goals. What I've done to you? Is that all you can say? What I've done to you?"

"Yeah, what you've done to me!"

"What have I done to you? You've felt nothing! No pain like I have. I've allowed you to remain a child and not carry the pain of what I did."

"Well, I think you're a coward for not telling me till now. Does Mom know?"

"No." Per sadly looked at a jet and its contrail cross the sky and shook his head.

"And why didn't you tell her and then me when I was younger? It would have been the honest thing to do."

"Maybe I was a coward. I tried once or twice but couldn't. Something always stopped me. I was in that Nairobi hospital once, and I tried, but the telephone connection was so bad. Then when I got home, everything was back to normal."

Jomo interrupted, again yelling at Per, "I can't believe any of this! This is not real! This is not happening!"

"Jomo, this is real. This is the truth," Per answered as his shoulders slumped in shame.

The two fell silent as an elderly couple approached, holding hands. They walked slowly in step as if they'd been walking side by side in just that way forever. When they had passed, Jomo began again, this time in a lower voice but with dangerous anger. "I don't think I can love you anymore. I don't! I really don't!"

"I still love you, Jo. I always will."

"I don't care what you feel. All of this is wrong. I should call the police."

"Unconditional love," Per interrupted. "I'm your father."

"I don't want your love. You've lied to me by omission all these years."

"If I lied, it was only because I love you. I let you remain a child, but I can't hold this any longer by myself. Can't you understand?"

"What's this? I should feel sorry for you?"

"You're successful. Don't you see it? My heart still hurts."

Jomo stood up, rinsed his mouth out with the water bottle Per had offered him, threw the empty bottle as hard as he could, and then stood squarely in front of Per who was still sitting on the bench. Per looked him in the eyes but offered no more.

Jomo spoke with a low boil in his voice. "What if I have children? What will they be like? Or do you even care?"

"Well, I don't know."

"You don't know? You don't even know!"

"Yes, I don't know. Birth is and always will be the eternal crapshoot. You turned out pretty good, didn't you?"

"Don't give me that existential bull. I don't give a damn."

"Grow up, Jo, and face it! It is! Maybe those old world genes are pretty damn good."

"What about Julie? You've ruined it for us. What will she think?"

"Look, I started with I'm sorry to even tell you."

"Sorry? You're sorry, and I have to live with this? You're sorry? Sorry is not good enough and stop calling me a child! I'm twenty-five years old."

"Then stop acting like a child. You came to me. I'd still carry this if you hadn't asked. You came to me, Son, remember? Something was bothering you."

"Sure, I came to you, but it was about some dreams and the pouch. I didn't expect some horror science fiction, some sick psychotic story."

"Ya know, I've been losing sleep for years and wondering how many times in how many ways I could say I'm sorry. I imagined being on my knees, begging for forgiveness, and I'm tired of being that man. I'm not going to apologize to anyone anymore, not even you. I'll say I'm sorry to Nice, but that's it. Grow up, Jo. I'll try to explain this to your mother, and I might lose her."

"I can't believe you're telling me you're not sorry! I hope Mom divorces you!"

"Sorry for wrecking your life? My God, you're in the top 1 percent of healthy and strong human beings on earth, and I'm supposed to be sorry for the rest of my life? There's emotion and reason here."

"Emotion and reason—what the hell are you talking about? My father is a Stone Age man."

"I'm your father! Just stop. Stop and think of all the good times we've had together. Are they nothing? Do they mean nothing to you?"

"No, I don't want you."

"Yes! Yes! I'm your father, Jo! I'm your real father."

"You mean you're not standing by me here?"

Raising his voice, Per yelled, "I've always stood by and for you. You trusted me. You love me, and I love you!"

"But you're not now. You're not standing by me now."

In a cathartic scream, Per answered, "What do you want from me here? Get on my knees? No, I will not! Not now! Not ever!" He stood up face to face with his son.

A jogger approached, giving the two a wider berth as the accusations and the yelling peaked.

"I thought you were becoming a man, and that I could tell you."

Jomo looked at this father and yelled, "I am a man!"

"No, I don't think so. If you want to know everything, I think you've hung on to being a child far too long. You're twenty-five, and still everything is easily solved with a hug and an 'I love you, Mom and Dad.' You're acting like a child now. My God, look at you! Look at your tantrum."

"I am not! This is not about me!"

Per countered quickly with a totally rational statement that threw Jomo. "Oh yes, it is! Now that I've told you, it's all about you! What're you whining about? Your life's been pretty exceptional as I see it."

Jomo tried to interrupt. "What are you trying to pull now?"

"We raised you as best we could."

"Yeah, but Mom didn't know!"

"Well, neither did I 'till you were nineteen. Look at who you are now or do you even know who you are after winning Olympic medals and making money in football? Hating me forever, I'm telling you, will be like cancer."

Per paused. "Yes, Jo, you're still a child, and now, if you want to live your whole life as a child in pity of your lot in life with your genes, then you can drown in your childish anger and self pity or you can face it all and move on. If you're man enough to hear the whole story, I'll tell you." Per began to sit down. His last statement had closed the door on any further harsh discourse.

The two were silent, and then Jomo spoke slowly, "I'm not going back home with you now. You go back to Mom. I'll catch a cab to Ocean Place Hotel. I've got to think about this. Tell her I missed a flight and called you. Tell Mom whatever you want, I don't care."

"No, I won't lie to her. I'll tell her we argued, and I'm going down to Ocean Place to see you tomorrow morning.

I love you, Jo. Go! This is not hug time, just go! When you come home, I'll tell Nice what I've told you."

"She may divorce you. I'll always stay with her. When I see you, I will know you're my Simba. Grandpa Jomo told me a time like this would come."

Per sighed. "This is real. This is you. This is me. This is us. Just go! This is not a Maasai spear in a young man's fantasy. I'm your real father, so forget Simba! Simba is your grandfather's life."

Per didn't return to his car. He stood there alone watching Jomo get into a cab, and as he watched, his son turned to him. Their eyes met before the door closed shut, and the cab sped off.

He walked and cried and walked, sometimes feeling better because some of the weight was lifting. It was five o'clock before he got home, exhausted.

Nice met him at the door and instantly knew something was amiss. She kissed him lightly and then, seeing his red eyes, asked, "What's wrong? Where's Jo? Where've you been?"

Per said nothing. He just walked past her into the living room, turned on the TV, then sat down with a long sigh. With glazed eyes, he looked at the carpet and barely acknowledged her when she entered the room. Quietly, in a monotonous voice, he answered, "We argued. He caught a cab."

Nice was silent, then asked him, "Where is he?"

"He's staying on the beach down in Long Branch at Ocean Place. He may come home tomorrow. I don't know. I'm going over there tomorrow morning."

"What on earth could you two be arguing about? You've always gotten along."

"I said things, and he said things. I said things, and I don't regret saying them."

"Per, you're talking in circles. What were you arguing about?"

"After I talk with him tomorrow, and he comes home, I'll tell you."

Nice turned her head like a dog hearing an odd sound. "Something's not right here, but I'll wait."

"Thanks, Nice. Tomorrow, I'll tell you. I promise."

Seeing he was spent, she went to the kitchen and returned with a bowl of homemade soup on a tray. She ran her fingers through his hair and massaged his shoulders, and then left him alone in his sorrow.

21

THE NEXT MORNING, Per was up and soon knocking on the door to room 857. Jomo opened the door, and without the usual friendly greeting, he simply said, "Come in."

As Per entered the room, Jomo handed him a cup of coffee.

Per started. "Well, are we done arguing? Can we find a way here?"

Jomo interrupted softly, "I didn't sleep last night. I understand, and you're right. Here I am, twenty-five years old and still a child. You try to tell me the truth, and I…" He stopped searching for the right words, and Per finished his sentence for him.

"And you rejected me!"

"Yeah, I rejected you and what you told me, what you tried to tell me when you finally had the courage."

"Worse, Jo, you rejected yourself."

They both paused to look straight at each other.

Jomo exhaled. "I looked at myself in the mirror this morning for a long time while I was shaving."

"Yes, and who did you see?" Per waited, and then continued, "Jomo Jorland or a Stone Age man you just heard about yesterday and know nothing about?" Per put his coffee cup on the table and asked again, "Who did you see in the mirror, Jo?"

Jomo got up and walked over to the window overlooking the Atlantic coastline. Per was silent, patient, waiting for his son's answer. Then he turned to his father, and all that could come out was an airy whisper as he raised his chin a little. "I saw Jomo Jorland." After those words, he pursed his lips.

"And did you like who you saw?"

Jomo thought then replied, "Yes, very much."

"So what do you think of all this? You in the mirror, your genes, me, your father, your anger?"

There was a knock at the door, followed by a voice, "Room service."

Jomo let out a long breath and put up his hand in a "just a minute and we'll continue" gesture. He opened the door and in rolled a cart with two stainless steel covers. He checked one—eggs Benedict, toast, and fruit—then gave the uniformed woman a generous tip.

As the door closed, Jomo turned to Per and gestured to the food. "Look at all this fine food in a fine hotel. You didn't give me money to check in here. I earned it. I like who I am. I'm proud of what I've accomplished."

"And so am I, Jo."

"What I'm saying is, when I look in the mirror, there's nothing about me that could be considered Stone Age. I'm a modern guy."

"Yes, you are, Jo, and an Olympic champion. Your genes may have helped you along the way, but we both know they haven't hurt you."

Jomo listened to this, and then turned to his father as if a light bulb had just turned on in his head. As he began serving the eggs Benedict, he asked in a lighter tone, "Tell me what you know about my genes."

Per took a bite of toast, surprised at this turn of attitude and tone. He waited as he found his words. "There's no one else on earth with genes as unique as yours. You are one among billions. Then again, so are mine, but you are unique because your mother is Maasai Tribe and your paternal genes are Cro-Magnon. They're your parents, separated only by time. Your father's genes are from a time when the earth was pure."

"Pure?"

"Yes, no toxins in the water, in the air, in the soil; a time when there were no pills, no x-rays, no PCBs, dioxin, no weed and feed. Listen, more than two hundred industrial chemicals have been found in the umbilical cord blood of unborn American babies."

"X-rays, chemicals?"

"Yes, none of the factors that cause disease and mutation that we live with now twenty-four hours a day. Theirs were healthy genes through natural selection. The pure earth, Jo. They talk in scientific circles about looking into the future that all life, even humans, are constantly evolving. I think your genes, physically, are the strongest the race of *Homo sapiens* will ever be. Just think what they had to overcome."

"What else?"

"Do you remember that hunt with Marty when you were gored in the shoulder by the buck?"

"Yeah, it must have been a deep cut. It still bothers me a little."

"Remember how I put dressing on it after sewing and cleaning it? I saved a sample of torn muscle tissue on that gauze."

Jomo took off his shirt and traced his finger over the scar. "I remember I ran the buck down, and it charged at me for its life."

Per continued, "I took the gauze to the lab and did a DNA test to verify what I told you yesterday. But more importantly after that, I started an ongoing study of your muscle—"

"Hold on," Jomo interrupted. "Why do you say *more importantly*?"

"Yes, on your muscle tissue with the electron microscope."

Per took a notepad from the telephone desk and drew a picture of a cell, then mitochondria within that cell. On the other side, he drew a diagram of the inner structures of the mitochondria as seen by the electron microscope.

"In your muscle cells are subcellular structures called *mitochondria*. In your mitochondria are submicroscopic structures called *cristae* that produce the power at the molecular level that you feel as strength and stamina." With a joking smile, Per continued, "Remember eleventh grade biology and the Krebs Cycle?"

"I remember the term Krebs Cycle, but I don't know anything about it."

"Listen, Jomo, there's a submicroscopic part of your muscle cells that are maybe 20 percent more numerous than those of modern humans. Your mitochondria contain 20 percent more cristae that help you have better aerobic respiration at the cellular level. They're where the reaction takes place at the atomic level. You can process more oxygen."

"Are you sure about this?"

"Well, no and yes. I got this idea to do the study when I noticed how you rarely seem to run out of breath or even go anaerobic in track or football."

"Have you been able to explain that?"

"What you're asking me is how it all works. It's simple cell physiology. What's the difference between aerobic and anaerobic respiration? We're talking about cellular respiration, not you and your lungs, okay?"

"Okay. Got it."

"In your case, you have the ability to remain longer in aerobic than any world class athlete."

"Why?"

"Aerobic respiration occurs in the cristae of the mitochondria. It's really at the atomic level. It uses oxygen and sugar to produce ATP molecules. ATP equals energy.

ATP enables your muscle to repeatedly contract and relax. Anaerobic does not occur in the mitochondria. It occurs in the cell cytoplasm and is far less efficient at producing ATP molecules. In fact, the aerobic respiration reaction can produce up to thirty two ATP molecules while anaerobic can only produce two to four molecules. So when you need a lot of ATP molecules for energy, which is the best way?"

"Aerobic respiration."

"Yes, and on top of that, anaerobic respiration produces an unwanted byproduct."

"What's that?"

"Lactic acid. Aerobic respiration does not. The lactic acid can build up in a muscle cell if blood flow is not enough to rinse it out. A runner has to slow down to keep the lactic acid from shutting down a muscle, as in a cramp."

"This explains it!"

"Yes, Jo. Great marathoners finish without breathing extra hard, but they are anaerobic none the less. They've had to run slower to control lactic acid build up and also because they're only producing two to four ATP molecules from the anaerobic reaction for most of the race."

"That explains why my muscles don't get used up."

"You do understand."

"Yeah, I never quite got something."

"What's that?"

"In the locker room back when I was at the Olympic trials, there were these guys who whined that they didn't make the team 'cause they went out too fast. So what really happened was they used up their aerobic too fast and ended up going anaerobic too soon. They ended up running on two to four ATP molecules, while I was still running on thirty two. Wow."

"You've got it, Jo. It's all because your genetic blueprint called for 20 percent more cristae in your mitochondria. There's more though. My research on your mitochondria is startling, but unless they get more oxygen, their potential is wasted."

Per gestured with an open hand. "Now listen, Jo, because I don't really know who's genes gave you your great heart and lungs. It's called your VO2 max. I'm sure they measured it at the Olympic Training Center."

"Yeah, I was on a treadmill and breathed into a pipe. They were all looking at me."

"That's the test! Remember when you were on the beach in Jamaica and won that breath-holding contest in the water?"

"Yes, I still remember that. My time was three minutes and twenty-two seconds."

"Jo, your heart and lungs are extraordinary. The maximum amount of oxygen you can deliver to your mitochondria is so high compared to other athletes that it compares more equally to the sled dogs in the Iditarod race in Alaska. Son, your heart and lungs are off the charts."

"Are you saying it's my genes that won those medals?"

"No, the genes are only a part of who you are, Jo. You had to train and have the innate talent to run, and that, I believe, you inherited from Nice, the blood of the Serengeti; a bloodline of runners going back hundreds of thousands of years."

"I always thought I could win a race because I wanted it more than the other guy. There's pain in competition at the world level. I feel it."

"Yes, and that's your greatest talent, Jo."

"What?"

"Your great talent is your will, your desire to win. Just stop to imagine, you could have been a couch potato and never realized your gift."

Jomo stopped all questions and went to the cart for another sweet roll, and then added a second to the plate. Per went to the window. They separated in the room, both lost in their own thoughts.

Jomo brought his father a roll. By the window, watching the coast, he again asked, "Why? How did you do it? I want to know as a man, not as a child."

"I'll tell you because you deserve to know. A short while after our wedding, Nice wanted to have a child. We both did."

"And then what?"

"Well, we tried, and she never became pregnant. At the time, it was not a good situation in our new marriage. We finally went to a fertility doctor, and he told us he would try to help us, but there would be no guarantee. He said in-vitro fertilization would be our best chance, basically conception in a petri dish."

"I know there's no guarantee."

"There's never a guarantee, but in our case he thought my sperm was inadequate to conceive. It was more than a little humiliating." Per looked down. "When I was able to regenerate the Cro-Magnon's sperm just as I had with the mammoth's, I decided to do a double-blind and gave the fertility doctor a sample of my sperm and one of the warrior's. Believe me, he was a strapping young man in his day. I remember that day I went to the lab. The whole place was shut down. Within one hour, I had regenerated his sperm. I took another three hours of intense study to validate that sperm. I mean every test the lab was capable of—broken DNA strands, for example. The sperm was as healthy as mine with no physical difference except for, of course, the male DNA it carried. I was convinced it was safe, and if I couldn't find any problem with it at AnGen, and then I knew Dr. Gorlin couldn't with his simple phase-contrast microscope. Somehow still, I knew it was wrong, but I thought he would make a far better father than a crapshoot from a sperm bank.

"If Nice conceived, I wouldn't know. Why would I want to know? Then as a baby, you were strong and healthy, and I didn't want to know. I could have run a DNA on a hair follicle at any time but didn't. I already felt so much guilt for doing the unthinkable."

"Then after the buck gored me, you did want to know."

"Yes, Jo, on an impulse. I've made a lot of impulsive decisions in my life. You always seemed a little different, and you know the rest. I checked your DNA from the dressing, and the Cro-Magnon is your biological father. There is no doubt."

"There's no doubt?"

"There's no doubt." Per sat down, put his hands on his knees, and exhaled. Jomo put his hand on his dad's shoulder to comfort him. "Let's go home and get this over. I have to tell your mother now before I lose courage."

"I agree. It's time."

"Thanks."

"And," Jomo offered, "I'll help in any way I can."

"I appreciate that, Son, but it's all on me."

Jomo grabbed his suitcase and they were out the door, soon heading home to an uncertain and potential fork in the road between his parents. As they took the elevator down to the ground level, Jomo remembered his most powerful recurring dream, "But, Dad, the strangest dream I've ever had happened on top of Mount Massive. I couldn't remember it for a couple of years, and then it came again last night. Something about a boy who says he's my brother, and he loves me. It's all so—"

Per put his hand on his son's shoulder, "So, Jo, it's true. I believe there is a strong chance you do have a brother. I'm amazed to hear this from you. A few months ago, I read a research article about dreams. Personally, I don't think they'll ever dig deep enough into the mystery, but there are documented deep dreams or special dreams. The only explanation for them is that these dreams are seated in brain neuron synapses where the actual dream is inherited on chromosome 16."

Without thinking of a response to Per, Jomo spoke by reflex, "His name is Tuk. I think he is—was or still is—about seven years old. His name is Tuk. He is my brother. I'm sure! He told me he loves me, and I should always walk in *The Truth*. Dad, that dreamed changed my life. I now believe it was God talking to me through my brother."

"Jo, this is fascinating because I heard those very words when I found the man in the ice. I felt like I was temporarily hypnotized or in a dream."

22

NICE TOOK THE TV remote out of Jomo's hand. Clicking it off, she announced, "All right, what's going on? I already know there's something going on between you and Per. You've been home six hours, and you have never, and I do mean never, been this quiet! Now, I'm asking you again! What's up?"

Jomo knew he'd be leaving soon. *It's now or never*, he thought. "This is between you and Dad. I'm going to make some coffee."

"What's between Per and me?"

"I'll be in the kitchen," he replied as he headed down the hallway.

Nice turned to Per with a questioning look. "What's going on? You told me it's between you and Jo!"

Per stood slowly, hands in his pockets, head down. "Well, I thought this day might come. I wish it had come years ago, but there never seemed to be the exact right moment or reason to tell you, and Jo was always so healthy, and now he's successful. His life's so good. I just never found the right moment."

"Huh? Get over here and sit down. Now, tell me what you're trying to say. You're scaring me!"

"I'll tell you. I tried to tell you long ago from the hospital, the day I got that snake bite. There's no easy way to tell you, Nice, but I am not Jomo's biological father! There, I've said it."

Nice looked at this man who had been her husband for over a quarter century as though he had turned into an alien. She opened her mouth, but no sound came. She was speechless.

Per forged ahead, "Do you remember when the delivery room doctor said Jo's eyes would eventually turn from dark brown to a much lighter shade?"

Nice nodded.

"That's when I started to wonder, and then on that trip to Jamaica when he was ten, even you commented how he was somehow different."

"Exactly what are you saying? That was only casual talk."

"Just that he is different. I am not his biological father. He carries your genes but not mine."

Nice shook her head. "I don't believe you! This is impossible! Whose genes does he carry then if they aren't yours? Whose genes does he carry, Per?"

Per could hear Jomo listening from the kitchen. "I told Jo yesterday morning. Remember when he was nineteen and got gored by the deer antlers on that hunting trip with Marty and me? I brought the gauze from one of his dressings to the lab and ran his DNA. I am not his biological father, as I suspected."

"And?"

"And what? There was a 0 percent chance that his DNA was from me. That's why we argued yesterday when I told him."

"So who is his father?"

"I told Jo yesterday, and now I will tell you. First, I want you to know how much I love you both, but I can't let Jo carry this secret like a cancer eating away at him his entire life without you knowing, and it's my responsibility to tell you and only mine."

Nice braced; her body language totally closed.

Jomo came out of the kitchen with three cups of coffee. He placed them on the table then sat down in a chair across from his parents and kept quiet.

Per reached for his cup, holding it in his shaking hands. "Remember the mammoth expedition I went on about a year before Jomo was born?"

Nice nodded.

"That last night before we airlifted out, I went down in the trench to check the straps. It was then I saw him in the ice, a perfectly preserved Stone Age man. Using my ice ax, I uncovered his face."

Nice looked at Per oddly then squinted her eyes at him.

"I took a muscle sample from his arm and another sample of his frozen sperm. I also took the leather pouch I gave to

Jo when he was a teenager. You've seen that. I put my ice ax under the man's arm and covered him back up with snow. Then I put the two samples, wrapped in my bandana, and placed it in the cooler with the mammoth samples. I told no one. I still have some his muscle and sperm samples in the freezer at the lab. Jomo's DNA matches his DNA."

She dropped her mouth and shook her head violently. "Stop, I don't want to hear this!"

"I must continue, Nice. I believe the man is still there in the ice. Yesterday, Jomo asked me why. I've grown up a lot since then. When we wanted a family, you couldn't get pregnant, and finally, the doctor suggested in-vitro fertilization. That warrior was a far better donor than some nameless guy trying to make a few bucks by donating his sperm."

"Per, for the love of God, Per, stop this crazy talk!" She was going ballistic, but Per continued. He was beyond the point where he could stop.

"I suspected all along in those days that the problem was with me, Nice, and not with you. Dr. Gorlin confirmed it. You heard him yourself. The day after we brought the frozen mammoth sperm to life, I went back to the lab alone and was able to bring this man's sperm to life by exactly repeating the same technique."

Jomo broke in, "Keep going, Dad. Tell it all."

"Jo, if you want to help you can stay but keep quiet. This is all on me!" Turning back to Nice, he continued. "I brought two samples—the first of my sperm and the second, of the Stone Age man's—to the doctor at the fertility clinic. Nice, I didn't even know for sure which of the samples conceived until the DNA test I did on Jomo's blood when he was nineteen years old! We were a happy family. Jomo was a healthy baby! It wasn't until after the deer hunt that I suspected gene activation. You know, where a gene turns on later in life. Of the two samples I gave Dr. Gorlin that day, only one conceived. He told me so." What followed was a long eerie silence, the air thick in their own home.

"No, on second thought, Jo, I want you to leave. Go down the hall and close the door, *now*! What I'm about to say is none of your business." Per then turned back to Nice. "Apparently you have selective memory because I still remember your words to this day."

"What are you talking about, what *I* said? I remember that time in our marriage. It was about six months after our honeymoon. We were trying. I know all this, Per."

"No, I don't think you do."

"Yes, I do. I wanted a baby."

"Well, so did I."

"But I wanted children, several children. In case you forgot, I always said I was an only child even that first night we met at your townhouse."

"You don't get it. That argument that night when our sex fell apart. You just quit. Then you lost your temper and said something that cut me in half."

"What? What argument? How should I remember something I said twenty-five years ago?"

"That's what I mean, Nice. You must have selective memory."

"So? Tell me then!"

"Okay, you want to know why? Why I did the unthinkable?"

"Yes."

"Because of you."

"What?"

"Yes. Because of you! You pushed me to it."

"I'm, Per, I'm sorry. What did I do?"

"What you did was what you said. You lost your temper. You lost your mind. You got out of bed screaming at me because you couldn't get pregnant after trying and trying. In fact, that next week we went to Dr. Gorlin's office. You know, the fertility doctor."

"Yes."

"Then you stopped your screaming and said in a quiet voice, and I still remember your exact words as you left me and slept on the couch. I was afraid of you. I actually locked the bedroom that night."

"Okay, tell me."

"You said, 'I always wanted children, and God had to give me you.'"

"Oh my God. Oh, I am so sorry."

"Yes, 'And God had to give me you.' Those are the words that pushed me over the edge. I still remember that night. I didn't sleep well, and I didn't talk to you the next day. I felt so inadequate. No, I felt so worthless, so unloved by you. I thought our marriage had failed. I'd been able to cope with anything in life until you said those words. So when I found the sperm to be viable, I knew this was the man worthy of fathering your first child since I couldn't. I wasn't crazy. I was trying to please you to save our marriage."

"Oh, Per, I am so sorry, so sorry."

"You never apologized in the days to come. The days turned to weeks then months. Then I began to think whether you truly loved me. We both looked forward to seeing each other after our trips. Sex was great again but still no child. Then came the Norway dig, and you know the rest."

"Will you ever forgive me?"

"I did years ago but could never forget your words. Our love continued to grow with each of us being faithful partners for life. There was never anyone else."

"So that's why you did it."

"Yes, Nice, that's why."

Nice placed her hand on Per's knee and rose, looking everywhere but at her husband. She let loose a string of Swahili, her hands covering her ears, not wanting to hear one more word.

"I love you, Nice. What would our life have been without Jo?"

"Please stop! Stop! I need to get out of here!" Hands on her hips, she walked out the front door and left it open. He heard her crying on the front walk, and then she was gone. A crack of thunder shook the windows. Jomo came to Per's side and they sat there motionless as the rain blew through the open door.

They were in the family room talking when Nice returned home three hours later. She stood in the doorway, cold and soaking wet from head to toe. Not entering, she looked first at Jomo then at Per. Her eyes were red and swollen from crying. Tear tracks lined her face. She stood limp, but no more tears came. When Per started to get up to comfort her, she held her hand up to stop his advance. He sat down on the edge of the sofa next to Jomo, afraid of what she was about to say. Catching her breath, still standing in the doorway, she began quietly, still not looking at him.

"Per, if you had told me this story twenty years ago, I would have called the police and divorced you on the spot. I would have been mad at you first, and then offended and hurt beyond all I could imagine, but this is now, and I love you too much to throw it all away."

Per heaved a great sigh of relief and then spoke softly, "Thank you, Nice. You'll never know how much weight I've carried for so many years."

Nice looked straight at him with unblinking eyes. "A secret is hard to hold and even harder to tell. I don't know if it hurts more to carry one for a lifetime than to confess it. Really, I don't know how it feels to confess. I don't have anything to confess. I have never hidden anything from you, nothing, I swear.

I don't know what I would do without you." She walked over to the wall and looked at a framed pictured of her holding baby Jomo with Per next to her. "Look at Jo. What would we be without him? How could I go on? I'm hurt, Per, but we've weathered some pretty big storms together over the years, especially those early ones. I can't throw all those years away, not after all we've been through, but why didn't you tell me sooner? Why? Why, Per? My God, did you really think all these years since you found out that I'd fold if you told me? I'm his mother! Look at me, Per! You're my husband, and I'm his mother! I don't fold that easy, and I will keep this family together!" She walked slowly, slightly bent from lack of strength. Her steps left wet tracks on the floor. She fell down on her knees sobbing. Both men rose and hugged her. As a family, they cried. Nice raised her head finally, and in a much clearer voice, she went on.

"My attitudes toward matters of heredity and family have changed. Yours have too, Per. We've all changed over the years. If what you have said is true, then I'd like to see this man. I'd like to know more about him. If you did this to begin a family, it changes nothing. We've always been family, a real family. I've always told you I'd support you. If this is something that has never been done before, the world needs to know."

Jomo nodded his head in agreement.

Per exhaled in relief. "I'll write a letter to the Smithsonian and a copy to Larry Calvert. Jo and I will go to the excavation site with you, and together we'll bring back his biological father."

Jomo jumped in quickly. "Good, I want to see him, Dad."

Per responded, a bit irritated by Jomo's statement. "Quit talking like a child, Jo!"

"Then let's do this soon," Nice said, heading for a hot bath. "I need some time to myself. I'm worn out, and I'm all cried out." She fired one last angry volley at him down the hall, "I can't believe it, Per. I can't believe you kept this—all this— secret! All these years! And one more thing—I might sound fine to you about all this, this, this science fiction pregnancy I went through. Well, I'm not! It's going to take some time for me to even look at you, but when that time comes, you'll know." She almost slammed the door but held her anger.

As she was drying her tears in the mirror, she noticed her jewelry box out of the corner of her eye. Slowly, she reached for it and opened it. She hesitated, and then pulled out fistfuls of necklaces and bling until the box was empty. Again she hesitated and listened. No footsteps in the hall. She carefully probed with her fingernail to find the hidden blue ribbon, carefully pulled it, and the false bottom rose to expose a perfectly cut large diamond wrapped in a scrap of pink paper with a faded area code 202 phone number inside. She put it in her palm and looked at it with sad eyes. She hadn't taken it out for so many years.

She thought, *You spineless coward. He confesses to you and you tell him you've got nothing to confess. Do it now. Go back in there and tell him. Tell him you've held your secret since before you met him. You're a coward! This is maybe your last chance. Are you willing to take it all to your grave? Smuggling, the longing to see him again in Paris, sex on the same day Per and Jo return from Kenya. If you don't, you're worthless, worthless, Nice.* Then she placed it back in the hidden compartment, sealed the false bottom tightly, put the necklaces back, and drew her bath.

As she slid deep into the soothing hot water, she thought of Michel and what he had said of secrets while walking along the Seine so many years ago. *"A secret is always, it is forever. To live in the present is to put it aside as not relevant." Should have listened to my mother before I said, "Roses are Red."*

23

PER AND JOMO went to the study, closed the door, and sat down face to face.

"Jo, listen to me. Before we start this letter, you have to realize the reality of what we're about to do. Right now our family holds the secret. This isn't like sports where you can come back the next game and begin all over again. This decision is forever. If we send this letter to the Smithsonian Institute, it won't be long before the entire world knows it, knows what I did, and who you are. After this letter becomes known, our lives will never, never be the same, Jo. I'm asking again. Do you need to see your biological father so much you'd risk it all—your future, my future, and Nice's future? You've got it all. You've made it. This is a gamble you don't need to take. Where did you get this need to gamble?"

"I have to keep the secret till I die no matter what happens, even when I marry and have children of my own? Carry it to my grave? Never tell my wife, never tell my children when they're old enough, life continuing like this never happened?"

"That's what I mean, and to be honest, I personally don't want to do this. I've broken no laws, nothing, but this could put my company and my reputation at risk for something I did twenty-four, twenty-five, years ago. Then there's Nice, who says she wants to see this man as you do? And I wonder about her career and what this announcement would do to that. Would her life in front of the camera end? Think of the absolute worst scenarios, Jo. We could end up being thought of as the freak family of the year in the tabloids. Those people are ruthless, and the unknown is whether our lives would be destroyed."

"You're right. I've made millions playing football, a sport I really love, so why would I blow my contract? Then, there's nothing wrong with me. I'm an Olympic champion. I've never taken steroids or broken any laws. I don't know how the fans would take this. Maybe I'm being naive. I want to think they'd still like me."

Per nodded in agreement. "Yes, Jo, they'd still like you. Think—the Olympic committee. You may even lose those gold medals you worked so hard for. Public sentiment can be harsh. One day you're a hero, next day a bum, a loser. This is real. You better be ready to handle disappointment. There are plenty of good men who've never come back when the big fall comes. Look, I can't be selfish here, and I think Nice would agree. You and only you bear the genes of that Stone Age man. Not me, not your mother. You're young, and let's face it, Nice and I are older. After we're gone, you'll live on. Do you understand what I'm saying, Jo?"

"No, why does it have to be my decision? I think this is a family decision to make!"

"I just told you, Jo, at some point everyone must choose on their own. Whether their parents are alive or have passed away, there comes a time when everyone must choose on their own. It's always different, and it's always hard."

"I know, that's why I've been quiet for two days after you told me. Grandfather Jomo told me my Simba would come one day or I would go to Simba. He said I would have to prove myself to become a man. He said my Simba wouldn't have a black mane. He said my Simba might be a disappointment or an opportunity. He told me to start preparing for Simba so I'd be prepared when I was tested. He said I must know myself. Well, I do feel like I know myself."

"You already know what I think about that Simba talk, but okay, what have you decided, Son?"

"I'll tell you tomorrow. I love you, Dad, but I need a little more time. We'll talk in the morning."

The following morning, Nice and Per were sitting on the couch just close enough to infer they had reached some sort of lasting truce. Both looked haggard, like neither had slept. She wore no makeup and her eyes were red and puffy from crying. They were talking quietly about how Per had put the secret on Jomo's shoulders the night before. He came in, picked up a big chair, and sat down facing his parents.

"I've decided to go public. I've done nothing wrong. We've done nothing wrong! I'm a champion. I want to see my biological father. This is a big gamble I think we'll win."

Per and Nice sat there expressionless. He drew a deep breath and slowly exhaled. Nice pursed her lips and said in a low voice, hands on her thighs, "Then it's decided. We'll go forward with the letter, and we'll find this man, your biological father, and bring him home."

Per added, "I don't like this, but okay. Now, there's just one last thing, Jo."

"What's that, Dad?"

Nice shifted her foot a little as Per was about to speak then she answered the question herself. "Jo," she paused, "you have to tell Julie and the sooner the better."

Per chimed in. "That's right, Jo, you can't leave for Norway not telling her and have her find out in the news. You and this expedition will be all over the news."

Jomo's faced dropped. He doubled over as if punched in the stomach. "Oh no, oh no."

"Jo, are you all right?"

"Jo," Nice raised her voice, "are you okay?"

Jomo looked up at the two, eyes blurred, and whispered, "She called me about two weeks ago. She's pretty sure she's pregnant. She said she did a home pregnancy test."

Nice was stunned. "Jo!"

Per looked down. "Oh. Oh."

Jomo continued, "And it's worse. She said she isn't sure she wants a baby right now, not even marriage." By now, he was shaking.

"Oh, Jo."

Per groaned at hearing this development, put his head in his hands, and said mournfully, "I'm sorry, Jo. I'm so sorry that I caused all this."

"It's a little late for sorry, but I accept your apology. I'm going to call her and drive up to New Haven on Saturday morning. We'll talk about her pregnancy, the dig in Norway, and then I'll tell her who I am. I have no other options here than tell her everything, do I?"

Per and Nice sat motionless and made no attempt to interrupt him.

Jomo continued, "If she leaves me and aborts the baby, I can't hold her. I can't stop her." At that, Jomo pulled his cell phone out of his pocket, walked out the door and dialed Julie. Per and Nice could faintly hear him talking on the back steps.

Dr. Carl Witkop
Director of Human Paleontology
Smithsonian Institute
900 Jefferson Drive SW
Washington, DC, 20560

Dear Carl,

If you check the Gene Pool Project archives, you'll find that AnGen did the initial genetic assessments on the Saami mammoth and subsequently participated in the first cloning efforts of that project for the Smithsonian Institute. That was so long ago, you probably are not aware that I, personally, was the one who retrieved the samples from the original dig site in Northern Norway.

What I am about to tell you has not only been classified since then, it has been my secret from the world until yesterday when I told my family. I am asking you to handle the disposition, study, and information dispersal. On the last night of the dig, I discovered what I believe to be a perfectly preserved Cro-Magnon man. I took a muscle sample, which is still in an AnGen freezer, and a sperm sample from him. I told no one and included the samples with the mammoth samples as I left the dig site. That is not all. I have since that time verified that this Cro-Magnon man is the biological father of my twenty-five year old son through in-vitro fertilization.

I am requesting the Smithsonian Institute to finance a return expedition to the site to retrieve the man, bringing him to the United States for further study and eventually share a display with the public. Carl, as you can well imagine, this is a highly sensitive issue with our family, and I trust you will handle it only with the utmost care. Please give me a call to set up an appointment next week, and please see that my good friend Larry Calvert will be there. I already have plans to be in DC at that time.

Sincerely,
Per Jorland, PhD
President, AnGen
PFJ/pj

Copy: Dr. Lawrence Calvert, Director
Smithsonian Institute
900 Jefferson Drive SW
Washington, DC, 20560

24

Late Saturday morning, Jomo pulled up in front of Julie's dorm. She stood with a relieved smile to see him, her soul mate since elementary school.

After a kiss and some small talk, Julie quickly got down to her unexpected pregnancy, and she tore right into it. "I'm serious. We have to talk. I don't think you're getting this. I'm pregnant!"

"Yes, I do get it, Jul, but I've got some things to tell you also. Why don't we go for a walk? It's a nice day. C'mon."

Julie folded her arms. "See what I mean? This is not a nice day kind of talk. No, my roommate's gone for the weekend! I want to talk in my room."

"Okay, Jul, okay, we'll go up to your room. No problem."

"Then don't interrupt me when I'm talking! Oh, I'm sorry, excuse me, Jo, guess I'm pretty upset about this." She looked down at her stomach. "I mean this baby!" She started back to the dorm, leaving him at the car.

They climbed the stairs to the second floor, entered her room, and closed the door. Jomo sat on her bed, and she sat on her roommate's. She put her hands on her knees, looked straight at him, and said soberly, "I'm pregnant. It's for sure. I feel it, too. So, now what do we do?"

"What do you want to do?"

"Not me, what do we do? And don't try to put this all on me. I mean it!"

"Well, I've been thinking about this all the way up here."

Julie was almost sarcastic. "Go on, and tell me what you've been thinking!"

He got up and went to the small refrigerator for a soda, popped the top, sat back down on the bed, and pressed on, "First, Jul, there's a few things I have to tell you. Why I came up here today, for starters." He searched for the right words. "I don't know how to tell you."

"Do you have another girlfriend? What's the big deal here?"

"No, Jul it's not that. I love you. There's more to all this though. There's more that I just found out myself, it's complicated, and I don't know how you'll take it."

"Found out what? Found out from who?"

"Found out from my dad. We had a fight."

"Your dad? How could he matter?"

"He told me a few days ago, and then we told my mom. Well, he did, but I was there."

"What are you talking about? They've got nothing to do with this!"

Jomo got up and started pacing.

Julie, impatient with this odd exchange, ordered him in a raised voice, "Jo, sit down! Sit down and tell me what this is all about!"

He sat back down. "I could start from the beginning, but I can't."

Julie, at a low boil, said, "I'm listening. Start anywhere. Just tell me what the hell is going on here! I'm pregnant, and you're playing word games!"

Jomo dropped his head on his hands. "Okay, I'll be going to Norway soon with my dad and maybe my mom. We're going to—"

"What? I'm pregnant! Do you hear me? We have no real plans, and you come here saying you're going to be traipsing off to Norway with your folks? Are you crazy? What about me and the baby? What about football? You're nuts!"

"Hey, let me finish, just give me a minute here!"

Julie frowned. "Is there anything real in your life, Jo? Let me put it another way 'cause I don't think you get it. This is already bad. Are you trying to make it worse?"

"Well, let me tell you why."

Her voice softened. "Everything to you is the next race. The next Africa. Look at me!" She pointed to her face. "I'm pregnant, Jo. Nobody can see it yet, but I'm pregnant. I'm in the mathematics master's degree program at Yale. Can you hear me?"

Jomo sighed, and plowed ahead in a low voice, "Before I was born, my dad went on a wooly mammoth dig in

Northern Norway. He found a perfectly preserved Cro-Magnon Stone Age man, marked the spot, and told no one."

Julie, surprised at the turn he was taking with the conversation, listened with her mouth open, not knowing where it was headed. "So?"

"That's where we're going, Jul, to dig him up and bring him back to the Smithsonian Institute."

She raised her voice again. "But what's the big deal you have to go with? I need you now, Jo, here! Don't you see it? We have to decide what the hell to do and make a plan! I'm so upset, I can't even think!"

"I have to go on the expedition to Norway, Jul!"

"Why? What? Leave? Are you running out on me?"

Just then, there was a loud rap on the door. "Security! Is everything okay in there?"

Julie went to the door and opened it. A uniformed campus cop peeked around Julie and saw Jomo. Jomo looked back at him and the gun in his holster. "Everything okay in here, Julie?" he asked again.

"Yes, Sam, it's okay. This is Jo. He's my boyfriend. We're trying to work something out. We're okay, really."

Sam looked closely at her eyes. "Okay? Sure?"

"Yeah, Sam, we're okay here, but thanks." She closed the door, sat down, and continued. "You can't go anywhere. Why do you have to dig up this man?"

Jomo grimaced with pain at Julie's pointed question. His body language showed he was cornered. He knew he would have to drop the bomb now. He opened his hands as if asking for mercy, and said, "Because he's my biological father, Julie. My dad has proven it through DNA tests. There's no doubt that Nice is my mother and the Stone Age man in the ice in Norway is my biological father." He stopped talking because he could see she had turned pale. She had both hands over her mouth and looked like she would pass out as she took in all that Jomo had just said.

With her hands over her mouth, she responded, "Then you're half Stone Age. So then what's growing inside me?"

Jomo jumped up, went to hold her, and laid her head down on the pillow so she wouldn't faint. She took a little of his soda then put both hands on her stomach. Looking at the ceiling, she cried, "What have I got growing in me? What have I got growing in me?" By now she was panicking.

Jomo interrupted, "I had to tell you. I just learned a couple days ago myself. My mother had me through in-vitro. My dad brought back that man's sperm from the mammoth dig."

Julie's eyes were like a caged animal's. "I thought I knew you, but I don't know you at all! How could I have—no, no!"

Both were quiet for a few minutes, as they tried to take in all that had been said.

"This is very wrong, Jo. This can't be happening to me."

Jomo moved closer to her, but she evaded him. "Don't touch me!"

"Maybe I shouldn't have told you, but it was all going to come out after the trip anyway."

"Maybe what?" She tried to pull herself together, but all that came out was, "There's a Stone Age baby growing inside me, and that's all you can say?"

"I love you. I love you, Jul."

"Why me?" Her anger turned to sadness, and she began to cry.

Jomo looked at the carpet for a full five minutes as she cried, and then he started again. "Listen to me. Per studied the man's genes. He says they're good, says he lived in a time when the earth was pure, no toxic air or water, no chemicals, no processed food, no preservatives." He stopped to watch her.

She just lay on the bed, shaking her head over and over in a trance. Then she stopped suddenly. "What if it's ugly? What if it's like a Stone Age? What if I hate it? What if I want to kill it?"

He grabbed her by the shoulders. "Julie, stop this, please look at me. We've known each other all our lives. Look at me. I'm healthy, normal. Remember when we were young? Did I look different to you then?"

Julie looked hard at him like never before, ran her hands over his face, and reached for his hand. He took it tenderly. "I'm normal," he pleaded.

Her hands went back to her lower stomach area, and she was still as she felt the area carefully. "What will I do now?"

"Well, we—"

"No, you don't understand. Maybe I should get an abortion, and I don't even know about you." She slowly pulled her hand away from his.

Jomo instinctively knew the meaning of this act. His heart hurt as tears fell silently down his face and landed on his pants.

"I love you, Jo, but you have to go now. I need time to think about this, about you, about me, and about an abortion."

"Julie."

"No, please, just go. I don't know when I'll call you, but please don't call me."

Jomo got up, leaned over to kiss her, and she turned her head. With tears still flowing, he went to the door, opened it, and turned back. "I love you, Julie," he said one last time as he shut the door. She heard him repeat, "I love you, Jul. I love you, Jul," as he walked down the hall.

She went to the window and watched as he walked to his car shoulders slumped. She thought, *You've got a game coming up.*

As Jomo got in, he looked up, but she didn't wave. As he drove away, she pulled the shades, went over to the desk, picked up an advanced mathematics text book and looked at a white sheet of paper she'd written some equations on. Eyes still glazed, she set the paper in the book, closed it, and placed it on the shelf with her other math books. She lay down on the bed, where she tossed and turned for hours. Finally, she slept.

25

Two MONTHS AFTER Per revealed his secret to the family, the Jorlands, accompanied by Dr. Carl Witkop, boarded the jet to Oslo. Because of a clause in his contract regarding extraordinary family situations, Jomo was allowed to miss one game a season—all the time he needed for the expedition. They were to meet up with representatives of the Norwegian government and elected Lapp politicians representing Finnmark immediately after landing, then quickly catch another flight further North. The unprecedented project was to be filmed for a documentary which would be shared with the world, revealing Per's and now the Jorland family's secret.

A month earlier, an advance team using a powerful metal detector had reached the remote site, and a definite positive metal reading was found exactly where Per's GPS log indicated he had placed the ice ax twenty-six years earlier.

During the seven hour flight, Carl discussed with the family a little of what was potentially known about the man in the ice, if Per's story was found to be correct.

"This is the farthest North a mammoth and this Cro-Magnon man have ever been discovered in Norway. So this is new. The site survived because of its altitude. The largest discovery of pristine mammoth and mastodon bones is at high altitude near Snowmass Ski Resort in Aspen, Colorado, so I'm not at all surprised at this high altitude discovery in Finnmark. Around ten thousand years ago, two thousand years after your biological father, a gigantic earthquake and resulting tsunami decimated the Norwegian coastline and lower areas. It has always been thought that this area was too locked in glaciers or ice to support life, but with this find, it could be said some early humans must have ranged this far North in search of food—that wooly mammoth, for instance. Further, this tribe was able to adapt to the colder temperatures.

"It's that simple. Who knows, perhaps life was easier in the cooler climate than farther South where tribal territory was lost and won by wars." Carl opened a bag of nuts, popped a few in his mouth, and then continued. "Look, Jomo, I may be talking out of school here, but Per told me you were having trouble with your girlfriend. I mean, about her, well, about her being pregnant and all."

Jomo looked down, closed his body language at Carl's forthrightness, and replied, "Yes, it's true, Carl. She'll probably get an abortion, and I guess we're done, over. I just don't know."

Carl interrupted, hoping to stop Jomo from a downward spiral of depression. "Listen to me. There are some important things you need to know about yourself that maybe no one's told you. Maybe you're secretly trying hard to put a good face forward here when down deep you wonder about this Stone Age blood running through your veins. Am I right?"

Carl looked at him without a smile as Per and Nice strained to hear the conversation over the hum of the jet engines.

"It's written all over your face, Jomo. You're in pain. I barely even know you, but I can see it."

Jomo looked at Carl blankly, feeling his armor being stripped from him. "Okay, then. What's so important? You can tell me. I've lost Julie. I'm unsure who I am. I think I've forgiven my dad, yet life is complicated right now."

"Then listen to me! You've been hearing the terms Stone Age and Cro-Magnon for far too long! There's more to it, Jomo, so much more to it."

Jomo exhaled. "Then what, Carl, what? Nothing can change that!"

"Now listen! The term *Cro-Magnon* is meaningless."

"What?"

"It's meaningless to you. It's simply the name of a place in a small town in Southern France where some early modern human bones and skulls were found in the 1860s! That's all! Since about twenty to thirty years ago, these people are referred to as simply early modern humans. Homo sapiens, just like you and me, right down to the subspecies."

"But I thought Stone Age people were subhuman."

"I figured that and so many others also. The term *Cro-Magnon*'s not used anymore. It was originally meant to separate these early modern humans from the Neanderthals, that classic cave look. You know that half-animal look with matted hair from all the old textbooks."

Jomo cocked his head to the side. "So I'm not Stone Age."

"No, Jomo, you're not. You're 50% early modern human. These early modern humans looked just like you and me. You could give 'em a haircut, sweatshirt and jeans, put 'em in a line at McDonalds, and you'd never know. They were about the same height as most Europeans today. They were built stronger, and surprisingly, their brains were slightly bigger than ours. And yes, their faces were as modern as ours, the same."

"But why should all this make me feel better?"

"Because you are a normal human being. Unique, yes, but normal just the same. And if I may be so bold here"— Carl paused, looked at Per and Nice—"that baby that Julie carries is normal too!"

"Dr. Witkop! I didn't know that."

"Jomo, you don't need to say anything. I understand." Carl put his hand on Jomo's shoulder as tears began to flow down his cheeks. Jomo broke down and cried quietly. Nice and Per were strapped in and could only watch their son as Carl comforted him.

"Okay, Jomo, glad you're back with me here. Some scientists believe the proud Basques of Northern Spain and the Western Pyrenees are direct descendants of the early modern humans that lived in that area. Again, no difference except for his time in history, Jomo, he was not different from us. Per's studied his DNA and says it's 99.999 percent the same as modern humans.

"Part of that minute difference is in their mitochondria. They were like us, the same, except maybe their mitochondria were more adapted to hunting and chasing big game rather than planting crops. Maybe their mitochondria degenerated a little in their ability to produce energy molecules due to an ever-increasing agricultural lifestyle. Call it a sort of reverse natural selection where the less fit became very successful in reproducing. The farmers got the girls for the first time in human history, just kidding. These were hunters, Jomo, but there were yet no gatherers for four thousand years."

Somehow, it all hit home with Jomo. His eyes opened wide, and he was astounded by this statement. "This guy goes way back! That's as long ago to us as when the pyramids were built!"

"Yes, he had a brain as large as ours, spoke a language, and most of all, was creative—the true mark of intelligence. There are seventeen thousand year old cave paintings in France that rival the great works of Picasso. I've seen them, Jomo. They're fascinating. Quality for the pure sake of quality.

"This man would have had a home, a family, and a tribe. Sure, iron or bronze had not been discovered yet, but he probably lived a good life. He cried, laughed, and at his age, was a leader, a hunter-warrior. He buried elders. He had leisure time and used utensils. Yes, utensils, Jomo. His hut probably was not much different than the Saami laavos you'll be sleeping in soon. And get this, talk about creative.

In Southern Germany, researchers found a forty-thousand year old flute made from a bird's leg! A flute, Jomo! Imagine them sitting around a fire playing a flute and singing songs.

"Jomo, like I first said, except for time, this man was just like us, and you, Jomo, are truly a man in time. And speaking of time, here comes dinner," Carl said, smiling as the flight attendant began placing their meals on the tray tables in front of them.

"I love the roast beef served in first class, don't you, Dad?" Jomo said, picking up his knife and fork, not waiting for a reply. His unexpected humor surprised Per and Nice. They all broke into a long overdue laugh. Jomo was back.

Haakon Bjornson from the University of Oslo's Department of Natural Science met the four as they deplaned the SAS flight from New York. After introductions, he commented with a degree of doubt in his voice, "I hope your clothing will be adequate. In December and January, temperatures can drop to minus thirty-five degrees Fahrenheit in the mountainous regions of Finnmark."

Per nodded in agreement but countered, "Oh, we'll be okay."

Jomo looked confused, having never heard the term.

Identifying his expression, Haakon continued, "Finnmark is the Northernmost county of the nineteen counties in Norway. In this county is the Northernmost town in the world. Only the Saami live there. They can take the cold of the Arctic winter. Come, we'll have to hurry to make our connection to Wideroe Airlines. We'll be stopping along the way in Narvik to refuel and take on mail, and then it's on to Hammerfest. Your supplies have already been airlifted from Tromso to Hammerfest.

"Six Saami workers and a shaman have been at the site for two days now. They've set up the laavos and are ready to dig when we arrive."

"What's a shaman?" Jomo asked.

"The Saami shaman is their medicine man. They believe he can predict the future. I think the workers are a little bit nervous about disturbing the spirit of the iceman, so they want the shaman there for protection during the actual dig," Carl replied.

Nice, quiet till now, was beginning to wonder what she'd gotten herself into. "Spirits, spirits, schmirits!" she huffed. "My father always talked of spirits, but to be honest with you, I never saw one, never heard one. Once my father broke out of a deep sleep in the hut yelling, 'Spirits! Spirits!' It was the neighbors throwing dishwater over their boma," she said laughingly. Haakon joined her in a hearty laugh.

Later, the flight from Narvik to Hammerfest was a bumpy ride. They were well above the Arctic Circle now, and it was becoming darker and darker below—the endless Arctic night. Even from eight thousand feet, the sun only cast a pink glow.

"How long will the dig take?" Nice cautiously queried, looking out the window into darkness.

"About a week," Haakon replied, noting her concern. "Maybe less."

"If I get too cold in that tent, will you make arrangements to have me flown to Hammerfest? I have to know what happens here."

Haakon chuckled. "Of course, but we'd have to radio for the helicopter. If the weather's bad, as it often is this time of year, they might come or they might not."

"Hmm. That's not very reassuring."

Haakon looked over at Per. "We have to do this in winter to assure the ice block containing the man doesn't begin to melt as it's being airlifted to Hammerfest."

"That's how it went with the mammoth," Per added.

Haakon went on. "Plans have been changed. From there, it'll be placed in a specially built and powered deep cooler aboard a Norwegian military cargo plane and flown to Oslo. The Smithsonian Institute has arranged a US cargo line to bring it across the pond. I've covered every detail. Oh, I should tell you all, the Saami are more than a little upset about the five million US dollars that the institute is paying the Norwegian government for the ice man. It's like in America where, if an artifact or sacred bones are dug up on a Native American reservation, the Indians believe permission must be first granted from their chief and their council. The Saami and the governor of Finnmark are in a flap because they were not involved in the expedition's planning, and worse, they received only part of the five million dollar payment."

"You don't expect any trouble at the dig, do you?" Per asked in worried surprise.

"No! It'll be too damn cold for any trouble in total darkness!" He laughed. "Can you imagine busing in for a reindeer sled protest? This whole deal's been authorized by the prime minister and cabinet. I've got the papers right here in my coat. I was there when they voted. Even the king, who delegates his power to the prime minister, was there."

"Well, I'll be glad when it's over, and we're back in New York," Nice quipped. "I'm a Kenyan, not a Saami."

Haakon nodded. "Maybe this is not for you, Nice."

Per added, "If you like, we'll set you up in Hammerfest in their best hotel with hot running water. Maybe you'd like a room overlooking the fjord."

"We've been married so long, you always know what I'm thinking."

"Thank you, but we both know that's not true."

"But if you're not there, Mom, you won't be in the documentary film of the dig. You won't be running your hands over six inches of ice with the man's eyes staring out at you."

Nice laughed so hard she nearly fell over. "Jo, I've had lots and lots of time in front of the camera lens over the years, and sometimes fantasy and reality never meet. I think there's something Swahili about that, but I can't think of it right now. Maybe when I'm warmer, someday, it'll come to me!"

"Yes, Jo, that probably won't be happening. Sorry," Per jumped in. "We'll be keeping him encased in at least three feet of ice all around. We'll probably just see a dark form, that's all."

Haakon, amused at the interplay of this interesting family, turned to Dr. Witkop who had just awakened from a travel weary nap. The incessant hum of the motors had changed. "We'll be landing soon, and then we'll all get a good night's sleep before meeting the chopper that'll take us up to the site." He turned to Nice. "Think about a hot bath and a good sleep. You'll have about twelve hours before you must decide whether you're in or out of the dig. You, Jomo, there's plenty of hard work ahead. We'll need you." Haakon thought about what a surreal ironic scene that would be: a son digging up his biological Stone Age father, who's holding a titanium ice ax while encased in ice at minus thirty-five degrees Fahrenheit far above the Arctic Circle—the stuff of a great adventure novel.

The bone chilling effect an Arctic winter has on a human accustomed to warmer climate hits home with the first breath of fresh air. In one physical act of hopping down from the chopper, the brain comprehends. First, you feel it on the tip of your nose, next your eyebrows, and then your fingers. You're a foreigner. This is the Serengeti of the North—snow, wind, ice, and stars. You quickly learn it's clothing, fire and shelter, or die.

As the chopper disappeared over the horizon, the popping sound of its blades morphed into a new rhythm; the sound of a single drum versus the eerie void of Arctic air.

The drum abruptly stopped, and a weathered face with a red cap peaked out from the flap of the third laavo. "Come in." Dropping their packs, the four entered the laavo to see a little man with twinkling eyes seated close to the fire with a reindeer skin drum between his knees. Two wooden mallets lay at his side, temporarily silent. He spoke few words, but when he did, each sentence was short, to the point, and followed by a long silence.

Jo thought, *He speaks with his silence as part of his words like Grandpa Jomo did in Kenya.*

"I am Shaman."

Per opened. "We are honored, Shaman. You have allowed us on your land. We will respect it, do our work, and leave quickly. My name is Per and with me are Carl, Haakon, and my son, Jomo."

The shaman had a raven on his right shoulder. It would not take its eyes off Jomo. Per was surprised when Jomo spoke first.

"What does the raven eat?"

"Reindeer meat. I give him what I can share, but he knows there is a reindeer carcass ten kilometers to the

North. He never goes hungry. When I have none, he brings me food."

"Why does he stay with you?"

"He has chosen me. He tells me the coming weather and when to turn."

"Turn where?"

"To another way. I see by looking outside of you that your word is good. You are all good."

Jomo joined. "Thank you for your trust."

"This is not about my trust, young man. This is about your trust."

Per nodded with a slight smile.

Jomo cocked his head. "What do you mean, my trust?"

"You all must trust me as the diggers trust me. You, Jomo, will be digging. Until you leave, both good and bad spirits will try to enter you. If you trust me, I will protect you from the bad spirits."

Per bowed at this. "What of the bad spirits?"

"The bad spirits will try to hold the ice man. I have been hired to protect you and turn their tricking back on them. When you leave here, you can give me a tip."

The four were silent at this carnival-like turn of play. The shaman closed his eyes, reached for a stick, and stirred the embers using only the sound and the feel of the stick. No one spoke as all eyes fixed on the end of the stick and how it moved through the colors of red and black. Then suddenly, the shaman opened his eyes wide, looked straight at Jomo, and spoke clearly and with purpose, "Let me see your hands."

Jomo took off his gloves. The gloves he'd brought were already inadequate, and he was glad when Per had told him before the chopper dropped them off that he had slipped some big lined leather mitts in his pack.

The shaman took Jomo's right hand, brought it close in the firelight, and quietly said, "You are right handed."

Jomo nodded.

The shaman slowly placed Jomo's right hand to his cheek and held it there. Then with a lower voice, he quietly mumbled in a broken English, "You're hand is cold, but it will be warm."

Puzzled, Jomo replied, "What? What did you say?"

"Your hand is cold, but it will be warm," the shaman repeated, this time more seriously, and then turned his attention to his drum and tightened his knees around it.

Jomo thought, *What's he saying? How did he know Dad put those mitts in my pack? I haven't even unpacked them yet. Dad just told me in the chopper! How could he know that?*

Per looked at Jomo as Jomo looked back at Per. As if to say he knew what Jomo was thinking, he simply shrugged and said, "I don't know, Son."

The shaman then picked up his mallets and began the tempo where he'd left off. Over the beat, he spoke loudly, "You must go now. Work and leave quickly. I have been beating on this drum for days in preparation. I am tired. If it stops, I cannot protect you."

The four arrivals left quickly and moved into their laavo. Time to work.

Jomo was sweating. His halogen headlamp had cracked in the deep cold. He and six Saami, each with their own six-by-six inch poles, levered the ice block up just enough to get the metal carriage underneath it. The heavy duty nylon straps would be woven into the frame the next day. They were all cold and tired from a week's worth of digging a six foot wide trench into the ice all around the dark block. The smell of oily chainsaws seemed to be permanently fixed in his nose. His fingers were swollen, cold, and stiff inside his gloves. Frost from his breath caked his face. Muscles between his shoulders and neck were pleading for rest. His parka bore the angry bites of a runaway chainsaw blade.

He thought of his mother and knew Nice had made the right decision to stay in Hammerfest. This was no place for her. She'd have her time but not now, not here, in this cold hell. *Maybe she was sleeping now or opening the door for room service or reading the headlines in* Verdens Gang, *the Norwegian newspaper, about the expedition in Finnmark.*

He thought, *What's going to happen with Julie? I had to tell her before it would be all over the papers and TV. I had to! It didn't go well at Yale. She told me not to call. Maybe it's done. Maybe we're done. All those years together, and it's done. I guess I don't blame her. What woman could handle marriage, sex, children, even going to the grocery store with me after what I told her? I don't blame her for getting an abortion. I'm too cold to think about what we could have had together. I've got to work now.*

Nothing in football was ever this difficult or were the Olympic gold medals. It was so cold. The Saami worked in thermal insulated Carharts covered by reindeer skins. They never complained, yet Jomo could see they were suffering just as he was. They were tough. Two hours of work in these temperatures is equal to eight in a warm setting. You start to get a headache. It consumes you as it turns into a body ache, and then you don't feel. Your steps are slower, and then you feel like you're getting sick but know it's only the cold. It's hard to think straight. A simple task becomes epic and always, always the cold pressing on your every square inch of exposed skin. Day never comes. Disorientation. A cold dream of something you came to do, a dream hard to remember.

Per was also exhausted. He and the two professors had tried to help with the digging and sawing ice early on, but they were older, softer, and their academic way of life was apparent when they could no longer continue. They only left the shelter of the warm laavo to bring hot coffee and jerky to the workers, monitor progress on the dig, and continue the filming for the documentary in shifts. This was a young man's job, and Jomo was determined to see it to completion. The older men were good cooks though, so delicious, steaming dinners and rich, hot chocolate were available in large quantities on request.

Funny, Jomo thought, *it came down to seven guys sweating and slowly freezing at the same time down in a trench in a forgotten arctic valley in semi-darkness when millions of dollars would be spent and millions of humans would one day come to view the efforts of this icy dig.*

They woke up, ate, worked, ate, and fell asleep to the endless cadence of the shaman's drums beating, beating, beating. Sometimes the wind played along in octaves. Sometimes when the air was still, the drum's concussions were accentuated on the laavos's frozen skin. The shaman was doing his job, all right. Maybe the spirits didn't like the chainsaws, but at least they stopped for twelve hour periods. The drums seemed to never stop. Maybe the spirits didn't like the drums. Maybe the spirit was still in the pouch Jomo had stuffed inside his parka. Maybe it didn't want to go back to the cold body. He thought, *Don't his arms ever get tired of beating? Maybe there is no spirit, and I've done all these things in my life on my own. He doesn't even look like a shaman anyway with that Nike sweatshirt and faded red Coca Cola cap. Too cold, it's just too cold to think about it all anyway. I must keep working.*

The cadence was acid etched in one's mind like granite claw marks on a slick wall in the Grand Canyon. *Beating drums. Beating drums. Continually beating on and on. Think. Think.* Then it was over.

Back in the laavo, the four ate reindeer meat, canned sardines, and the last of the hot chocolate but were too exhausted to talk. Even the shaman could manage only one drum beat every half hour. The once lively expedition had withered.

Per, Haakon, and Carl were already asleep. As Jomo stoked the fire one last time and retreated deep into layers of reindeer hides, he wondered, *Will one drum beat be enough to keep away the bad spirits while I sleep until the chopper arrives tomorrow and we're up and out?*

Jomo drifted deeper and deeper into an exhausted sleep. *He quietly got up, slipped out of the laavo, and found himself down in the dig. Not a sound. He moved around the cube as if floating then spied the hand extending out of the ice block, beckoning yet motionless.*

He took it in his right hand and clasped it. He clasped his father's hand. It was warm. Oh my God, it's warm! Jomo was paralyzed, mesmerized. No! Where are the drums? No drums. The drums, oh, where are the drums? Instantly, he snapped his hand back. He collected himself and cautiously reached out his hand to again grip the extended hand of his ancient father. He touched a finger, then the thumb, then three more, and then a light yet firm grip. Warm. The hand was warm and warmed his hand.

Jomo stopped, relaxed, and thought, There is no danger here. My father is warming my cold hand just as the shaman said he would, as a father would his child.

The drums began again. Now they were faint, very faint, far off, then growing slowly, becoming louder, and then melding into that hypnotic rhythm—that mindless rhythm of no space, no time, no thought, a blankness of empty yet full, of cold yet warm.

A crack, no, a crackle. Jomo opened one eye. There was a crackle from the fire. He opened both eyes to see an odd pattern traced in the coals. He sat up. Per and Carl and Haakon were still deep asleep under their hides. He saw the pouch by his pack and reached over to pick it up. It was warm. Jomo fell back into a deep sleep.

Per watched with his arm around Jomo as the Navy Sea Stallion withdrew the cube of evidence past from its place. "Those 12,175 years, just an eye wink on a graph of time," Per waxed. "As I was a younger man then, now I'm an older man, and you are the younger. It is the circle of life, Jo."

Carl and Haakon watched the two embrace; their stiff parkas hardly allowing their arms to circumvent each other's backs. The helicopter was waiting. The shaman hitched a ride back to Hammerfest. He had told the raven to leave the night before the storm. Jomo made certain his drums were buried back with the cargo in the other helicopter. Then, to show his respect for a job well done, Jomo gave him his official players' team cap from the New York Giants. Inside the inner band, he had slipped five one hundred dollar bills.

The weathered expression of gratitude was enough to tell all had gone well with the spirits. Gratefully, with a five tooth smile, he removed the Coca Cola dozer hat and donned the colors of the Giants. Jomo nodded with approval.

The rotors hummed. They were going home.

Simultaneously, the screen went blank as the lights came on.

Reporters from world news agencies streamed through the exit doors and were directed to the conference room set up for the media beforehand. Sitting behind the microphone at the head table were the Jorlands. The paparazzi jostled for the best camera angle.

A spokesperson for the Smithsonian Institute tested the microphone and began to speak, "All you've seen in this extraordinary documentary of the excavation and analysis of the early modern human is true and thoroughly documented. His genetic profile has been verified by three independent genetic laboratories in the United States, Sweden, and the United Kingdom. There is absolutely no doubt the 12,175 year old Stone Age man is indeed Jomo Jorland's biological father. Next week, an enhanced version of the film you just saw will be broadcast worldwide on the Discovery Channel. A complete transcript of the film is available at the door. Now, regarding the family's wishes, we ask you to make no moral judgments in your articles. The family has no statement to make at this time.

They simply wanted to be here to show you, the press, they stand unified as a family. By going public, they have made an enormous contribution to science. I know it was a hard decision for them. This truly is an exciting day not only for the Smithsonian Institute, the Jorland family, and AnGen but the entire scientific world.

"The knowledge we will gain from the Stone Age man and his son, Jomo, will help us rewrite the genetic history of the human race. Ladies and gentlemen, this is big! Some hypotheses will fall, and some will survive the scrutiny. This new mitochondria discovery has the potential to be a game changer. Thank you all for coming."

With cameras flashing, and security guards clearing a path, the Jorlands made their way to their car and sped off.

It was just as Per had predicted. Jomo went under the media microscope like never before. It was too great a story for the tabloids to resist: NFL Star Is a Stone Age Caveman! *The thing about it was, it was partly true. At first, I thought he might be falling into a depression because of his decision to go public, but as I watched it all play out, I changed my mind. Jomo kept it all inside and tried not to show it. All he really had left was football. Julie was gone. After they delivered the massive ice block to the Smithsonian, he'd changed. He stopped all interviews. But I liked him.*

At the time, I hadn't yet heard about his dreams and meeting his younger brother in the afterlife. Much later, as I interviewed him for my story, he spoke of the gift of how to walk through life with the fullness of family those dreams gave him. He had found his place and lineage among the seven billion people on earth.

26

PER FLIPPED THROUGH the channels and stopped on the FOX News Network. The *Olympic Update* show was about to begin. "Nice, could you please hurry? It's on," he called to her from the living room.

> This is a big one that suddenly came on the world scene. A consortium of countries led by the Kenyans lodged its formal complaint with the International Olympic Committee in Lausanne, Switzerland. They're challenging Jomo Jorland's seven Olympic gold medals won two years ago at the Summer Games in India.
>
> The issue surrounding the huge brouhaha is whether or not Jomo, with his Stone Age father's genes, is a hybrid or not. If the vote goes down that he is, he will be stripped of all that gold. His defense is that his entire DNA genome is naturally occurring, and that only time separates his biological mother and father. Nonetheless, our sources indicate there are some members of the voting committee who are sympathetic to their challenge. Our sources tell us, this one will be decided quickly. One thing is certain: the vote will be close. Stay tuned, FOX News will keep you up-to-date and informed. In other news...

"Now, let us address the matter of Jomo Jorland of the United States."

The aura of the Kenyan ambassador still filled the room. The fourteen fixed their gazes at the letter now situated squarely before their president. Finally looking up, they raised their eyes almost in unison to the gray-haired gentleman for his guidance. Removing his bifocals, he slowly leaned back in his chair and cleaned them with his handkerchief. As he pushed himself forward, he covered the letter with the palm of his right hand. "This will be hard and unpopular either way, but we are charged with the mission to judge independently of government agencies, all, and any groups or other interests. Our objectivity is crucial. Granted, our voting on this issue before us will be extraordinary. However, we will not be and never have been swayed by outside opinion. We must remain autonomous of all influence."

With purpose, he put his glasses back on, frowned, and continued. "Now for the track and field protest. We will review the evidence and discuss the issue of the Kenyan protest today and interview Jomo Jorland's parents by internet conference call tomorrow. Following that call, there will be the final vote. Are there any questions or objections to this protocol?"

Hearing none, the president went on, "Then it is decided. We'll proceed with that plan then."

The next morning, Per waited at the computer with Nice at his side. The conference call from the voting Olympic executive committee was scheduled for 7:00 a.m. US Eastern time. Before the final vote, the committee wanted to hear Jomo's parents' statements.

Nice looked squarely at the screen as the committee members appeared. Behind her in plain view of the voting committee was the display case containing Jomo's seven gold medals.

The Olympic Executive Committee president began. "Hello, Dr. and Mrs. Jorland. We have reviewed the Kenyan protest over Jomo's seven gold medals. In a nutshell, the Kenyans believe his medals should be stripped because of his unusual genetic makeup, as you know. If Jomo's medals are taken away, the Kenyans stand to gain three of those medals, the Brits and the Jamaicans, two. Before we vote to either grant or strip Jomo of his medals, the committee would like to hear from both of you as to why you believe he should be allowed to keep them. Mrs. Jorland, by coincidence, you grew up in Kenya. You may proceed first."

Looking at the camera, Nice smiled. "Yes, thank you for this opportunity to speak. Jomo is our son and we love him. There is nothing about his genes that have been modified. His DNA is 100 percent naturally occurring. Only time separates the two who contributed to it. Furthermore, you must stop to think and consider that he and his extraordinary will to win earned him the medals. I'm saying to you, he did it on his own and did it fairly. The medals belong to him. I trust your ability to make the proper, rational judgment."

"Thank you, Mrs. Jorland. Dr. Jorland, you may begin."

Per, sitting next to his wife, looked into the camera. "Yes, thank you for hearing my statement. The will to win, to never give in, never give up, is not an inherited trait in humans and never has been. There is no DNA makeup that can replace that which lies deep inside every champion— whether it be in sports, academics, military, or the arts, and that factor is desire.

"Yes, I have determined that Jomo's mitochondria are different from modern humans, but all that can be deduced from that is this is but one theory why he is an Olympic champion on the track. After all is said, no one can prove that his mitochondria made him a winner. Here in the US, we have a term, *couch potato*. Without great desire, he never could have risen to such great heights. There are so many other factors, but desire is the greatest of these.

"Instinct is inherited. Desire is not. Do any of you honestly believe a man can inherit the insignia of a Navy SEAL or an Army Ranger? Let's talk specifically about Olympic competition.

"I see most of you are old enough to recall that Olympic hockey game of 1980 where a US team of college kids beat arguably the best hockey team in the world, the Russian Red Team. The term *miracle on ice* was coined by the media, not by any of the US players. Anyone on that team including their coach, Herb Brooks, who now has left us, will tell you that game was not won on a miracle, genes, inheritance, or any of that bologna—it was hard work, a never-give-up, never-give-in attitude, and that's desire.

"Ladies and gentlemen of the executive committee, Jomo is our son, and we know him. Through his life he has shown his courage, good judgment, and determination to accept a challenge, but most of all, he has shown us those two unique factors all winners have and those are love of life and desire. No doubt about it. He earned those medals! Thank you."

"Thank you, Dr. and Mrs. Jorland. We are ready to vote and will be back to you shortly. Please stand by. We'll phone you with our decision."

One hour later, the phone rang twice, and Per said quietly to Nice and Jomo, who had just arrived, "This is it. They've decided. You answer it, Jo, and put it on speaker."

"Hello, Dr. Jorland?"

"No, sir, this is Jomo, but my parents are sitting here with me and the speaker is on."

"Hello, Jomo. My name is Jean Claude Tricet. I am president of the Olympic Executive Committee. Now, listen to me carefully. First of all, every member of the committee witnessed your performance at the Summer Olympics in Delhi, India. We have reviewed films of each of the seven individual men's track events you medaled in, including close ups of the starts, mid race, finish line, and even up to one-minute post race of each event. In addition, we reviewed similar films from the last three Summer Olympics.

"I can tell you, this attempt to gather this kind of information is unprecedented. This is not a performance drug doping case. It's about genetics. As you know, the Kenyans have lodged a protest. Their complaint is that your mitochondria are more efficient than modern day athletes, giving you the advantage of not—bear with me here—not running out of breath in each of the seven events you gold medaled in, leading to your victories and your new world records.

"Now, for the record, you received and now own Olympic gold medals in the men's 100 meter, 200 meter, 400 meter, 800 meter, 1500 meter, 3000 meter, and 10,000 meter events. Are you still with me?"

"Yes, sir," Jomo responded in a concerned tone.

"Now, for the committee's vote: Jomo Jorland, I regret to tell you the committee voted 8 to 6 with one abstaining in favor of the Kenyan's protest. I am sorry, Jomo, truly sorry. Do you understand?"

"Yes, sir, I do." Jomo sat down, his expression blank.

"However, it was a double vote. It was unanimously agreed to grant you one gold medal to keep; the men's 100 meter. The remaining six will be awarded to the second place finishers in those events. In addition—this will hurt, and I'm sorry—but every team event, such as relays, you participated in will be disqualified. You will be allowed to compete in future Olympics only in the men's 100 meter.

"I am very sorry, Jomo. You are so talented. Personally, I believe in you and your desire. You are the most amazing athlete I've ever seen in the Summer Olympics, but our vote is final. You are allowed to keep the men's 100 meter gold because, going back three Summer Olympics, the first and second placers in each final were not out of breath. The race is too short to make that happen. Therefore, all racers are equal in this event. I'm sorry this is parsing. You will receive a letter from me to document our vote and to arrange for the transfer of six of your gold medals. Now, just between you and me, I hope to see you in the next Summer Olympics."

"Well, sir, after this news, I don't know. Of course, that's two years from now. Maybe I'll feel like defending my record then."

"That's the spirit, Jomo! That's what I was hoping to hear and do tell your parents how impressed I was that they fought so hard for you. Goodbye, Jomo."

"Goodbye, Mr. Tricet." Jomo slumped in the chair and shook his head over and over.

Nice put her hand on his shoulder, "Oh, Jo. Oh, Jo, I thought we had it. I really did."

Jomo looked up at Per and Nice. Both were stunned.

"This is my entire fault. It was my choice to go public. You warned me, Dad. I know. I worked so hard, and now, my six world records are gone. I earned them." Jomo exhaled and slumped farther into the chair, put his hands on his face and elbows on his knees, and cried. The medals he had in his lap fell to the floor.

Per spoke quietly, "Yes, Jo. I thought we had it too. When we gave our statements, it all seemed so positive. He sounded like he was on our side. I'm so sorry, Jo. We tried. We tried so hard."

Nice gave him a hug. "Yes, Jo, we did all we could. We know you earned those medals, and we'll get through this. You'll get through this. We'll get through this because we're a family, and we love each other, and we give each other support."

"Thanks, Mom. Thanks, Dad."

In a natural move, the three came together in a hug, the one they'd done so often when Jo was a child.

Just before he left for football practice, Per caught him in the driveway as he was pulling out. "Just think about this. Once you've won the medals, you're no longer relevant. Your next life begins. The media grinds and tries to peel you. You're better off with one medal than the seven the world knows you earned. Jo, it's called going out when you're on top. You took the stairs up. Now don't take the elevator down. The 100 meter is the big one; the signature event in track. You're still the fastest-man-in-the-world. Tell you what, Jo, after practice why don't you catch the train back here and spend the night in your old room? I know the Meadowlands are three hours away, but we'd love to have you here."

"Good advice, Dad, and thanks. I might just do that."

That day at practice, Jomo was a non starter. It was all he could do to just go through the motions. Coach took him aside.

"Jo, is something bothering you? You're missing blocks, and you're late on your patterns."

"Coach, the Olympic committee took my gold medals this morning, all of them except the one hundred."

"Oh, Jo, I'm so sorry to hear that. I was really hoping."

"I do feel bad about the medals. I never liked running track. I never liked a coach telling me how to run, so I really don't care about losing them that much. Only one thing that bothers me."

"What's that?"

"The only reason I trained so hard was to beat the Kenyans again."

"I heard that story."

"Yeah. To prove it. No one believed they were really trying."

"Why didn't you like track? You're the best."

"Organized track is so confined. It's not spontaneous like a run in the woods or mountains. That's who I really am, Coach. I feel it."

"I'm listening."

"Why run? I mean, why run? Why should it be such an honor to be the fastest-man-in-the-world?"

"You're one of billions."

"Running in itself is meaningless unless there's an objective such as food or escape. The goal has to be more than some cast gold. Running is pain, but it doesn't take courage like, say, descending a rain slicked mountain at sixty miles per hour in the Tour de France. It's not as impressive as original thought like, say, inventing the light bulb. It's not even enough to be a hero. The term *hero* is used too easily. That's a marine who brings back two injured buddies under fire."

"You know, Jo, you're making sense. I didn't know you had all this in you."

"I'm just working through losing a few medals to the Kenyans I beat."

"I see."

"Now, every time I catch a touchdown pass and the crowd cheers, I think of how it all started that day in the bush and after what my Grandpa Jomo told me."

"May I ask?"

"After we win the Super Bowl."

"Deal."

"Thanks, Coach. Don't worry. I'll get my mojo back. I will!"

"Yeah, I know you will. Fortunately, we've already mathematically clinched a good berth in the division playoffs. I was planning on giving the rookie a lot more game time anyway. Oh, yeah, while you were up in Norway, I had a good talk with the team about you and your, uh, genes. They're all good men. A lot of them voiced their opinions, and I can tell you they're all behind you 110 percent."

"That's good to hear, but I'm surprised."

"Why is that, Jo?"

"Bobby told me the guys are starting to not like me."

"I know about that. All I can tell you is they voted to support you. Can you take a little advice?"

"Okay, I'm ready."

"Self control. Find that fine line between confidence and arrogance."

Jo began to walk away. "Thanks, Coach."

"Not so fast, Jo! Come back here. You're a great player. Tough. I honestly don't think you're even aware of it; this arrogance thing the guys talk about. Have you been this way since you were a kid?"

Jomo raised his eyebrows at the question. "I crushed a kid's hand once, broke a lot of bones. Went to the principal. Never felt bad about it."

"As a kid, what else?"

Jo hesitated, "I don't know if I should talk about this."

"What else? It's just you and me here. Did you get in trouble with the police?"

"No."

"Then?"

"Okay. While I was in Africa with my dad, I killed a guy with a spear."

"My God, Jo!"

"Then I killed another guy with a Rambo knife."

"Jo!" Coach looked down and frowned in pain.

"That's not all, Coach. I killed another two guys with my bare hands. They were gonna rob and kill me. They both died in the hospital."

"Jo, I've got to sit down. With your bare hands? I thought I knew you after rookie camp. Why didn't this come out before the Olympics?"

"Nobody ever asked me. Don't ask me anymore. They were all bad guys. The Kenya National Police liked me."

"Then…one more thing."

"What else?"

Coach lowered his voice and looked at Jo with steel-blue eyes. "Your girlfriend, Julie. Remember when we sat together at the team banquet?"

"Yes. Great night."

"Ever hit her?"

"No, sir. Never!"

"Ever a close one?"

"No, no, sir. Honest."

"Now you listen to me carefully, Jo. Bottom line, if you put one of my players in the hospital, you're done on my team."

"All right, Coach. You have my word."

"Okay, Jo, so you get back out there and get through the day. Tell you what, why don't you take tomorrow off to work through this. The offensive coach is going 100 percent on the rookie anyway."

"Thanks, coach. I was thinking of driving back home to Washington. I'll sleep in tomorrow and spend the day with my parents."

"Stay healthy. We're going to need you in the playoffs." He slapped Jo on the back.

That following morning I gave Per a call at six thirty and woke him up. I was so excited and shaking, I could barely dial the phone.

"Hello?"

"Per?"

"Yeah, it's Larry. Larry Calvert. Wake up!"

"Yeah, Larry? You woke me up. What's going on?"

"Per, this is so exciting, and you don't even know yet?"

"What?"

"What? Your picture's on TV. You're all over the radio."

"Why?"

"You won the Nobel Prize in Medicine and Genetics! It was announced in Sweden while we were still asleep in the US."

"Larry. Wow! I cannot believe it. Larry, I've got to sit down. What are they saying on TV?"

"Listen. They made a last minute vote to include you in this year's ceremony. And not only that, Nice and Jomo are also recipients because this was the family genetic story of the century, maybe of all time. They got honoraries."

"Oh, Larry. Thanks so much, my friend. I couldn't have done this without you. This makes it all worthwhile. Sometimes I thought I was going crazy, but I kept on."

"It wasn't easy for me either, my friend. You know that, and I'm happy for both of us. Now, go wake up Nice. The ceremony in Stockholm is coming up soon. You've got to get crackin'."

"Okay, Larry. Okay."

"Congratulations, Per. Stop by when you get back. Oh, and after you calm down, check your emails. I've sent you one with all the particulars about your Nobel Prize. I'm sure it's an email you'll save along with your letter from the committee."

"Will do. So long. Oh, wait, Larry. Buy a first class airline ticket to Stockholm. I'll pick up the tab. I'm inviting you to the award party. Love to see you there."

"I might just do that, Per. Thanks. Bye for now."

I couldn't help but think about that conversation we had fishing on the Chesapeake so long ago before Nice and Jomo. He talked about impulse and how he lived his life, right or wrong on it, and now he's getting the Nobel Prize.

Per put down the phone and stood by the window, thinking of the huge up-and-down swings in his life and how his secret had caused so much pain. Now was the time to reveal his last secret. He thought, *I'll never keep a secret from them ever again, for the rest of my life.* He exhaled, smiled, and walked quickly to the bedrooms.

"Wake up! Get up! Wake up! Come down to the kitchen. I've got great news."

Bleary eyed still from Jo's previous day's disappointment, they shuffled into the kitchen.

"Per, what's going on?"

"Yeah, Dad, what's up? What's all the commotion about, and why the big smile at seven o'clock in the morning?"

"Okay, you two. Just sit down. My heart's going so fast. I have to settle down."

"Alright, Dad, go. What?"

"I've waited all my professional life to tell you this, and Nice, you know what I mean."

Nice cocked her head and straightened up in her chair.

"Now it's time to tell you my last secret. There will be no more secrets from me ever again." Nice's face turned serious, but Per pushed on. "This secret is about five years old. Remember when I suspected Jomo's gene activation after the deer hunt? I secretly began sending my DNA research on you, Jo, and your biological father to my friend Larry Calvert at the Smithsonian Institute. I could trust him to hold the secret. Our deal was that he would publish the research when I was ready, and then about a year ago, he asked me if he could forward it all to the Nobel Committee in Medicine and Genetics. I agreed knowing that soon I'd have to tell you and Nice.

"I got a call from Larry Calvert this morning. We're on the radio and TV! The Nobel Executive Committee has cast an unprecedented vote to award a second Nobel Prize in Medicine and Genetics to our family for our contribution to research in human genetics! Only the Curies and a handful of others have ever had such a family honor. We are Nobel laureates!" Per said with a smile. "The awards ceremony and banquet is in seven days. I'll make reservations for the Flag Suite at the Grand Hotel in Stockholm."

"Pack your best," Nice said over the mens' voices and immediately took charge.

Per added, "Jo, you and I will be in white tails. I'll arrange to have them at the hotel when we arrive. This is going to be so much fun!"

Nice interrupted, "Well, I have an idea. Per, you call Tambo and have him bring my parents to Stockholm. Except for the wedding trip, they've never been more than a few hundred miles from their village."

"Yeah, and I've got a lot to talk with Grandpa about. I'll start with that spear. I'd like to hear more about that story and a few others."

Nice put up her hand. "Stop, Jo, but what about your football?"

"Oh no! I'm sure coach will let me go. I'll take a pay cut, and the rookie is going to start next game anyway. We've already clinched the playoffs. I'm going. I'll call coach. I'm going, no matter what." Then his mind went to Julie. "I wish Julie could be there."

Nice put her hand on Jo's shoulder. "Jo, you're living in the past. Live in the present. Let the past catch up to you, if it can. Move on. If she still loves you, she will find you. That's the way it works. Otherwise, Jo, you're a Nobel laureate—well, honorary—and you have an appointment in Stockholm you don't want to miss."

Per was across the kitchen, but he could hear in her voice that she was also talking to him.

Nice pulled Per to her and looked straight into his eyes. Jomo took the hint and headed off down the hall.

"Per, you're the best, and I love you," Nice said to him, laying the kind of kiss on him that's hard to forget.

Later, Per went down to his study to read my email.

> *Hi Per,*
>
> *Yes, this is all so exciting. I'm glad I was the one to tell you first. I just talked to my contact in Sweden. In a nutshell, here's how it all went down:*
>
> *First of all, you are getting the big one, the Nobel Prize in Medicine and Genetics. Jomo and Nice are*

receiving honorary Nobels (after all, you couldn't have done it without them).

Second, the recognition of your work: among the most interesting finds from the early modern human and Jomo's DNA is that irrefutable proof has been found that Neanderthals (before they disappeared) did indeed mate with early modern humans and, in doing so, greatly increased our ability to fight infections, disease, even cancer. All of us know of some people that rarely get sick, but if they travel to another part of the world, they can get very sick. This is a phenomenon across the gene pools of the world.

On chromosome 6 are found a small set of genes now believed to be inherited from the Neanderthals. They're known to researchers as the human leukocyte antigen (HLA) class 1 genes. As you know, they carry instructions for making the HLA proteins. Per, your research on Jomo's chromosome 6 was spot on proof.

When early modern humans began their epic trek out of Africa, some mating with the Neanderthal gave the newcomers (us) a speedy way to combat regional-specific parasites, bacteria, viruses, and infections, i.e., we flourished because of our ability to adapt quickly to new regions of the world at the genetic level. Per, I don't need to tell you this will undoubtedly lead to gene splicing research in chromosome 6 to rid specific diseases caused by these bugs.

For example, Jomo is one among billions with his pristine genetic genome. Only you, as his father, could have picked up on the fact he'd never had a cold. Your work discovered he inherited another extremely rare gene sequence from Neanderthals on chromosome 6, and that your results prove that gene sequence creates a genetic-based resistance to the common cold. By attaching a copy of Jomo's unique nucleotide sequence to a virus that is harmless to humans (a vector), the new gene sequence can enter the epithelial surface cells of the sinuses and nasopharynx. Over time, the faulty gene sequence is replaced by another, immune to the common cold virus.

Your work at AnGen to create the nasal spray was genius. Given to babies and toddlers, it's the first true genetic vaccine. I apologize for doubting you. I was wrong. I thought you'd gone off the deep end that day when you showed me your latest research. Instead, you were creating the genetic cure to the common cold. This is really big, Per. I was at the meeting last week, and they wanted me to give you the surprise. Well done. You get the Nobel, my friend, and it's not some cheap, political, hand-greasing prize.

Best regards and congratulations.

Your friend,
Larry Calvert

27

THE JORLANDS ARRIVED in Stockholm five days before the awards ceremony, time enough for walks and sightseeing. Nice dropped an idea. "These last few months have been a real roller coaster ride, haven't they? When this is over, why don't we go somewhere, Per? Just get lost where no one can find us, call us, and email us, nothing. I think it's time, don't you?"

Per smiled and agreed. "You're right. No one in the history of the world ever went through what we've been through. When we get home, it'll be just long enough to pack, what, two swimsuits, four T-shirts, sandals, masks, and fins? Anything else needed, we'll buy when we get there. It'll be kind of like a second honeymoon, Nice. I like the sound of that."

"Sorry, Jo, three's a crowd. Besides", she laughed, "you've got playoffs and a Super Bowl to win."

Per looked at Nice and put his arm around her. It was quiet for just a bit, and their pace had slowed. While walking on that beautiful day around Skeppsholmen and Gamlastan, Stockholm's historic Museum Island not far from the Grand Hotel, Jomo tried to sum it all up.

"Who am I? I know who I am. Not to brag, but I'm the fastest-man-in-the-world. I've got a bio dad I never knew. What's odd about that? There's a guy on my football team who's adopted and another guy whose mom is on her third husband. I had to actually dig through the ice to find him, but now he'll always be in there. I can just drop in to see him or maybe he will visit me in a dream. I'm okay with it."

Then more seriously, he continued, "Only a few weeks ago, I learned who I am. At first, to be honest, I was mad. I've always thought I was different, but never in a bad way."

"It's okay, Jo."

"No, I have to say this. I've always thought I was different in a good way, but there's something natural here. I can live with this now."

Nice and Per looked at their son as a grown man. The three continued on with the walk. An old pelican with a gray face, maybe listening, held its ground in front of them. The old bird nodded, flapped its tattered wings into the breeze, and soared.

Then Jomo broke the silence with a happy tone. "Everything I could have been is because of my ancestors, but the love you've both raised me with has made me who I am. I am Jomo, a man in time."

Nice listened and then elbowed Per gently. "Jo, aren't you forgetting something?"

"Give me a minute. I'll come up with a few more."

Nice stopped her son. "Jo, you're a Maasai warrior. The respected kind, I mean. Remember what those trackers told you around the fire?"

Per chimed in. "Yes, Jo, you are of Nice and you are of Africa."

The Jorlands continued their walk around Gamlastan. Jomo looked to the sky. "Yes, I am Jomo, and I have found my place."

Later, back at the Grand, Per and Jomo were standing at the window admiring the three-masted tall vintage ship moored in Stockholm bay and beyond the Royal Palace. There was a knock at the door, and Nice went to answer it. A hotel steward, dressed splendidly in a white jacket, greeted her. "This is the Flag Suite. This is the room of the Nobel Prize recipients in Medicine and Genetics?" he asked in English with a smile.

"Why, yes it is."

"A gift, compliments of the Grand Hotel, ma'am."

Just then, Jomo and Per walked down the spiral staircase of the glass tower.

"Thank you," Nice answered as the steward placed a huge silver bowl on the table. Even before it reached the table, Jomo grabbed a few grapes. Wrapped in gold and blue ribbons was a magnificent selection of fruits, Swedish cheeses, chocolates, champagne, and aquavit, the infamous Swedish alcohol elixir. The official note read:

> Looking forward to meeting you,
>
> King Karl Gustav

"You might want to get dressed," Per commented, awestruck after reading the note. "The Swedish Foreign Ministry guy will be here soon to escort us to the Stockholm Concert Hall for the awards ceremony." Trying hard to knot his white tie, Per was rescued by Nice.

They had been in Stockholm for five days, each one filled with symposia, parties, and press conferences, but tonight was the grand finale; the awarding of the Nobel diplomas, medals, and of course, the one million dollar prize. Then following the banquet and dance at the Stockholm City Hall, the evening would end with a party at the Grand Hotel's famous Hall of Mirrors, the perfect ending to a perfect week.

Nonkipa and Jomo Nkoe had left Kenya only once before about twenty-seven years ago when they traveled to New York for Nice's wedding. It hadn't been an easy task for Tambo to convince Grandpa Jomo to travel again. Now, they were far older and had never heard of the Nobel Prize nor were they even sure where the country of Sweden could be found. Truth be told, Nonkipa could close her eyes, all these years later, and remember room service and the amazingly soft New York City hotel bed.

Tambo had found an ally in Nonkipa that easily sealed the deal in convincing the elder Jomo. Per had hired Tambo again to travel with the couple and act as translator and guide until they met the family at the Grand Hotel. Nice wanted her parents to have a few days to rest up. She was so proud to have them with her. She had been right. They needed those days not only to absorb beautiful Stockholm but to have times together, perhaps their last.

Per twirled Nice around. "Nice, you have never looked more beautiful, and you were so right to choose a sarong and beads for tonight. Pinch me, please."

"Ha, and look who's taking me to the party", she gestured grandly, "two of the most handsome and strong men to be my escorts and dance partners. Imagine, my men in white ties and tails. Hmm."

All three came together as they had so many times when Jomo was young, but this time Per and Nice knew he had grown to be a man.

"Now, Jo, don't spill on that white tie," she fussed. "I don't have an extra one in my purse."

"Yikes. Mom, I can't believe you just said that," Jo replied, and they all laughed. Then came a knock at the door. Jomo was first to the door. Expecting to see their escort, he opened the door to see Julie standing there as beautiful as a princess in a storybook.

"Julie! I didn't expect to see you here!"

Julie smiled. "Do you remember the day when you told me your secret? Well, I told you then I needed some time. We've been together since fifth grade, Jo, and all this about genes changes nothing. I love you, Jo, and besides, you know me well enough to know I would never miss a great party!" She kissed him.

Jomo pulled back to look at her beauty, and he made no effort to disguise his lowered eyes to a bulge in her belly. He kissed her on the forehead and then took her arm.

Nice smiled and took Per by the hand.

"Mrs. Jorland, do you mind if Jo and I go into another room for a few minutes?"

"I'm not surprised at that. Of course not, Julie. It's so good you came. The king's escort is soon arriving. Go in the bedroom. Quick."

They closed the bedroom door and embraced in a kiss.

"I went to women's services at Yale New Haven Hospital five times. I never told them. They did every test, even a few new ones, checking on DNA-inherited diseases. Everything, Jo."

"What? I know that smile, Jule. So what were the results?"

"My main doc told me before I left for Stockholm our baby is perfectly healthy."

She grabbed him by his shoulders and shook him. "Jo, our baby is healthy and normal."

Jo took her in his arms. With a smile as wide as his great-grandfather's in that faded old lion picture, he said, "Told ya, Jule. Let's get married after all this."

Julie drew back. "Yes, let's get married. I choose you, Jo."

They kissed and went out to tell Nice and Per. Then there was another knock at the door. It was time to go.

The awards ceremony at Stockholm Concert Hall was concluded by a rotund hilarious former laureate who knew when to end his speech when he spied the first yawn in the audience.

The party at the Grand Hotel was well underway. Academic stuffiness had given way to jokes, handshakes, and occasional raucous guffaws and cheers as the champagne was liberally poured.

Nice had not worn the traditional Maasai red kikoi since a shoot for *Vogue* magazine many years ago. Proud and glowing, she sat next to Nonkipa at the round linen table. Nonkipa wore a robe similar to her daughter's.

To her left, Jomo and Per looked resplendent in tuxedos. Grandfather Jomo stood first, a striking sight in his ceremonial Maasai robe, as King Karl Gustav of Sweden approached their table. His eyes fixed on Nice's beauty, and then he smiled individually to each at the honored table.

Raising his glass, he announced to the expectant room of revelers, "A toast to the three laureates in the field of Medicine and Genetics!"

Around the Hall of Mirrors, everyone rose up and raised their glasses to the trio. Per, Jomo, and Nice turned 360 degrees to see all arms high. The laureate party was peaking at the Grand Hotel.

"Now, how does such an interesting family such as yours plan to split the money?"

A loud roar of laughter erupted at this well-timed royal quip.

Someone handed Per a microphone. He waited till the raucous crowd of intellectuals quieted down, and then spoke in all seriousness.

"That truly has been a question we've been considering, what to do with a million bucks? Tonight, we can announce it will be given to the Smithsonian Institute as an endowment to construct and maintain a cold room display for our Stone Age warrior and Jomo's biological father. Thanks to my good friend, Larry Calvert. Please stand, Larry. Oh, and we will also buy more cows for my father and mother-in-law from Kenya, Jomo and Nonkipa Nkoe." Per gestured to the two.

A crescendo of applause erupted as the laureates' black mortarboards turned to party hats.

As the three embraced, with young Jomo in the middle, Grandfather Jomo raised his glass high. I stood at my table, knowing all what this family had gone through and raised my glass high. At a nearby table, a single Kenyan government dignitary dressed in full ceremonial red acknowledged the impending toast with an unexpected smile and raised his glass straight-armed to the chandelier. At the same table, Dr. Purcell, the carbon-14 London sleuth who had crashed the party, continued the cheer. Spontaneously, the old warrior bounded up onto the center of the table. He gestured for young Jomo to join him on the impromptu stage. Jomo ascended, first standing on his chair. He placed one solid foot on the table to check its stability, remembering the Swahili proverb "Never test the depth of a river with both feet." The crowd grew silent as Jomo stood at the old man's side far above the crowd in the storied Hall of Mirrors.

Without further hesitation, the elder Jomo shouted in Swahili, which no one in the intimate ballroom understood except Nonkipa, Nice, Jomo, Tambo and the Kenyan official, "Toast kwa simba muuagi! (A toast to the lion killer!)"

The king turned quickly to Tambo, heard the translation, and with a broad smile, stood up with his arms above his head, applauding.

In English, he yelled, "Yes! Let us have a toast to Jomo, the lion killer!"

Dr. Purcell approached the impromptu stage and when the crowd had sufficiently quieted, announced in his best cockney accent, "And a second toast to Jomo, a man in time!"

Everyone stood up on their chairs and applause could be heard clear across Stockholm bay.

Their wedding on Sir Richard Branson's island of Mustique was exquisite and very private. I know because I was one of the few invited. Only one journalist and photographer were there to cover the ceremony. Marcus Balieau—he is so New York— was there to photograph and celebrate this family whose roots went back to his drive from Mombasa to the Kenyan foothills of Mount Kilimanjaro and then the chance meeting with Nice and her mother in the marketplace.

It was a beautiful day with a thousand hibiscus flowers in full bloom behind the minister. I sat next to Per and Nice and had ready a clean handkerchief to hand to Nice. Jo was a lucky man to marry such a lovely, dynamic woman as Julie, and I told him so in a short speech I gave at the reception.

28

Larry Calvert

So I guess I should have raked today. These leaves are getting ahead of me. Anyway, I'm coming to the end of my story.

I still see Per and Nice occasionally. We're the best of friends. Just before I retired, I invited Per and the family to the institute and was especially looking forward to meeting Jomo and Julie's son.

A white limo pulled up in front of the Red Sandstone Castle entrance. The driver got out, went around, and opened the door for the Jorlands. I just stood there smiling as they walked to the front door.

"Welcome, Per and Nice! It's so good to see you and Jomo and Julie! I've been looking forward to seeing you all."

"Hello, Larry. It's great to see you, too. Thanks for the invite," Per replied as we held open the door.

Per stopped to make a proud introduction. "Larry, I'd like you to meet my distinguished grandson, Ken, Ken Jorland. Ken, I'd like you to meet our friend, Mr. Calvert. He works here."

I reached down to shake hands with the child and greet him. "I've heard so much about you from Per and Nice. It's so good to finally meet you, Ken. You know what? You can come here anytime you want. I think you'll like the interesting things you'll see here today."

He stood up straight. "It's good to meet you too, Mr. Calvert. It's my birthday! I'm six!"

"Well, happy birthday," I answered with a chuckle. Per beamed at his grandson's grace.

I switched my attention to Jomo. "Ken? Ken, as in Kenyatta? Am I right?"

Jomo laughed. "Larry, you're as quick as ever! We're going to Kenya next June. His great-grandparents, Jomo and Nonkipa, are in their nineties, and we'd like Ken to hear a story or two spun properly in their hut."

Nice added, "As I did many times, over and over. It is the Maasai way, but they're good stories, especially the one about the old picture and the spear. We're all going, actually."

As we entered the venerable building, I gave my usual respectful nod to James Smithson in his crypt. God rest his soul. The place was empty. We walked past the small coffee shop area and took a right to the end of the hall. I surprised them all, especially young Ken, when I opened a secret panel that led to a passage under the Mall to the National Art Gallery and the Museum of Natural History. Our steps echoed. Per asked a few questions about who the board might have in mind to replace me when I retire.

Jomo and Nice laughed as they told the story about when Jomo wandered off and got lost. I still remember it. Nice was beyond frantic. A security guard found him fast asleep in the cockpit of a World War I era biplane.

As we neared the Cold Room Exhibit, I turned to Per. "It's been quite a ride, hasn't it?"

"Yes. Oh yes, it has, my old friend."

I kept going, "Nice, the dig, Jomo, the Nobel Prize, Julie, and now, young Ken."

"Friends like you, Larry, well, they broke the mold."

"No, Per, it's friends like you and Nice."

"I guess we're pretty even after all these years."

"Hold it! What about what Julie and I've been through?" Jomo asked.

"Thank you. So I stand corrected!"

Nice smiled. "Your sense of timing comes from your grandpa, Jo. He could turn a lion attack into a stand-up comedy act." They all laughed. "I miss him and Nonkipa. It'll be good to see them again. I hope they're in good health."

When we approached the Human Paleontology Hall, I stopped the group and paused. "I'll leave you now. Sometimes, it's just about family. I'm honored I was a small part of this destiny." I embraced Nice and Per, shook hands with all, and walked alone back down the hall. Suddenly, I felt a little sad. I guess, because I knew my time as director here was over.

As they walked the remaining steps to the hall, Jomo asked Per, "How many generations ago did he live?"

"Well, Son, the common accepted years per generation is 30. So if this man lived 12,175 years ago, then approximately 404 souls have lived and died through the years since his demise. Most all of them loved, laughed, and cried as we have. It just shows how little we really are in the grand plan, the history and future of *Homo sapiens*."

Per turned his key that opened a high-tech door, and the Jorlands entered. This was the first time Ken would see the cold room exposition of his biological grandfather. The elders had been here a few times, but the youngster's eyes bulged out at the realness of the man on display.

"Hey, it's cold in here. I can see my breath. Look! That man's dead. He kind of looks not dead too, alive! Wow! Dad, look, he's got big claws around his neck. See, Mom?"

"This is the man we brought you to see," Nice said. "Your Dad and Grandpa Per worked very hard to bring him here for people to see and for you to see. He came from Norway."

Julie added, "Yes, Ken, we brought you here to see him. If you look real close, his eyes look a lot like yours, like yours and like your dad's."

"I can't see his eyes, Dad. Lift me up, please!"

Jomo came over behind the six year old, and in one easy move, Ken was riding on his father's shoulders.

Young Ken looked closely at this stranger inside the cold glass case. "Oh yeah, I can see him better now." He put his nose to the glass to get as close to the man as possible.

Then he shouted, "Look! There's a little blue line in his eye! I've got one too, just like it! Teacher found it!"

"What?" Julie looked startled.

Ken was leaning on the glass and pointing with his right index finger.

All four elders crowded in to look closely at what Ken had spied. They were so amazed, no one could speak. Sure enough, there was an extremely thin blue line, so thin it was almost invisible in the warrior's left iris; its location, about two o'clock on the eye.

Fascinated, Ken kept his hands on the glass while looking deep into the early modern human's face.

Per, a scientist with a lifetime of study in genes and heredity, softly whispered, "The beginning of blue eyes. We may be looking at the beginning of blue eyes." Per then quickly turned to Ken. "Ken, look at me straight so I can see your eyes."

Jomo bent over so his father could get a good look.

Per held Ken's face still with one hand as he looked carefully at his left eye. "He has it also, left iris at the two o'clock position."

"I asked teacher about it, and she told me when I was very little, I couldn't decide what color to make my eyes." Ken again turned to the Warrior. "Maybe he couldn't decide either!"

Per looked at Jomo's eyes. "No, you don't have it, Jo. It skipped a generation." Per again turned to Ken. "He couldn't decide what color, Ken, but he sure took his time to tell us all what he decided, didn't he?"

Ken laughed at his Grandpa Per's comment and then Per turned to Jomo. "I think it's time to try to tell him."

Jomo, with his son still on his shoulder, ventured a try at it. "I'm your father, Ken, but—"

"I know that, Dad."

"But he's kind of like your second grandfather."

"What do you mean? Did you know him?"

"Well, no, not really, but kind of." Jomo looked at Per. "I've felt him a lot, and your Grandpa Per knew him. He met him a long time ago, before you were born, even before I was born."

"Yes, Grandpa Per met him long ago, in a cold place called Norway," Julie explained. "And they each gave something very special from their lives that you now have to carry on."

"Carry? Carry what? What do I carry?"

"It's easy, Son. Be good. Be proud of who you are. Be proud of your family, your heritage, and do your best to leave a legacy beyond your time here."

"Ken tapped his dad on the head. "You're all talking different. Who is this guy?"

Julie smiled. "It's okay," she said, as Jomo handed Ken down to Julie, and she hugged him close. "We'll come back next year with Grandpa Per and Grandma Nice and tell you a little bit more about him."

"Hey, could I bring my class from school?"

"Sure, of course. Someday we can all come and see him again. All together," Jomo replied.

Nice came over to give him a hug. "Yes, Jomo, we're all together again."

Per joined in and then Julie. Finally, with everyone laughing and hugging, the young one found his way to the center. All loved.

Jomo looked closely at the man, nodded, and then spoke, "I saw him years ago in my dreams, and I believe he was a good man, and I think he led a good life. I think he shared his fire and food. If it's all right, I'd like to name him Toruk. I don't know why, but I believe his name was Toruk, and he had a wife and child named Tuk, who loved him. We should honor him because he's part of us, only separated by time. To be honored as much by those who follow us on this beautiful earth is all we can hope for."

The rover crawled closer down the four-wheel-drive road and came to a stop. Nice and Per opened their doors and walked to the front of the vehicle. A gentle breeze hinted of rain somewhere to the Northeast, bringing life to the Serengeti once again.

"I know that smell—rain. It might be the last storm of the rainy season. No one's home. They'd be outside by now."

"Probably the pasture," Per replied.

Nice licked her index fingers, placed them in the corners of her mouth, and blew a distinct series of whistles. She waited and then repeated the call. The answer whistle came from just beyond the bush a few hundred yards away. They smiled to each other and looked around, taking it all in— Mount Kilimanjaro, the Serengeti, the blue sky, and the clean air. She took his hand as they went over to the two wooden crosses on her parents' graves.

Nice sighed. "She died, and then he died of a broken heart. I'm so ashamed I didn't come for either funeral." She shook her head. "If I only could live parts of my life over. Per, I have done things you don't know about that have caused so much pain and sorrow."

"Whatever you've done, I forgive you."

Per said a short prayer, his first prayer out loud ever, and they kissed.

"Per, I don't think they'd mind if we went in for a peek."

"No. It's been so long since you've been back."

As they approached the hut, Nice crouched by the door. "See, look here, my initials in this brick. I helped repair this wall before I left for America. I asked Father that they never be covered over, and here they still are. I loved Nonkipa and Jomo so much. Even though they've gone on, I feel their presence. Now I must carry on. It's still all the same here, only I am different. Let's go in. Lower your head, Per."

"I know. Every time I went in here, Nonkipa said that."

"So lower your head."

"I'm lowering my head."

"It's cool in here, just as I remember, and there's the fire pit and my bed. It's all still here."

"Jo slept on it when he was here."

"And these books." She opened the top one of a large pile. "Basic mathematics and look at this one, *Homeschooling Your Child: The Dos and Don'ts*."

"Looks like young Ken is in summer school. Do you think Julie's qualified to teach third grade math?"

"Very funny, Per."

"Looks good. This all looks good, Nice."

She placed the books back and made a far off look she'd seen her father make when he spoke of something important from the past. "Nonkipa told me something a long time ago. We'd gone to market and were having coffee in town. You know that café. I was in college, and it was just before I went to America. She told me to live a life that would please God, and I should *always walk in The Truth*. I rebelled and was lost for so many years. I believe I am finally there. I've taken a long look inside. And yes, Per, God did have to give me you. I believe this is all good, finally all good. Let's go out and find them. Oh, would you mind? I'll be out after you in a minute. I'd like a little time."

Per replied, "I understand."

"Thanks. It's where I grew up. Just this little hut."

Per ducked out the door into the bright sunlight. When she could hear his footsteps stop by the rover, she reached into her jeans pocket and withdrew a folded scrap of pink paper. She listened again. No steps. She unfolded it to reveal the large diamond. She lit a match and burned the pink paper over the fire pit and then held the diamond in her palm for a moment. Her hand tipped till the stone silently fell deep into soft ashes. Before she left the hut, she rustled through some papers and found a letter from Detective Choge. The first sentence read,

> "Heard you're back, Jo. Remember my offer? It still stands. I'm serious. Would you like to join the brotherhood?"

> Detective Choge

She gave another whistle as she walked out into the bright sunshine. Out of the bush walked six cows. Next appeared Jomo, carrying his grandfather's spear. Young Ken instantly spied his grandparents and ran the hundred yards to their embrace, but he was crying.

Jomo walked slowly. His eyes were red and lost. As he approached, he spoke, "There were two bad men. It happened yesterday. A little boy who hid behind a bush told me. They came asking for me. Ken and I were in Nairobi for supplies. The boy said he heard her say, 'He is not here. I love him. I'm telling you the truth.' There was a lot of yelling and then five gunshots. The boy got a partial license plate. Why would two men with guns come for me? They killed Julie. They killed her, Mom. The funeral is tomorrow. I will bury her here next to Jomo and Nonkipa. I am so glad you're both here."

Jomo broke down and cried, and then all came together as a family with Ken in the middle.

Acknowledgments

SPECIAL THANKS TO the following: Jarl Aarbakke, rector at University of Tromso, Norway; a Kenyan I never got the name of on an overseas flight to Stockholm, Sweden; Robert Bellig, retired biology professor, Gustavus Adolphus College; Hald Morten, University of Tromso, Norway; Lannie Williams, for her patience and expert grammatical editing.

Our very special thanks goes to Michael Sears and Stanley Trollip, authors of the award winning Detective Kubu Series by pen name Michael Stanley. Without their professional advice, encouragement, and numerous manuscript readings, this book would have died an early death. Michael's kindness, honesty, and patience for several reads went far beyond most anyone we've ever met. He is a great author and a fine gentleman.

Finally, thanks to Mike Lange, our good friend who grew up in the Washington, DC area, and his dog, Shamus.

Glossary

boma. Protective fence made of thorn bushes

chai. Kenyan tea

Finnmark. Inclusive area of the most Northern Norway and Finland

kikois. A cotton multi striped sarong worn on the Indian Ocean coast of Kenya and Tanzania

Kikuyu. ("Kee-*ku*-you") A tribe that lives only in Kenya

laavo. ("*Law*-vo") Mobile Saami tent consisting of poles and reindeer hides

Maasai. ("Ma-*sigh*") A tribe that lives both in Kenya and Tanzania due to the artificial boundaries set when Kenya gained independence from England in 1964 and Tanganyika and coastal Zanzibar were renamed Tanzania

Makonde. An African wood carving

Moran. A young Maasai man from a traditional Maasai family. Generations ago, a young man became a Moran as a passage to warrior. Nowadays, some consider a Moran an unruly young man or even a thug or gang member rungu. A big club-headed stick

Saami. ("*Saw*-mee") Indigenous people of Northern Norway and Finland (Finnmark)

Swahili. ("Swa-*hee-lee*") The common language of Kenya and Tanzania. It is not a tribal language, and is not spoken out of East Africa

ugali. ("Oo-*gal*-ee") A heavy, starchy maizelike porridge meal

Bibliography

Africa: Timeline Index & Other Issues. *Africa, Timeline Index & Other Issues.* Accessed May 22, 2015.

Ardrey, Robert. *African Genesis: A Personal Investigation into the Animal Origins and Nature of Man.* New York: Literat S.A., 1961.

Ardrey, Robert. *The Territorial Imperative: A Personal Inquiry into the Animal Origins of Property and Nations.* New York: Athenaeum, 1966.

Ben-Aaron, Diana. "Retro Breeding the Wooly Mammoth."

Technology Review, 1984.

Brown, Eryn. *"Humans Got Immunity Boost from Neanderthals Study Finds; Synopsis Of Research by Laurent Abi-Rached."* Los Angeles Times, August 25, 2011.

Colbert, Edwin H. *Evolution of the Vertebrates: A History of the Backboned Animals through Time.* 3rd ed. New York: J. Wiley & Sons, 1980.

"Cro-Magnon." Wikipedia: The Free Encyclopedia. en.wikipedia.org/wiki/Cro-Magnon.

"Cro-Magnons: Why Don't We Call Them Cro-Magnon Anymore?" About.com. archeology.about.com/od/earlymansites/a/cro_magnon.htm.

"Cro-Magnon." *New World Encyclopedia.*

"*Cro-Magnon 1.*" Human Evolution by Institution's Human Origins Program. Accessed May 22, 2015.

DeWitt, William. *Biology of the Cell: An Evolutionary Approach.* Philadelphia: W. B. Saunders Company, 1977.

Diamond, Jared. "*The American Blitzkrieg: A Mammoth Understanding.*" *Discover*, 1987.

Distefano, Matthew. *Homework Helpers: Biology.* Enhanced & Updated [ed.]. ed. Pompton Plains, NJ: Career Press, 2011.

"*Dwight D. Eisenhower.*" Wikipedia. Accessed May 22, 2015. http://en.wikipedia.org/wiki/Dwight_D._Eisenhower.

"*Early Histories: Cro-Magnon Man.*" Early Histories: Cro-Magnon Man. Accessed May 22, 2015.http://www.mikedust.com/history/cromagnon.html.

"*Fossil Hominids: Cro-Magnon-Man.*" Fossil Hominids: The Evidence for Human Evolution. Accessed May 22, 2015. http://www.talkorigins.org/faqs/homs/cro-magnon.html.

Gould, Stephen Jay. *I Have Landed: The End of a Beginning in Natural History.* New York: Harmony Books, 2002.

Gould, Stephen Jay. *Full House: The Spread of Excellence from Plato to Darwin*. New York: Harmony Books, 1996.

Jueneman, Fred. *"More Mammoths in the Mist." R&D*, 1999.

Kluger, Jeffrey. *"Free Wooly Out of the Cold." Time*, 1999.

Kurten, Bjorn. *The Age of Mammals*. New York: Columbia University Press, 1971.

Lambert, Pam, Jerry Krammer, Lorenzo Benet, and Cathy Nolan. *"On a Frigid Siberian Plain, Arizona Paleontologist Larry Agenbroad Meets the Mammoth of His Dreams." People Weekly*, 1999, 111.

Levine, Joseph S., and David T. Suzuki. *The Secret of Life: Redesigning the Living World*. Boston, Massachusetts: Stoddard Publishing, 1993.

Llanos, Miguel. *"Bloodhounds Used to Sniff Out People Killing Elephants for Ivory."* MSNBC N. http://worldnews.nbcnews.com/_news/2012/03/05/10582934-bloodhounds-used-to-sniff-out-people-killing-elephants-for-ivory?lite.

Maeder, Jay. *"Bring 'Em Back Alive."* U.S. News & World Report, 1997.

Meyer, Stephen C. *Darwin's Doubt: The Explosive Origin of Animal Life and the Case for Intelligent Design*. New York, New York: Harper Collins Publishers, 2013.

Moskowitz, Clara. *"Comet May Have Collided With Earth 13,000 Years Ago."* Space.com. March 6, 2012.

Moss, Cynthia and editors. *Elephants*. International Wildlife. 1999.

Pobst, Sandy. *National Geographic Investigates Animals on the Edge: Science Races to Save Species Threatened with Extinction*. Washington, DC: National Geographic, 2008.

Sagan, Carl. *Pale Blue Dot: A Vision of the Human Future in Space*. New York: Random House, 1994.

Spence, Lewis. *Myths of the North American Indians*. New York: Gramercy Books, 1994.

"Stone Age Atlantis." The National Geographic Channel. Archeologists Investigate a Former Landmass in the North Sea Now on the Sea Bottom. October 2010.

Tangley, Laura. *"From the Tundra: A Big and Wooly Discovery." U.S. News and World Report*, 1999.

The Times Atlas of the World. 10th ed. New York: Times, 2000.

Welsh, Jennifer. "40,000 Years Ago: Live, from the Cave—Flutists!" msnbc.com. May 24, 2012. Accessed May 22, 2015. http://www.nbcnews.com/id/47555197/ns/technology_and_science-science/t/years-ago-live-cave-flutists/.

Wilson, Edward O. Letters to a Young Scientist. New York, New York: Liveright Publishing Corporation, 2013.